Shattered
Shields

Shattered Shields

Edited by
Jennifer Brozek &
Bryan Thomas Schmidt

SHATTERED SHIELDS

This is a work of fiction. All the characters and events portrayed in this book are fictional, and any resemblance to real people or incidents is purely coincidental.

A Baen Books Original

Baen Publishing Enterprises
P.O. Box 1403
Riverdale, NY 10471
www.baen.com

ISBN: 978-1476-7-3701-0

Cover art by Todd Lockwood

First Baen printing, November 2014

Distributed by Simon & Schuster
1230 Avenue of the Americas
New York, NY 10020

Library of Congress Cataloging-in-Publication Data

Shattered Shields / edited by Jennifer Brozek and Bryan Thomas Schmidt.
    pages cm
  Includes bibliographical references and index.
  ISBN 978-1-4767-3701-0 (paperback)
1. Fantasy fiction, American. I. Brozek, Jennifer, 1970–, editor. II. Schmidt, Bryan Thomas, editor.
  PS648.F3S53 2014
  813'.0876608—dc23

                                        2014027497

10   9   8   7   6   5   4   3   2   1

Pages by Joy Freeman (www.pagesbyjoy.com)
Printed in the United States of America

This anthology is dedicated to the men and women across the ages who've fought for freedom, safety, and better lives for their families and fellow countrymen. We salute your courage, sacrifice, and honor.

CONTENTS

INTRODUCTION

MILITARY AND FANTASY HAVE GONE TOGETHER FROM THE EARLIEST days of fantasy storytelling with tales of soldiers, armies, and battles often intertwining with those of knights, kings, and wizards. In some people's minds, they are almost inseparable, a key element of stories from the likes of J. R. R. Tolkien, C. S. Lewis, and so on, in whose tales enormous battles play key roles in the overarching stories and serve as backdrops to the main quest.

But like military science fiction, a clearly defined and popular genre, military fantasy can be so much more than an element of epic fantasy plots, with tactics, strategies, and battles taking center stage inside Warhammer, for example, or the works of modern fantasists like Glen Cook's Black Company tales, Myke Cole's Shadow Ops, and Steven Erikson's Malazan.

Some of the most exciting action in fantasy takes place in the context of military engagements, and some of the most memorable characters are warriors, so we decided to bring them together in a collection of such tales here for fans of both military history and tactics and epic fantasy action.

Included are seventeen new tales from top authors such as Glen Cook, Elizabeth Moon, and David Farland writing in their bestselling Black Company, Paksenarrion and Runelords universes, respectively. Larry Correia, Sarah A. Hoyt, and others are writing in new universes. Seanan McGuire gives us an epic fantasy prequel set thousands of years before in her popular October Daye urban fantasy universe, while Robin Wayne Bailey revisits the setting of his Frost novels. In between, we have tales from exciting newer voices like Wendy N. Wagner, Joe Zieja and

Annie Bellet, as well as original tales from popular writers like Dave Gross, James L. Sutter, and Cat Rambo.

While each tale is unique, all are fast-paced, with plenty of action. Some are dark and deep, others light and funny, but together they should satisfy whatever mood strikes you as you read. Our mission as anthologists is to first entertain and second introduce readers and fans to new voices which they might have not yet discovered. We hope you'll get plenty of both here as well.

Above all, we hope these tales will inspire you to escape into journeys of the imagination to distant lands where true heroes of courage and honor reside and hope reigns eternal for better days. As Aragorn said at the Black Gate: "A day may come when the courage of Men fails, when we forsake our friends and break all bonds of fellowship, but it is not this day. An hour of wolves and shattered shields when the Age of Men comes crashing down, but it is not this day! This day we fight! By all that you hold dear on this good earth, I bid you stand!" (*Return of The King* movie, based on the book of the same name by J. R. R. Tolkien.)

—Jennifer Brozek and
Bryan Thomas Schmidt,
November, 2013

Shattered Shields

Ashes and Starlight

A Runelords Story

DAVID FARLAND

AS THE KNIGHTS OF MYSTARRIA RODE THROUGH THE DUNNWOODIN evening, all grew quiet. Avahn knew that her guards rode in silence in part because they were weary to the bone and in part because they feared the Toth.

The creatures were still a mystery.

They'd appeared two days ago, floating in the Carroll Sea on great gray ships that appeared to be carved from stone. The boxlike vessels were like nothing any human would construct.

What the creatures wanted, no one knew for sure. There was no way to communicate with them; they had not tried to parlay.

Instead, some of them merely stepped off their ships and walked along the bottom of the sea, and then climbed out along the coasts only to set fields of crops afire.

Winter would be hard, Avahn knew. Famine was coming.

An animal cry rose in the woods, like the keen of a hound—desolate, bereft.

A shiver raced up Dval's spine as his mount leapt forward a pace. He whirled to see King Harrill upon his warhorse, the gray color of cold ash spotted by snow. The king gazed upward, hazel eyes blank, brow crinkled, and merely wailed like a trapped animal.

The dark pine boughs overhead echoed the cry and diffused it, so that the wail seemed to both rise from the ground and descend from the sky. "Mehrel?" the king called to his dead wife.

"Mehrel?" He stretched his hands out, palms outward, begging heaven for succor.

Eleven-year-old Dval had never seen a man so broken.

He knew that King Harrill suspected Dval of the queen's murder, though Dval's only crime was to have found her dead. That, and to have been born into an enemy clan, to have been born a Woguld.

Among the Woguld, grief was for children. True men did not wail like this. Dval wondered if such excesses were common among these day-lighters, these Mystarrians.

From the corner of his eye, he studied King Harrill. The man was hefty, short, and unimposing, with old muscle going to fat. He wore a deep blue riding robe over his breastplate, and no helm, only a simple crown carved from oak, polished smooth and darkened by age over the centuries. Aside from a haughty bearing, nothing suggested that he was a king.

He began to blubber and sniff, wiped his nose with one sleeve.

Dval's own father had been found murdered six months earlier, yet Dval had never wept for him like this. Dval wondered if he should have wept.

No, Father would not approve. It is not wailing that he would want, but vengeance.

So far, Dval had not been able to grant his father vengeance, or shed tears on his behalf.

Dval looked to the king's retinue to see their reaction to this mad howling.

Ahead and behind, the king's knights rode with hunched shoulders, faces forward, as if distressed to hear the king's outburst. Their mail jangled with each plop of a hoof.

So, it is not common even for these savages to cry. Dval suppressed a mocking grin. Mystarrians were no better than animals.

Weariness tugged at Dval like an undertow. The air so close to the sea felt thick and wet in his throat. Even in broad daylight, he rode through a landscape that seemed more shadow than leaf and tree.

Twisted pines brooded above, keeping the road in perpetual gloom. He could feel the trees all around, as ancient as legend, moldy and rotten, like King Harrill himself. With the dying of the day, linnets had begun to flutter upward, wings of amber flashing in the slanting light, glimmering like garnets. The woods smelled of mold, decay.

The king noticed Dval's smile, and whirled. "*Warum starren Sie?*" the king hissed, flashing his teeth.

Dval did not understand his uncouth tongue, but guessed at the question. He answered proudly, knowing that it might cost him his life. "I see a king who cries like a girl." He did not hide the contempt in his voice.

The king growled and pulled a long dirk from his boot-sheath, waved it threateningly, though he was well out of reach.

Dval urged his mare forward, ignoring the mad king's glare.

"Father, stop!" Avahn cried. She rode next to Dval, painfully aware of the older boy's color as they passed through a crop of sunlight.

Dval had a Woguld's skin, white as a swan, with long silver locks and eyes so pale green that they were almost colorless. For two hundred years, his people had warred with Mystarria.

"Oh, am I to take orders from a child now?" the king demanded.

"What I ask," Avahn said softly, in order to appease him, "I ask out of love. Spare him. Dval saved my life. I am in his debt."

Dval's stomach growled, and she realized that no one had offered him food since his capture. Yet he showed no sign of fatigue. He held his back straight, head high—every bit the warrior, from a race of warriors.

King Harrill's voice cracked like a whip: "Don't get too comfortable with that ... *grosse wurm* at your side." The epithet *grosse wurm* was a slur used when speaking of the Woguld. Their skin was the sickly color of giant earthworms found in Southwest Mystarria.

Avahn had just turned nine. She was not used to her father's unsteady temper. She'd been sheltered at court, raised among nannies, learning the lore that every princess should know.

"I want to keep him, Father," she pleaded. "He fought back the wolves again and again." Her father bit his lip. "Please? I never ask you for anything."

"It's not so simple," her father grumbled. "He's not a pony or a bear cub." He gave Dval a dark look, and the king's entire demeanor changed. His eyes narrowed suspiciously. "How do we know that he's not a spy? If I do as you bid, take him to court, train him as a guard, he'll learn our deepest secrets. He could kill you in the night."

"What more does he need to do?" Avahn asked. "The world is falling into ruin, what with the Toth. Shouldn't we plan on fighting our real enemies?"

Her father grimaced, glanced at the boy, with the hood of a green riding cloak pulled protectively low over his eyes, his long tan loincloth and moccasins, and the deep blue tattoos of a tree winding up his right leg. Dval couldn't be more than twelve, Avahn felt sure. He wasn't a warrior, out to learn the kingdom's secrets. He was hardly more than a child.

The king stiffened, as if he'd come to a decision. "There is only one way that the boy can prove his loyalty: he must betray *his own* people. He must lead our troops into the Woguld's underground strongholds and help us wipe them out."

Avahn's heart hammered. It seemed impossible. He could prove his loyalty only by being disloyal to his own people? "But—"

Her father cut her off. He said firmly, "His people have rejected him. He owes them nothing."

Avahn glanced at Dval to see if he reacted, but he merely stared ahead. He showed no sign that he understood.

In her mind's eye, she remembered the archer in the woods, his silver elk's mask gleaming in the sun, its antlers wide, as he drew an arrow on his crimson bow. She heard the whistle of the arrow as its goose feathers winged through the air.

Dval's own people had tried to kill him—simply because he'd saved her life. Perhaps it was true that he no longer owed them anything, but she doubted that he would turn against them.

"Train him then," Avahn begged. "Let him learn to love Mystarria, make it his home. In a year or two, perhaps he'll do what you ask." She said this last only to appease her father, not because she believed it.

"I'll not have that worm in the palace," King Harrill affirmed.

"Take him to the House of Understanding then," Avahn suggested. The House of Understanding was more than a house, of course. It was a great school near the Capitol. In ancient days, it was a school where lords and soldiers trained at an inn, but soon grew in reputation so that one building could not contain it all. Now there were dozens of "rooms" to the house; entire buildings and arenas where one could specialize in various crafts. "He can train in the Room of Arms to develop his fighting skills, and he can learn our language in the Room of Tongues."

The king did not answer.

The forest had begun to thin ahead, and suddenly a war horn blew, deep blats that sounded like three sharp barks.

Immediately, Sir Adelheim, her father's captain, pulled his horseman's battle axe from the sheath on his back and charged ahead. Her father reined in his own mount, which leapt a pace, eager to join the fray.

"Stay back!" Avahn's father warned her as he reached for his own battleaxe.

The horses danced in place, and the troops that had been riding behind charged forward, their faces set like stone, drawing weapons as they streamed into the forest.

Avahn peered forward, straining every sense. She smelled ash, and realized that they were coming out of the Dunnwood. She smelled smoke—not the smoke of a campfire, but of burning fields.

She spotted a tree that had been blasted by lightning, stripping it of bark. She remembered this place. Ahead, a small town named Moss End hugged the woods. It had an ivy-covered fortress, quaint but stout, while a beautiful stone bridge arced above the river. A trio of inns hugged the shore near the forest, while on the other side of the bridge squatted rows of ancient cottages, their roofs piled with heavy straw thatch.

Ahead, warriors' cries echoed through the wood, and for several moments Avahn listened to the sounds of battle. Soon, Sir Adelheim came cantering back on his black destrier. As the sun dipped behind the mountains, darkness deepened, almost as if he brought the night with him.

"Milord," he called. "A few miles ahead—we've been attacked!"

Here? Avahn wondered. *Why would anyone attack Moss End?*

Dval rode from under the ancient trees after sunset, just as stars had begun to come alive in the dying day, lanterns swinging in the rafters of heaven. Beneath the shadow of the old forest, they came upon the site of a massacre.

Cottages lay in ruins beside the road, roofs ripped off as if by a tornado. Stone walls from fine hostels had been shoved inward, and a bit of smoke still wound up from the rubble of hearths.

Of the fortress, an ancient tower, only a pile of rubble remained.

In the courtyard lay a woman, her belly ripped open and guts strewn all about. A child was not far away from her, and she reached toward its corpse. Nearby, Dval spotted the head of a knight, still in its helm with visor down, staring blankly from the roadside.

All had been murdered, as senselessly as his father had been murdered.

Seven red hens raced from the courtyard at the approach of the troops.

Dval had never seen such destruction. Last night, he'd witnessed the fires burning from the mountains and had wondered if the folk of Mystarria were at war. But this was like nothing he had ever imagined.

"*Kommen hier!*" a soldier shouted at the backside of the ruins, and other soldiers raced toward him across the green, past more bodies. Behind the fortress, Dval came upon one of the king's champions, the hill giant Bandolan. The giant stared down at a monster.

"Toth!" the savages whispered in hushed tones, some of them aiming war lances down to a dead creature at their feet. "Toth."

Dval stared, amazed. The beast looked to be two times taller than a man, but it was nothing like a man. It had an exoskeleton covered in thick gray hide, much like that of a reaver, but it was thinner than a reaver. It had four legs and two long arms, each of which ended with three talons and a thumb-like claw.

Its head was large, with a bony plate fanning out from the skull. On the end of the plate were wormlike philia, with which it tasted. In life, the philia could stand up and move, much like snakes rising to peer about. But now that the creature was dead, they hung limp.

The creature's long jaw had dozens of fangs, and a purple tongue filled its mouth, but did not extend to the teeth. It had nine air-holes on each side of its snout.

In many ways, it resembled a reaver's head, but there was one amazing difference: reavers have no eyes. This creature had four. They were nothing like human eyes. One pair was as large as Dval's fist, its surface a bloody red. A smaller eye just beneath it was purple-black.

There were few plants or animals that had adapted to living both in the underworld and the outer world. Obviously, this was a creature of darkness that could still somehow see in the light.

The Mystarrians backed away from the monster in terror, like children, but Dval had lived most of his young life in the underworld among his people's burrows.

He was familiar with the plants and animals that grew deep

underground, where heat from thermal vents allowed life. There were huge wormlike glue-mums there, and strange spider-like creatures, and cruelest of all, the reavers.

But this was something new. "Toth," he repeated aloud.

He crouched down near the creature's abdomen. It had been crudely hacked with axes, and the air vents there were broken and fouled.

He sniffed at its rectum, trying to catch the creature's "death scent," and smelled something very much like lavender and rotten garlic.

The Mystarrians sniggered.

"He's a butt sniffer," Sir Pwyrthen jested. "I've got a hound that does that to me."

Avahn stiffened in embarrassment for the Woguld, but said nothing.

Dval stood up straight, strolled around the creature. He reached toward a soldier who held a spear, gave a hand-it-hither gesture. The soldier smiled dubiously, gave the Woguld his spear.

Dval took the spear, went to the creature's thorax, leapt in the air, and tried mightily to plunge the spear into the monster's exoskeleton. But even with three tries, putting all of his weight behind the blow, he could not break the beast's skin.

The men laughed. Captain Adelheim joked, "It's dead enough, boy. Give it up!"

Most of her father's men were runelords with endowments of strength. Perhaps they would have not had such a tough time piercing the monster's hide, and so they mocked Dval's efforts.

But Avahn's father leaned forward on his mount, peering into the gloom. The boy took his spear, stood back, and plunged it beneath the creature's forearm, into its armpit, and this time the spear entered a good foot.

"The boy is testing its defenses." The king's tone was curious, but not convinced. "Watch him, lads. We might learn something."

Now Dval went to its head, stabbed at the eyes, and once again the spear was rebuffed. But he sought out a point between the eyes, where three prominent points met, and once again threw all of his weight behind a blow.

The spear pierced the dead Toth's skull, its tip driving six inches into its brain, and then snapped.

"Huzzah!" the men cheered.

Dval looked up triumphantly. The lesson was learned. The men who had killed this creature had hacked at its thorax ineffectively and had barely managed to slay it. But Dval had just discovered two points where a man might strike and make a quick kill.

King Harrill's eyes narrowed, and he peered about the dead town. "Why here?" he wondered. "What are they up to? This place has little strategic merit."

Sir Adelheim suggested, "We're at the edge of the forest. Maybe the Toth are creatures of the wood."

"Right," Sir Pwyrthen agreed. "The Toth could be like dogs, marking the edge of their new territory."

"Or the mountains." King Harrill sounded uneasy, as if he did not want to assert motives quite yet. "We're at the feet of the mountains here."

Off in the trees, a soldier called out, "Milord, there are tracks leading into the woods. Two more of the monsters came this way."

The king smiled. "Light some torches, men. We'll run them down!"

He peered at Avahn. "You'll stay here with your . . . the *wurm*. Sir Bandolan will watch over you."

He nodded toward the hill giant, who puffed out his chest and brandished his war staff. The troops raced off toward the forest's edge.

Dismissed from the action, Dval did not concern himself with the monster any longer. The giant and Avahn climbed up into the remains of the old stone fortress, found a corner of standing walls perhaps twenty feet off the ground, and crouched there. Night was coming quickly, and bats danced overhead, taking gnats on the wing.

Dval had not eaten for a day and a half.

He remembered the red hens, decided to eat one. They would be sluggish with the coming night, trying to settle on their roosts. The stars were coming out, but the waxing moon had not yet risen.

He walked through the town, and found many dead villagers. He eyed the bodies, searching for gold or silver, but King Harrill's soldiers had already claimed everything of value.

Yet Dval noticed something odd, a mystery. The men had all been clubbed to death, but he found three women, and each had been gutted, as if a single talon had pierced her beneath the navel and ripped upward. Then her entrails were flung about.

This was not the kind of work performed by reavers. Reavers went mad from time to time and committed terrible atrocities. But there was a surgical precision to this attack.

But why had the monsters defiled the women?

Dval spotted the remains of a henhouse behind the ruins of a cottage, a few cages still standing on stilts. He drew close to one, smelled warmth and feathers. A hen was inside.

He reached in gently, hoping to ease her from the roost, but the hen squawked and leapt out, flapping her wings as she took to the air.

To his surprise, Dval missed grabbing her.

All he got for his trouble was…an egg, lying warm in his palm. He'd seen hens crap eggs in fear before, but he'd never had one lay an egg in his hand.

He laughed, cracked it, and swallowed the fluid.

Dval checked two other boxes, but they were empty.

Still hungry, he went to the dead Toth. He'd smelled the creature's death, and instinct warned that the others would return. There was a secret known among the Woguld about reavers. Their death cries were carried in their scent.

The smell of a dead reaver confused its fellows, made them cower in fear.

He hoped that the same was true of the Toth.

So he took his hand and wiped it on the wormlike philia hanging down at the back of its abdomen, then spread the scent in a bar across his forehead, painted stripes on his cheeks, and one on his chin. Thus he wore a war mask that only a Toth might discern.

When he finished, he climbed up into the old fortress, stood in the shadow of the giant Bandolan, and peered across the horizon.

To the west were plains, with fields aplenty. They'd been burned, and the ground lay blackened under a net of stars. In some places, where brush was heavy or logs lay in the grass, little fires still sputtered, so that the stars seemed to light the ground in the distance.

The Toth burned the fields. He wondered why, and could think of only one reason. *The Toth didn't come to conquer this people, but to supplant them completely. That's why they tear the wombs from women.*

✧   ✧   ✧

King Harrill's men charged along in the night, over fields of dry ash black under the starlight, crossing a shallow river several times, sluggish from summer and never rising higher than his mount's withers.

He was so weary, so weary, and he struggled in vain to remain awake.

In the soft sand at the water's edge, his men stopped to study some Toth's footprints, like those of a giant bird. In the darkness, the starlight shining on the sand left an impression, something like a human face.

King Harrill suddenly imagined his dead wife again, lying beside the wreck of the royal carriage, her beautiful features torn by wolves, leaving only a mouth of perfect teeth surrounded by bloody meat.

The image overwhelmed him, a whirlwind bowling him over. He hunched in his saddle as if he'd taken a blow.

"Damn the heavens," he wailed. "Blot out the stars! Let rot cull the tender seeds from our ground!"

He was dazed by fatigue, and his head spun. He clenched his legs tightly against his horse's ribs, trying to hold on.

He blacked out from the emotional pain, and roused moments later to find Sir Adelheim at his side, holding his elbow to keep him from falling from his mount.

King Harrill was keening uncontrollably, a low whine emanating from his throat. He bared his teeth, struggled to regain some control, but continued to sob.

"Are you better, milord?" Sir Adelheim asked.

He fought for control, reeling.

"Hold me, my friend," King Harrill begged. "Hold on to me."

"I'm here, milord," Sir Adelheim whispered. He leaned close, his forehead almost touching the king's, and held him firmly, as if to lend him strength.

"Do you know where we are?" Sir Adelheim asked.

The world was spinning, night and darkness and stars turning above. Thought came slowly.

"I forget," King Harrill whispered, and he struggled to hold on to a thought, but sleep was like a quicksand, pulling him under.

"Toth," Adelheim whispered. "We're tracking them. Remember?"

"Yes," King Harrill whispered, clinging to the thought. Two Toths had survived. It was terrible to think that such creatures could be so powerful that they could take out a garrison of twenty good troops, and kill a hundred villagers, with only one casualty.

He hoped that the Toth had suffered for it; he looked at the ground, hoping for signs of blood, but saw none. One of the monsters had three toes on each foot. A much larger Toth had four.

The tracks were very fresh, their sides crisp.

"They seem to be wandering," Sir Adelheim said. "They've moved around tonight, but never moved more than about five miles from the fortress."

King Harrill seemed to struggle free from his stupor.

They're aimless, King Harrill thought. *Maybe dazed or wounded. Perhaps my men have pushed them beyond their endurance.*

The Toth had circled back toward the fortress twice now, and he'd managed to send lancers ahead to cut them off. But what could they want there?

The only thing at the fortress was his daughter.

The thought unmanned him. He'd lost his wife to these monsters already.

Now he recalled the women he'd seen in town. He'd only seen one up close, a couple of others from a distance. All had had their organs ripped out.

My daughter? he wondered.

A gentle breeze had begun blowing in from the sea for the evening.

"Send the men ahead to chase those bastards," King Harrill suggested. "But let's keep a few men back. I think they'll try to head for the fortress again. We'll go to the far side of that stand of pine over there and wait under the trees."

Sir Adelheim nodded, cut three lancers from the group, and sent the rest ahead.

King Harrill smiled. His madness earlier today could be forgiven. King Harrill the Cunning was back.

Avahn, Dval, and Sir Bandolan sat in the rocks atop the keep, and peered about. Sir Bandolan said in a grumbling voice, in the way of such giants,

"*The stars grow tired,*
"*Night runs deep.*
"'*Tis time for a child*
"*To go to sleep.*"

Avahn smiled up at him. Sir Bandolan shook his head, the rat skulls in his beard rattling together.

"Is that an order?" she asked.

Sir Bandolan grumbled and pointed with his heavy oaken staff toward the ground. His was a weapon favored of giants, bound as it was with iron rings and tipped with a brass point. It could be used as either a spear or a cudgel—and, in a pinch, a walking stick.

"All right," Avahn said, and she crept to the corner and lay down. The stones here still carried the heat of the day.

She pulled part of a tapestry over herself.

Avahn lay in the starlight, eyes gritty and tired. She and Dval had been trapped by wolves the night before, and she found that she could not sleep, she was so worried.

She opened her eyes and saw Dval crouched on a stone. A rising moon had turned his skin to silver. Somewhere he had managed to scavenge a spear, and now he peered down at her gravely—a silver gargoyle with death shining from his eyes.

"Ashoo. Ashoo," he whispered softly. Sleep. Sleep, and she obeyed his command.

Above her, Dval watched and waited. There was a clearing around the fortress. The land had been burnt off each year, kept free of brush. Nothing could reach them without being seen.

Yet he worried. If the Toths' sense of smell was as strong as he believed, they would come for Avahn.

His heart hammered, and he watched the fields.

There was a villager lying askew at the edge of the woods, a knight in ringmail, his cape twisted around him.

Dval's own father had been found like that, dead at the food of a crevasse.

Most in the burrows thought that he had taken a fall by accident while on guard duty, but Dval did not believe that. His father had been a warrior, honored as a Supreme Man. He was not careless or blind.

He was so much better than me, Dval thought. *I have not even earned a title beyond my family name. I suppose now that I never will.*

Dval had been convinced that his father had been murdered, but the elders of the clan had not investigated.

Who would want to kill Dval Kartinga, hero that he was?

Suddenly, Dval recalled his uncle, with his crimson bow and silver elk mask, taking aim.

Never had he imagined such a thing. His uncle, Dval Oormas, had shared a womb with Dval's father.

Could Dval Oormas have killed his father?

The pieces fit together like the scales on a fish.

Of course. Dval's father, as the Supreme, had been the chief elder to the clan, next in line to become its leader. If he died, it left an opening for those who might want to take his place.

Dval's uncle might harbor such hopes. As an uncle, it was Oormas's responsibility to raise Dval to be a warrior, like one of his own. But it was a responsibility that Oormas had hated.

Dval remembered the constant sneer in his uncle's tone, the insults and belittling.

His uncle had sent Dval over the mountains into enemy territory to find his blood mare, and Dval had seen moccasin prints while following her trail. He'd imagined that one of his cousins had driven the horse over the mountains, playing a cruel trick.

But what if it was his uncle who had done it?

Of course, Dval thought. *Why else had he shown up at just the right time?*

Dval was a strong young man. As his mother had put it, "Your father's blood runs strong in you. You shall be Supreme someday."

That was reason enough for someone to try to kill me.

Perhaps when I entered the carriage, Dval reasoned, *my uncle hoped that the wolves would finish me, so that my blood would not be on his hands. Or perhaps when the Mystarrians showed up, he imagined that they would kill me.*

But neither had happened. The Princess Avahn had begged her father for mercy.

So Oormas had taken matters into his own hand, and had shot an arrow at Dval.

Suddenly, it all fit together in Dval's mind, and he was so excited, so eager to take the idea back to the burrows and tell the clan, that he almost did not see the two Toth emerge from under the trees.

Before he knew it, they were halfway across the clearing, racing soundlessly, four arms folded tight against their chests. One of them was small and fast, about twelve feet tall. The other was much heavier, a large female, and ran sluggishly.

She held what looked to be a long rod of crystal that glimmered under the starlight, and blazed red, as if fire leapt up from its heart.

The grass had been burned all around the city, so she could not have intended to burn that. Only one thing stood to reason. She would burn the last of the humans standing atop the fortress.

"Ya-chaa!" Dval whooped a war cry as he leapt over the fortress wall and charged the enemy.

"Oh, *schiesse!*" Sir Bandolan shouted, and Avahn leapt up from her corner, fighting sleep.

The giant grabbed his great war staff and stood firm, a wall between Avahn and the Toth. Avahn peered out into the darkness, and could see little.

A huge Toth was out there, and it wielded a club that blazed like living fire, whirling it in the darkness. On the ground beneath it, the boy Dval was shouting, his white frame turned red beneath the spinning flames.

He had his spear out, and did battle with two Toth at once.

"The boy is fearless!" the giant said in amazement.

More than that, he moved now as quick as a serpent. His foe was a smaller Toth, one with the shadows, and Avahn could barely see it in the darkness. It leapt and twisted away, teeth gaping. It hissed and shrieked, an alien sound, and bore a huge axe with three double heads.

It swung at the boy, but for some reason, as Dval pressed the attack, the creature kept fading back, the philia waving madly upon the frills of its head-plate, as if terrified and unbelieving of what it faced.

"Go save him!" Avahn shouted to Bandolan, for she feared that no mere human could face two Toth at once.

But the giant shook his head, wagged his great black beard. "My duty is to save *you!*"

Dval dodged beneath the smaller Toth's swing, leapt back. No fighter of Mystarria could have evaded that blow in darkness, Avahn thought. None of her men could see so well in this infernal dark.

But Dval leapt away, and for a moment, he disappeared in the shadows.

Suddenly his enemy gave a keening shriek and halfway collapsed to its left. The bigger Toth swung her flaming club overhead, and for an instant, Avahn saw the image of Dval, engaging the smaller monster.

He'd stabbed it beneath the arm, plunged his spear into its chest. Now he danced backward and disappeared into the shadows again.

The wounded Toth staggered a bit, fell back, and then swung its mighty axe. Dval was a white shadow in the starlight and moonlight, dancing away.

But he went flying, and Avahn shrieked as she realized that the Toth's axe had found its mark. With a sickening crunch, Dval flew back a dozen feet.

The smaller Toth stopped and peered up toward the fortress, and for a moment it held its axe in both hands, then staggered forward and crashed to the earth.

Only one Toth was left. The big slow one.

"Get down!" Sir Bandolan grumbled, his voice issuing from his cavernous chest like rolling thunder. He shoved her to the ground.

Dval's head spun. He felt as if he were caught in a tornado, his head spinning around. He clawed his way out of the darkness, and found himself on the ground.

Blood smeared his chest.

The Toth. The male had given him a mighty battle, and the end of the axe had nicked him, sent him flying.

A sense of urgency filled him, and Dval leapt to his feet. "*Ya, kanah!*" he shouted. To eternity!

He leapt up, thinking that while he was unconscious, the female must have charged the fortress, but to his surprise, she stood not more than a dozen feet from him.

She whirled and raised her flaming crystal staff overhead so that it whistled and hissed at the same time. The staff was at least fourteen feet long, and as thick as a large sapling.

His chest hurt, and Dval was in terrible pain. He staggered forward and realized that his feet would not move. He felt shocked, wounded.

He suddenly realized that he had dropped his spear, and he bore no weapon at all in his hand.

His ears were pounding, blood drumming in tune with his heart, and he stared for one moment into the maw of the Toth as it gnashed its teeth, huge eyes peering at him without moving, much as a spider's eyes will.

His whole world was reflected in the Toth's eyes. He could see himself there, blood streaming from his wound, his face pale as death. The monster's fiery staff whirled toward him, and time seemed to stand still.

The Toth lurched forward, a lance piercing through its abdomen, and a charger came out of the night, a warhorse with a leather helm painted white like a skull, and leather barding.

The Toth fell on top of Dval, crushing him, so that for a moment he lay on the ground and struggled to breathe.

King Harrill rode out of the woods, only a few strides behind Sir Adelheim and Sir Pwyrthen, and watched the big Toth succumb to death, her armored body crashing to the ground with a sound like trees falling.

To his dismay, Avahn came leaping down from the fortress in the starlight, as if eager to finish killing the Toth herself, and Sir Bandolan the giant was too slow to stop her.

Avahn raced to the dying Toth and grabbed her giant staff, then struggled to use it as a lever.

Only then did he see the fallen Woguld lying beneath the monster.

The giant came trudging down, too. He grabbed the Toth, rolled her over, and pulled the boy out.

The Woguld lay in the moonlight, struggling to breathe, and King Harrill drew near, wondering if the boy would survive.

To his surprise, Dval climbed to his feet and staggered to the fallen Toth. Only then did he reach into the pocket of his tunic and pull something out.

He laid it upon the dead Toth's thorax, then grunted and pointed at it meaningfully. By the light thrown from the fiery staff, King Harrill saw a cracked shell.

"By the powers," King Harrill said, "the damned creatures have laid eggs!"

The pieces came together for him then—the reason the Toth had wiped out this city, and why so few had invaded. Now he understood why the Toth had refused to leave the ruins at Moss End.

Avahn demanded of Sir Pwyrthen, who had some skill as a surgeon, "Sew up the Woguld's wounds. I think his ribs are broken."

Indeed, Dval now squatted beside the dead Toth, admiring his handiwork, as if there were nothing special about it.

By dawn, King Harrill's men found the Toth's nest, hidden on a sunny sandbar near the river, high on the bank. Two thousand eggs they shattered that day, and then combed the riverbank looking for more, just in case. Only a few eggs were kept whole, for King Harrill insisted that he learn how long a Toth took to hatch.

So Avahn found herself that afternoon, riding across fields of barren ash toward the Courts of Tide, its magnificent towers rising up from islands in the distant sea. The setting sun shone golden-red upon them, making them look like beaten copper, while ash swirled at their feet.

So much destruction, she realized, *and from so few Toth. They never even bothered to land their ships.*

Her father had sent men ahead to warn his knights, to warn the kingdom, to search everywhere for the monsters' eggs. Fortunately, they were huge and easy to track, and she dared believe that they'd find them all.

As she rode, she glanced over at Dval, slumped in his saddle, his green robe pulled over his face. He clutched at his mount blindly, as if in pain.

"So, Father," she said at last. "Can I keep him?"

King Harrill glanced at the boy. "There are some honors that cannot be given," he said wearily. "They must be won." Then, as his weary scowl transformed into a thin-lipped smile, she realized that she had won. "He saved you twice, I suspect, and he may well have saved our kingdom. I'll let him train as a guard, and be glad of it."

Avahn's heart seemed to soar, and she smiled up at her father, but his face became haggard and drawn, and he warned, "Don't become too attached. His training must be hard, if it is to be of any worth. He cannot be coddled. You will be forbidden to show him any favor. You will not be allowed to speak to him, or speak *of* him. Do not even think of him. He is a soldier, a shield. In times like those that are to come, such shields will be easily shattered."

Avahn could only hope.

The Fixed Stars

An October Daye Story

SEANAN McGUIRE

The bay trees in our country are all wither'd
And meteors fright the fixed stars of heaven.
—William Shakespeare, *King Richard II*

The Castle Brocéliande, Albion, 572

THE RAVENS THAT DIPPED AND WOVE THEIR ARCANE PATTERNS IN the sky above the castle walls were out in full force, their black wings painting prophecy across the dusky purple sky. I wanted to look away, leaving those transitory etchings unread, but I could not force my eyes to close. Too much death and too much dying were scrawled there, spelling themselves out one scavenger bird at a time.

A footstep on the battlement behind me told me that I was no longer alone. I started to turn, and stopped as Michael's voice rumbled, "No, sister. Stay as you are; I need your eyes to guide me."

"Guide you to what, a hard fall to the rocks below?" But I smiled and did not turn. Michael was the youngest of my brothers in those days, still feeling out his place in the hierarchy of our strange family. His antlers were only as broad as two hands splayed wide, and his parchment-pale eyes could almost seem to track motion across a room, even though they had not seen a

21

single thing in the eighty years he had lived thus far in Faerie. All his sight was borrowed from the eyes of others.

"To your side, fair sister," he said and stepped up next to me, almost towering in his nearness. He had grown quickly to a man's stature and had been the taller of us since he was scarce ten years old. Not that I was possessed of any great height; my nature had always been protean, inclined to twist and change as need demanded, but when I allowed myself to sink into my natural shape, I was a small, slender woman, easily lost in the crush of a crowd. I could be overlooked, if I so willed it, and I willed it often.

But the time for silence and solitude was past. I kept my eyes fixed on the fields outside the castle walls, letting Michael see what he would never be able to behold on his own: men, camped close enough that the shit and feathers dropped by the flocking ravens landed on their heads. So many men, and all of them touched by our manipulations. They must have numbered in the hundreds, and before that day, I would not have thought that so many merlins lived in all of Albion.

Michael was quiet for a time before he asked, "Has Father come?"

"No." The word was small, and simple, like a key being slipped into a lock. "No," I repeated, and this time jagged laughter followed the word, impossible to catch or to contain. "The great Oberon come here, for us? The least of his children, guarding the least of his frontiers? Eira will come to fight beside us, and feed you sweets and braid my hair before our father comes to us. There is no cause to count on him. His mercies have never been ours to claim."

"Antigone." Michael's voice was almost chiding now, like he had somehow become the elder, and I the stripling child in need of soothing. "Father loves us. He has always loved us, and he always will."

"I wish I shared your certainty, Michael." I turned my eyes away from the battlefield-to-be as I leaned up and pressed a kiss against his cheek. His flesh was cool from the evening air. "Do not stay outside too long. You'll catch your death of chill."

He chuckled. "Yes, sister." My eyes were useless to him now; he would be borrowing vision from the ravens, using them to gain a hundred views of the men who camped below us. By the time he came back into the castle, he would know everything there was to know about their defenses, the weapons they had brought with them, and the items they were scavenging from our land. His information would be invaluable, as it always was during times of war.

A pity that we were going to lose this fight, as we had lost so many others since the merlins took up arms and rose against the many cruelties of their fae progenitors.

I turned my back on him, glad that he did not have eyes of his own, and that he could not see the marks of my betrayal on my face. Shoulders bowed with the weight of a burden that should never have been mine to carry, I descended the rough stone steps toward the waiting castle door.

There are those who yearn to know the future. You can see them at every fair and gathering, skirting around the edges of the crowd and looking for someone who claims to have the Sight. Will I live long, will the crops be good, will I have many children, they ask, and the fortunetellers tell them what they want to hear—those who have the ability to lie, that is. I have never been able to force my lips to form falsehoods, and so I have never found favor in the courts of kings or queens, whether they be mortal or fae. Too many dark truths have fallen from my mouth like poison berries, and no one wants a fortune teller who will not pretend that tomorrow will always be better than today.

The upper halls of the castle were deserted. The household staff would be below, shoring up our defenses, while the nobility prowled like chained beasts, eager to wet their swords on merlin blood. The fact that the men outside our walls were our distant descendants didn't matter to them. My brothers and sisters had raised their children to believe that nothing outside of Faerie had value, and merlins were outside of Faerie from the moment of their births.

Brocéliande had been one of Titania's places to begin with, intended for the pleasure of her children and designed as a beautiful poem of a building, rather than a properly defensible fort. Fortunately for the fools who gathered in the halls below me, the construction of the castle had been given over to Trolls and Gremlins, Coblynau and Hobs—people who understood that a wall needed to do more than simply decorate the landscape. It needed to keep the people inside safe and dry, and it needed to keep the people outside at bay until they were invited to enter. They were not difficult tasks, and the castle performed them well.

But there are other tasks to set before a castle: tasks involving secret passages and hidden ways through the walls, tasks best performed at noon, when the uncaring sun sends most children of Faerie to their beds to sleep the daylight hours away, and such private assignations as must not be seen by the ever-judgmental moon may be carried out. These, too, were performed by the palace at Brocéliande, and performed well enough that even though I made my way from the top level of the castle all the way down to the lowest in the wakeful twilight, not a soul saw me, nor marked my passage.

I stepped out into the courtyard, shivering from a chill that had nothing to do with the temperature of the air. What I was doing...it was unforgivable, and yet I had been given no choice in the matter by the people who claimed to love me best. They would not listen to reason. They wanted blood.

The castle gates were latched, but it was a simple matter to murmur my desires to the sturdy oak, which remembered me well and warped itself enough to allow me to slip out of the stronghold and onto the smooth cobblestone of the castle bawn. Here, too, could you see Titania's arrogance at work: the moat was deep and wide, yes, and home to strange beasts that would rend and tear any flesh that came too close to their terrible jaws. And at the same time there was the bawn, wide and smooth as a village square, and there was the bridge, which could easily hold a palanquin drawn by two Dragons walking side by side. There was no safety here. Even if the battle went in Faerie's favor, blood would flow like wine.

Full dark had fallen, blinding Michael's ravens. My cloak was the color of the sky, blue-black edged with runnels of red. I pulled it close as I hurried across the bridge and toward the camp on the other side of the field. The smell of smoke and unwashed human skin assaulted my nostrils as I drew near, reminding me that I ran toward a different world than that which I left behind me. This was a rawer place, harder, because it had been given no other choice.

The first watchmen were stationed near the boundary fires, where the light was bright enough to dazzle sensitive fae eyes and buy a few precious seconds to sound the alarm. I heard them rustle in the brush as I drew near, doubtless reaching for their weapons. I did not stop or slow, but continued walking forward with my chin held high and my eyes fixed on the distant tents. If they killed me here—if a spear crafted of rosewood and tipped with blessed silver found my heart, and iron nails were driven through my flesh—then the tides of war would turn. Mankind would lose, and my family would maintain their position over all. It was not the right outcome, I knew that much, but if things should go that way, it would be outside of my control and none of my fault. I would betray no one. And so I walked, and waited for the spears to fly.

No one raised a hand against me. I was, in my own way, as well-known here as any of their own forces. So I continued on across the moor until I came to the second ring of fires, this one set around the main encampment, as if keeping the dark at bay could do anything to dissuade the creatures that called it their home.

"Halt!" called a voice. "Who goes there?"

"I have many names, and I cannot tell you which of them is true," I replied with utter honesty. "But your leader calls me 'Nimue,' and so that is my name, to you."

"How do we know you are who you claim to be?"

I rolled my eyes, glad for once that the fire hid the face of my challenger. It would have been difficult to keep the claws from my fingers, and thence from his throat, if he had looked me in the eye and challenged my honesty. "You don't," I said flatly. "But here is a riddle for you: Nimue, it is said, never lies, although her truths can be ribbons that a man may use to tie himself in knots. If I am Nimue, then I am not lying to you, and will be direly offended by your question. If I am not Nimue, then what's to stop me from reading the future in your entrails before any man could come here to your aid?"

There was a chuckle from the darkness, rich and slow and beautifully familiar. "You never have learned to suffer fools gladly, have you, Auntie?"

"No," I said. "I have never seen the need. Come out of the firelight, Emrys. I wish to see you, and I am tired of standing here alone."

"The firelight is my friend, Auntie; it keeps Faerie's wolves from my door," said Emrys, even as he walked forward and out of the flickering distortion. He was a tall, strong man, with black hair and a bushy beard that he had allowed to grow since the siege began. His eyes were very green. If any had questioned his heritage, they need only have looked at those Roane-bright eyes and known him as a member of my line. "I wasn't expecting you tonight."

"Give me your arm and lead me to your tent," I said.

He frowned. "My men will talk."

"A pox upon your men," I spat. "They will have more than enough to talk about soon, if you and I do not have this conversation now. Will you take me, or have I come all this way for nothing?"

Emrys's frown deepened as he moved to stand beside me, linking his arm firmly through mine. I put my hand against the hard muscle of his forearm, matching his pace as I allowed him to lead me into the encampment.

"I do not like this," he murmured.

"You were not meant to," I replied, and we walked on. "You put too much faith in fire, Emrys. There are people fighting on the side of Faerie who are born in fire, who can juggle flame like a human man juggles a ball. It would be a small thing for a child of the Fire Kingdoms to turn your wall against you."

"And are there any children of the Fire Kingdoms come to fight for Brocéliande?"

"No," I said, with absolute honesty and no small satisfaction. The binding that keeps my tongue true was set upon me by Eira, looking to win the favor of her mother, the fair Titania. It was intended as a punishment, and it has been, in its way. But it also allowed me to betray my people without hesitation. How could I be blamed for telling the truth when Eira saw fit to steal away my choice in the matter?

Emrys nodded, satisfied by my answer. "That is good to know. Has the Undersea come?"

"Not yet," I said. There were men in the shadows, creeping forward as they watched me walk through the camp on the arm of their leader. I kept my eyes on the path ahead, not acknowledging their presence. I was the intruder here.

It should never have been like this.

"Good," said Emrys, and together we walked on.

✧   ✧   ✧

His tent was as plain as any of the others on the outside: plainer, even, with visible patches on its side and no banner flying overhead. His personal coat of arms flew above an empty tent on the other side of the camp, a decoy against attacks from above. I smiled a little when I saw that. He had listened to my advice after the last battle and was adjusting to the tactics of the fae.

Inside was another matter. Inside, the tent seemed to go on for the length of a great feasting hall, with an oaken table suitable for gatherings of men, and a bedchamber almost as large as the one which I enjoyed at Brocéliande. The air smelled faintly of heather, the single-note signature of his magic. Unlike their pureblood and changeling forebears, merlins were too thin-blooded for complexity. It was a small price to pay, given all that they had gained.

Emrys walked me to the table and guided me to a seat on the long bench like the gentleman that he was. I unclasped my cloak and slipped it from my shoulders, before folding my hands demurely in my lap. In the fire-lit tent, my white samite gown glimmered like a star.

"Why are you here, Nimue?" he asked. "It can't be to tell me not to march against Brocéliande. You know that I will not call off this attack."

"No," I said with a small shake of my head. "You will not, and more, you *cannot*. If you stand down now, the war is over, and you will head the losing side. That cannot be allowed to happen." If Faerie won, everything would change, and not for the better.

Emrys frowned as he sat down beside me. "You say that every time we speak. Why won't you tell me your reasons?"

"Is it not enough that I will side with you against my own kind?" I unclasped my hands, reaching up to touch his cheek with the back of my fingers. He was a handsome man, in his way, more like his father than his mother, who had shown her Roane blood more clearly in the curve of her neck and her longing for the sea. She had been my granddaughter, and Emrys was my great-grandson, and when I looked at him, I was still looking, in some small way, at her.

"Believe me, I am more grateful than you can know, but Nimue, I need more." He pushed my hand gently away. "My men wonder why this is the battle we press above all others, when there are Faerie mounds and hollow hills near-undefended all over Albion. This is a castle."

"This is an icon," I corrected gently. "Fly your flag above it and assert that you have a place in this world, even if you are not allowed a place in Faerie. That is what must happen here."

"And how many will die for an icon?"

I turned my eyes away, lest he somehow see the fields of carrion birds reflected in them. Ten merlins for every fae warrior, that was to be the cost of a free and fair tomorrow. His breed would be near-decimated by the battlefield at Brocéliande. "Too many," I said softly.

"Then give me a reason, Nimue, or leave my tent. You have given us enough information to know the castle's weak points."

"I didn't think my brother would come." The words escaped before I could stop them, a truth compelled by Eira's damn geas. I looked back at him, the near-mortal man with my family's eyes, and said, "His name is Michael. He won't die tomorrow—it is difficult to kill the Firstborn, and none of us will fall, win, or lose—but his presence changes the field. He can borrow the eyes of any living thing. Your men. The birds that fly above the battle. There is nothing you can do that he will not see."

"Then we are lost."

"No." I shook my head fiercely. "I would not be here if you were lost." I would be far away, sunk deep in the grieving tides, weeping into the sea, who would always, always forgive me my shortcomings. "There is still a way you can emerge triumphant from the bloodied day to come. But you must trust me now, and you must decide, once and for all, to believe me when I say that I have never lied to you."

Emrys looked at me silently for a time. Finally, he asked, "Nimue, what happens if we do not carry tomorrow's field? Why are you so willing to betray your people?"

I closed my eyes. "Please don't ask me that."

"No." His fingers closed around the flesh of my upper arm. Because he was family, I did not pull away. Because I loved him, at least a little, I did not sink my teeth into his throat to punish him for his transgression. "I have come here because you told me that this battle was the one to turn the tide. I have listened as you changed your song a dozen times because something had shifted. I have told my men that you will not betray us, and watched their faith in me weaken every time you went back to your own kind. I may die tomorrow. We may all die tomorrow, and grant Faerie the victory it so dearly wishes. You *will* tell me."

"I am willing to betray my people because my people betray themselves by taking up arms against you. Faerie was..." I hesitated, searching for the words to frame a truth too big to be contained. "Faerie was pure in the beginning. Untainted by mortality. We were always a house divided, but we were all one family."

"You, too, Auntie?" Emrys pushed himself away, releasing my arm at the same time. I heard him stand. I did not open my eyes. "I always thought that you were different, but you're just like the rest of them, mewling over blood purity and hating us for what we represent."

"No, Emrys. That's not it at all. Faerie was pure, and had Faerie stayed pure, we would not be here. But my brothers and sisters couldn't resist the mortal world—the candle that burns the briefest often gives the brightest flame, and they were drawn to touch the fire. They had children, and those children had children, and the children of those children had children. Faerie is so joined with the mortal world now that there's little sense in pretending the two can ever be separate again." I opened my eyes to find him scowling at me, mistrust written plainly on his face. "The changelings were our responsibility. We failed them. Their children were our responsibility. We failed them as well. Now we're on the verge of failing you."

"And this would make you betray your kin?"

"You *are* my kin," I said. "All of you, through one parent or another, are kin to us. If we kill you..." I faltered. Again, the words seemed too small for something so great and so terrible. "Faerie stands at a crossroads. If we lose here at Brocéliande, our parents will step in. They will say 'You have managed your children poorly,' and my father will change the rules." I had seen them in my dreams, Oberon's hope chests, with the power to make changeling children fae, or to rip the magic from the hands of merlins. We needed them. I didn't know why yet, but I knew that one day, all of Faerie would depend on those trinkets.

"And if you win?"

"If we win—if the tide of battle runs toward Faerie, and not toward her descendants—then our parents will keep their distance, as they always do. The merlins on the field will be slaughtered without mercy, put down as dogs who dared to bite their masters." I closed my eyes again. It didn't stop the images that flowed like water through my mind, but it saved me from the sight of Emrys's face as I continued. "The children of fair Titania will call for a cleansing, and the children of Oberon will be blood-mazed enough to agree. The children of Maeve will argue against it, and we will lose, and the Wild Hunt will ride."

"Who will be left for the Hunt to take?" Emrys sounded horrified, as well he might. It was the slaughter of his people that I spoke of.

"Your wives and daughters; your sons," I said. "Your mothers and your fathers, until every heart that beats with a mingling of fae and human blood has been extinguished. They will kill you all, Emrys. Every changeling, every weak-blood, every merlin, and when the gutters run red, they will say, 'We have done well,' and go back to the arms of their mortal lovers." And when those unions brought forth more children, they would be left on the hillsides to die, until the night-haunts were reduced to a flock of squalling babes, none of whom had been allowed more than the first fragments of their lives.

Silence fell between us. I opened my eyes to find Emrys staring at me, his cheeks as pale as paper and his eyes filled with unshed tears.

"We will carry the field," he whispered. "Only tell me what must be done, and I will see to it that it is so."

I nodded gravely. "You are a wise man," I said. "Sit beside me."

He reclaimed his seat upon the bench.

I told him what he would have to do.

May Faerie one day forgive me.

Morning dawned bright across the fields of Brocéliande. The air grew heavy with the stink of dying magic as the sun ripped down the small illusions of the night, and an army of men appeared at the gates.

Illusions are strange things: when cast simply enough, using primitive enough methods, they can become undetectable to the strongest among us. I leaned against the wall of my secret passage, catching my breath, and listened to the guards on the battlements above me as they sounded the alarm. Emrys's merlins had crept close under cover of their single-natured spells, until they covered the broad, boastful bridge and stood near the very walls of Brocéliande. Feet thundered in the hallway outside.

"Now?" hissed Emrys. I turned to find him all but dancing

in place, eager to join the battle that was even now getting underway. It had grieved him dearly to come with me, rather than standing by his men. Some of them would never trust him again, nor follow him anywhere; that would come to trouble him more and more in the days to come. But his was the hand that held the sword. I knew that.

"Not yet," I replied. More feet thundered past. "Wait."

"I will not wait forever," he snarled. The men behind him— five good men, hand-selected for this mission—grumbled their agreement. My hold on him was wavering, and without him, I had no hold at all over them.

"You will not need to," I softly replied. "Soon."

Men roared both inside and outside the gates. The battle would be joined by now, merlins casting their subtle spells and swinging their swords as fast as they could, and my siblings and their children mowing them down like wheat in a field. Ten for every one that fell, that was the cost of this battlefield. Ten for every one.

The sound of footsteps finally faded. I pushed myself away from the wall, looking to Emrys, and asked, "Do you remember what you must do?"

He nodded. "Yes."

"Then we move." The hidden entrance to the castle proper was not far; I led them there and pushed it open, revealing the empty hall. All who could answer the alarm had gone already, and those of us who were not warriors were expected to be high on the battlements, casting support spells, or hiding in our rooms, waiting for the carnage to pass. No one would question my absence from the field.

Together, the seven of us ran fleetly down the hall. Two serving girls peeped out from a closet, and two of Emrys' men stopped to subdue them, tying their hands and covering their mouths to keep them from screaming. Those men would live. We continued on as five, until we could see the open castle gates ahead of us, and the backs of my brothers who held the field, and the carnage unfolding beyond.

The clash of metal and the stink of a thousand mingled magics drifted on the wind, obscuring the smells of blood and shit and urine that were the true perfumes of battle. A hawk the size of a stallion dropped from the sky, grabbing a merlin in either talon before soaring away again, and a volley of arrows pursued it. A Silene who had come to the fields of Brocéliande only to please her mother fell, her skull cleaved in two by the axe of the merlin who now stood across her body, waiting for his next challenger.

"Now," I murmured. Emrys—dear boy, who understood what we did this day—grabbed me from behind, one arm locking around my neck. I cried out, the sharp, anguished sound of a dying seabird. It pierced the other sounds of battle, washing them away.

When my siblings turned, this is what they saw: a merlin man holding the oldest of Maeve's daughters, an iron knife in his hand and pressed to the soft flesh beneath my chin, which was already beginning to blister from the metal's nearness.

"I have silver," he shouted. "This castle is ours now, or you can explain her body to your parents."

Aoife stepped forward, one hand raised in the beginnings of a spell. "Let her go, merlin, and you can walk away."

"Leave this castle," he replied. "It is ours now."

I closed my eyes, sagging in his arms. It was all down to choice now; all down to how my siblings played their fated roles.

The twang of a bowstring came from somewhere close, and I heard the arrows strike home in the breasts of Emrys's men. They fell. Emrys did not let me go.

"Leave this castle," he said again.

Oh my brothers, oh my sisters, you spent the lives of your descendants like so much coin, but the deaths of our own? Those had always been rare. Those had always mattered. I heard the horns blow to call off the men still fighting in the fields, and still Emrys held me. The servants and the noncombatants were moved from the castle, and still Emrys held me. My throat ached where the iron burnt my skin, and I did not move, and he held me. The surviving merlins came in from the fields. I opened my eyes to see the gates swing shut on the forces of Faerie, standing on the bridge with murder in their eyes.

"You will need to unmake the bridge," I rasped, my voice low and strained from the iron against my skin. "They cannot attack the castle walls, but the bridge..."

"It will be done," he said, and ran the knife across my throat, and I knew no more.

I awoke on the moor, face down in the bracken, the front of my white samite gown stained black with my own blood. Michael crouched nearby, his hands on his thighs and his milk-colored eyes turned in my direction. A raven perched on his shoulder, doubtless lending him its eyes.

"How long?" I rasped.

"A day," he replied, and offered me his hand. I took it, allowing him to pull me from the muck. "He should have used the silver as well, if he wanted your death to keep."

"Mercy is a virtue," I said, standing on unsteady feet and feeling the smooth skin of my throat, already healed from what Emrys had done—what I had ordered him to do. "Brocéliande?"

"The merlins hold it. The spells in the walls were woven well. Too well. We can't reclaim what's ours."

I nodded. "Then the battle is lost."

"Yes." The raven on Michael's shoulder looked at me intently as he asked, "How were you taken, Annie? You are my cleverest sister. You shouldn't have been caught so easily."

"Ah," I sighed. "That is easy, dear brother. I betrayed you. I betrayed you all."

Michael nodded. "I thought as much. Father is here."

". . . truly?"

"Truly." He smiled. "Let us go and tell Oberon that his stronghold is lost, but his daughter lives." There was no judgment in his expression. Michael understood better than most that what I did, I did for good reason.

"I would like that," I said. "Borrow my eyes." There was a tingle as his magic slid into my mind, and then the raven that had been serving him took flight, racing to join its family in the feast that covered the fields. Together, arm in arm, we walked away from Brocéliande.

The Keeper of Names

LARRY CORREIA

"THE DEMONS MUST BE EMERGING FROM THE SEA AGAIN," THE overseer said as he entered the storehouse.

Alarmed, Keta the butcher sprinted to the entrance, meat cleaver in hand. He looked toward the distant shore, but saw no monsters. The ocean was its normal blue, not blood-red like the last time. "Are they coming?" he gasped. It had been nearly twenty years since their last incursion into the lands of House Uttara. "How do you know? Have you seen them?"

Yet the overseer wasn't panicking like most men would if they'd seen such horrors. "Calm yourself, butcher." The large man scowled as he moved one hand to the whip at his side. He was a hard man but, unlike most appointed to his station, not a totally unkind one. Such disrespectful questions could earn a beating. They were both casteless, but even amongst the lowest of the low, there was order.

Keta bowed his head. "Forgive me. I was little the last time the demons came. They slaughtered everyone." Realizing that he was still clutching the sharpened cleaver, Keta quickly dropped it onto a nearby table. The Law said his kind were not allowed weapons, only the tools necessary to perform their work. "Fear made me speak out of turn."

The overseer let go of the whip. "I've seen the ocean beasts myself. Only a fool would be unafraid. There have been no raids yet." Remarkably, he took the time to answer the young man's questions. "This morning I was told that one of the Protectors of the Law is on his way here."

Keta's mouth was suddenly very dry.

"A Protector is coming all the way from the capital." The overseer scratched his head. "That's a long journey, and this house isn't so big to warrant such a visit. I bet demons have been seen along these shores again. What else could attract a Protector's attention?"

An uprising... But Keta didn't speak. The Protectors kept order between houses and the castes in their place. He could only pray to the Forgotten that it was demons from the Haunted Sea and not another purge that brought such a perfect killer into their midst. *What a horrible thing to wish for.*

"Regardless of the reason for the visit, the master wants his holdings in top shape for a visitor of such high status." The overseer glanced around Keta's storehouse. Cured meats hung from chains. Barrels of salted fish were neatly stacked in the corners. The storehouse was already extremely neat and organized, as Keta had learned a long time ago that the best way to avoid trouble was to never cause any. "I can't imagine a warrior who can kill demons with his bare hands inventorying meat, but clean everything just in case."

"As you command, it will be done."

"And one other thing." The overseer leaned in conspiratorially. "I heard the master giving instructions. If it is demons, and we're raided, the warriors are to protect the master's household first, then the town, then the livestock next, and once the cows and pigs are safe, only *then* see to the casteless quarter." The overseer's disgust was obvious. "It's nice to know that years of loyal service has made it so that our master values the chickens more than he values the lives of my children."

Was this a test of his obedience? "That is how they are valued according to the Law."

"I don't think demons honor the Law." The overseer's eyes darted toward the discarded meat cleaver. "I'd keep that handy if I were you."

"That is just a tool necessary to fulfill the responsibilities assigned to me," Keta said automatically. "I would never—"

"Of course." The overseer nodded. "It's just a tool. I forget myself. That's not a wise thing to do with a Protector coming. I will spread the word. Get back to work."

He waited until the master's man had left the storehouse before returning the meat cleaver to its place on his apron. The overseer was correct. The master and the Law were correct. A sharpened piece of steel was just a tool. The spears, knives, and clubs Keta had been secretly stockpiling beneath the barrels of fish were also just tools.

His mind was the weapon.

"I think the overseer might join with us when the time comes," Keta whispered to his fellow conspirators.

"He strikes me as the master's man," Baldev said. "I wouldn't trust him."

"I don't know. He seemed truthful. I think he's had enough of the Law. Same as us."

"The overseer's words are worth salt water." Govind's teeth were visible in the dark when he grinned. "Besides, he's given me the whip one too many times for no good reason. He's getting his throat cut, same as the rest of the master's pets, when the time comes."

There was a constant low level of noise in the bunkhouse, as was bound to happen when you packed over two dozen casteless men, women, and children into one shack, so they weren't too worried about being overheard. There were many other bunkhouses just like this one on the master's lands, and each one had its own conspirators as well.

"When the time comes? We keep talking about that like it's the return of the Forgotten." Baldev was casual about his blasphemy. "If this Protector is on his way because of us, the time needs to be *now*. We need to strike soon."

The dirt floor was covered in straw. Everyone slept on top of their personal belongings to keep them from getting stolen during the night. Keta rolled over on his meat cutter's apron to stare at his friend. "Are you mad? We're not ready. There aren't enough of us."

"The master's house only has a hundred warriors. We've got twice that now."

"Have you been out in the sun too long, Govind?" Keta was actually surprised the fisherman could count that high. "Your duty is to mend the nets. That's all you do. Sleep, eat, shit, screw, and mend nets, and then complain about mending nets to us before you repeat it all the next day. Your whole life you've worked on nets. How good are you at mending nets?"

"I'm really good at mending nets."

"So, if I grabbed any two men here, and sent them to the

beach tomorrow, they together would be able to handle nets as good as you by yourself?"

"Of course not. It takes time."

"Exactly, stupid. The warrior caste's only duty is to fight and train to fight. That's all they do. That's all they care about. You hear them on the other side of that fence, hitting each other with wooden swords from dawn to dusk. They're as good at their duty as you are at yours. No, we wait until we have enough to overwhelm the house all at once. And then when we win, we win fast and clean. All of the casteless in this province will rise up and kill their warriors, too."

Baldev was the strongest, but he knew Keta was the smart one. "And there's so many of us that even the other houses won't be able to do a thing."

"This province is the ass end of the land. We've got cursed ocean on three sides. The other houses are too busy fighting each other to send an army to deal with us, and by the time they do, we'll have formed our own army. A real casteless army. Only then, we won't be casteless anymore. We'll be whole men, like them, and even the Law will have to recognize us."

"Just because you're the only one of us who can read makes you think you're so smart," Govind snarled. "You steal one of the master's books about strategy, and you think you're such an expert. You're a dreamer."

The book had merely given him new ideas. Govind had no idea just how much of a dreamer Keta really was. They were focused on freeing themselves, but Keta wanted to free *all* of the casteless in every province. He wanted to see the great houses in flames. Even though they weren't allowed to speak of the old ways or practice any of their traditions, Keta knew in his heart that the Forgotten was real, and though they had abandoned their god, their god would never abandon them.

"We keep doing what we're doing. Find more like us, willing to fight and smart enough to keep their mouths shut. When the day comes, we'll know. Soon, my friends, it'll be very soon."

Govind grunted. "Fine. We'll wait then. And while we wait, this Protector will show up, breathing fire, kill us all, eat our souls, and we'll be so much better off. I'm going to sleep."

Keta lay on his back, stared at the logs of the ceiling, and tried to ignore the screaming of hungry babies.

Baldev waited a minute before whispering again. "What are we going to do about the Protector, Keta?"

"Nobody will talk. Our plan is safe."

"And if it's not?"

They'd all heard stories about what the Protectors of the Law were capable of. "The Protectors are only men, Baldev. They're only men."

"You are wrong."

Keta woke up with a start. He sat up in the straw, and his first instinct was to move his hands about to make sure no one had stolen his belongings or the meager amount of food he had stashed. It took him a moment to regain enough sense to understand that it was very late, and the bunkhouse was too quiet. The snoring, grunting, and farting of the packed in bodies seemed muted, like his ears were plugged. But he'd heard a voice. Keta looked around and flinched as he realized somebody was sitting in the straw behind him, only a few feet away.

"The Protectors are more than men now. It is best to think of them as a one-man army, or perhaps a one-man inquisition. They are warrior monks of the highest caste, whose bodies and minds have been broken by hardship and reformed by magic, and if one of them is trying to kill you, then you will more than likely die."

Keta slowly put one hand on the handle of his cleaver. Squinting, he tried to make out the visitor's features in the dark. The stranger was very old, probably forty years at least, thin even by casteless standards, and dressed in fabric made of the coarse woven fibers common to one of their station. "Who're you?"

"Someone who has been listening to your plotting and been rather amused by it. Our people were thrown down forty generations ago. Do you really think in all those years you are the first who has thought he could destroy the Law?"

"Quiet!" Keta hissed. The old man wasn't even whispering. He scanned the room, but everyone appeared to be asleep. "Are you trying to get us killed?"

"You are doing a fine job of that without any help from me. Besides, none of them can hear us. We may speak freely."

Keta snorted. "What? Are you supposed to be a wizard or something?"

"Yes, Keta the butcher, something like that. I am the Ratul, Keeper of Names, and I have come to help you shake the foundations of the world."

Keta did not speak of the strange visitor to anyone, especially his fellow conspirators. They would've either thought he was mad, or that it was some sort of elaborate ploy to expose them. But a Keeper of Names? They were a tale that casteless mothers would tell their children to give them enough hope to sleep at night. Even talking of the Forgotten's clergy was a violation of the Law. Only a babbling madman would claim to be one. Yet, Keta had to know the truth.

The next night he waited for everyone assigned to his shack to fall asleep before sneaking out the back window. His sandals didn't make much noise on the grass. There were so few warriors here that he wasn't worried about being seen, but even if he was, he'd never been caught violating curfew before and more than likely could plead his way out of it by saying that he was going to visit one of the women assigned to a different shack. He'd probably only get a beating to show for it at worst. As much as the higher castes would never admit it, Keta suspected he was far too valuable at his duties to start chopping his limbs off for such a minor infraction. He did the work of a butcher and a storekeeper, and it would take far too long to teach another casteless to read the inventory ledgers.

The tide was high. The surf was crashing against the black rocks. Ratul was waiting for him there.

The madman did not turn to look as Keta approached. "Did you know that in the days before the sky opened and the demons fell from the heavens, that man actually moved across the waters in great vessels?"

"That's foolishness." The ocean was pure evil. There were only two things to be found in the ocean: death and fish. And fish were only good to feed to the casteless, as whole men would never touch something tainted by unclean salt water. "Why would anyone do such a thing?"

"Because we are not alone, or maybe we are now, but we were not then. There are other lands, as big or bigger than this one, and isles, so many isles, thousands of them in between."

Keta knew that there were islands. On a clear day some could even be seen on the horizon. He remembered a time many years ago when some of the casteless decided to try and make it to one. A false prophet had a vision, saying they could go live in a place beyond the Law's reach, and be whole men there. He said the Forgotten would protect them during their journey. Many fools had gone with him on their pathetic cobbled-together boat, while the rest had watched, curious, along the shore. Of course, the demons had come from the deep and consumed them, and the master of the house had laughed and laughed at the foolishness of his non-people.

"There used to be trade, of ideas, things, animals and crops. Men explored and settled and made new lives and bore children who'd do the same. Now that the demons own the sea, I wonder if those other lands have become as dark and isolated as this one, or if they still live at all. Here, Ramrowan pushed the demons back into the sea. Maybe the Forgotten didn't send other lands such a hero."

He had heard so many conflicting myths and stories, but this was new. "Ramrowan?"

"They've done such a fine job stomping out our history here." Ratul looked at Keta for the first time. "When God defeated the demons in the War in Heaven, they fell here and began a great slaughter. Mortals could not slice the hide of a demon, so God sent one of his generals to the world to protect us. It was Ramrowan who united all the houses and pushed the demons back into the sea. Thus Ramrowan became the First King. We built a great temple at the spot where he fell to the world, and a city sprung up around it. It is still the capital today."

"The Law says that there are no gods and no kings," Keta said suspiciously. "There is no temple in the capital, and there is certainly no king over the houses."

"The Law did not exist then. In those days there were prophets who taught God's will. After Ramrowan died, the prophets said that the demons would return again, and only the blood of Ramrowan would be able to smite them. If this bloodline died out, we would all perish with it. The Sons of Ramrowan were to defend us, and their bloodline could never die, or we would be defenseless before the demons. They each took a hundred wives and had many more sons who each took many more wives. Their lives were sacred, and far more important than lesser men, so the first caste was born."

"There have always been castes!" Keta insisted. "I read it in a book!"

"Heh. You can read? I knew that I chose well. No, butcher, the Sons of Ramrowan were the first caste, and as time went on other castes were created to serve their whims. First were the workers, then the warriors, then the merchants and most of the others that we still have today, all of them created to see that every desire of the Sons was granted. All wealth was theirs to take. Any woman they desired was granted as another wife, because what are the wishes or property of any one house compared to our eternal security from the demons? The priests enforced the will of the ruling caste. They began to replace their god's teachings with the desires of the Sons of Ramrowan. As the numbers of the first caste grew, so did their greed and pride."

"We will rise up and kill them all," Keta spat. "They are still horrible today!"

"Yes..." Ratul turned back to the waves. "Yes, they are." He sighed. "Things changed over the generations. The priests began to forget their god, and the prophecies were merely tools to gain riches. The church and the Sons of Ramrowan became one and the same, and the priests even bore their name. Eventually, the great houses grew in unbelief until they only saw the priesthood as oppressors. The Sons of Ramrowan, who had grown fat and indolent, were no match for the brutal warrior caste they'd created to protect them. The great houses were so angry that they destroyed the church and killed every priest they could find. The temples were burned and the statues were smashed. The Law was written to correct the excesses of the First Caste, but it went too far. It declared there was no before and no after, so it only set in stone corruption. And thus our god was Forgotten."

"You claim to be of the old priesthood." Keta didn't know what to believe. "Why are you telling me this, Ratul?"

"Because the Protector of the Law isn't coming here for your pathetic rebellion. He is coming here for *me*."

Govind, the net mender, was at his left, and Baldev, the stone lifter, was at his right. Today they were not casteless net menders, stone lifters, or butchers, they were soldiers, and they were striking back against the house that had kept a boot on their face their entire life. Twenty more casteless were crowding against the doorway behind them, eager to begin.

This is what it must feel like to be a whole man.

The sound of woodcutter's axes falling on sleeping heads was far louder than expected. The warrior's barracks was coming to life. Men were springing from their beds—*the warrior caste got actual beds*—and taking up their swords.

"Kill them all!" Keta lifted his meat cleaver and hurled himself, screaming, at the nearest rising warrior. He lashed out and caught the warrior's wrist as he reached for his sheathed sword. The stump came back, pumping red. Keta snarled and hacked away. Steel parted flesh, opening the warrior's neck clear to the vertebra, and he flopped back into this blankets.

Keta had never killed a man before, but he found they died not so different than butchering a pig.

Until they fought back.

The warriors collected themselves far too quickly, and then their swords were slicing back and forth through the darkness. They stood shoulder to shoulder, each one knowing what to do because they'd practiced together for thousands of hours. A handful of assassins rushed them, and casteless blood splattered the walls and pumped out onto the floor as a result. Another group hit, but the warriors split the wave like a cliff rock.

They were a wall of steel. The warrior's backs were to a stone wall. Keta had expected this would happen. They needed to be pulled into the open, so Keta could surround and crush them with superior numbers. "Outside! Everyone run!" Keta slipped in a puddle, but then Baldev had him by the arm, hoisting him and carrying him back toward the door. "Run!"

Of course, the warriors gave chase, because that was what a predator did when its prey fled. Even naked and barely awake, the warriors didn't hesitate. They rushed out the door after the assassins, and right into the waiting spears and hurled rocks of a casteless mob. The pursuing warriors had not expected so many foes, and they died quickly as a result.

There were other barracks, but they were made of wood, so they'd been set on fire. As the coughing warriors tried to come out, they were shoved back with spears. Impaled or burned, Keta didn't care. The manner of their deaths didn't matter. Only that they all died.

Keta climbed on top of a barrel so that everyone could see him. He waved his bloody cleaver overhead. "Tonight we show them we are whole men. To the master's house!" If everything had gone as planned, the master would already be dead, throat slit by a casteless pleasure woman who was part of the conspiracy, but Keta didn't want to dampen his new army's enthusiasm. "Onward!"

"Drag him from his hiding place and hang him on the punishment wall!" Govind bellowed as he brandished the dead overseer's whip.

The mob surged toward the master's house. Other warriors would be waiting, and these would be alert, ready, and possibly armored, but there would be no stopping the tide of blood tonight. Keta hopped down from the barrel.

A hand fell on his shoulder, so hard and strong that at first he thought it had to be Baldev, but instead it was the frail old Ratul, the supposed Keeper of Names. "What are you doing?" he demanded.

"Creating an army. Creating a future!"

"All the time I spent teaching you the old ways, and you've learned nothing, hot-blooded fool!" Ratul pointed toward the gateway of the master's house. "You've doomed them all."

Shadows created by several torches bounced wildly across the stone walls. There was a lone figure silhouetted in the entrance, blocking the way. Keta had to squint to see. There was a man, tall, broad of shoulder, just standing there, without so much as a tremble before the rushing mob of furious bodies. He had a forward-curving sword in one hand, the tip resting on the steps. His armor was strange, and ornate, each piece of steel intricately etched and filled with silver. The stranger looked at Keta's army... and *smiled*.

It was the Protector of the Law.

"He's not supposed to be here yet," Keta stammered. "There's no way he can—"

The Protector stepped forward, directly into the mob. His movements were quick, difficult to follow, impossible to predict. Spears were thrust into the space he'd been filling and rocks were hurled uselessly through the air. The Protector took another step forward as the first wave of Keta's rebellion fell dead and dying behind him.

Only a few seconds had passed. The rest of the mob didn't even know that there was a nightmare in their midst yet, but then the screaming began, and blood sprayed into the torches and burned, sizzling with that familiar smell. Arms and legs were separated. Heads went rolling. And still, the Protector was untouched. Some tried to fight. All of them died. Others tried to run, a few of them made it.

It wasn't a sword. It was like a farmer's sickle. And the caste-less were wheat.

He walked through the trailing edge of the mob, only it was no longer a mob, it was a mass of severed tendons and broken bones. It was like the floor of Keta's butcher shop on the busiest day of the year, magnified and spread over the entirety of the master's grounds.

Baldev was the strongest of them all. He roared as he swung his mighty hammer. The Protector stepped aside and let it shatter the stone where he'd been standing. With barely even a flick of the wrist, Baldev's guts were suddenly spilled everywhere in a tangled purple mass. Govind struck with the overseer's whip. It was clumsy, missing the *snap* of the overseer's skilled touch. The Protector merely caught the leather, tugged Govind toward him, and sheared the top half of the fisherman's skull off.

Calm as could be, the killer strolled down the path, silver reflecting the light of torches dropped from nerveless fingers. And, at that moment, the uprising against House Uttara was broken. Keta's brothers dropped their tools and ran like the sea demons had come to swallow their souls.

Keta would not run. This was his doing. He lifted the meat cleaver in one shaking hand. "Damn your Law!" he screamed at the Protector. "I will die a whole man!"

"No." Ratul pulled Keta around to face him. "Take this." He shoved a heavy bundle, wrapped tightly in oilcloth, against Keta's chest. "Keep it safe. Go south to the Ice Coast."

"I can't—"

Ratul shoved him away with surprising strength. "Flee, Keta the butcher. A new prophet has been called in the south to guide us. God will choose a general like unto Ramrowan of old to lead us. You will serve them both as they forge a true army. God will guide your path. I have seen it." Ratul reached down and picked up one of the fallen warriors' swords. He spun it smoothly once, as if testing the weight, and the old man did not seem unused to such an implement. Ratul began walking toward the approaching Protector. "It is time for our people to remember what has been forgotten."

Keta watched, horrified, as the Protector approached. He stopped several feet away from Ratul, and then did something that Keta had never seen nor imagined he would ever see from someone of such a high station. The Protector politely *bowed* to Ratul. "Greetings, Keeper."

"Good evening, Devedas." Ratul returned the gesture, as if he were an equal. "I'd always hoped it would be you."

The two lifted their swords, their stances a mirror image of the other.

Keta the butcher ran for his life.

He ran for hours, across rocks, down the beaches, through the tide pools shallow enough to be free of demons. When he didn't think he could run any farther, he ran some more, vomiting in the sand, but never slowing. When he thought his heart might burst, he still pushed on, terrified, afraid to look back toward bloody House Uttara. He tripped and gashed his head open on the rocks, but he never dropped the heavy bundle Ratul had given him.

When Keta could run no more, he collapsed into a quivering mass of burning muscle, crawled into the hollow of a tree, and pulled branches and leaves over his hiding spot as the sun rose. He'd sleep during the day and run at night. There would be a purge. There was always a purge when the casteless sinned against the Law. Everyone he had ever known was dead or would be soon.

When he awoke hours later, Keta found that Ratul's bundle was still in his hand. The oilcloth had been wrapped tight and cinched with leather straps. Curious, he carefully unwrapped the package.

It was a book. The thickest book he had ever seen. It was nothing like the plain things he's stolen from the master's library over the years. This was bound in a thick, black leather, unbelievably smooth when handled one way, but sharp enough to draw blood if rubbed against the grain. He'd heard of such a thing. This was the supposedly indestructible hide of a demon. Keta opened it hesitantly. Each yellowed page was magnificent, packed with letters so small he could barely make them out.

They were names. The book was filled with names and numbers that had to be dates. Linking the names were lines. Page after page, there had to be as many names and lines as there were grains of sand on the beach. It wasn't that different from the ledgers he'd kept all his life, only these were people, not supplies or animals. The master had such a thing for his house, a wall painted with the names of fathers and sons, stretching back for generations. The master called it a genealogy; only that one had been insignificant in comparison to this.

One page had been marked with a folded piece of parchment. That page said *House Uttara* across the top, and it was dense with inked names and lines.

He recognized many of the names. These were *casteless* names.

But it couldn't be. Each entry had *two* names. Non-people didn't get two names. Only whole men had a family name. The Law did not allow the casteless to have families. Casteless were property. Not people.

Hesitantly, Keta traced his finger down the page until he found his own family name.

Ramrowan.

Heart pounding, hands shaking, he closed the book, then wrapped it tightly in the oilcloth, extra careful to make sure it was sealed and the straps were cinched tight.

Then Keta, Keeper of Names, began his long journey south.

The Smaller We Are

JOHN HELFERS

THEY ATTACKED JUST AFTER NIGHTFALL.

We'd just finished making camp in a clearing after scouting routes for our main force all day. After setting guards, we were sitting down to cold mushroom cakes when the hum of whirring wings made Syreth's pointed ears twitch. The satyr and I looked up as a blur of motion streaked toward us.

Tliel's small, skinny body decelerated to hover in front of my face, his wings beating too fast to see. The pixie's entire body was shrouded in darkcloth, with only his glowing, silver eyes visible. The crack of breaking branches and thud of footsteps shook the ground behind him.

"Six tallest coming! To arms!" Not waiting for orders, Tliel shot up into the air, intending to survey the battleground, then assist where needed. But as he rose, a bow *twanged*, and a black streak hit and carried him into the tree canopy.

The rest of my unit was already moving, but it was too late. Before we could organize, the tallest burst through the tall elms and maples and rushed at us. Clad in black leather armor, faces shadowed under iron helmets, they attacked in pairs. One was armed with the usual long sword, its scalloped edge capable of cleaving any of us apart if it connected. The second held a large net, which was thrown at a designated target.

Tliel's warning did allow us to avoid being taken completely unaware. While flight was probably the best option, we were too close to enemy lines to risk abandoning each other. And besides, we hadn't had a straight-up fight in a long time.

Fzith and Bzith, surviving brothers from a large goblin family who had been fighting since the war began, threw their wooden plates at the lead warriors while drawing double-bladed daggers. Rethgar, my fearless redcap, grabbed his worn pikestaff and charged straight at his two, evading the thrown net by speed alone. Crouching on equine legs, Syreth sprang into the air, also avoiding the net sailing toward him. His ironwood-shod hooves came down with a loud *clunk* on an enemy warrior's head. Nereas, her face unlined yet weary amid long, white hair, danced away from another spinning net and into the trunk of the nearest oak tree, disappearing as she merged with the living wood.

And me? As the net intended to catch me flared out overhead, I simply sank into the earth.

Below the surface, my gnomish vision was gone, but I homed in on the nearest enemy by tracking his heavy footfalls shaking the ground. To my left, the roots of Nereas's tree flexed and shifted as the dryad brought the mighty oak to life. I grinned at the painful surprise about to be visited upon our enemies. They may control the plains and their noxious cities, but the woods are still *our* domain.

As I stalked my target, I was jarred by a distant, heavy footfall that shook the earth around me. I'd felt that kind of impact before, and quickened my pace, even as my spine shivered. *Please don't let it be one of* them.

Drawing my granite dagger, I rose out of the ground into the midst of furious combat, all frenzied movement, grunts, yells, and screams. Pike head clashed with sword as Rethgar battled a blade-wielding tallest. A few steps away, Syreth defended himself with his foot-long horns while threatening his two assailants with a gnarled oak cudgel. Blood sprayed from a nasty cut on his arm with each powerful swing.

The creak of old wood sounded as one of the satyr's opponents was grabbed by several oak branches. Nereas lifted the man high into the air, then threw him against another oak on the other side of the clearing. The leather-clad warrior hit headfirst, fell to the ground, and did not rise again. With a feral grin, Syreth pressed his advantage on the remaining tallest, forcing the swordsman to retreat in the face of those razor-sharp horns and a thick wooden club.

Lying next to me was the net-bearer who had tried to capture the redcap, moaning and clutching his privates. He smelled of blood, sweat, and fear, and I knew exactly where Reth's first stab had gone. His eyes locked with mine. Before he could move, I bent over and slashed the wounded warrior's throat, his blood gushing out to stain the dirt black. The tallest reached up to try and dam the tide of life's blood flowing between his fingers, but was too late. The scent of copper filled the air, his arms going limp as his panicked choking faded to dying gurgles.

I felt the same heavy, crushing footfall I'd sensed before, closer this time, and looked around to see whom I could aid before the enemy reinforcements arrived.

A goblin curse made me glance at Fzith and Bzith facing the last pair of enemy warriors. The mottled brothers stood back-to-back, twin double-bladed daggers in both hands, fighting *broznich* style, their left feet heel-to-heel so each could sense the other's movements and plan his offense or defense accordingly. It allowed two or three goblins to vanquish twice their number. Against equal numbers, it was only a matter of time before they prevailed.

Meanwhile, Rethgar advanced relentlessly on his opponent, leading with well-placed stabs and slashes of his iron pike. The tallest defended himself valiantly, but the tireless, feral redcap kept pushing the fighter backward—directly toward me.

When he was a step away, I stabbed my blade into the back of his knee, penetrating the softer leather at the joint. The dagger point sank deep into his flesh, grating against bone. With an agonized shout, the warrior fell to the ground as I pulled my blade out and sank it into his side, underneath the armor straps. He screamed again, keeping his sword up to fend off Rethgar while clawing at me with his free hand. The redcap slashed the blade away with a mighty swing, then brought the pike around and down to cleave through the tallest's raised arm and into his nose. The iron spearhead rose and fell twice more, and when it was over, the man's face was a bloody ruin.

Another footstep shook the ground, making Reth look up, alarm flitting across his face. He exchanged a nervous glance with me. "Is that—"

A shout from the other side of the meadow made me look over to see Bzith clutching his side, where the fletching of an arrow jutted from between his ribs. *The archer!*

"Help them!" I snapped as I turned to run for the tree line.

Before I'd taken a step, a high, terrified yell tore the air. The tallest archer dangled in midair, held captive by the branches of the tree he'd been using as a perch. The living wood wrapped around his arms and legs, pulling his limbs apart unmercifully. His helmet had been knocked off, and pain contorted his brutish face as he strained against his bonds. His mouth gaped open in a scream of pure agony, and when I saw the lower part of his breastplate bulged out, I knew what Nereas had done.

The smaller branches uncurled from around the archer's arms and legs. Sliding off the thick limb that had impaled him, the tallest flopped to the ground. His trembling fingers plucked at the straps of his armor, but he was too dazed and weak to remove it. Drops of his own blood fell on his face from the dark-stained branch above. Even with aid, he would die from the terrible wound. Eventually.

My face remained impassive as I watched him twitch and shudder. I knew Nereas was merciless—a dryad who survives the destruction of her grove has nothing left but revenge—but I had never seen that trick before.

A strangled grunt drew my attention back to the goblin brothers. With Rethgar reinforcing them, the last pair of tallest was on the defensive, the net-bearer having drawn a flanged mace to assist his partner. They stood next to each other, their weapons a barrier of steel against the two goblins and one blurred redcap.

Beginning to sink into the earth, I stepped forward to help. As I did, a caprine form hurtled down out of the darkness, staving in the swordsman's head. The satyr screamed in triumph as he crushed the tallest's body to the ground. His partner gaped in shock at the sudden death of his partner. Before he could move, he was pierced three times: twice by goblin blades, and once by a needle-pointed satyr's horn. He convulsed and began to drop as Rethgar wound up and swung his pike with all his might.

The last tallest's head bounced across the clearing and rolled to a stop at my feet, his shocked eyes glazing over into death. Panting hard, we all looked at each other as another thundering footstep sounded, accompanied by the snap and crack of breaking timber.

We all knew what was coming, but Nereas spoke first, using the leaves and branches of her tree to whisper the words. "A *Ravager approaches.*"

"Then leave that tree. We have to get out of here—" I began.

"More humans follow it . . . gooo . . . I will hold them here—"

"Damn it, Nereas, I'm ordering you to come out of there right *now!*" I said.

"Gooo now . . . before it's too late."

"She's right, Topkir," Rethgar said, blunt as a stone. "We gotta go, afore we're all nicked."

I didn't move, even though I could sense more footsteps behind the Ravager. "Nereas—"

An oak branch bent down to push me, not unkindly, toward the far end of the clearing. *"Nooo time . . . gooo!"*

Fists clenched with rage, yet knowing she was right, I stumbled to the other side of the clearing. A blue-white glow from the forest warned where the Ravager was coming from, and as I pushed into the underbrush, I glanced back to see it explode into the glade.

A head higher than any tallest I'd ever seen, the Ravager was a cold-iron monstrosity, one of our enemy—at least I was pretty sure a tallest was inside it—who was encased entirely in iron. Some kind of unknown, fearful magic allowed the person inside to see, because there was no viewport on the blank face, only smooth metal. Its hobnailed feet sank an inch or two into the ground with each step, but it strode forward with ease. Blue-white light flashed from the joints of its arms and legs each time it moved. Several tallest trailed behind it, using the Ravager as a merciless battering ram to clear the forest before them.

Nereas reached for it with every branch she had, entwining its arms and legs in wood. The Ravager plowed relentlessly forward, its jointed fingers grabbing oak limbs, snapping them off, and casting them aside. I knew every broken limb hurt Nereas—a dryad feels damage to the tree she inhabits as if the injury is inflicted on her—yet I still didn't move, hoping she would flee before it was too late.

The Ravager marched toward her oak, breaking tree limbs as thick as my body like they were brittle twigs. Reaching the trunk, it encircled hard metal arms around it and strained. Nereas screamed as the iron pressed into the tree. With a mighty heave, the Ravager ripped the mature oak from the ground and dropped it, the once majestic tree now dying—and with it, one of my best scouts.

Hands clutched my jerkin and pulled me into the brush. Blinking tears from my eyes, I let myself be led deeper into the woods as we fled.

We ran for what seemed like hours, until we were sure we had left all pursuit behind. No one complained, although Bzith panted hoarsely with every step. His brother and Rethgar took turns helping him along. Although the tallest have a longer stride than us, they do not know the forest like we who have grown up in it.

Night shrouded us when I finally called a halt. We staggered to a stop amid a cluster of elms, their leaves fluttering in the slight breeze. Normally I would have had Nereas merge with the biggest tree to sense for nearby enemies, but that wasn't possible anymore. I merged with the earth for a moment, reaching out for anyone following us, but felt nothing. Pulling back up, I rubbed a grimy hand over my face, the strain and lack of sleep weighing on me as the rush of combat and flight faded. Even so, something about that fight bothered me.

"What now, Top?" Fzith asked. "Tallest are pushin' deeper in. We need t'report back, yah?"

Still deep in thought, I didn't reply. Then I realized what was strange. "They had a Ravager."

Rethgar spat on the ground. "Yeah, so? See more and more damnable things from them every day. What's special bout this one?"

"Intel says Ravagers don't operate on the front lines unless there's a tallest caster nearby—something about needing them to make the construct work. We didn't see any caster sign, which means they're hiding him somewhere." I raised my head to stare at my squad. "We need to find that caster."

Rethgar shook his head. "Orders were to scout and return, not cross enemy lines—"

"We can do both," I interrupted. "Send Tliel back to head-quarters with our report while we go locate the tallest camp. We can't let any units blunder into a caster unaware." They're the most deadly tallest—able to warp natural energies into their own foul magic. A single one could destroy an entire company. For that reason, any casters spotted were killed on sight. I looked around. "Where's Tliel?"

We all checked around for the pixie, but saw no sign of him. "Where'd he go after sounding the warning?" Syreth asked.

"The archer." I cursed my lack of awareness. I'd been so focused on Nereas' sacrifice that I'd forgotten the pixie took an arrow during the fight. "He was hit, but I thought he was still flying." My gut twisted at the thought of losing another soldier. "We have to go back."

"I left a trail," Rethgar said. "If he was up, he'da found it—and us—by now."

"Syreth, you and I will backtrack and look for him. Reth and Bzith, do what you can for Fzith's injury. We'll be back as soon as we can." Snugging my battered, pointed leather cap tight on my head, I turned to the satyr. "Let's go."

He picked me up and settled me on his shoulders, then bounded off through the woods, accelerating until the passing trees and brush were nothing more than a black blur. Rethgar could go as fast in a straight line, but he couldn't maneuver like a satyr. All I could do was hold on to his thick gray pelt and not cry out every time we came within a hair's-breadth of hitting a stump or rock. But Syreth adjusted our trajectory every time, whizzing between the towering trunks and ancient boulders jutting from the earth.

When we reached the clearing, he set me down at the edge. We both scanned the area, in case the tallest had left a force behind. The dead bodies had been removed, and only black patches of drying blood and dozens of large footprints—including the deeper ones of the Ravager—remained. There was no sign of Tliel.

Syreth sniffed the air. "Tallest stink everywhere . . . can't pick up his scent."

I swallowed past the lump in my throat when I saw Nereas's toppled oak, its limbs torn or chopped off and its bark scored with dozens of sword cuts. Like us, the tallest were not merciful to their enemies.

We cautiously entered the clearing, ready to run at the slightest sound of the enemy. "Guard me." I sank into the ground again. Concentrating, I extended my senses, searching for any sign of our comrade. *There.*

Rising, I trotted to the far side. On the ground, amid a line of tallest boot prints, was a lone, glowing drop of blood. Walking a few steps into the woods, I found another one. Next to it lay a single, tiny, broken arrow, confirming my worst fear.

"He's been taken."

Our reduced unit traveled swiftly through the forest, ready to slaughter anyone who got in our way. When we returned, there was no discussion about what had to be done. We never left one of our own in the hands of the tallest. Ever. Even Bzith had nodded when he'd learned where we were going. Although his seamed face was drawn and pale, and his side must have pained him with every step, he hadn't uttered a sound of complaint.

Twice we avoided tallest patrols, although we were forced to double back and circle around the second enemy party. We weren't sure they were specifically looking for us, but it made sense—we'd killed theirs and escaped with our lives. Well, most of us. After dodging the second group, caution slowed our steps—no sense losing four to save one.

After calling yet another halt, Syreth returned from point and bent to my ear. "Edge of the woods is just ahead. Suggest we take a look before going in."

I nodded, and we all crept through the underbrush to where the woods ended and the realm of the tallest began.

Before us stretched endless plains, once mighty forest like what we were being pushed deeper and deeper into, now denuded and bare, so that more tallest could build their villages, "towns," or even the largest and most offensive of their settlements, a city.

We crouched near one of these smaller holdings now. Once, it had been a thriving settlement we'd been friends with long ago, living next to them in harmony and trading for what we needed.

Now the village was mostly razed wreckage. Only a few scattered homes were left, all damaged from the skirmishes ranging along the edge of our forest. Thatched roofs were burned or holed, doors and walls smashed in. All that was left of the mill where we'd once bought flour was a single wall near the dry creek; the rest had been reduced to rubble.

It wasn't always this way. Years ago, we smallkin lived in peace with the tallest. We had been allies, fighting side by side in the Great Trollent Wars. The alliance had been powerful enough to shatter the Trollent King's attempted conquest of the other races. It had even freed the goblins, who had supplied invaluable intelligence before the final battle on the Plains of Toolk, and they had been rewarded by being allowed to live in the forest among the rest of us. The several years of peace afterward were wonderful.

But as the peace continued, the tallest began chafing under

it. Restless and aggressive, they began pushing their borders out more and more, encroaching on our lands, countering any protest by saying they needed "just a bit more space."

We tried reasoning with them, but all attempts failed. The elves sought an accord first, seeking to ratify borders for both sides, and halt the increasing skirmishes between the two races, but the tallest accused them of plotting to take over their own lands. They warned the elves that if their demands were not granted, they would take what was rightfully theirs. War was declared soon after.

At the time, we kept out of the conflict, not wanting to choose one side and risk the wrath of the other. The Tallest-Elven war shook the countryside, laying waste to kingdoms of both races before the fecund tallest practically wiped out the elvish race. A scattered few may have survived, but they were hiding far, far away from here.

We thought there would surely be peace after that, but the tallest next turned their greedy gaze to the mountain kingdoms of the dwarves, saying those industrious people were hoarding their best gems and gold for themselves, and trading the poorest ones with the rest of us. When the drums of war sounded again, still we did not participate, feeling that as long as they left our homes alone, the tallest would be content when they had again taken what they felt they deserved. It was a terrible mistake for both races. The dwarves have barricaded themselves inside their mountain fortresses, thinking themselves safe, but we know the truth—it is only a matter of time until the tallest eradicate them as well.

Only when the tallest launched their war on our homeland did we realize the extent of our folly. They would never be content until they had conquered everything, controlled everything they could see. And we had foolishly allowed them to expand their holdings until there was no choice left but to come at us.

We fought, of course—we still fight today. I have battled the tallest through many campaigns, watching friends and family fall underneath their relentless advance. Burying my husband and children, carrying on the fight in their memory. Deep in my heart, I know we are losing, as we retreat a bit more every day. The tallest seem to have been placed on this world to do two things—make offspring and make war. From the smallkin to the dwarves to the elves, our long-lived races do not reproduce as quickly, a critical disadvantage against them. Add to this the terrible magics their casters wield, and sometimes I wonder if any of us will survive.

"Top?" Rethgar whispered. "There's a light on the far side."

"Movement, too," Syreth said. "One, maybe two of them."

"If the rest are in the woods looking for us, this is our best chance to save Tliel," I said. "Let's go." We were taking a huge risk, but there was no other way. By the time reinforcements could get here, the pixie would surely be dead.

With Rethgar on point, we began sneaking into the ruins, pausing every time we took cover so I could sense if anyone was approaching. We scurried from shattered wall to pile of rubble, every sense alert for any sign of detection.

After many tense minutes, we crept within sight of the building with the flickering light in the window. It was a keep tower, once part of a larger stone building, now standing alone. The structure was quiet, but four guards were posted outside. Tliel had to be inside—there was nowhere else to keep a prisoner.

"The rest of you lure as many guards away as you can," I whispered. "I'll go under, enter the tower, and free Tliel. We meet back here in ten minutes. If an alarm is sounded, or we don't make it, you all head back to base. Everyone understand?"

The others all nodded.

"Give me a count of thirty, then begin." Orienting myself and estimating the distance to the wall, I took a deep breath and sank into the ground. With so little movement around me, it was difficult to be sure I was heading in the right direction, but I pressed on. After forty paces, I cautiously poked my head up.

Light assailed my eyes, making me blink furiously through my tears. I was right where I wanted to be—inside the keep tower. Freezing in place, with only my head above ground, I looked around.

The first thing I saw was the Ravager, not more than two paces away. In the candlelight, the motionless iron construct cast its bulky shadow over a wooden table beside it. Although its featureless face looked right at me, it made no move to attack.

Maybe the operator isn't inside it now, I thought. Slowly I withdrew from the packed earth floor, my gaze locked on the metal monster, ready to descend again if it reached for me or lifted a giant foot to stomp me into jelly. It did not move. Other than the construct, the room appeared empty.

In the distance, I heard the distinct *clip-clop* of Syreth's hooves on what remained of the stone streets. He bleated once, then again. Seconds later, I heard heavy footsteps heading toward him; the carnivorous tallest no doubt thinking they'd heard a wild goat. Syreth would lead them on a wild-satyr chase for their trouble.

The faint clink of chains on the tabletop drew my attention. Spying a three-legged stool nearby, I climbed on it to see what was making the noise.

My breath caught in my throat when I did. Tliel lay there, naked, his normal, bright silver glow dim and wavering, tiny arms and legs stretched wide by slender chains. A large, dark bruise covered his chest where the arrow had hit him. Angry black welts marked where the iron cuffs bit into his flesh. Wide, panicked eyes stared at me while he made desperate noises behind the wooden twig strapped in his mouth. I smothered a scream when I saw the worst injury of all—his wings were gone. The barbaric dogs had cut off his wings!

My plan had been to have Tliel fly away once I'd freed him, but now I wasn't sure how we would escape, since I can't carry another being with me underground. Nevertheless, I had to help him.

"We're getting you out—" was all I could whisper before he shook his head violently. At the same time, a key rattled in the door. I jumped down and hid underneath the table, drawing my dagger as the door creaked open.

A pair of sandaled feet, their shins wrapped in white strips of cloth, walked to the table. Tliel rattled his chains furiously, then quieted as the tallest did something I couldn't see.

"There now . . . this will all be over soon." Although the words should have been soothing, they were spoken with all the warmth of a trollent. "Just another moment—"

The tallest's words devolved into the harsh language of their magic, and a familiar blue-white light filled the room, throwing everything into harsh shadow. The chains shook as tiny hands and feet beat a frantic staccato on the wooden table. On the wall, the shadow of Tliel's body arched in agony as the tallest caster tortured him.

Rushing under the caster's legs, I stabbed up with all my strength. The tallest's arcane words turned into a shriek of agony, and the light flared even brighter. I pulled my blade out as the tallest stumbled away, his hands clutching his groin. Ignoring him, I leaped onto the stool, intending to free Tliel, but froze in horror.

Whatever spell the tallest had begun was still going. Dozens of tiny bolts of energy arced from the pixie's body to the Ravager. Tliel's hair stood on end, the tips of his fingers and toes singed black as arcane power was drawn from him. The construct began glowing as it absorbed more energy from my comrade. The blue-white light streamed into its joints, making them glow like when it had come after us in the forest. With a final strangled scream, Tliel collapsed, his last breath rattling out of his sunken chest. Acrid smoke wafted from his eyes, nose, and mouth.

The Ravager swiveled its head toward me. As if recognizing who I was, it raised an iron fist to crush me where I stood. I leaped aside as its hand came down, pulverizing the table. Knowing there was nothing I could do to save Tliel, I kept going, sinking down into the earth.

"Stop . . . *Alten!* . . . I command you!" the bleeding mage gasped as the Ravager lurched toward him. "*Alt!—ALTEN, I SAY!*"

The last thing I heard was his dying scream as the iron monster crushed his chest with a heavy foot.

Shuffling through the dirt for a few yards, I came up outside the keep tower. Two guards threw the door open and ran inside. One flew back out almost instantly, sailing through the air to slam into a partially collapsed wall, breaking off a large chunk of it. He fell onto the stone street, his head bent at an unnatural angle. The other retreated to the doorway, but was jerked off his feet and hauled back inside. His screams were also brief.

More tallest ran to the tower, now trembling under blows from the rampaging Ravager. I ducked back down and retreated from the chaos, stopping only when I felt a loud rumble shake the ground.

Poking my head back up, I saw the tower had collapsed, apparently brought down by the construct. Tallest ran everywhere, shouting orders and calling for help. No one noticed me slink into the darkness.

I rejoined the others back at our rendezvous point. "Where's Tliel?" Syreth asked.

I shook my head. "I didn't reach him in time." A partial

truth, to keep my unit quiet until I could talk to my superiors. "Let's head back and report."

The memory of what I'd seen in that tower was seared into my mind. I knew the tallest could be capable of terrible cruelty—they'd proven that when they had killed my husband and children; revenge for deaths inflicted on their own. But if they were capable of this kind of monstrousness, what hope did we possibly have against those who would use the very lives of our people against us?

I have racked my brain for a solution ever since we returned to headquarters, deep in the heartswood. Now, as I am about to give my report to our leaders, I have come up with what I hope is the answer. It is savage and dangerous, and will require the sacrifice of more lives. I will volunteer to lead this special unit on what can only be described as a suicide mission. But I see no other choice.

We must seek out and kill all of the tallest casters that know this magic. We must destroy their ability to make the Ravagers. It is the only way we will survive.

I only hope that we are not too late—that we can kill all of them before they kill all of us.

Invictus

ANNIE BELLET

BRIGADIER-CAPITAN ALONSO XABI TOOK THE SPYGLASS FROM HIS first mate and Navie-Capitan, Mateu, and stared out across the foaming waves. NC Mateu had the sharpest eyes of any man Xabi had sailed with in his twenty-year career, and unfortunately they hadn't failed him this time.

Sails on the late-morning horizon, sails rigged to the standard of the Zerrijkan Navy. The ocean swelled, pushing the stern of his ship toward the heavens, and for a moment, in his glass, Xabi caught the flash of a red hull. He handed the piece back to Mateu and ran his hand through his thinning hair.

"It's the *Tyger* all right," Xabi muttered. Deep in his belly, he felt the familiar nervous thrill he always felt before a fight. The brine-and-tar scent of ship and sea turned to smoke and blood in his nose as the old battle-hunger rose, blurring his vision.

"Men in the rigging, Capitan," Mateu cried. "We're spotted. I think they are prepping the turn."

The *Tyger* was a ship Xabi knew from the reports. She was suspected of sinking Eregensian trade vessels, but no one had ever been able to bring proof enough for a war declaration. If Xabi tangled with her now, it was quite likely none of his crew would survive to carry this tale, either. Not that the *Senyera* wasn't a fine vessel, but she was built for speed and show more than battle. Good for taking the two Ineo ambassadors and the signed treaty back to the Whispering Isles, piss and culo for outfighting the heavy Zerrijk galleon.

Xabi's mind raced, listing their advantages against the enemy.

They had just sailed out of a spring storm, and many of the sails were still stowed to ride out the gale, but they had the windward advantage on the *Tyger* and would be able to maneuver more easily than the heavy galleon for a little while. But the *Senyera* lacked the sail power and top speeds of the galleons and was loaded down with gifts for the Ineo; riding low and pregnant in the water.

Not that it mattered. It wouldn't be one ship he'd have to outmaneuver and outrun.

"Where goes Berkhout, goes Van Zeyl," Prime Teniente Porras said. He and Xabi had come up on the ships together, through the line from Guardiamar. It hardly surprised the Capitan that Porras seemed to read his brooding thoughts.

The *Tyger* and her Capitan, Berkhout, never sailed without the sister ship the *De Brack* and Capitan Van Zeyl. Two war galleons lurking in these waters left no doubt in Xabi's mind that they were laying in wait for his smaller ship and her precious cargo. It was an act of war, if anyone made it out alive to report home.

How the Zerrijk had found out about Eregensia's plans and the treaty, he couldn't speculate. Not yet, at least. Though the word "traitor" teased his mind.

"Capitan?" PT Porras tapped Xabi's arm gently.

Xabi looked down at Porras's weathered and scarred hand resting on his green coat-sleeve. Orders. He had to give orders. Now. He felt the weight of his men's eyes on him, at least those who weren't in their hammocks catching up on needed sleep after the gale.

"Rouse the full crew. Set the sails. Send Mar Alben and Mar Tosell up top mid and mizzen. I want to know where the *De Brack* is as soon as she shows herself. For all we know, Berkhout might be pushing us right into her, showing his sails so that we'll run." It was what Xabi would have done in his place.

His men left the rail of the poop deck, crying out his orders and adding their own. Pride lifted his heart from its black reverie for a moment. At least the Almirante had let him choose his crew for the journey. Escorting the Ineo was a punishment duty disguised as an honor. The treaty was important, granting Eregensia the right to sail her trade ships through the Southern Passage. It was the first such agreement signed between a human empire and the elusive Ineo.

But a Brigadier-Capitan should be commanding war-class ships and keeping the waters off his kingdom safe from encroaching powers like Zerrijk. The Zerrijk had been skirting open war for a year now. He shoved his resentment away. It was that sort of blunt anger that had him hundreds of nautical leagues from his home waters, playing host to two foreign civilians. He was, as the Almirante had put it, supposed to be out here on the Southern Ocean cooling his boots and considering an early and graceful retirement.

Xabi snorted, thinking he'd retire when the sea herself closed over his balding head and not a breath before.

The call came down from the foremast nest as Xabi descended to the quarterdeck, trying not to crowd his Capitan-Navie as the huge man gripped the wheel and looked to him for direction.

"Sails sighted fifty degrees east," Mateu repeated.

"Make for the west, three-hundred," Xabi said, pleased his voice carried none of his agitation. The *De Brack* was between them and the Barren Coast, where, with a little skill and a lot of the God's luck, the *Senyera* might have been able to slip through and hide in the shallower water. The only options were to fight or sail to the west, where the two war galleons would eventually hunt them down on the open water.

There was, of course, a terrible option. From the look in Mateu's eyes as he pulled the wheel and called out the orders, Xabi knew that his Navie-Capitan had thought of it as well.

A smooth blue-green head that seemed carved out of jade and painted for a child's fancy crested the steps to the deck. The Ineo's thick, muscular body barely shifted with the movement of the galley, even as the wind caught the unfurling sails and pulled the ship starboard. The afternoon sun glinted on the Ineo's scales and off his flamefish-skin robe. Xabi acknowledged the Ineo, who went by the name Sun Sin, with a nod.

"My sister and I offer help, Capitan," Sun Sin yelled over the creak of lines and snap of sails catching wind and shifting.

The offer made Xabi smile. He had taken this assignment with great protest and decided before even meeting the two sea folk that he wasn't going to like them and that they'd better just stay out of the way. The Ineo had done just that these last five weeks, but they'd slowly won over the crew with their steady ways, their lovely singing voices, and their uncanny ability to lose at dice and cards.

Out of pity for Sun Sin and Min Yi's cache of personal coin and jewelry, Xabi had started inviting them to dine in his cabin and taught them the board game of King's Defense. Apple brandy flowed, conversation followed, and a tentative friendship based around admiration for the sea and love of tactics and strategy.

"I accept your offer," Xabi said, "though I'm not sure of the diplomatic consequences."

"If we are killed, treaty dies." Sun Sin's expressions were difficult to read, his broad facial muscles less expressive than a human's and his large green eyes pupil-less and unblinking, but Xabi caught the dark amusement in his tone.

"It would help if we dropped weight. We can't outrun them on open water, but we might be able to lose them if we can find shallows."

"Shallows?" Sun Sin tipped his head to the side in question.

"He means the Boneyards," Mateu said, spitting over his left shoulder as he named the cursed atolls.

Sun Sin's thin lips split over his sharp black teeth. "Good, put risk onto enemy," he said. "Drop whatever gifts you wish into sea. In face of danger, it becomes . . . how you say? *Baboui geum*, false riches."

"Thank you, my friend," he said with a slight bow, praying his idea would put risk, as Sun Sin phrased it, onto the heads of his enemy.

Xabi saw Fraga Teniente Banxar's bright copper head ducking and weaving among the mizzenmast shrouds and descended, yelling for the young Teniente to join him as he moved for the hold.

"Come, Fraga Teniente," he said, fighting the nervous, thrilling urge to grin, "let's go feed a fortune to the Lady of the Sea."

The Boneyards were a string of bleached and barren coral atolls that stabbed up through the churning sea around them like discarded monstrous bones. Sailing south from Eregensia, ships always took the inner passage, staying a score of naut leagues off the cliffs where the water was deep and the winds stable until the continent curved away to the east. To sail near the Boneyards was to beg trouble. The currents were wild there, and the winds changed at the whims of the gods. Depths were unpredictable due to the breaking and shifting of the coral reefs and the constant rumbling of the seabed.

Xabi strode the length of the main deck, watching his men, calling out instructions when needed, his shoulders tight with anticipation and his heart full of quiet pride in his men. There wasn't a man among his crew of sixty he hadn't sailed with before and found as steady in a storm as in a calm. Even his youngest officer, Castel, one of the Guardiamar, had bright, excited eyes unclouded by panic.

Of course, the young man hadn't ever seen combat. The way sails and rigging tore and crushed men beneath them under the onslaught of sail-rippers fired from shipboard ballistae, the giant crank catapults bolted into the decks of most warships. The way man and metal and wood burned in the unquenchable fires of Foc'deu, the green fire that burned on water. Once the warships got within range, there would be no more options. No escape. No retreat.

"Depth-finders!" Xabi called out. He strode up to the forecastle, joining the two Ineo who stood silently out of the way at the bow.

"Capitan," FT Banxar said as he brought two Mar with him carrying the fathom weights and line used for checking depth when sailing in uncertain, tight passages. "The *De Brack* has swung away to the south, but the *Tyger* stays the course."

"They mean to cut us off if we cross the Boneyards, Capitan," said Mar Roig, a cheerful young man who had been on ships since he graduated his smallclothes.

"But we do not mean to cross," Xabi said with a slight smile. He and the Ineo had come up with a plan so stupid it might have turned the edge of midnight back to bright again. If it worked.

"Capitan?"

"Turn the foremast, slow the ship," Xabi called out and a dozen Mar leapt into the rigging, pulling the sails perpendicular the main and mizzen sails, dragging the ship to nearly a full stop.

"Depth?" Xabi asked. The waves were choppy here and water swirled in tiny maelstroms beyond the bow of his ship. The ivory bones of the nearest atoll loomed closer with every wave roll even as his crew shortened sail.

"*Tyger*'s gaining, Capitan," his hirsute Segund Teniente, Laque, called out, the message passed down from the nest.

Xabi looked at Sun Sin and raised an eyebrow in question. It was the Ineo woman who answered him in her softer, lower toned voice.

"We need twelve fathoms," said Min Yi. She was a twin to her brother, same gemlike eyes and muscular body beneath a shimmering robe.

"Prime Teniente Porras! Men ready?" Xabi called down to the main deck.

"Men ready," came the relayed call back.

"We're losing the light, Capitan." FT Banxar shifted from boot to boot on the deck.

"When I need you to point out the obvious, I'll give you the order, Fraga Teniente," Xabi growled. He didn't mean to be rough with the man, but timing was key now, essential even, if he hoped to pull his ship and his crew free of this trap alive.

Among the treasure below decks, he had found a ship-wrecker chain, clearly intended as a novelty gift and show of goodwill to the Ineo. It was a large, spiked chain made for holding entrances to bays and protecting harbors, designed to crack ship hulls. There was no time to set it up at a narrow point in the Boneyards, even if they had known the terrain enough to try. The best that Xabi and the two Ineo had come up with was to find a place where his ship could sail over and the *Tyger* or *De Brack* could not quite touch. That meant at last ten fathoms but no more than twelve.

It also meant letting the *Tyger* close enough that they could potentially get off their ballistae or launch pots of Foc'deu.

"Twelve fathoms, Capitan," Mar Roig called out.

Xabi took a deep breath. Then a second. Out to the east he saw the sails of the *Tyger*, the galleon sailing close enough now that the blood-red hull leapt above the waves like an unsteady flame. All commands carried risk.

"Drop chain! Furl sail!" he yelled and listened to the echo as the commands were given down the length of his ship. The heavy chain went over the stern, lowered like an anchor and draped out behind the *Senyera*, an invisible and deadly fin beneath the waves.

The *Tyger* drew closer, shapes resolving themselves into red-uniformed men crawling the rigging and decks like vermin. His own men loosened their swords and readied crossbows, but Xabi hoped it would not come to a fight. The enemy ship was half again the size of his and carrying over double her crew. As much as his blood sang for a good battle, blade to blade, he had long and many scars ago learned the folly of such glory. If only he'd learned to keep his tongue as sheathed as his sword. He shook the thought off.

The chilling scream of a ballista spring, the shrieking release of wire and rope cranked tight and now freed to fire a thick bolt, as though from a giant crossbow, whistled across the churning waters. Sail-rippers.

"Make room!" came the cry from the poopdeck Guardiamar, a serious and capable lad called Mata for how many men he'd killed in a pirate raid his first summer aboard ship.

The sails were pulled in; making smaller targets, but the thick missile with its toothy, broad head caught the rigging in the mizzenmast. Braces and halyards caught and tangled, ropes ripping free. The second sail-ripper finished the port lift on the topmast and yard, tearing the whole rig free as it swung and dragged itself down.

Xabi moved without thinking, leaping off the forecastle to the main. There had never seemed to be so much room on a ship before, and yet so many things in his way. Men yelled and screamed, and the ship herself tipped to port as the mizzenmast groaned. It was too far.

"Capitan!" A huge, sweaty body shoved Xabi back as he gained the quarterdeck. The top mizzenmast and yard hit the poop deck only a few strides ahead of him. He looked up into his Navie-Capitan's eyes as men screamed and others rushed to pull rigging and the splintering yard free of the wounded.

Xabi shoved Mateu aside and drew his long knife, diving in among his men as they cut rigging and tried to restore order to the deck.

"Crossbows aft!" Xabi yelled as he dragged a bloody but still conscious man free from a tangle of halyard and lines.

"Fire pots!" came the cry down from the nest.

"Sand!" came the order, given so in tandem with his Navie-Capitan that Xabi wasn't sure who had spoken first. They'd laid the sandbags along the rails and around the masts as they sailed for the Boneyards. It was the only way to quell the endless rage that was the green Foc'deu.

"I've got him, Xabi." Noguerra, his ship's surgeon, gently pulled at Xabi's bloody sleeve as he helped the injured Mar to his feet. "This blood his or yours?"

"His, his," Xabi said, waving the doctor off.

"Good, this is not the time for stupid heroics," Noguerra said. He lifted the aging soldier half onto his broad shoulders.

Xabi bit back his response that this was *exactly* the time for stupid heroics. He staggered to the rail, eyes on the enemy as the crimson uniforms scurried to reload and crank the ballistae, this time with pots. Where was that damned chain? The galleon was too wide to have missed it. Had they misread the depths or her draft?

A deep and echoing crack answered his doubts, and for a moment, men and ship seemed to quiet and grow still. Then a terrible cry went up from the *Tyger* and the red shapes moved more quickly. The big galleon groaned again, her creaking and splintering cries carrying easily over the water to Xabi's grateful ears. The *Tyger* stopped her forward push through the water, foundering as her deck pitched and buckled. Smoke and green flames leapt into the air as the fragile pots of Foc'deu dropped and cracked.

"We've knocked her knee and stem, Capitan!" Mateu grinned.

"Capitan! Capitan! Capitan! Eregensia Invictus!" echoed from his own ship, and Xabi found himself taking up the cry along with his men.

Then he dropped his sandbag and turned, calling out for Mateu. The work wasn't done. The sun had dropped to a burning smear on the horizon in front of them, temporarily restoring some of the coral pink to the Boneyards' grim shapes.

It wasn't over. The *Tyger* wouldn't trouble them, even if she managed to put out the fires. Her stem and hull were damaged beyond ocean-bound repair. The best Berkhout could hope for would be to put the crew into cockboats and hope Van Zeyl could rescue them.

"Capitan," Segund Teniente Laque called to him from the quarterdeck, and his voice sounded far from victorious.

Laque knelt over a still, stout body on the quarterdeck, blood staining the scrubbed wood at his feet. Men parted for their Capitan but Xabi moved forward reluctantly. He recognized the weathered boots with their silver buckles tarnished and pocked by the salt water. He knew those strong, scarred hands dusted with gray hair.

One of the heavy wood and iron braces had swung free of the mizzenmast and caught Prime Teniente Porras full in the side of the head as he tried to help his men clear the deck before the yard came down. His chest rose and fell and his eyes were open but his life was leaking away from his broken head in a slick, dark stream.

"I can't...move...my toes," Porras said, his voice thick and halting, as though he spoke around a mouthful of sailcloth.

"I'll move them for you, if you tell me where you want them to go," Xabi said softly, kneeling down beside his old comrade and friend.

"Order me...not...to die."

Xabi blinked hard, willing his eyes to stay dry. There was no crying in the Eregensia Navy.

"I order you not to die, Prime Teniente. If you disobey me, I'll have you keelhauled and feed your jewels to the Lady of the Sea."

Porras groaned, and his lips pulled in a terrible parody of a smile. "Gillipollas."

The insult was the last word he spoke. As the light died in his friend's eyes, Xabi rose, pulling the mantle of command around himself like armor. Like a shroud.

"Clear the decks, give me the damage reports. Casualties. Injuries. Carry on, men."

Besides Porras, they lost three others, all Mar. Petit, Alben, Flor. Xabi committed their names to his memory, adding them to the long list of the fallen who haunted his dreams, grim reminders of his failures as a commander. They had lost the use of the mizzenmast until they could repair the rigging and jury-rig a new topsail and yard. The burning *Tyger* lit the night behind them. Xabi had the men lower a cockboat and head out in front of the *Senyera* to test the depth and find a way forward through the ghostly Boneyards.

Sun Sin and Min Yi moved quietly among his crew, helping Noguerra get the wounded below deck and offering their muscle wherever it might be needed. As twilight turned to full dark, the two sea folk came up beside Xabi where he brooded at the rail, watching the lanterns of their guide boat blink and bob. Sun Sin carried a long wooden case, decorated with mother-of-pearl in swirling shapes. Xabi wondered if that held the treaty, and if so, why they would bring it up on deck.

"The chain worked," Xabi said. "Thank you for letting us use your gift."

Sun Sin snorted through his flat, thin nose. "You are welcome. Better to use and live than die over meaningless courtesy."

"I wish the Almirante had your feeling about diplomacy," Xabi said, offering up a tired smile and a half bow.

"It is not over," Min Yi said. She rubbed the smooth rail with one webbed, six-fingered hand. "I wish we could be more help."

The Ineo were excellent swimmers and deadly hand-to-hand fighters, with the capacity to hold their breath underwater for as long as a whale might. They weren't good in wide open water, however, preferring to stay to the channels and inlets of their islands. They controlled their waters with net and trident and sank ships that dared to trespass. Without the treaty, no trading vessel would risk trying to shorten the journey around the Capo de Esperanza by cutting through the channels of the Whispering Isles or Sogsag Im, as the Ineo called their kingdom.

"Not unless you have ship-sinking magic up those shiny sleeves," Xabi said. Legends said the Ineo had great powers over wind and wave and the beasts of the sea, but Xabi had learned there was little to those stories beyond bored seamen's fancy. The only magic he'd seen was that their strong legs fused in the water, turning into a powerful tail that would be the envy of any fish.

"Do you feel ready to lure another ship, Capitan?" Sun Sin asked, his eyes almost black in the lamplight.

"Even if I did, we don't have another chain. Nor do I think we could lure the *De Brack* into the Boneyards the same way. We were more lucky than not with the *Tyger*."

Xabi watched curiously as Min Yi opened the box. It did not hold the treaty. Instead, a strange brace and auger lay inside, the handle thick and dark as though carved from stone and the heavy shaft sporting nine bits, each two fingers thick and wickedly spiraling.

"Sal Inja. To kill ships." The Ineo woman smiled, her teeth like obsidian knives in the flickering light.

Xabi rocked back on his boot heels, some of the exhaustion draining away. The *De Brack* was out there, beyond the Boneyards. If he couldn't find a way to give her the slip and sail south, or if Van Zeyl chose to give chase instead of trying to save his stranded men on the *Tyger*, Xabi would be forced to fight again. To risk his ship and his men.

"It will be a challenge," he said, "if you need them close?"

"Yes. Distracted, or they will notice us boring their hull. At home, ships have nowhere to sail in the narrow channels; we fix them with nets and use Sal Inja to teach a lesson. In open water, we need time. Cannot bore in one breath, not with only two." Sun Sin shrugged, tipping his head to the side.

"It will be dangerous," Min Yi added.

"There is always risk at sea. And in war," Xabi said. "Come. Tell me more about what you need and how the Sal Inja works. Whatever dawn brings, we'll face it."

They moved away from the rail as the wind shifted, carrying a call of "fifteen fathoms" across the water, and the answering cry from Mateu at the wheel of "Steady on!"

Xabi met the eyes of his men as he passed them, heading for his cabin. He saw only trust and respect in their tired faces, though it barely warmed his sad heart. He had failed Porras, Petit, Alben, and Flor. He would do better on the morrow.

"Eregensia Invictus," he whispered, and the wind stole his words, lifting them up into the sails and out across the speckled heavens to the gods' ears.

Rising Above

SARAH A. HOYT

FREIHERR MANFRED VON RICHTHOFEN KNEW HE'D FALLEN INTO A trap when he came out of the lake with the boar in his jaws.

There was no moon. This far within the forest La Chaussee no artificial light intruded. But the vision of his dragon form was keen.

Several men waited in the shadows around the lake, stepping out of cover in the underbrush as Manfred rose out of the lake with his prey. The scant light of the distant moon was enough to establish that they wore the black uniforms of the *Zauberkunstnie-derwerfungsdienst*, commonly referred to as the ZND, the police who guarded against magical infractions in the ranks—and out.

He swallowed, a human gesture in this reptilian form. His mouth filled with the taste of the boar's blood. For days he'd dreamed of blood. For months he'd longed for the freedom of his shifted self, for wings to the sky, for freedom and flight. While working as a courier in the trenches, surrounded by humans on all sides, smelling them, almost tasting them, he'd worked hard to discipline the dragon and convince it that the humans weren't prey. But he longed to let go.

I could kill them all, went through his head, as he rose farther out of the lake, his leathery red wings streaming water. It was followed by *I could fly away*.

Both were the dragon's thoughts, instinctual. Manfred's human mind knew the meaning of the wide-belled, silver weapons in the hands of the ZND. His late father's voice rose in his memory. "Do not go imagining you're invincible in your monstrous form, young sir. Do not go dreaming that nothing can overturn you. The ZND have weapons aplenty to deal with your kind, weapons that fire rays of magic poisonous to shifters, weapons that reduce you to your human form and worse."

He swallowed again. The boar's blood was like intoxicating wine to the dragon's senses. He'd lain in wait for the animal in the shrubs around the lake, seen her go across the lake to the potato field, and back again, for three nights, before gratifying his desire.

"Freiherr von Richthofen," a voice called, somewhere against the taller shadows of the centuries-old trees. Scents of pine and oak, of moss and growing grass played in the dragon's nostrils, ineffective against the symphony of taste and the smell of blood in his mouth. Were it not for the blood he might have been able to tell how many ZND agents there were, and exactly where, by smell alone.

"You are under arrest for being a shapeshifter, a violation of the laws of Aethelbert," the voice came again. "You are surrounded by men armed with weapons that are effective against your kind. You cannot take them all at once. Attempt nothing. Do not worsen your case."

How can I make it worse? Under the law, being a shifter is a capital crime. But Manfred knew well it could be worse. It was one thing for his mother to read a dispatch saying her first born had been taken for a shifter and executed. Another for her to read newspaper reports of how Manfred, in dragon form, had killed fifty men before being brought to ground. One was a shame, but endurable. The other was Mama knowing all her moral teachings had failed.

Even if there were few enough ZND agents that a full-throated flaming would get them all, the commander's voice from beyond the trees indicated there were men farther on. If they were armed with magical weapons, they could still hit him. He knew that the dragon recovered from wounds with miraculous capacity, but these weapons were designed against magical beings.

"Freiherr Manfred Albrecht von Richthofen!"

He took a deep breath. He closed his teeth hard on the boar's body. Blood squirted down his throat and around his face. He opened his jaws and dropped the animal. It fell into the water with a splash. Men stepped back. The front row aimed weapons at him. From the sounds, another two rows stepped back and, likely, also aimed weapons at him.

There was nothing for it. He'd have to face his fate with what dignity he could muster. If they left him any dignity. He searched his mind for stories of shifter executions. Such things were usually done in secret and published only, if at all, as *Herr So-and-So*, executed at such and such a place for violation 46 of the laws of magic of Aethelbert—the oldest set of Germanic law codes in existence that dealt with magical violations. Manfred suspected few non-lawyers even knew what violation 46 was.

He forced his body to change. It was neither easy nor pleasant. Shifting into the dragon felt like when you turn in bed in your sleep, and take your ease, and spread yourself, finding your most comfortable place. Becoming human again always felt like shrinking in, like forcing oneself into an unnaturally small space.

It was easier when the dragon had been allowed his way, when the thirst for hunting and killing and for eating his prey had been sated.

Hungry, angry, scared . . . yet he must shift.

His father had sent him to Wahlstatt, a military academy, at the age of eleven. It was judged a strange choice by people who didn't know of Manfred's peculiar difficulties. His lady mother, who did, had cried and tried to dispute with her husband. She'd said that Manfred, surrounded by so many young people, whom his dragon-self would view as prey, would go insane. Constant vigilance would make it impossible for him to have even a moment of freedom. And besides, Wahlstatt trained cavalry officers, and horses shied away from the carnivorous forms of shifters.

"Do you think I don't know that, Madam?" Richthofen's father had answered. "The only hope of survival for your wretched son is to learn to control the beast. That is the only hope for his life and our honor. He will learn control or die."

He had learned control. Other than an escapade when he'd flown to the top of the spire at the school and tied his handkerchief to the lightning rod, he'd never given anyone a chance to suspect his other form. And that one time, he'd passed it off as a daring adventure, claiming he'd climbed the spire. That had inspired punishment from the masters but admiration from the other boys.

Now he called on all his control, on all his strength. His body twisted. The excruciating pain of bone grinding on bone, of flesh and bone compacting, diminishing, made his mind a blank. He coughed, and the dragon's immense, membranous red wings flapped against the cold water of the river, once, twice, in spasmodic contortions.

When he could command a coherent thought again, he was a man standing up to his neck in cold water. His teeth hurt. His head ached. His own blood flowed in his mouth. He must have caught his tongue in his teeth.

His own eyes, human and not at all dark-adapted, couldn't see the ZND in the shadows, but he felt them there, in the dark, pointing their weapons at him. His bare feet dug into the pebbled mud of the lake bottom.

"If you'd step out with your hands up, Freiherr," the commanding voice called from the shadows, seemingly closer to the lake.

They couldn't think he was armed, could they? Not in water up to his neck, not when he'd just shifted from his dragon form.

But one thing he'd learned early on, from his father's implacable discipline, long before his father had found out Manfred's true nature, and then from the various school masters and commanders, it was that no good came of arguing with those who could hurt you.

Besides, he supposed having seen what he was, what he could become, the ZND were scared, and he couldn't fault them. Fear was not often rational, and scared men can kill because they're afraid.

Manfred lifted his arms above his head, feeling the night air bite, colder than the water. It made walking forward more difficult, robbing him of balance, but he struggled on. It should have been easier to walk when the water was down to his waist, but it wasn't. By then the shaking had set in, the reaction-shaking from the shift.

By the time the water was down to his ankles, he could see a dozen men nearby, holding the silver weapons on him, and beyond them an older man, who didn't need a weapon because he wore the star of the commander of the ZND.

Manfred stepped out of the water. Nausea had set in. Not unusual when the dragon had been hunting and feeding. The taste of blood in his mouth, the boar's and his combined, made him wish to retch.

The men closed in as though he were still the dragon and terrifying, in military formation, surrounding him.

More than anything, Manfred was conscious of his nudity. Part of his human form, part of his self-control, was in the donning of his uniform. He'd worn a uniform since he was eleven. It was his armor against the world. "*Entschuldigung!*" he said, but his apology came out thin and reedy, shaking with his tremors. He meant to ask for the uniform, which he'd left rolled up and folded beneath a tree to the north of here.

One of the silver guns let loose.

His short blond hair stood on end, and it seemed to him as though he'd been flayed alive.

It was just a second. His senses shut down.

He woke up feeling bruised and beaten. He woke up midsentence, having just said something and having no idea what it was. He was sitting up on a hard chair. He was still naked and shivering.

It was like waking in the middle of a walking dream, something that had happened a lot when he was nine or so, just before the shifting had started.

Five men watched him intently—two on each side, with the silver, bell-shaped magical weapons trained on him. The other man stood behind a desk, a middle aged man with white hair and dark, suspicious eyes. They wore the uniform of the ZND.

A weak light shone above the desk. The walls were made of stone, and Manfred had the impression he was underground. They were probably afraid he'd shift and flame. Stupid. There wasn't enough room for the dragon in here. To shift would be a complex way of committing suicide. Not that it didn't have its temptations.

He ran his tongue inside his teeth. It felt as though he'd been gargling with blood, and he suspected he'd vomited, too, in the time before full consciousness. His mouth tasted like the gutters of hell. He was dying of thirst.

Before he could rasp out that he couldn't remember the question, the older man's eyes changed expression, and something almost a smile twisted the corner of his lips. "Ah," he said. "I see you're full awake now."

"Yes," Manfred said. "I beg your pardon. I don't remember the question?" He lifted his head. He was not tall, but he was a muscular and well-formed man. He could be imposing.

He wished to heavens they'd give him his uniform back, but he supposed prisoners who'd revealed themselves half-beast and therefore not worthy of human dignity weren't allowed to dishonor a uniform by wearing it.

The commander smiled. There was something like understanding in his eyes. "Freiherr," he said, reasonably. "You know what the end of this is."

"Yes," Manfred said. "You execute me. I don't understand this pleasant little excursion on the way there." He turned, in a desperate gambit, and spoke to the nearest man holding a gun, as though he were one of his servants in the ancestral estates at Schweidnitz. "You. Get me a glass of water."

By the corner of his eye, Manfred saw the commander nod. The man shrugged, holstered his weapon, and left through a door somewhere behind Manfred. Manfred heard the door open and close, but didn't turn. He didn't need the dragon's senses to tell him there were more men back there, all armed.

The door opened and closed again, and the man returned. He proffered a tall glass of water to Manfred at the end of an outstretched arm, then jumped back to stand with his comrade, gun at the ready.

The commander waited until Manfred drank, which Manfred forced himself to do in small, disciplined swallows, and not in the wild gulp he wished to.

"Come now," the commander said. "You know the law doesn't just punish those who shift shapes into dangerous forms, but also those who willfully hide them."

"My father knew," Manfred said, and then bluntly, "He is dead."

"So you told us," the man said. "And...no one else? Your mother, your sister, your brothers—all ignorant of your true nature? How is that possible, in the closeness of family life?"

"I don't know, *Herr* Commander." He bent and set the glass near the leg of his chair. Wild images ran through his head, of throwing it at the commander, of disarming the man nearest him, of—

Of getting shot and eventually beheaded. A purpose that would shortly be accomplished without exertion on his part. At least he hadn't given the rest of his family away. Better not tempt them to hit him with the magic discharge again. Clearly he could talk while out of his mind. Instead, he said, "You must tell me all about a close family life, Commander. My father sent me to Wahlstatt when I was eleven."

The commander frowned at Manfred. It was clear this was not the answer he'd expected, nor one he knew how to respond to.

"No one at Wahlstatt suspected—" he began, in tones of disbelief.

"If anyone did, they didn't tell me," Manfred snapped. "Unfortunately, being a shapeshifter doesn't give me the ability to read minds, *Herr* Commander. Or I would not be in this position."

The commander made a click of his tongue on the roof of his mouth, then stared at Manfred. "You did not spend your seven years there without shifting shapes."

"No."

"And no one saw you?"

Manfred shrugged.

"You commanded a cavalry detachment, *Rittmeister*?"

"On the Eastern front, yes."

"And not one of your subordinates suspected? And you managed the horse without its going mad with fright?"

Manfred sighed. "Obviously," he said. "I managed the horses at Wahlstatt, too."

The commander glared disapprovingly at Manfred. "I don't believe you, *Freiherr*. There is nothing you can say to make me believe you. I know there is a group of you, a conspiracy of shifters, probably all dragon shifters, all known to each other. We found you because we detected the magic given off by changing shapes—but there was far more than yours in that area of the trenches. Our instruments detected it."

Manfred shrugged. "And what has that to do with me? Perhaps I give off more magic than normal. My shifted form is large."

The commander shook his head. "I'm afraid, *Freiherr*, that we must delay the end of your case yet a while. The magic of dragons interferes with the magical charges of our rifles and the discharge of the cannons. You might think that you're being loyal to your comrades by not talking, but the truth is that you're costing the lives of more men.

"Take him to detention cell A."

"Not," Manfred said and, as he spoke, he twisted his ankles behind the legs of his chair. "Without my uniform. A uniform, at any rate."

"*Freiherr*—"

"Oh, yes. Doubtless you can hit me with a low discharge of magic and carry me unconscious. Though there is a good chance that I'll freeze in this position and you'll have to carry the chair with me. All I'm asking for is my uniform. You can strip it of insignia."

The commander hesitated. Then he nodded to a man nearby.

The uniform they brought Manfred was his own, folded as he'd left it. He removed the pine needles from it fastidiously, and dressed carefully—underwear and socks, pants, shirt and tunic and cap. He slipped his feet into the boots that had been his grandfather's, the boots of a Prussian cavalry officer. Then he stood and saluted, before turning to head for the door.

There were six more men there. They fell in on all sides of him and, by his bearing, he contrived to give them the appearance of a guard of honor as they led him down a long rock corridor to a door at the end.

The cell was more comfortable than Manfred had expected. It was, in fact, much like officer's quarters. It had two camp beds, against opposite walls, and a small table holding a pitcher of water and two glasses. There was no dresser or trunk for his clothes, but there were pegs on the wall. The beds had sheets and blankets.

On one of the beds a man sat, looking dazed. He was darker than Manfred, and probably taller, but more importantly, the uniform he wore, even if it looked like it had been dragged through a mire, showed an insignia of three stars and a pair of wings.

Manfred snapped a salute. "*Hauptmann!*" he said.

The man lifted lusterless eyes, then smiled, or at least attempted to. He stood up, and offered his hand to Manfred, "In the ante-chamber of hell, does that matter?" he asked. "My name is Oswald Boelcke. *Hauptmann Fliegerabteilung* 62. And you?"

"*Rittmeister* Manfred, *Freiherr* von Richthofen," Manfred said, and snapped a salute again.

The other man turned away from him. "They . . . captured you?" he asked.

It occurred to Manfred that the man might be a spy, but what he said was, "They are almost for sure listening to us."

"Undoubtedly," the other man said. He went back to sitting on his bed. "If there are secrets you would keep— I have none.

They think that other fliers are also dragon shifters." He shrugged. "I was discovered because my plane was hit, and I couldn't help but shift and save myself on the way down."

Manfred made his way to the water glass, searching in his pocket for a handkerchief. He poured some water onto the folded linen cloth, and rubbed it on his face. "I was pig hunting," he said.

"Oh," Boelcke said. "Wolf?"

"Dragon." Manfred resumed cleaning blood from his face. "I used to listen to the airplanes overhead and dream—" He stopped.

Boelcke laughed. "It's not much easier. You want to... You want to do things you can't do in a plane. I needed so much discipline to fly." He shook his head. "But at least you're in the sky, and almost alone." He paused a moment. "It was good while it lasted." He paused again. "This will kill my parents. And my brothers."

"My mother and my siblings, too," Manfred said. "Only... Violation 46. Many people will not know what that is." He chose to lie with a straight face. "Perhaps not even my family will guess."

Boelcke looked at him. The look passed between them. Boelcke's family also knew, and neither of them was going to say it aloud or make a gesture that would endanger their relatives.

"How long will they keep us before they execute us?" Manfred asked.

Boelcke shrugged. "It depends on how long it takes the commander of the ZND to become convinced we know nothing. They believe that there must be at least thirty fliers and thirty or so support personnel below who are shifters and likely, they say, dragon shifters, from the burst of magic they received, all from the same area. They think when my fliers impinged above the trenches, the magic caught and amplified."

"Is there any chance they're right?" Manfred asked.

"No. There were twelve of us on the mission, flying patrol to keep the British from bombing our positions."

"And yet they got some great burst of magic," Manfred said.

"Perhaps," Boelcke said and shrugged, "The British bombs give off a magical charge."

Manfred frowned. All the large weapons they'd seen used in this war so far had been nonmagical. He couldn't imagine the need for magic in something such as that.

He felt tired suddenly, and fumbled in his pocket for his watch. He did not find it.

"I have no idea what time it is, but it must be close to dawn. I was hit with what I presume was a low magic charge, and I'm sore through. I'm going to sleep till they wake us to execute us."

He woke up in total darkness. From the sounds of breathing, he thought his cellmate must be asleep.

Manfred felt as though he'd just discovered something important, but he couldn't tell what. He stared into the dark, his heart beating rapidly. There was something he knew, something—

He got up, stumbled toward the little table, found it by hitting it and making the glass rattle. "Richthofen?" said Boelcke's voice from the general direction of Boelcke's bed.

"Yes," Manfred said. "I need water." He poured water from the pitcher to a glass by touch, then drank, feeling as though it were the freshest water he'd ever had. His mouth still tasted vile.

And then he wished they'd let him bathe before killing him, but another thought intruded, a memory of a . . . dream?

"Boelcke?" he asked.

"Yes?"

"What if the ZND aren't lying? What if their instruments aren't defective? What if there really was a burst of magic that big from that area? What if out of that burst of magic, there were only you and I, shifters, on our side? Surely we can't be the only shifters in the world. The English have their own shifters."

"They put shifters to death."

"Everyone puts shifters to death," Manfred said. "Except the Americans. And yet, we are still here."

Boelcke's feet hit the floor. "What do you mean?" he asked. "Precisely?"

"I know we have an Imperial air service, but I heard the men in the trenches grumble that you people up there are doing nothing. They hear the planes, they look up and see our planes. And yet, bombs still fall. I've never been up there. I can only guess at what happens. But . . . is it possible that bombs come not from the English planes but from above?"

The air in the small cell was still and too warm, and Manfred smelled the warm wool of the uniform, his own sweat, and remnants of pig's blood.

"I don't know," Boelcke said. "It's so noisy, and your goggles limit your peripheral vision. And you're paying attention to the enemy in front who might shoot at you. There might always be planes above you that drop bombs, though we're trained to listen for their engines, of course. Because that's a vantage point from which to shoot at you."

"I didn't mean planes above you," Manfred said. "That's not what I meant at all."

There was a long silence, and then Boelcke understood. "Oh."

Manfred rushed to the door, started pounding on it with his hand. When that didn't answer, he joined kicks of his feet.

"Hey, there, what are you doing?" Boelcke asked, sounding alarmed, as though afraid Manfred had lost his mind entirely.

"They wanted us to talk," Manfred said. "We're going to talk. Why should they sleep softly in their beds, while we're in here, desperate to talk with them?"

It was odd how, in perfect darkness, and Boelcke such a new acquaintance, he could tell the other man had smiled. Presently, he joined Manfred in pounding on the door, but not before he said, "I have no idea what you hope to gain by this, but the worst they can do is execute us earlier."

A few moments of this racket, and the light came on, and there were sounds of running feet down the stony corridor outside.

The key turned in the door, and Boelcke stepped back, hands up. Manfred imitated him, which was a good thing, because when the door swung open, four men stepped in, each of them holding the belled, silver magical guns, but these were longer and thicker, and Manfred suspected they'd deliver death at an instant's notice.

Behind them, the commander appeared, his hair tousled, his uniform looking like he'd dressed before he was fully awake, both of which gave Manfred a great deal of comfort.

The ZND commander glared at them. "What is the meaning of this? Have you decided to stop pretending you don't know anything, and to tell us the names and the posts of the other dragons?"

Manfred shook his head. "We told you we didn't know any other dragons, because we don't," he said. "It is like this—did you run sweeps after that burst of magic? Is it still so elevated?"

"It would only," the commander said drily, "be that elevated if the dragons were in shifted dragon form. We followed you and *Hauptman* Boelcke to your shifted forms, from that burst."

"Yes? And you think that so many infantry soldiers, so many cavalry officers, so many airmen shifted—unnoticed?"

The commander looked stunned. He stepped back. He was silent. Manfred knew the silence wouldn't last. He spoke quickly. "Listen, what if the English have a dragon corps, which flies above their planes, unseen, in the clouds? Would that explain how their bombardments are so successful, despite our best attempts to stop them?"

"The English are civilized," the commander said. "They execute shifters."

"Do they now?" Manfred asked. "But what if they didn't? What if they thought our kind, abominations though we are, can do a greater service alive than dead? What if they have recruited their guards to supplement their as yet ineffective air force? What if that explains their dominance of the air?"

"You're trying to escape."

"We're most assuredly not. Where would we escape to? We're both men with well-known families, *loyal to the Kaiser.* Where could we go, if we escaped?" Boelcke said in a reasonable tone.

Manfred joined in. "Have there been other such bursts of magic recently? During heavy bombardment?"

"Naturally," the commander said. "During bombardments, dragon shifters shift and escape."

"What? From the trenches? Don't you think someone would have noticed?"

The commander drew in breath through his nostrils and let it out through his mouth with an explosive effect. "I will have to ask. I will have to talk to... *This might go to the Kaiser himself.*"

"Undoubtedly," Manfred said. "And meanwhile, I'd like a bath and some coffee."

There had been coffee, and bread and butter, but not a bath, or not for some hours yet. But if the matter had gone *all the way to the Kaiser,* it must have been resolved with unseemly haste, because it was not yet noon when several ZND guards escorted Boelcke and Manfred to separate rooms, and each was given the use of a bathroom and the luxury of a bath, then proffered clean uniforms.

When they met again, they both looked like new men. They were escorted into some sort of a meeting room, with a large round table, and around it were seated men Manfred knew only by name: the strategists and planners of the war.

It turned out they didn't want to ask either of them much, only to make a proposal. Whether the British were making use of dragons in the war or not couldn't be fully decided, of course, until the Germans tried it. The Germans proposed to try it. If the British were indeed deploying sixty dragons each time they made a bombing raid, there might be no defeating them—certainly not with Manfred and Boelcke alone. In time they would track down and find more German dragons. They thought they might have another one, right now. But even three would be ineffective against that many. So it might be a suicide mission, but if Boelcke and Richthofen were willing to try....

Boelcke had spoken, then, with some good sense. If the English were doing this, their dragons were not armed. They were bomb carriers, no more, no less. Could the magical guns used by the ZND be adapted so that a dragon could carry one of them? Also, he added, having been up there, he knew the dragons would need goggles. Their eyes were as sensitive as human eyes. Or more. And if they were to go that far up above the clouds, they'd need something for the cold. And how were they to know friend from foe up there? Sure, if it was just two of them and maybe this other dragon they were tracking. But with so many English dragons, wouldn't it be easy to be confused?

The planners and generals nodded, and agreed, and made suggestions.

Two days later, they had their trial. The third dragon was a dark-haired young man called Werner Voss. Manfred would later learn that, on capture, he'd been offered the chance to join them and had taken it eagerly.

They were provided with cannon-sized magical-ray-firing guns, and their process explained. The guns could be set on high or low charge. A low charge would not kill, but falling from the sky almost certainly would, particularly since, when unconscious, shifters tended to revert.

They had been allowed to practice their flying only once, in the dark of night, handling the cannons. Manfred's red dragon had been joined by Boelcker's golden one, and Voss's shimmering green.

The identification mark, essential, in case the English had dragons of the same color, was an imperial cross in a circle of white, painted on their wings.

And the solution to the cold had been to have the dragons' bodies rubbed with goose grease, something that long-distance swimmers in cold waters often used.

The dragons sat side by side in a huge, temporary tent, while mechanics who had been briefed and told they must keep absolute secrecy rubbed them with wool impregnated with goose grease.

Manfred imagined how that requisition had gone off, and what the suppliers must think. They must assume that some really big dishes were being cooked. He had stretched his wings helpfully, half-amused at the mechanics' skittish behavior. If they told anyone, they wouldn't be believed, but the truth was the men didn't like this assignment.

While the last segment of his left wing was getting greased, the phone had rung. The English were on their way. The three dragons looked at each other and nodded, then lumbered to the exit of the tent farthest away from the battle front, and one after the other, they took off.

Boelcke, an experienced air fighter, took the lead.

Up, up, and up, above the clouds, above the roar of the approaching English planes, and above the takeoff of their own fighters.

Manfred felt dazed, having shifted in full daylight, having taken off in full sight of Germans, who had saluted as they took off. It seemed to him as though reality had been suspended. He was up there, in the clouds, in a mad dream.

For a moment, he thought that he'd been wrong. He could hear the English planes below, but nothing up here, nothing above.

Then suddenly the air shimmered in the distance, with seven approaching dragons in a V formation—green and red, white and purple, and that intense golden that Boelcke also displayed.

Manfred gave himself a moment of silent congratulation. He'd been right twice. The British were recruiting dragons. And there would have been confusion but for the insignia painted on their wings.

Closer still, flying full tilt toward them, he realized that he'd been right on another count. The English were not armed, except with curious round pots that he assumed were the bombs.

He was rushing headlong to engage, but Boelcke's dragon gave a sign. They'd worked out a short number of signs for "stop" and "rush," and "go this way." Boelcke's sign was to stop their advance, and Manfred imitated the gesture, to make sure Voss saw it, on his right.

The rules which Boelcke had developed for airplane combat he'd given them, thinking they'd apply to dragon combat as well. And the third rule was to fire only when close to the enemy. But that, Manfred reasoned, was for machine guns and magical rifles. Not for these wide-dispersion magical weapons.

He saw Boelcke point his weapon, almost dropping it from his claws for lack of practice, but grabbing it again. Manfred pointed his own weapon, making sure neither of his friends was likely to be caught in the ray. To his right, Voss was in position.

They let fly with the magic at low power. There was a sound like the screaming of a thousand banshees.

Manfred's mother, an educated noblewoman, was fond of Milton's *Paradise Lost*. Now Manfred imagined that the angels falling must have looked like this. As the front line of the dragons was hit by the magical ray, the lead dragons lost consciousness and became naked men, falling to Earth, sometimes dropping the bomb they carried, sometimes taking it with them.

The bombs fell, too, but they were not yet over the German lines, and Manfred hoped they were minimizing the damage. In future, they must make sure to have some way of stopping those bombs.

But before he could think more on that, his weapon had run empty. It must be the same for his comrades, because he saw Voss drop his weapon, and Boelcke toss his aside with an almost contemptuous gesture. Of the dragons who had faced them, there were now only six, who, as though realizing that the enemy was disarmed and in smaller number, surged forward to attack them.

Caught in between two charging enemies, Manfred had a moment of heart-stopping panic before he thought of Boelcke's rule number eight: if possible, avoid two aircraft attacking the same opponent.

It wasn't so much a thought as an instinct. He waited till the two opponents were close to him—and close to each other from opposing sides—then, remembering that Boelcke also said to always attack from above, he flapped his wings desperately, climbing up above the two. He'd judged right. They'd been so close to him, they had no time to avoid the collision, and while they were entangled, he turned and flamed them both.

A flame attack by itself wouldn't be effective, and besides it left you feeling as though you'd just been gutted. But with them so close, it caught both their heads, and it must have worked, because both changed into young men, their hair on fire, falling full tilt toward the Earth.

Manfred heard a roar to his side and turned to meet a golden dragon. But the golden dragon lacked insignia on the wings and couldn't be Boelcke. It must, therefore, be an Englishman. This took a second to determine, and then Manfred attempted to climb above the Englishman, but not so fast that a singing flame didn't catch the tip of his wing. He couldn't flame in turn, because Voss, engaged in combat beyond the Englishman, would likely be caught in the return flame. So he let out a scream, and even as he did, he struck out with his back claws toward the other dragon's head.

His claw went into the Englishman's eye, causing an involuntary reaction. The Englishman's wings came in and up to get at Manfred. And Manfred somersaulted midair, and clamped his teeth on the dragon's neck.

The dragon shifted and suddenly, instead of a dragon, Manfred was biting a man, almost severing head from body. He let go quickly, appalled, shaken at breaking the taboo of a lifetime.

In that moment, he'd have been vulnerable. In that moment—

But as he turned to meet a dragon flying near him, he realized by the insignia on the green wings that it was Voss.

There were no more enemies. Boelcke, victorious, was already flying down ahead of them by a circuitous path to avoid being seen by ground troops or aviators. At least as much as possible. Manfred imagined the secret wouldn't long be kept.

There were baths and proper accommodations waiting for them this time, after the hellish ordeal of shifting back into humans, exhausted and low on energy.

Boelcke and Voss came to meet Manfred in his room, where, stripped to the waist, *Freiherr* von Richthofen was having a wide, long burn that ran from the outside of his shoulder to the inside of his waist seen to by a medic.

The location and size of the burn amused Manfred, as he didn't think that it had been that large a burn. And it had been his wing tip.

The other two looked as morose as he felt. Voss, who sported a sling on his right arm, said it was just a sprain, but looked pensive. "Is it right," he asked, when the medic had left, "that we should kill our own kind, just to serve our homeland?"

"Why not?" Boelcke asked. "Didn't we always do it?" And to Voss's surprised look. "We killed other men. How is the fact they're also shifters any different?"

Manfred frowned, putting his shirt on, and then his tunic over it. "It would be different, if we were dragons attacking humans," he said. "After a while, it would be hard not to think of all men as food. But the others are dragons also."

"Speaking of food, I understand they are to serve us dinner. And the two of you are to go to flier school."

"What? Dragon flier school?" Voss asked.

"No, to learn to fly airplanes. That way we'll be able to form our own squadron, supposing we find some more of us, and then we can keep things secret more easily."

"I always wanted to go to flight school," Manfred said. "I did not enlist to deliver eggs and butter." He finished buttoning his tunic. "But it occurs to me we should paint some wilder patterns on our wings to make recognition easier. You know, stripes and dots and such. In vivid colors."

Boelcke looked at him and tilted his head doubtfully. "We shall look like a flying circus."

A Cup of Wisdom

JOSEPH ZIEJA

THE FLAPS OF THE TENT BLED THE SILVERY-GRAY LIGHT OF THE MOON. The boy sat in the center, thin wisps of smoke rising from the sticks of incense buried into the soft dirt of the Calchaka Plains. It smelled like sandalwood and rosemary, smells that reminded the boy of his mother's kitchen and her soft cheeks.

The boy banished the memory; this was not the time for childish daydreams. This was the time for war.

His father, standing with his back turned, twisted the pestle into the mortar with smooth, rhythmic motions, the hardened muscles on the back of his arm writhing hypnotically. The light vest he wore over his sweat-slicked back was more than many others in the camp wore that night; the summer heat of another military campaign made clothing unbearable for most.

The sound of the guard changing outside told the boy that it was nearly midnight. He wished he were out there, sweating with the men, instead of in here, sweating in fear.

You are not afraid, he told himself. *You are ready to fight, to lead men, to kill.*

"Father," the boy asked, "why do I have to do this? There will be fighting tomorrow."

His father did not look back. "Are you ready to face the Ferendi?"

"I will crush them," the boy said, his jaw hardening. The Ferendi, those twisted invaders from the north with their curved swords and dark magic, had been a plague, a disease that needed cleansing, for half a century now. Finally he'd have his chance.

93

His father turned around, his expression grim. The sharp lines and angles of his face were softened by the large black beard that hid no few scars. In that face lived the boy's motivation; just looking at it made his hands itch for his sword. The boy would make his father proud on the battlefield, earn his right to command.

His father transferred the substance in the mortar to another bowl, this one a blackened wooden thing with small holes in the bottom. This he placed over a small pit in the center of the tent, where smoldering coals added their dying heat to that of a sweltering summer night. The boy shifted in his seat.

Silently, his father raised his hand and held it over the bowl. The talisman of knotted iron hanging from a cord on his father's neck began to glow with a pale blue light. The source of ancient magic joined itself with his father's spirit and unlocked the power with a sound like crackling fire; his father was doing something to the substance in the bowl. Nervous, the boy grasped his own talisman, imagining calling on the old magic to cut down Ferendi soldiers and help free his people from their fear. His time would come, and soon.

The change in smell was instantaneous; the scent of his mother's kitchen was replaced by the stench of war. Sweat. Blood. Burning. The acrid odor of decomposing bodies. He willed his face to remain still, not wanting to let his father see him flinch. Suddenly, the distance between him and home was very tangible.

"I am one of the highest ranking generals in this army," his father said. "You will rise to replace me someday." A thin smile that was anything but warm spread across his face. "Consider this my first lesson."

"But Father," the boy said, still stroking his talisman. "You have given me many lessons."

His father said nothing. He took a small copper cup and pushed it into the top of the wooden bowl over the coals. A thick, oily liquid seeped up out of the iron-black porridge and crept down the side of the cup. Stepping forward, he offered the cup into the boy's hands.

"Drink," he said.

Hiding his revulsion and refusing to dishonor himself with more unanswered questions, the boy threw the liquid back and swallowed. It tasted like hell.

The world vanished.

Hadran took two arrows to the chest, and that made me the commander.

"Archers!" I screamed, grabbing the talisman that hung from Hadran's neck. It was slick with dark blood and a slimy green-black liquid that I was careful not to touch. Ferendi poison. "Concentrate your fire on this location!"

I tapped into the power of the talisman and sent out a brilliant beacon of blue light. It soared across the open field and toward the Ferendi and settled just on the left flank of the charging horses, where they hadn't formed a solid line yet. Their cavalry had finally overtaken their own archers, and this was the moment where they were the most vulnerable. I'd been here before. They wouldn't launch another salvo for fear of hitting their own men, but that left me plenty of time to pepper them with arrows and magic until they ran us through.

"Captain!" someone called to my left as a cloud of arrows rose from our ranks and headed toward my marker. "Look!"

I spun, sending a wave of flame billowing outward toward the weak link in the cavalry line before pulling my attention away. I didn't wait to see if it hit. It wouldn't matter anyway.

Even before I turned, I knew what was coming. The cavalry had been a distraction; the real threat was coming from the west. An entire brigade of Ferendi Spin-Devils sped toward us, kicking up so much dust and dirt that it turned the Calchaka Plains into a giant bowl of green and brown stew. Those battlemages were destruction incarnate, and they were advancing unopposed.

"Stand fast!" I called. "Aldan, Chari, Tumeni, with me!"

I didn't look to see if the men I called had followed me. They always came.

The archers were still firing on the cavalry, and a brief glance told me that our position would be overrun in just a few minutes. That wasn't my concern; I was worried about the Spin-Devils. If they broke through us, they were only minutes from the main camp. Women and children were there. I thanked the gods I had never taken a wife. Knowing she was back there would have broken me. I was a man with nothing to lose, and that made me dangerous.

Power coursed through me as I drew upon the talisman, sheathing my sword. I wouldn't need it anymore.

"You know what we have to do," I said quietly. The sounds of dying, screaming, fighting were all around me. But it all seemed too quiet. War, to me, always seemed too damn quiet.

I heard grunts from the men behind me. Ten years of friendship and sharing pain and loss had come to this moment. I felt our magic joining, the burning sensation that came with using too much at once, and the peace of knowing that it didn't matter.

One deep breath was all I had time for. Then the Spin-Devils were upon us. I know, before they ripped my body apart, that I killed at least one of them. I pray to the gods that I killed at least one of them.

The boy's eyes snapped to alertness, his lungs heaving with heavy, ragged gasps. He could feel the cold steel of the Ferendi Spin-Devils' spears digging into his skin, feel their magic tearing away at his mind and body and reducing him to dust.

"Father," he said. "That . . . that was Captain Gannis the Fearless, wasn't it?"

Gannis had been a hero, a thing of legends. His stand against the Spin-Devils had been told in every tavern, sung by every bard. But this didn't feel like a story; it felt like a desperate grasp for a small advantage by a captain staring defeat in the face. And he'd only been in charge because someone else had died. That didn't seem very grandiose at all.

"You must be ready to sacrifice," his father said. "Are you ready to face the Ferendi?"

"I will be as Gannis was," the boy said, though it didn't feel quite right even as the words left his mouth. His father was just trying to discourage him, to keep him safe and coddle him. It was no way to treat a warrior. He *would* fight tomorrow, and he *would* bring his family's name honor.

"Drink," his father said, refilling the cup and extending it to the boy.

The boy looked his father straight in the eye and drank.

I fingered the rank on my shoulder that marked me as the High Commander. Surrounded by my staff, in the safety of a command tent miles away from the front, I didn't feel like I was in command of much.

The thick parchment that showed a drawing of the battlefield, crudely replicated by one of our Bandala fliers, was filled to the edges with small figurines representing my field commands. Ferendi troops, black stones, were quickly beginning to outnumber mine.

"We need to pull back, Commander Shen," Karn, my deputy, said. Always cautious, but I was always reckless. We had balanced each other for decades.

"Pull back to what? The city? There's nowhere else to go."

The rest of my staff was arguing over where to place troops and when to tap into our reserves for magic. Talismans were in short supply, and the power that the mages could draw from them was getting weaker by the second. Soon we'd be a primitive band of pikemen and archers, trying to contend against a swarming tide of darkness from the north. I didn't even know how to negotiate a surrender if I wanted to save my men. Nobody spoke their language.

I stopped listening to them. I'd learned long ago when to probe for advice and when to act on my instincts, and right now my instincts were telling me that I was missing something.

Looking at the western edge of the map, I noticed a small hole in the terrain that I hadn't seen before. The Ferendi mass was strangely shaped, like it was defending itself from an attack that wasn't there. They'd been spread out to avoid concentrated archer fire, but now, according to the Bandala scouts, they were bunching together. Like they were making room for something.

"There," I said, breaking through the chatter. I pointed to where I saw the hole in the enemy lines. "That space is too big. Not by much, but too big. It's exposing their army's left flank, and we have Hadran's brigade helping to pave the way for a cavalry strike there."

"So?" Karn said. "That's a good thing, Commander."

"It would be," I said, "but the Ferendi aren't that stupid."

Karn, his face tired and worn, swallowed.

"Spin-Devils," I said, tapping my finger on the parchment. "Battlemages. That's why they've been holding back. We need to get—"

Cold steel pierced my armor and sheathed itself in the center of my ribcage. I didn't know what had happened at first, but as my body pitched backward and I grappled with my lungs for air, I finally tore my eyes off the map. Everyone else around me was already dead. Everyone but Karn. Dear, dear Karn. He withdrew his bloody hand, and I saw the thin glaze of magic that had been hiding his face evaporate, revealing that near-black skin, those watery, yellow eyes. Ferendi. How long ago had the Spin-Devil taken my deputy, my friend? How long had I been inadvertently feeding the enemy information through him? Worse, did they speak *our* language now? So many questions unanswered.

The world blackened like tree bark in a forest fire, and I reached up to grab the High Commander rank on my shoulders. I tried tearing it off, but my fingers would not close.

The boy clutched his chest, and sweat dropped from his forehead onto the thirsty dirt below him. A single sharp intake of breath told him that his lungs were not filling with blood, that the steel in his heart was not real. Dreams. Illusions. The lingering love for Karn was so great, the sadness at his death so enormous, that he could not stop the sob that escaped his tightened lips. Panic threatened to overtake him until he realized that the Spin-Devils weren't actually about to crest the hill and destroy Hadran's brigade and Captain Gannis with it.

"No," he said, though he didn't know whom he was talking to. It felt like a great void was opening up inside of him.

"You must be ready to command," his father said. "Are you ready to face the Ferendi?"

"Yes," the boy said, feeling some of the fire return to him. He *was* ready. Of course he could command. He *understood* war. Why was his father showing him these things? Was he trying to make him run home? There was no honor in that.

A familiar copper cup snuck through the darkened edges of his vision.

"Drink," his father said.

Trembling, the boy took the cup.

The Bandala's wings beat feverishly underneath me, sending me undulating up and down with nauseating rapidity. Two years as a Bandala flier and scout, hundreds of times flying over the Ferendi, and it all boiled down to this one moment, this one piece of information.

Shina had four arrows sticking out of her hide, and she was losing altitude with every second. Her panicked cries had started out as screeches that split the sky, sounds that would have made any other animal run in terror. Now the beast was barely making a whisper. Screams had turned to wheezes. Gray-blue foam appeared at the corners of her mouth and flew backward in the wind as we rushed toward friendly lines.

"Come on, girl," I said in time with the beating of her enormous, powerful wings. "Come on, girl. We have to tell them."

The Spin-Devils had been like a dark storm cloud that had lost its place in the sky and landed on the earth instead. I saw the bodies of our scouts and patrols littered across the fields like the discarded toys of children, watched the Bandalas of my comrades turn into ash in the air as the Ferendi battlemages lit them on fire like dry straw. Scouts fell from their backs, arms flailing. Their screams were almost louder than the creatures on which they flew.

I was the last. And if I didn't get back to High Commander Shen's tent with this report, they were all dead.

Shina's head lilted to the side, and her wings stopped beating. We pitched sideways.

"No!" I cried. I pulled the reins hard as we began to spin. "Shina! Wake up!"

I had hoped at least she could get me to the ground safely. If I could get ahead of their charge, I might be able to get back in time to warn them. Now I didn't know what I hoped.

The long, dark croon of one of the Ferendi's flying beasts called out behind me. They'd followed. I couldn't tell what direction they were coming from. I couldn't tell what direction anything was coming from. We were spinning out of control, the world becoming a dizzying, rotating mess. My stomach crept up to my throat. Another arrow, fired from the back of the Ferendi's beast, lodged itself in Shina's back. She didn't make a sound.

I pulled the reins. I slapped Shina's side. I screamed my message out as we began to plummet, hoping that someone, anyone would hear me.

"The Spin-Devils are coming!"

The ground. *The ground!*

The boy was looking up at the top of the tent, his head spinning. He'd felt his own bones crumble like old parchment as he'd hit the ground, felt his stomach rise into his throat with the rapid descent. Had that just been the impact of him falling off the stool he'd been sitting on?

Groaning, he sat up, the vision of the injured and dying Bandala still fresh in his head. Dizziness overwhelmed him and he pitched sideways wildly, knocking into a table full of arrows. They scattered to the ground.

"He never made it," the boy said, his throat tight.

"You must be ready to fail," his father said. "Are you ready to face the Ferendi?"

"Fail?" the boy said, looking up at his father's cold face. "Why do I have to be ready to fail? I will not fail." His voice hardened as he repeated himself. "I will *not* fail. I *am* ready."

His father extended the cup. "Drink."

With the slightest of hesitations, the boy reached out and took the cup.

I ran into battle only because there was an army running behind me and stopping would have meant being trampled. Death behind, death ahead. The open field throbbed with the beating rhythm of tens of thousands of footsteps, hoofbeats, the sound of falling bodies. The Ferendi host charged forward, their black armor sucking in the light. We ran, screaming to hide our own terror, weapons raised.

Somehow, I was in the first rank of soldiers. The lines clashed. Someone hit me from behind; I felt it all the way through my armor. A friendly soldier stepped on my ankle. I thought I could hear the bone break even over all the noise.

I looked up. A rearing horse, its rider holding a barbed spear high in the air. Time froze for a brief moment before he brought it down.

Oh, gods.

"That's it?" the boy shouted, incredulous, furious. The feeling of emptiness, of pointlessness, was so great inside of him that it threatened to swallow him whole. He nearly forgot the incredible pain that still lingered from where he'd been stabbed in the stomach by the Ferendi cavalryman. "What is the purpose of this? What am I learning?"

He wasn't sure to whom he was asking the question. Was he wondering at the purpose of these visions, clearly intended to frighten him? Or was he wondering what the purpose of such a short, futile life was? The simple soldier had barely even lifted his sword. Instead of charging forward into glory, cutting down enemies, valiantly sacrificing himself for the greater good, he'd simply ... died.

"Are you ready to face the Ferendi?"

His father did not even offer advice, that he must be ready for futility and meaninglessness. That he must be ready for his life to mean almost nothing. That he must be ready to be forgotten and left on the field to die.

Was *this* war?

The boy nodded. He could change this. He could avoid that fate. It wouldn't happen to *him*. *He* was different. Not pointless. Not just a target for a Ferendi spear.

"Drink," his father said. Through tear-blurred vision, the boy could see the copper cup in his father's hand. He did not reach for it.

"Only once more." His father's voice was almost soft. Almost.

The boy snatched it from his father's hand.

"You are just trying to make me go home," he said. "I will not. I *am* ready. The Ferendi will die by my hand."

He threw the liquid back in one gulp.

I kept an image in my head for times like these, a mental picture of my daughter dancing with my wife in the middle of our house. I saw both of their dresses twirling as I stood in the corner slapping my hands on the drum head and shouting out the words to an old song that my mother had sung to me when I was a boy. That was how I preferred to remember them: their dark skin healthy, shiny, smooth. Thinking of the peal of my daughter's laughter coaxed a broad grin from my dirty, grimy face.

"What are you laughing at?"

I looked up. Tomani was looking at me across the fire as he sharpened his barbed spear using a slick rock. He'd done it so many times that he didn't even have to watch; a less experienced man would have cut his knuckles to pieces. Behind him, his black armor gave off an ominous sheen, reflecting the firelight along wet traces of blood left on its surface.

"Home," I answered honestly.

He clicked his tongue at me. "Home is far away, Samcha. And we may not see it again."

I shrugged. "I know. But if I don't think of it often, I worry that I will forget that it ever existed."

Tomani laughed. He had no time or interest in family, like so many other Ferendi who had chosen the path of the Spin-Devil.

"Home may be gone already," he said, and his laugh suddenly turned bitter. "Let us just hope that the pale dogs keep scattering like lambs. Then maybe we can talk of home again."

I thought back to how Ferend must look now, with the sickness killing off all the crops, making the land infertile and useless, the people starving. I hoped my wife and child could still eat. I hoped they were still alive.

"Let's go, Samcha," Tomani said, standing. He gave a great stretch and a yawn before reaching for his armor. "Our home is on that field now."

I looked out on the grassy plain that would certainly bring us another day of tireless fighting and tried hard to see them dancing again.

Ten years had faded the memory, a bit, but . . . it was still there, for now.

When the boy came back to reality, he found his father sitting on a second stool, staring at him with a blank expression. His father did not hold the copper cup in his hands; the coals behind him that had helped him distill the potion had long since died out. How long had he simply been sitting here, doing nothing? The guards changing outside again told him that hours had passed, but all of this had felt like mere seconds.

"I was . . ." he said, having trouble bringing the word to his lips, "a Ferendi soldier. A Spin-Devil."

His father nodded. "And are you ready to fight them?"

The boy swallowed. "I don't understand," he said. "That Spin-Devil had a wife and child. He missed them." He put his hand across his chest. "The pain in my heart . . . I can feel it."

It was more pronounced than any of the terrors he'd experienced; the fall from the Bandala, the spear through the gut, the cold knife in the chest. It was a pain of duality, of complexity, that settled like a great weight on his shoulders. He felt at once very wise and very heavy, and found himself wondering if there had ever been a way to separate those two sensations. What had happened to the Ferendi homeland? Did fighting for his own home mean robbing the Ferendi of theirs? Was that right?

"Never forget," his father said. "This is not black and white. It is not all glory. Sometimes you will lose. Sometimes you will need to bear the heavy pain of your decisions. Sometimes your enemies are not dogs to be put down. They fight for things just as we do. They bleed, and die, and mourn. When you dishonor your enemy, make him less than human, you dishonor yourself." He reached out and placed a hand on the boy's shoulder.

Suddenly, bells began ringing somewhere in the distance. The boy looked out the tent flap and saw thin fingers of dawn creeping in through cracks in the canvas. He'd been in here all night. He should have felt tired, but for some reason he couldn't bring himself to feel anything. Sounds of people putting on their armor, shouts from commanders to get people into position, and sounds of horses whinnying broke the silence of the early morning. Battle had arrived, whether they were ready for it—whether *he* was ready for it—or not. The Ferendi were coming.

"So," his father said. "Are you ready?"

The boy stood up, frowning. He shook his head as he clutched his chest again. He could still feel the loss, even though the visions had faded. Two girls, dancing in a living room that had looked frighteningly like his own.

"No," he said. "I am not."

"Good," his father said. He threw him a sword, and the boy caught it without flinching. "You are in my detail today. Get to your mount and meet me at the head of the camp in five minutes."

The boy looked at his father, looked at the sword, and looked inside himself. Then, silently, he went off to a much different war from the one he had come to fight.

Words of Power

WENDY N. WAGNER

KÁDÁR SCRUTINIZED THE FLAKE OF CLAY ON THE BLADE OF THE screwdriver. "He's just getting too old to be a war truck," she said. "Look at this clay. The *logos* barely flickers in it."

Zugsführer Warren spat on the packed earthen floor of the machine house. "You know I can't see that magic shit," he growled. "And it wouldn't matter if I did. An order is an order, Gefreiter Kádár, and the Oberst needs every last golem out on the field."

The small woman wiped the screwdriver clean on her shirt-tail and restrained a sigh. There was no point arguing with the big American; if anyone was a stickler for following orders, it was the Zugsführer. They'd butted heads before, and Kádár had come away with a headache.

She stroked the pitted side of the golem. Even the Amero-Hungarian state seal, painted on each of its shoulders, looked worn out. "Poor old Benchley."

"You *name* them?"

She didn't bother glancing at Warren. Instead, she studied the dull gray places where the field operators had patched the injured clay. She narrowed her eyes. "This patch clay is shit," she growled. "Even the clay I used to convert him from a fighting man to a war truck was better than this, and I wouldn't have used that crap to make a singing teapot."

She said this as if she'd been a clay artist or wizard before the war broke out in '29, when even an NCO like Zugsführer knew she'd only been discovered during basic training and that she barely had enough talent to patch the clay creations' wounds. The real ceramic workers—the ceramic wizards, the ceramicers—were working night and day at the capital, making golems to protect the Emperor and government offices.

"Patch it up," Warren growled. "I'm losing golems fast out there."

Kádár folded her arms across her chest. "I'll get to him." She jabbed her chin in the direction of the two twenty-foot-tall clay men stretched across the vast hangar floor. "Those guys are almost done."

Warren rolled his eyes. From experience, Kádár knew he didn't care about the weapons-class golems. Warren oversaw the unit's supplies, and the war-truck golems were his only interest. They pulled his carts of munitions and tents and foodstuffs.

"Just as long as I get my golem," he said.

"I'll get to him," she repeated.

The American turned around and trudged toward the exit. Kádár resisted the urge to sigh. She didn't like talking to people much. After four years as a ceramitech, she'd learned to prefer the company of the clay men. And anyone's company would be better than Warren's.

She rolled her shoulders. She'd been working the past ten hours, and she had at least another ten ahead of her. The next wave of injured would probably arrive soon. Not for the first time, she wished the Empire could spare another ceramitech for the unit—one with more talent. Some of the spells she was using pushed her to the very limits of her power.

She kicked over a barrel full of magic-enhanced clay and rolled it toward the stricken clay giants. A canvas-wrapped table stood beside the nearest golem, a jug of water on top. Her tools, ready to work. She'd already patched the worst of this golem's wounds: he'd taken an artillery shell in the upper chest, losing one arm and a good chunk of his chest armor. His new arm looked better than the original, the joints smoother and more carefully formed. She was proud of her arm and leg work.

Quickly, she removed a few pounds of clay from the barrel and worked it into a thin sheet, the word magic within glimmering blue and gold to her trained eye. She should be able to finish patching the golem's chest in no time.

His new chest armor still cooled in the logomantic kilns. Soft, unfired clay formed most of the golem's body, the magic giving it stability and firmness. In the safe harbor of Vienna, most of the serving golems received only soft clay shaping, but out here on the battlefield, armor was a necessity. The time in the kiln hardened the ceramic to twice the strength of steel. Words of magic kept it from chipping or shattering.

Kádár hesitated. Before she could apply the chest armor, she needed to seal the golem's *animus* into its chest cavity. Of all her tasks, she hated this one the most. She had just enough talent to keep the balls of magical energy under control—but only just. Any distraction, any lapse of focus, and the damn thing could go rogue.

The unit's last ceramitech died in an *animus* explosion. That kept the danger in perspective.

Something creaked behind her. Kádár jumped.

The battered war-truck golem now listed sideways. A little trickle of steam puffed out his stylized mouth. Someone had given him bull's horns as a joke, giving him an endearing animal quality. Kádár smiled at the old thing. "I'll be right with you, Benchley," she called. As if he could hear her. As if a golem understood anything beyond the order scrolls the officers shoved in its order hatch.

She rolled her eyes at herself and covered the worked clay with a piece of dampened canvas. Then she turned her attention back to the war golem. Even without his chest armor, he looked every inch a knight. Not much could penetrate a golem's *logos*-infused chest armor, but the empire's enemies worked at it. This golem had been felled by a Chino-French artillery round: Kádár recognized the signature crimping on the bits of shell case lodged inside the golem's ruined chest cavity. She'd been seeing a lot more of them lately. The enemy had made a leap in technology no Imperial spy had seen or expected.

She forced away such thoughts. She could muse on the state of the enemy's technology, or she could get to work. Only one of those alternatives would get her out of this hangar and into her bunk.

She hurried across the hangar to the sealed case of *animus* spheres. Her hand trembled as she unsheathed her knife. She didn't mind pricking her finger to draw the bit of blood that opened the spelled lock; what she hated was the way all those artificial spirits pushed and jabbed at the edges of her control.

During the seconds the case stood open, the *animus* threatened to break free.

Kádár scooped up the closest ball of *logos*-infused mesh, slitting her eyes against its burning brightness. The hairs on her arms rose up; her close-cropped hair prickled. Magic played over her skin, but she clamped a mental shield over it. With a toe, she kicked shut the chest.

She hurried to the golem and placed the mesh ball inside the chest cavity. The shaking in her hands intensified as she lowered the thin slab of clay over the glowing orb. This was the worst part. Until the magical energy bonded with the golem's clay, it would struggle to get out. She had to keep her mental shield firmly covering herself and the golem to keep the energy from escaping. She wished she wasn't so damn tired.

A puff of steam burst from the warrior golem's lips, and she sagged with relief. Its softly glowing amber eyes opened and closed.

"You're re-energized," she said. Her voice sounded creaky to her own ears. She needed a break. Better yet, some food. "I'm going to grab a snack, then get you armored up. You'll be back on the field in no time, warrior."

The thing blinked a few times. Its flat clay face showed no emotion, and of course, it made no sound. Golems couldn't speak.

Behind her something thudded. She turned around. "Anyone here?"

No one answered. In the brilliant glare of the work lights, nothing moved.

Kádár rolled her shoulders and moved back toward her little desk. Benchley sagged beside it, his silly horned head cocked.

"You next, Benchley." She stopped in mid-step, realizing that not only did Benchley sag sideways, he'd actually knocked into her desk. Her snack drawer had slid open, revealing her secret cache of dried fruit and canned beans.

"That's just what I needed," she admitted. "Thanks, buddy."

She patted his arm as she took out a can of beans and a can opener, then shook her head. As if he could hear her. As if he could know what thanks was. She'd been working with clay men for far too long—they almost seemed alive to her.

The hangar doors burst open and a half-dozen men charged through, a war-truck golem running behind them. The can opener fell from Kádár's fingers.

"What the—"

"Gefreiter Kádár!" Leutnant Breuer bellowed.

The sight of the highly decorated officer launched her into action. Kádár ran across the hangar just as Zugsführer Warren slammed shut the hangar doors and jammed them with a stretch of iron post. Someone shouted as he ran to undo the ropes tying down the cover on the sledge the war truck had dragged in. The chaos made Kádár's head spin.

A bandaged field operator stepped out from behind the leutnant and caught her by the arm. "Can you save Freddy? Is he going to make it?"

Kádár's gaze went to the work sledge the war truck had brought in. Something writhed and twisted inside it, but canvas shrouded the thing. Zugsführer Warren grabbed the edge of the canvas and whipped it off.

"Jesus," Kádár breathed.

Two golems lay twisted in each others' arm, both of them smoking, writhing. The Imperial golem gleamed a soft white, its clay the same bisque as tableware. The other's sullen red clay swallowed the sunlight. Kádár had never seen a golem like it before. Its long flexible limbs twined around the Imperial golem like snakes, four rust-colored pythons squeezing the life out of its prey. They hadn't loosened their hold yet, either, despite the smoke boiling out of the thing's mouth and nose.

The war-truck golem gave a nervous puff of steam. Kádár could tell at a glance that it wasn't a modified warrior golem, like Benchley. This poor thing had been meant for labor on the streets of Vienna. It had probably pulled a fancy carriage—its shape even echoed a horse.

Horrible thumping sounded inside the sledge. Then the Imperial golem shrieked.

"Freddy!" The operator threw himself at the sledge, but a flailing red arm launched him across the room.

The war truck rose up on its hind legs, shrieking like a horse. The leutnant shouted at it, but the golem had fallen back on its original order scroll. Kádár threw herself at its knees, pinning them together and throwing the beast off-balance. It came down on its feet, hard. Steam puffed all around her. Kádár barked a word of power. The horse-shaped golem went still.

For a moment, she thought she'd killed it, that she'd picked the wrong word, that she'd used too much talent and over-spooled its order scroll. Then its yellow eyes blinked back on. It backed away from her until its back pressed against the wall.

"What the hell did you do to my golem?" Warren bellowed, but the leutnant was grabbing Kádár's arm, shaking her, screaming in her ear. She had to do something about that red golem before anyone else got hurt.

She wrenched herself away from the leutnant's grasp and scrambled up on the edge of the sledge. She wasn't sure she had the strength for another word of power like that.

The Imperial golem suddenly sat upright. Its left arm, the one Kádár had designed, drove into the bottom of the red golem's face. A horrible crack resounded throughout the hangar.

Steam boiled out of the Imperial golem's joints, its eyes, the scroll hatch in its chest. A high-pitched wheeze filled the air, so shrill and pained Kádár clapped her hands over her ears. Then it twitched, once, twice, and went still.

Silence settled over the golem repair hangar. Kádár lowered her hands. The white golem's face was pressed close to hers, its eyes flat planes of yellow glass.

"Bravely done, Sir Knight," she whispered.

"They're dead?" the leutnant snapped.

She nodded.

"Then get to work. I want a full work-up on the Chino-French machine. I want to know what powers it, who built it, and how we can kill it: now." His lips tightened. "In fact, I want it yesterday. I've got an entire battalion of those things coming our way, and they've already destroyed twenty of my best units. That's an order, Gefreiter!"

He unblocked the door and stomped outside. His men followed him.

"What did you do back there?" Warren said.

"What?"

He took a step closer. "You heard me. What did you say? You took down my war truck, and you knocked out both these golems."

"That wasn't me!" Kádár waved her hands. "The golem did it all on his own. I definitely don't have that kind of power."

Disgusted, she squatted beside the unconscious field operator. "I can't believe none of those guys stopped to check on this man." She knew enough about first aid to guess he was all right, just knocked out. "I'm going to move him out of the way, just to be safe."

She worried, moving an unconscious man, but she didn't want anyone too close to that Chino-French machine. Some golems were equipped with a self-destruct, even Imperial models. It was impossible to tell merely by looking. Kádár dragged the man toward her desk.

Benchley cocked his head at her.

"Look after him, okay?" she asked. His head bounced, almost as in reply. In fact, it nearly looked like a nod.

She went back to the sledge, where Warren still stood. She put her hands on her hips. "Going to help me?"

"I'm not going anywhere until my truck can move, and I don't think it's going anywhere right now."

She spared a glance at the horse-like golem. Its eyes were dim, half their usual brightness. The thing had gone into its rest mode. "It's sleeping," she snapped. "It probably needs to re-spool its order scroll and restore its *animus*. They need rest, too."

She turned her attention back to the task at hand. The red golem made her nervous. The long arms, the intensely armored construction: this was all new design. The Chino-French had been stealing Imperial technology for years, but this was the first original creation she'd seen. She scrambled up on the sledge to get a better look. She had to push aside the cold hands of the Imperial golem to really see the red golem's face. The long crack running up its skull exposed something strangely damp-looking. What kind of magic were the Chino-French using? Some kind of alchemy, maybe?

She reached out to its cheek and wriggled a finger into the crack. She pulled out her finger, now stained red. She sniffed it and made a face at the copper smell.

"Is that blood?" Warren asked.

"Sure looks like it." She leaned forward and gripped both sides of the cracked clay head. It creaked in protest—then snapped open.

Kádár stumbled backward.

"Holy shit!" Warren grabbed her shoulder. "Is that what I think it is?"

She forced herself to move close enough to look at the pink thing. Her stomach twisted. "It's definitely a brain, and I'm pretty sure it's human."

"What does that mean?" Warren's voice had climbed in pitch. "How does that even work?"

"I don't know," she murmured. She held her hand over the brain, not touching it, just trying to feel what kind of magic had bound it in place. A faint aura clung to the organ, a sense of pain and darkness.

She shook her head. "I wish we had a ceramic wizard in the unit. They'd be able to get a lock on the magical system. This just feels… evil." She sat back on her heels. "I had no idea human energy and magical energy could even mix. The applications are incredible."

He leaned over Kádár's shoulder. "There's something blinking at the base of the brain."

Kádár peered at the tiny light. "Self-destruct!"

Warren's arms closed around her, throwing her backward, but it was too late. A blast of white filled the hangar, blotting out the golems, the sledge, the world. Kádár clamped shut her eyes, but she was only falling. Falling into the brightness.

And then black. She blinked hard. Her head wobbled as if her neck had been replaced with spaghetti. Her stomach flipped over at the slight motion. Everything hurt, and her head wouldn't stop moving. A horrible pealing like the world's largest bell rang in her ears.

She tried to sit up, but her body was pressed tight against a wall of ceramic. Kádár forced herself to breathe deeply and look around. She lay on the floor of the hangar, everything gray upon gray. She pulled herself to her feet despite queasiness. A set of softly glowing eyes appeared in the gloom, and with it, the faint outline of a broad, horned head.

"Benchley?" She reached out with tentative fingertips to stroke the clay machine's warm arm. It felt surprisingly soft and supple.

"Kádár. You're okay." Warren's voice sounded nearby.

"Because you saved me. Good thinking, Sarge." She blinked again, struggling to find him. "Where are you?"

"Here," he whispered. She could barely hear his voice through the ringing in her ears.

The voice came from the ground. Kádár dropped to her knees beside his shape. She was beginning to see colors now. There was much, much too much red.

"Oh, shit. I'll go get help."

"No. I'm not going to last much longer."

Kádár shook her head. "I can't let you die like this. You saved my life!"

"That's an order, Gefreiter. Plus, the infirmary's probably retreating." The thin shriek of artillery fire penetrated the ringing in her ears. The ground shook beneath them.

"We're under attack," she gasped.

"For a while now," he said. He coughed, and a bright bubble of blood popped on his lips.

"We've got to get out of here," she said. "If there are as many war golems out there as that leutnant said, this whole base is dead."

Artillery screamed again, and the ground bucked beneath Kádár's feet. She pitched forward as the far side of the hangar exploded in blue-and-gold light. She could feel herself screaming, but she couldn't hear anything.

The earth went still.

Kádár managed to lift up her pounding head. This second explosion had been worse than the first, but at least she hadn't hit her head again. She tried to take stock of the damage.

One half of the golem repair hangar no longer existed. A crater stood less than half a meter to her right, blue smoke rising out of it. The spot where her desk had stood—where the field operator had lain—was gone.

Twilight sky winked down at her, streaked with the fire of a hundred fighter balloons. "Oh shit," she breathed. "The *animus* chest. The fucking French blew it up. Benchley—" she began, but the war truck was no longer at her side. The golem's shoulders sprawled across her legs, his empty face turned to the ceiling.

"No!" She shook her head. "Warren?"

He didn't answer, but his breath gurgled in his throat.

"Don't die!" she barked. She tried to wriggle out from under Benchley, but nothing happened. She couldn't even feel her toes. She felt around her waist, her hips. She must have fallen on something, and the weight of the golem pressed her spine down on it. She was paralyzed. A cry caught in her throat.

"Warren, I can't move. They're bombing us. We're all going to die," she said. "We're all going to die."

"Fuck," he said. "You've got to get out of here."

"I'm trapped. Benchley fell on me. I think I'm hurt." She eyed the big war-truck golem. A tiny light flickered in his eye sockets.

"Benchley?" She held her breath. If she could get him up and running, maybe he could carry them out of this place. There had to be some Imperial squadron retreating to safety. They could help her.

The light flickered, then went on again, but dimmer than the light of a birthday candle. "Damn it," she breathed. "He's still alive, but his *animus* is failing. There's no way he's going anywhere."

"You ... can do it." Warren choked on the words. He didn't have much time left.

"If I could get him another *animus* sphere, maybe. But there's none left." Tears stung her eyes. She didn't bother wiping them away.

"Blood," Warren gasped. He jerked once, twice, and then went still.

Benchley suddenly lifted his head. His eyes flashed and flickered, lighting up the ruins of the hangar, the barrels of clay, the crumbled remains of injured golems. Shards of red ceramic lay all around like bits of frozen blood.

Blood.

The French were using it. The locking spell used it. If she knew more about magic, she could modify some of the power spells to give Benchley a boost. She bit her lip.

Benchley blinked at her. The light in his eyes was going back out.

She wasn't a wizard or a witch or even a real ceramicer. She had just enough training to handle clay and pack a pre-made *animus* sphere into a golem's body. She could never do it.

Up in the sky, something exploded in a burst of magnesium whiteness. A few Imperial red-and-gold balloons shimmered in the brightness, but only a few. The unit was losing. They were holding the most distant inches of Amero-Hungarian soil. No one would know what happened if the French won. She and Warren wouldn't even get a proper burial.

A sudden fierce fire burned in her chest. Those assholes weren't just going to take out her entire unit and all her golems and let them be forgotten. She wasn't going to let that happen.

Kádár reached deep within her, searching for the golden warmth of her talent. It wasn't always easy to find, but today it burned with molten heat. She had never felt so much power inside of her, such strength.

She stretched her fingers to Warren's cooling body. Blood covered every inch of it. She twisted her palm in the stuff. It felt damp, lifeless. She shook her head. That wouldn't work. She needed living blood.

There was only one place for that.

She fumbled along the ground for a chunk of broken ceramic. She gave a dry laugh. This wouldn't even hurt.

She plunged the shard into the top of her leg. Blood, hot and sticky and pulsing with life, poured out. Kádár gasped. With her senses shifted into the magical spectrum, she could see the energy in it, not the blue-and-gold of word-powered magic, but a white hot liquid gleaming that spilled out of her thigh.

She had to get it onto Benchley. She twisted the knife to widen the hole and jammed her fingers down into the wound. Blood covered her hand, soaked into her uniform. A wave of dizziness washed over her. She was losing a lot of blood.

She strained her dripping fingers toward Benchley's chest. The way he was lying, his scroll hatch faced upward, a neat round opening at the base of his throat. She couldn't get at his animus sphere, hidden away in his armored chest, but she could at least get her blood inside that hatch. The living liquid seeped inside him.

"Come on, Benchley. Open your eyes." She tried to remember the words of power, any command that would make him reboot, but her training felt very distant. Her head spun. "Please," she whispered.

As if he could understand her. As if common human politeness could have any effect on a being made of magic words and clay.

His eyes lit up like a light bulb.

She laughed. "Come on, Benchley. Let's get out of here."

Slowly, the big bull-like golem pulled himself to his feet. Blood ran down his shoulders and streaked his sides. He cocked his head, and she heard his order scroll spooling in his chest. He looked around the hangar.

"No," she breathed. "Please! Don't go! Whatever your orders are, please don't go!" She fell backward as another wave of dizziness washed away the last of her strength.

The golem suddenly brought his fist down on a cask of clay. From the ground, Kádár stared at him. She couldn't understand. That couldn't be in any of his orders. He dug into the clay with his blunt white fingers.

Black dots clustered at the edges of Kádár's vision. Blood still poured out of her leg; she would black out any minute. Black out and then die. She didn't even have the strength to cry.

Benchley's horns reappeared, his golden eyes bright. He bent over her. She watched his fingers stretch the *logos*-enriched clay over the gash in her leg and up onto her back. A sudden warmth filled the lower half of her body.

"I can feel my toes," she breathed.

He snorted and scooped her into his arms. He paused a moment to stare at Warren's battered body, then got to his feet and stepped into the night. He marched into the tree line and away from battle, following the tracks of Kádár's retreating unit. She pressed her cheek against the golem's warm chest, feeling a hint of her own living energy moving inside him. He was alive. The golems had felt alive to her, but Benchley was *really* alive now—because of her blood and her magic.

She closed her eyes, feeling the thrum of magic, a different kind of magic, pulsing in her legs and spine. It was part of her now, too. She and Benchley were both hybrids now, neither fully human nor fully golem. She risked a glance at her leg. It didn't look so bad, even if it meant her army days were done.

Benchley looked down at her, his eyes incandescent with power. Something reverberated inside him, a dull rumbling like steam building up inside a teapot. And then paper poured out of his scroll hatch, steaming shreds of all his old orders. By all the rules of golem construction, he should fall down, go still, shut down, but bits of paper kept bursting out of him, and he kept walking.

Under the glow of moonlight and the flash of artillery fire, it was like a ticker-tape parade just for two injured veterans. Kádár smiled and wondered where they would go without orders, without words of power.

Lightweaver in Shadow

GRAY RINEHART

ACROSS THE FOG-SHROUDED VALLEY, FROM THE DEPTHS OF RELLAM Wood, Varrikar war drums welcomed the day. Their deep, resonant blasts echoed off the fog itself.

Tyrol shifted at the sound, his boots still heavy with inch-thick mud that seemed to glue them to the hilltop. He strained to see the signal from Captain Hallern's position on the right flank. The thin shaft of light wavered through the mist, Milligan's shapes less distinct than they should have been: sloppy, even considering the fog. Tyrol had to concentrate hard to interpret. "Cavalry formed, infantry in place, sir," he said. "Enemy positions consistent with scouting. Archers ready...no visible targets yet."

"Damnable fog," Marshall Innolik said. "But we've used it to our advantage so far, eh?" His horse snorted when the big man stood up in the stirrups, as if that extra height might give him a clearer eyeline down into the mist-darkened valley.

He reseated himself and went on, in that voice that sounded like the murmur of a turning grindstone, his rhythm matching the Varrikar drums a bit too closely for Tyrol's comfort. "Do we trust the reports? Make the push now? Confuse the bastards? If we wait too long, will they have time to set their lines?" No one responded; they all knew the marshall answered his own questions, in his own time.

The wind shifted, blowing from Rellam Wood, and Tyrol caught the scent of oily smoke from the darkwood incense the Varrikar burned before battle. He choked a little as the smoke bit the back of his throat. Each heartbeat rattled the thin armor

117

of his breastbone, and he guessed that up and down the line his Dvornian brothers had the same hammering inside, urging them to move, to charge, to fight. He touched the hilt of his sword— his father's once—as if it might support him, and fingered the putty-filled indentation where a red stone had been set, long ago traded away by his mother. His hand itched to draw the sword, to join the others in the front ranks, but at fourteen he was too young and too small, even if he were not a lightweaver.

"Weaver, signal the captain to begin the first phase: release his cavalry to maneuver," the marshall said.

As if he were about to caress a porcupine, Tyrol opened the lantern's shutter and began stroking the light. The first time he had tried—when he realized that he had his mother's gift of manipulation—he had reached too far into the fire to grasp its light; at times like this, the flesh-memory of the blisters on his hands washed over him. He grasped for the heart-memory of his mother tending his hand, and made sure he kept his fingers free of the lantern flame.

Tyrol looked toward the distant hill where Captain Hallern waited. With quick, deft movements, as a common man might tie up a package with string or a musician caress the strings of a lute, he gathered vapor and twisted the watery air to concentrate and shift the lantern's light. His signals went direct where he aimed, which for now meant to Milligan to pass on to the captain.

Milligan's reply was succinct. "Cavalry released, sir," Tyrol reported, trying to keep the sudden exhaustion out of his voice. He stepped away from the lantern just long enough to grab a cold sausage. As the peppery meat began to revive him, he wiped a dribble of grease from his chin.

A couple of paces away, Kelflen rubbed the tip of a drum stick over the drumhead. The whispery sound cut through Tyrol, and his chest seemed to clamp down on his heart. Anticipation shrouded him; he supposed it shrouded them all—Kelflen, Ghilly the piper, the marshall's advisors and hangers-on, the men on the field below—as effectively as the fog.

Tyrol closed the shutter on his lantern. It had oil enough to last until midday, unless he had to send very many more messages.

The anxious moments piled on one another until the marshall said, "Sound the general advance. We will serve them our best, and see how they like it."

Kelflen beat out the familiar rhythm. Seconds later, Ghilly's drones and chanter joined in.

Tyrol barely heard their army's distant drums and pipes echo the call, so effective was the fog at swallowing the sound; yet the Varrikar drumbeat still came through. Then, as sudden as a pot boiling over, came the distant, inconsistent sounds of infantry and cavalry charging, weapons clashing, innumerable triumphs and dreadful pains delivered to men and beasts.

The fog hung over the valley, and the battle continued unseen.

The noise of the battle shifted from right to left and right again. Tyrol messaged Captain Hallern twice more, but the troops could not achieve a breakthrough. Kelflen and Ghilly continued to play out signals to the wider army.

A nearby scream of pain and alarm from the slope behind them cut through the pipe-and-drum call.

Tyrol glanced away from Captain Hallern's position and forgot to look back.

Near enough that the fog blurred but no longer hid them, a squad of Varrikar climbed up the slope. Lieutenant Pilkus, the marshall's adjutant, shouted a warning, drew his sword, and ran downhill to meet them. Others of the marshall's staff followed close behind. Tyrol's hand found the sword hilt again and even he took a step, but he kept his place by the signal lamp.

Marshall Innolik cursed.

The Varrikar were men, sharp-featured with wild dark hair, but even looking down on them from the hilltop this squad seemed peopled with giants. Yet several of them collapsed before Pilkus and the others reached them; could they be so greatly fatigued from fighting their way around the valley? The lieutenant threw himself at the center of the squad and struck at a behemoth in gray-green armor—but it was a glancing blow, and the big man stepped inside Pilkus's sword and hacked down at the young officer's knee. Pilkus screamed as his leg collapsed, but the Varrikar wrapped his arm around the lieutenant's sword arm and held him upright; he looked Pilkus in the eye as he drove the point of his sword up under the adjutant's breastplate.

The rest of the marshall's staff fared somewhat better, and others from the camp joined the melee. But in a moment, two, three, and then four of the Varrikar resumed their climb toward the marshall's position.

"Dear God, we are undone," Marshall Innolik said. His shoulders slumped. Then he straightened his back and a fierce purpose blazed in his eyes.

"Drummer, sound general alarm," he said. "Weaver, signal Captain Hallern to take command. And here"—he flung his leather case to the ground at Tyrol's feet—"if you live, carry that to Hallern and tell him . . . tell him I have been proud to serve with him." The marshall drew his broadsword, as long as Tyrol's leg, and spurred his horse toward the oncoming enemy. "And so have I been proud to serve with you all," he called as he descended the hill.

Tyrol forced his attention away from the marshall and onto his work. He raised the lantern's flame to its brightest. Kelflen's drumbeat changed and Ghilly's pipe roared out a new alarm as Tyrol sent his message in quick bursts like tiny lightning flashes. *Overrun here*, he signaled. *Take command.*

He started to repeat the message when Ghilly's pipes went silent. Tyrol turned.

One of the Varrikar dropped the piper to the ground and hacked at the pipes with his axe. The drones splintered and the hide bag wheezed a final breath.

The soldier stalked toward Kelflen, who stared wide-eyed but continued beating out the alarm.

"Run!" Tyrol shouted, and grabbed the lantern because it was the nearest thing to his hands. He yanked it off its pole and threw it at the huge man. It hit the Varrikar soldier's hip, and what was left of the oil sloshed out and took flame. The man yelled, jumped back, and beat at his burning clothes.

Tyrol picked up the marshall's pouch, then took hold of Kelflen's arm and pulled him away. They ran down the rocky slope, into the fog-strewn valley.

They picked their way between and around barrel-sized boulders, climbed through a split in one stone almost as large as Tyrol's mother's cottage, and crashed through stands of young pines, trading caution for speed as they ran, slid, and fell away from the doomed hilltop. Kelflen's drum was an early casualty, lost in the first few minutes. Tyrol held the marshall's pouch close to him, lest he drop it as they made their way.

Trees and rocks took on ominous shapes in the mist.

"The marshall was right," Tyrol said. "This fog is damnable."

Kelflen said, "The adjutant said it was a Varrikar invention."

"Then damn them three times."

They tried to snake along the line of lower hills that ran generally east toward Captain Hallern's position, but in the mist the only certain direction was down. Too far down meant into the wide part of the valley, and the worst of the fighting. Tyrol was no longer sure that was where he wanted to be; he told himself that his prime concern should be the pouch Marshall Innolik had entrusted to him, but he wondered if he had lost the courage he thought he had.

"Stop, Tyrol," Kelflen finally said. The boy's breath came so heavy he could barely make the sounds. He leaned and then slid down against a boulder the size of a wagon wheel. He still clutched a drum stick in his right hand.

Tyrol understood. Kelflen had been drumming hard before they started running. Tyrol knew that if he had repeated the marshall's message once or twice more he could never have run so far so fast. He supposed he had been lucky to have only had time to send it once, but he wished he knew if Milligan had seen it.

Tyrol let the place they were in soak into him, as his father used to say. The mist robbed everything within a few yards of color or clarity. The scent of clay mixed with moisture and mildew, but the air also carried a gritty gypsum tang and a hint of wild honeysuckle. War drums and pipes still sounded in the foggy distance, though down here it was harder to tell their directions or what they were signaling.

Tyrol bent close to Kelflen and whispered, "We can't stay here long."

Kelflen nodded. He kept his voice low. "They might find us."

"And I have to deliver this."

"Could we hide now, and move at night?"

"I don't know this area well enough."

"There's a river that runs through the valley," Kelflen said. "I saw it on the map. Some creeks flow into it from the hills. We could hide along the bank, and get water."

Tyrol doubted it would be so easy, but he was thirsty—hungry, too, now that he thought about it—and he could not understand maps. He was impressed that Kelflen could.

"How far away?"

"I don't know," the drummer admitted. "I've gotten twisted around. If we could see better, we would know."

Tyrol cursed the Varrikar again. Did their manipulators make the fog? That might explain how their soldiers made it so deep into the Dvornian lines without being detected. Tyrol remembered the front rank of the attackers collapsing before Lieutenant Pilkus even reached them. Were they all manipulators?

Tyrol waved his hand through the fog and gently pulled a few vapory tendrils as if he were going to make a lens... and recalled a time when his mother manipulated shadows on the wall to entertain him and his little brother. If he could weave shadows as well as light...

"I have an idea," he told Kelflen.

His idea should have worked, but the damnable fog diffused the light so much that Tyrol was unable to do much with it: he made shadows, but they seemed insubstantial, transitory, and the effort sapped him. So they moved as quickly as stealth and fatigue would allow until they came to one of the brooks Kelflen had promised.

Kelflen made a move toward the water, but as much as Tyrol wanted to charge ahead with him, he held them back to be sure no Varrikars were about. The noises of the battle seemed far removed from this spot, but neither of them admitted to being sure of what they heard.

"You drink, and I'll watch," Tyrol said, "and then we'll switch."

The water was clear as truth, and more refreshing. Tyrol wet his hair after he drank, and as he sat up and Kelflen bent to drink again, a trumpet blast tore the air. It was answered by another, farther away, and another, and then clearly recognizable Dvornian pipes and drums called out.

"Secure the line," Kelflen said.

Tyrol recognized the next notes. "Do not advance."

Part of the next signal was overwhelmed by another trumpet, but they got enough of it: form up, retrieve wounded, do not engage.

"Is it over?" Kelflen asked.

Tyrol wondered if he was imagining the growing light or if the Varrikars' fog was actually lifting. "And barely noon? I think this is only a reprieve."

They drank more, and huddled in the midst of a stand of young pines where they could see down into the valley. The fog burned away inch by inch, and to their left they saw the hill where they had stood with Marshall Innolik at daybreak. They had not gotten as far as Tyrol thought, or wished.

As the battleground cleared, they first saw the rough shape of Rellam Wood, closer than expected; then its distinct edge; then the bloodied, muddied ground in front of it.

Every standard in the field bore the color and crest of a Varrikar tribe.

They had come generally east, away from Marshall Innolik's old headquarters, but neither knew exactly how far they were from Captain Hallern's new command. Tyrol grumbled at Kelflen for not having a better memory of the map he had seen. Kelflen countered that he had not seen the whole map: other papers had covered parts of it. They stifled their argument by common assent, stole another drink of water each, and moved on.

They crept back up the hill, still angling eastward, from rock to rock to bush to copse to rock. Now that the fog was gone, Tyrol feared some Varrikar soldier gleaning the battlefield would see them in the early afternoon sun. He struggled to move even slower than he had earlier: instinct told him to dash from shadow to shadow, but he was sure any quick movement would catch an enemy's attention. Tension seized his muscles with the inescapable grip of a hawk striking a field mouse.

At another up-thrust of rocks, Tyrol chanced to climb high enough to look toward Captain Hallern's outpost. He lay flat and wriggled his way to the edge, where he sighed out almost all of his built-up tension when he saw the Dvornian flag still flying on the far hill.

Most of the ground in between was devoid of his country's troops, however.

Kelflen climbed up beside Tyrol. The drummer pointed out the line of Varrikar flags. "How did we lose so much ground?"

"How are we going to cross?" Tyrol countered.

"In the dark."

"It's a long way to go," Tyrol said, but bit off the rest of his words at a gesture from Kelflen. The drummer pointed uphill, and Tyrol heard the sounds of stumbling, sliding steps; then, indecipherable but clear enough to sour his stomach, the jabbering of two Varrikars in conversation.

Tyrol glanced around, but none of the possible hiding places looked promising. A moment later, two Varrikar soldiers—normal men, not like the near-giants who had attacked the Marshall's headquarters—crested the hill. Thankfully, they were angled away from Tyrol and Kelflen. Tyrol slid backward, pulling Kelflen with him into a crevice between the big rock and a smaller, wagon-sized boulder next to it, and in desperation grasped for the light and shadows to try to hide them.

The shadows felt slippery—the first word to occur to him—compared to the air and water and light Tyrol usually manipulated. He began to understand better why other people couldn't manipulate the light the way he could. He used to think that since everyone cast regular shadows, why couldn't they just as easily gather the light and focus it? These greasy shadows reminded him that he had not yet progressed as far as his mother, who could form a lens between her thumb and forefinger and use the earliest rays of the morning sun to start a fire to boil water for tea. But the battlefield would have been no place for her.

Fatigue and hunger gnawed at him the more he tried to twist the shadows around himself and Kelflen. The shadows felt like cool oil, and made even manipulating the warm light more difficult than usual. Tyrol wondered if he was misinterpreting some sensory elements of working with the shadow, and if his mother could have taught him more about it. Next to him, Kelflen squirmed and then was gone—

Tyrol nearly lost his grip on the shadows, and concentrated so hard on restoring them that he missed the first thing the Varrikar soldier said. The man held Kelflen by the hair, but the drummer had not cried out.

"...a spy?" the soldier said in thick, accented Dvornian as he pointed a long dagger at Kelflen. "Or a rat, hid in the shadows?" The man thrust Kelflen toward the other soldier, who wore intricate facial tattoos.

Tattoo-face jabbered at Kelflen, but dagger-man said, "Not understand? You'll understand this," and put the point of his dagger under Kelflen's eye. "You're a pretty thing," he said, but his rough accent made the words vile.

Tyrol shuddered as the dagger-man rubbed the flat of his

blade against Kelflen's face. The other Varrikar held the drummer's arms and leered; when Kelflen turned his head, the tattooed face was right there, eyes wide. Kelflen closed his eyes, and a tear slid down his cheek.

Tyrol could barely track the tornado of his thoughts: that his shadows had been incomplete, so it was his fault that Kelflen had been seen; that he could not risk being caught if he was to deliver Marshall Innolik's pouch; that he stood no chance against two grown men; that—

"Tyrol! Run!" Kelflen yelled.

The dagger-man slapped Kelflen, but he and tattoo-face looked around. "No one," he said, and put the blade against Kelflen's throat. "But quiet now, or you'll bleed." His partner laughed and jabbered, and the two went back and forth in their language for a moment. "Zholav says you'll stay warm long enough, even if we gut you."

The two Varrikar laughed, and Tyrol drew his sword while they wouldn't hear. It was hard to hold on to the shadow with his left hand while he maneuvered the sword in his right, especially since he had little room in the cleft of the rock; he was grateful that his father's blade was short, barely longer than the Varrikar soldier's dagger but twice as wide.

"Won't matter," Kelflen said.

Tyrol almost stopped moving when he heard the drummer speak, but he could not afford to wait. His fatigue was so acute that if he paused too long he would collapse and be found. He crept ahead, shadowed, as Kelflen said, "I'm plagued. We'll be dead soon."

Dagger-man poked Kelflen in the chin with his blade, and studied the drummer's neck. "Don't look plagued," he said, and jabbered to tattoo-face. The other man stepped back, and held Kelflen at arm's length.

"Just got exposed," Kelflen said. "That's why I told Tyrol to run. To get away from the plague."

Tattoo-face made a short speech in the Varrikar tongue, shaking Kelflen as he did so. Dagger-man jabbered back at him.

Tyrol moved in a crouch and kept dagger-man between him and tattoo-face. His sword felt heavy as a bucket of water, and he tried to keep his muddy boots from squelching too loud.

"You lie!" dagger-man said. "There's no tur-roll, no plague."

Tyrol put the point of his sword at a joint in dagger-man's armor. He dropped the shadows, stood from his crouch, and said, "Tyrol is the plague."

Tattoo-face's eyes widened as Tyrol drove his sword upward into dagger-man's back. Tyrol almost lost his grip as dagger-man turned; the soldier screamed out quiet bubbles of blood, but he swung at Tyrol's head as he tried to pull away. Tyrol ducked and pushed forward, his sword blade moving inside the man's body. Gore suddenly slicked his hands, and shit stench filled his nostrils. Dagger-man fell, and twisted, and Tyrol fell with him, fell on him, gasped for breath as he hit. He rolled and pulled the sword free, searching through fatigue-dimmed eyes for tattoo-face.

Tyrol's muscles quivered like baitfish struggling in an overfull net. Between the tremors and dagger-man's blood, he could barely hold the sword tip up. He had no strength—

—the tattooed Varrikar was nearly on him—

—but the man moved strangely, one hand to his throat and the other to his eye—

—from which protruded part of Kelflen's drum stick. Tyrol smiled and in triumph found strength enough to swing his sword again. He was still on the ground, however, so he swung at what he could reach and hacked the soldier's knee. Tattoo-face tottered, and Kelflen knocked him from behind. Tyrol lifted the point of his sword as tattoo-face fell on him and the upturned blade.

The daylight dimmed as a cloud passed overhead. Tyrol lay under the Varrikar, exhausted by the shadow-weaving and fighting. He tried to tell Kelflen he was ruined, spent, but could not form the words.

The drummer pulled the Varrikar off him and helped Tyrol stand and retrieve his sword. Kelflen almost dragged Tyrol away to the east, unheeding the need to hide from watchful eyes.

"Hurry," Kelflen said. "A little farther. A little farther."

Tyrol lost all sense of time and distance. The first time he stumbled, Kelflen somehow gave him water from a skin. "I took their satchels," the boy said, and pressed a hardcake into Tyrol's hand. "But come, a little farther."

The stolen food revived him. As the afternoon waned the shadows lengthened and were easier to manipulate; after more hard-baked biscuit and some nuts, Tyrol wove cover for both of them. They marched on.

They were within sight of the Dvornian line when they crept past the final Varrikar sentry. The man exuded arrogance, and a wave of hatred washed over Tyrol. He stepped toward the soldier, sword ready within the shadows.

Kelflen touched his arm. "No, Tyrol."

Tyrol stopped. He nodded. "Not yet," he said.

He remembered what his father had told him, a year or so before he died. "Late or soon, son, late or soon, the fight will come to you. And when it comes, you must go to meet it."

He had met the fight, and hoped his father would be proud. But he would follow his last order, and deliver the pouch to Captain Hallern if the captain still lived.

"Not this one," Tyrol said. "Not this time."

No doubt there would be other fights that came his way, and he would meet them—for as long as it took, for his countrymen and his mother and his brother—in his own way. Tyrol could be a plague of shadows on their enemy, but for now he had another duty.

And above all else, he did his duty.

Hoofsore and Weary

CAT RAMBO

THE NEW RECRUIT WOULDN'T ANSWER TO HER BATTLE NAME, SMITTY. She was the last of the new musketeers who had come on at the last minute to swell the unit's ranks. Now here that unit was, battle-diminished and trapped in hostile territory, the last of Captain Laws's fighting centaurs. Hoofsore and weary, as the song went, but somehow still mustering enough energy to snap at each other.

Sarge shouldered her way past the others to look at the new recruit and Jolanda, faced off, fists clenched and tails swishing irritably.

"What's all this?" she said, swatting away yet another stinging fly.

The new recruit was skinny. Insect bites blotched her fair skin around the leather breast harness. She said, scorn in her voice, "I don't have to answer to any name other than my own!"

Jolanda's temper was as quick as her musket. "You're in the army now, hinny. You'll answer to anything your superiors call you!" She shied as though about to wheel around and kick. Male centaurs reared on their hindlegs to fight. Females cared less about appearances and more about the power of a back hoof.

Sarge stepped forward between the two of them. "Go check the guns, Londa."

"Ain't no use with no shot nor powder."

"If we chance on some, I want them ready."

Jolanda grumbled but stepped away.

"Recruit," Sarge said.

The younger centaur snapped off a salute with folded paper precision. "Sir, yes sir!"

129

"At ease." Sarge eyed her youngest soldier. They were down to a couple of fingers over a handful, and had she been able to pick who survived this far, it wouldn't have been this raw newbie, who didn't know how to survive off the land, didn't know the little tricks that kept a soldier moving, and most importantly, didn't know that sometimes you bent for the good of the unit.

"In battle, there's no time for strings of syllables," she said. "Whatever they call you, you answer. Mine's even longer. So 'Clytemnestra' when you're in conversation, but names won't matter when we're fighting. Got that?"

Sarge ran a hand back through her close-cropped hair as the younger centaur nodded reluctantly. The recruit's attitude wasn't endearing her to the veterans. The usual pranks had been going on. But no time for that now, in the middle of enemy territory. They'd come down through the mountains—and hadn't *that* been a rabid bitch of a journey?—to hit at the capital, thinking their company would reinforce the siege there. Only to arrive in a broken landscape, devastation and fire all around. They'd missed the battle, and found only its aftermath.

They'd fought their way out of that, losing most of the company, including the captain, and struck south, somehow managing to avoid farmers. All but one of them were centaurs, and the territory was hard going, mucky ground that hid deep stones inside it.

What would the captain have done? Alyssum was scouting and still not back. Sarge fumbled for her pouch and extracted the map yet again, unfolding it.

She'd never been one for books. It was boys' stuff, staying indoors with scrolls and chanting. But the captain had gotten them all to beat their heads against it, even on the field when all they had to read from was their army-issued copy of *Rotterdam's Rules and Regulations for Field Cavalry.*

No use spending daylight on squabbles.

"Gear up," she ordered.

Seven, counting herself and the newbie.

Jolanda, shrew-eyed and quick to argue, but the best shot among them. Not that it did them any good with their ammunition all expended fighting their way out of those blood-filled streets. Limping now.

Penny, looking cheerful as always, despite the burns weeping along the side of her face, glistening with the last of the field kit's salve.

Alyssum, off scouting, who had drawn black around her face with the ashes of that last fire, till she looked like a tiger with her spiky orange hair. She'd lost her harness, but at least she was small-titted and lean enough to carry it off.

Unlike fat Karas, who was breathing in uncomfortable gasps. Her flesh hung loose on her from the mountain journey, and that was back when they'd had rations to carry.

Finally Janna, the only non-centaur among them, lean as a willow, the wicker panniers carrying her snakes sitting low on her hips. At least the snakes were well fed. The Jade Woman's arms were bandaged from their last bivouac, where she'd let her blood into a battered tin cup for the two serpents to lap at. The rest of the company had crowded away, tails and ears flicking, as the snakes, eggshell white and black as jet, crawled over Janna's green skin in a parody of moonlight and shadows before slithering back into their homes.

Now the Jade sat in a patch of sun, eyes half-closed. She had the knack of the soldier's doze. She opened her eyes as though sensing the sergeant's look and pointed her chin in question.

"Still waiting on Alyssum." Sarge folded the map and put it away, resisting the urge to look at it one more time. She knew it by heart. A narrow strip of forest edged the settlement ahead, orchards planted to keep back the impassable, bog-ridden marshland. If they could find shelter for tonight, they could slip through that forest and into uninhabited territory, deep woods and thornland where they could make for the coast. Risky but better than the alternatives.

If the captain were here, she'd know what to do. Instead, Sarge was playing it by ear. She'd accompanied the captain on three campaigns now. Twice down south to the Windy Plains, where they'd fought in the sands against serpents and the Jades. Where their own Jade had enlisted, along with the rest of her tribe when they had inexplicably converted to the flag under which Sarge and her captain served.

The Jade had proved herself well enough in the following campaign, a season pursuing bandits along the coastline. Still, Sarge never felt sure of the green-skinned, red-haired woman who stayed silent whenever possible.

Alyssum slipped back through the whip-edged underbrush. Her forearms and ribs were slashed red with its marks. "Hunter's shack up ahead. No one's been in there recently. Spring nearby. No food, but we might scare up some."

"You're sure? How far past it did you scout?"

Alyssum bared her teeth. "Teach your granny to pick ticks... sir." She drawled out the last scornfully. They had been together in that first campaign where Sarge had been promoted. Alyssum's resentment at being passed over still lingered.

Sarge looked to see where the others were. Jade had slumped back. The new recruit sulked to one side. Karas and Penny were examining Jolanda's hoof. From here, Sarge couldn't tell if it was a lost shoe or sprain. Neither was good, when they had a hundred miles to go still. And no guarantee that the promised boat would be waiting there for them, but they would jump that fence when they got to it.

She stepped forward, shouldered into the smaller woman, using her greater mass to impose.

"I know a cat crawled up your ass about me being in charge, Ally," she said. "But for the love of the triple Goddess, if you don't lay off, it's going to get us all killed."

"If I don't salute right, it's going to see us all dead... sir?" This time, ten times the insolence filled the other's tone.

"Strike off on your own if you want no one in charge but yourself," Penny said, sidling up.

Alyssum wheeled with a convulsive sweep of her hair, ears back.

The air was heated with the smell of sweat. It dripped down Sarge's neck. A fly landed to sip from the sweat between her shoulder blades, and she hitched her shoulders, twitching her skin to shake it off. She had a chained set of lumps along one haunch that she suspected harbored parasites already. If they could get someplace where they could build a fire, she could burn them out. Better now than before they grew and swelled, egg-sized lumps. She'd seen plenty of those in her year of duty here.

Sweet Lady's tit, she hated this country.

She let none of that show in her face.

Alyssum's gaze tracked between the other two before she dropped her eyes and combed fingers through her hair, wincing at the knots. "Whatever."

"Whatever what?"

Alyssum's head snapped up, eyes narrowed. But she said, "Whatever . . . Sarge."

Sarge had once asked the captain why she'd been promoted rather than Alyssum or any of the others.

"Why do you think?" the captain had replied. An irritating answer, but it was the captain's way to teach.

"Jolanda's a better shot," she said. "And Alyssum's tough as nails."

"Why does that make them better choices?"

She struggled for words. She'd never been good at explaining things. "They come from solider families. Grew up training, thinking about it. They're not . . ."

"Some hoity-toity, high-blooded flibbergibbet who ran off to join the army because she thought it'd be exotic?"

She flushed. She hadn't thought the captain had caught the words Alyssum had flung the previous day.

"You can tell each's strengths and why they'd make a better sarge," the captain said. "You think about the squad overall and where you fit. That's why I picked you."

Those words still warmed her. Of the forty-eight they'd initially had, they were only a fraction now. But she'd see those few to the coast.

Or die trying, more probably.

They pushed forward. Dangerous territory. If one human glimpsed them, alarms would go up. People would come hunting them. If there was a way to avoid that, it should be taken.

The hut wasn't big enough to shelter more than two of them, plus Janna. But there was overhang from its roof, and a fire circle near its front step. They scattered, looking for food. Sarge rummaged through the hut, but found only a short length of rope and a broken clay jar.

Outside nearby, the recruit was picking berries off of a bush, harvesting them into her helmet.

Sarge said, "You know the drill, soldier."

"But Sarge! These look just like the ones back home!"

"Empty them out. You don't know for sure." Sarge stood over the newbie while the berries tumbled onto the ground. "Now mash them."

"What?"

"Stamp. With your hoof." She illustrated, placing a hoof on the ground and bearing down until it squelched. She lifted her foot to reveal the pulped remains. "That's an order. Squash them."

Step slow and reluctant, Clytemnestra obliged.

"I don't fault the effort," Sarge said. "But stick to what we know we can eat."

They built the smallest of fires. Sarge had Jolanda take the steel needles from the field kit and heat them in boiling water before she lanced the itchy, pulsating lumps, extracting each occupant. They had beef tea still, and Alyssum caught a scarf full of frogs, while Penny dug cattail tubers up by the stream.

All in all, it was not the worst meal Sarge had ever eaten, despite the raw circles along her leg. Afterwards, Jolanda and Penny sang old battle ballads, quietly but sweetly.

"*Hoofsore and weary, my darling,*" Jolanda sang, "*But you are gone and I continue.*" One of the saddest of the soldier songs. Penny laid her fingers on the other's hand in signal, glancing at Sarge, and they switched to something brighter, one of the funny songs they'd been singing at court a few years ago.

She looked around at the faces. They were managing to keep it together even though they knew as well as she did that chances were slim that they'd get out alive. Still, they put a brave face on things and pressed forward.

That was what one did. What one's duty was.

In the middle of the night, Karas roused her. She came awake instantly, not sure where she was until Karas said, "I don't like disturbing you, sir, but the new recruit's suffering bad."

Sarge squinted at her, running possibilities through her mind. "Give it to me straight."

"Bellyache and the shits. Bad, both ways."

"Will she be able to travel tomorrow?"

The plump centaur shrugged. "Somewhat. Not as fast as usual. Giving her the last of the ginger from the kit."

"And you woke me because?"

"You're CO. Figure you'd want to know."

Sighing, Sarge followed her back to where Clytemnestra lay on her side. Centaurs rarely lie down, and the sight of the girl's still face, the hair clinging to her skin in sweat-dampened ringlets, made Sarge's belly twist in uneasy sympathy.

"Ate some berries after all, didn't you?" Sarge stood beside the girl and folded her arms.

The girl moaned something incoherent upward. "Take my braid..." she said. She still wore her hair uncut in the noble's fashion, wound around her head, though it was twig-strewn and matted now.

"Not time to think of that now."

"You don't understand. It's the custom among the high families. You'll give it to the one that loved me."

"I know what you're talking about," Sarge snapped. "Think you're the first highborn I've ever dealt with?"

If the other newbies had been alive, Sarge would've made an example of her. Would have toughened her up while teaching the others.

The captain had been good at that sort of thing. But she was dead and so were the other newbies. No point in anything till they were all out alive.

"We have to stay today, give her a chance to get her legs back underneath her," Karas reported in the morning.

"We don't have time!"

"If she can keep up, we'll be able to move faster. And if your plan depends on slipping through too quick to be spotted, we're going to have to choose between leaving her here or just making up our minds to get caught."

Sarge chewed her lip, tasting blood where it had cracked.

"Penny says there are more tubers, and with that rope we can put up snares and catch a few rabbits."

Saliva flooded her mouth at the thought.

"All right. But just one day."

The dawn was clear and bright. Sarge told them all to keep low and watch the skies for spy birds. Still, they managed to bring water in the canvas bucket and wash each other's hair. The recruit was still ailing, curled up quietly. The others groomed each other and mended tack.

Jolanda methodically cleaned all the guns, as though they might chance upon an ammo trove any moment. There was enough to eat that afternoon, and that night, at least by recent standards.

But at dusk, Alyssum, who had been standing lookout, crept in to confer in an urgent whisper, "Think we been made, Sarge.

Was a fellow skulking about in that stand of birches near the spring. He saw me, too. He was off quick when he realized I'd made him."

Sarge swore under her breath. "Send Jade to me."

She fingered the paper pouch holding her map. The settlement, once warned, would be waiting for them. The slim hope of the woods had been removed.

Now there was only an impossibility, one the captain herself had warned Sarge away from.

The Jade woman came quickly.

"I need a foretelling," Sarge told her.

Janna nodded. She crouched beside the slumped recruit. Sarge shook her head. "It's for a choice."

Janna quirked an eyebrow.

"Which way to go." In the face of the Jade's silence, Sarge added, "It's that or nothing."

"Then you don't need a foretelling. One choice is no choice."

"There are always others," Sarge said irritably. "We could tie ourselves hands and ankles and hope they'll be kind when they come to take us. I prefer something more active."

Janna's hand hovered on a basket's lid. "What is the question?" she asked.

"If we go the way I'm thinking of, will we die?"

Janna nodded. She reached into the basket, and took out the white snake. It came slowly, winding its head around her arm and then questing outward, tongue flickering, flickering.

Sarge held herself still to avoid flinching back. Janna came closer, snake winding around her shoulders. As she approached it swayed outward, bringing its face close to Sarge's. Its tongue flickered out, so close to her face that she thought it might lick her nose. She tried not to breathe.

The snake hung in the air, then, in a single motion, curved back to face its handler. It hovered in front of her face, gone slack-jawed and distant-eyed. With unsettling quickness, the snake shot forward, its head striking at the hollow of the Jade's neck, which bore a multitude of small scars. Her eyelids fluttered as the venom struck. Her eyes sank back in their sockets, and her cheeks hollowed.

She said, her voice pitched in the low register that she assumed at these times, "Yes, of course some of you will die."

"Who? What path leads to the fewest deaths?" Sarge said.

But it was already too late. Janna's head hung forward in front of herself, heavy as an over-laden vine. Sarge caught her as she fell, and laid her beside the whimpering recruit.

She didn't want to tell them what the captain had said about this path, but it seemed unfair not to.

When she repeated the words, silence met the declaration. Then Karas said, "You mean, the captain said that it was the very most dangerous place of all on the continent?"

Sarge nodded.

"Well, ain't that something," Penny said, slapping away a fly. "The sort of thing you get to tell your grandkids." She flicked a look back at Jolanda. The two of them frequently vied over the cuteness of the progeny appearing as a third generation in their families.

"Tough going, I suppose," Jolanda said.

Sarge nodded again. "First thornland," she said. "Worse than any you've ever seen."

"Better than sitting here waiting for them to come get us," Karas said.

They packed up the camp, and figured out who would carry Janna and who would help the recruit along.

They struck east, along a side road, then over fields to what the captain had indeed described as "the very most dangerous place on all the continent." Where the great barrier surrounding most of this kingdom had originated, through rituals and experiments. The heart of the Hedge. No one knew exactly what lay inside.

"I thought the Hedge surrounded the border here. Didn't we come in through a split in it?"

"We did." The mountain's rocky foot had given the great vines, as wide around as a centaur's barrel chest, no foothold, and so they'd slipped in despite the infamous living wall. "This is unconnected to that heritage. It's the plant they took the magic from."

"Ain't no understanding magic," Penny said.

"Naw," Jolanda said. "You can sometimes, and it gets at what she's saying. Magic *leaks*, it seeps back and forth, and so the original's got a little more magic pumped into it, by virtue of the Hedge holding so much."

"It will be a forest, but bad forest," Sarge said. "Remember that time we went overland to get that bandit camp on that cliff they'd halfway carved into a skull?"

Alyssum's face darkened. That had been terrible going: coarse, saw-edged grass that bit through cloth and leather, midges that clustered on any moist membrane, tufted, hillocky ground that tilted one way, then another, span by span. "That bad?"

"And dangerous."

Alyssum grinned at her. "Don't get much more exotic than this, do it, Sarge?"

They'd enlisted together. Standing in line waiting to talk to a recruiter, Sarge had confided her reasons for joining up—travel someplace exotic, she'd said, meaning but not saying anything was better than idle days. It had taken too long to find out the other's circumstances—a war orphan, raised by the state, and full of little habits inculcated by years of living in institutions. No wonder Alyssum had mocked her words.

The tone could have been a jibe, but it was friendly, if not particularly respectful. "Aye," she said, and left it at that.

She glanced around. They were ready.

"Let's go."

The journey through the mountains had been bad. It featured broken bones and frostbite, short rations and shorter tempers. Half a dozen lost their lives on the trails carved into the mountain's side, usually traversed only in the summer months.

This journey was worse. Thorns and grasses lashed at them, and the stinging insects became great hornets, the size of one's palm, cranky and capable of stinging five or six times in rapid succession, stings like fire that left blood-red sores around the stings. The flies *bit* now, taking thumbnail-sized nips of flesh.

At first, their destination was a green smudge on the horizon, then a wall, stretching up, forty or fifty feet of thorny trees. Brambles snarled the open space between their trunks. Everything was silent except for occasional muted bird noise from outside the trees.

"You have got to be kidding me," Alyssum said.

Sarge looked at the trees. She hadn't expected them to look quite so grim. "We don't have another choice." They followed as she made her way to the clearly delineated edge. You could see bare earth around each tree's foot, except for the wiry black brambles. Outside those margins, grass grew. Within them, it or any other small, weedy plants were unknown.

Everyone's wide-eyed glances showed an edge of panic. Sarge straightened her back and made her tone matter of fact. "Stay close," she said.

Within moments, the outside world had vanished. Spindly trees towered all around them, even their trunks covered with wicked thorns. The brambles grew at just the right height for tearing at fetlocks, and flies swarmed whenever the thorns raked a bloody path across flesh. Sarge had hoped things would be cooler here along the trees, but somehow it wasn't.

They stumbled on. The recruit had recovered enough to walk on her own, although Penny stayed near her, keeping a careful eye out in case she stumbled.

The sunlight filtered through layer after layer of leaves, made the world gray twilight. Now that she was unable to see the sky, Sarge wasn't sure how much light they had left. They needed shelter, and soon. She called Janna up to her.

The woman came with weary eyes. Restless scraping shook the baskets as though the snakes knew where they were, and did not approve.

"We need to know the way to go," Sarge said, almost apologetically.

Jade only nodded. She didn't ask the obvious question: How will you stay on track once I point the way? She knew as well as Sarge did that this would not be the first time she was asked.

"I don't need to know the route to the coast yet," Sarge said. "Find something that will help us." She laughed, and the sound of it surprised her. "Bonus if it includes food."

Bitter merriment dried in her throat as the Jade unpacked the snake. It flowed restlessly up and down her arm before sinking its teeth deep into the scar-dimpled flesh. She didn't speak, only pointed.

Within a half mile, the ground sloped down abruptly, leading to a thin rivulet, a few yards across, dark-watered and edged with more brambles.

They argued beside the bank whether or not it was safe to drink. Was this the thing that would help them, Sarge wondered.

With a thrash and roar, something exploded from the rivulet, seeming too large to have been contained by the scant water, tearing away the arm Karas had been reaching toward the surface. She screamed, falling backward.

Sarge drew the only weapon she had left, the captain's sword. She charged forward even as the others scattered. She slashed at the thing's dripping black scales. The blade bounced off ineffectually, the thwarted blow staggering her. It smashed at her, driving her back. She felt ribs crack under the assault.

The thing reared above her for the deathblow, then paused. She stared up at it in a blaze of pain.

It slumped to the ground, almost crushing her. A spear quivered in its back.

Looking across the stream, Sarge saw a knot of humans in strange spiky armor. She rounded on Janna. "What have we done, that you led us to this treacherous pass, you bitch?" she snapped.

Janna stood her ground. "This is our help," she said, as the others began to wade toward them across the stream.

Sarge tried to take another breath, but pain and blackness overtook her.

When she roused, she was in quiet almost-darkness, inside some structure. One of the humans squatted next to her. She was on the ground, but her ribs had been bandaged and the sharp pain had faded to a soft, woolly awareness of its presence.

Despair managed to insert its fingers around that cloud, pulling it to pieces.

"So we're captured, then," she said, more to herself than to the figure. Capture meant being killed, or worse, taken to be interrogated.

The human cocked its head to the side. This close, she could see that the thorny armor was actually its skin, as though thorns grew out from its very bones.

"Captured?" it said, its voice soft, sinuous, and sexless. "No, you have come to succor. This is the village of thorns, where many find refuge."

Hope surged in her. "Refuge?"

"If they choose to give away their memories of what they were once, they can stay here. Most do not come until they are ready for that decision."

She shook her head. "Not that. But will you set us on our way? We are making for the coast."

"In the morning. When all of you have made the decision." He rose to his feet. "Rest now."

Lying in the darkness, she ran through the list in her head. She didn't think Karas would have survived. And the others? Who might take such an offer?

Clytemnestra. A chance to escape the life she had chosen, not realizing what choice she had made. Surely the recruit would leap at the chance. And Janna.

And what would the sergeant say to that?

What would the captain have said?

In the morning, when they gathered their things, surrounded by the quiet, thorny beings who watched them but said nothing, Sarge didn't see the recruit.

"Stay and find her?" Alyssum questioned.

"No," Sarge said, and left it at that. She turned to look at Janna with a raised eyebrow. The green woman shook her head. "We have stories yet together, you and I," she said.

Sarge wasn't sure whether or not that reassured her.

But the girl was waiting a little outside the village.

Sarge paused when she saw her. Why had the recruit pressed the issue this way, rather than letting Sarge simply allow her to slip away? But she waited as the girl fell into line, next to Jolanda.

Sarge looked at her hard.

"It's my duty," the recruit said, shortly. "I thought about it, Sarge. And I thought, what would you do? And I chose."

What could she say to that?

She gestured at them to fall in. Perhaps they'd make it to the coast. Perhaps they wouldn't. But they'd try.

And as she led the way, she stroked the braid of hair around her wrist, the gray-strewn black braid that was the only thing she'd taken, beside the sword, from the captain's body.

Hoofsore and weary, my love. But I continue on.

Vengeance

ROBIN WAYNE BAILEY

SAMIDAR SWUNG UP INTO THE SADDLE AND SETTLED HER BOW AND quiver upon the saddle horn. She turned for one more look at the rubble of the village, the ruined and smoking homes, and the desperate faces of people whose names she barely knew.

Serafia, a young priestess of the temple, stood close by, trembling and wide-eyed. "No one has ever been able to ride this beast," she said nervously. "Yet, it takes to you."

"You see things, don't you" Samidar said. "All you priestesses see things."

Serafia cast her gaze downward. "Some see more truly than others," she admitted in a soft voice. "Jannica foresaw your coming."

"Now Jannica is dead." Samidar nudged her horse forward.

"Ride westward," Serafia called after her. "The sun will guide you."

Toward the sun, Samidar thought glumly as she rode beyond the village and into the woods. In the spongy earth, she easily picked up the trail of the soldiers who had attacked Shaloneh.

By late mid-afternoon, she left the forest behind and paused on the edge of a grassy, sun-scorched plain. Ahead, a range of low sloping hills rippled against the horizon. They reminded her of far-off Esgaria, her homeland, which was no more, and she felt a rare moment of homesickness. She brushed a hand over the moonstone circlet she wore, the Esgarian diadem, a last artifact of her people.

She despaired to find herself once again in armor with a

sword in her scabbard and a demonic dagger at her side. She had hoped for a brief time to find peace with Jannica, but now that hope was lost.

Twilight crept across the sky, and the first stars of evening dotted the heavens as she reached the hills. An easy breeze began to stir her hair, and she tied it back with a leather thong. The breeze turned cool as the shadows deepened, and Samidar shivered. The soldiers' tracks still led westward toward what remained of the sun. On an impulse, she spurred her stallion to a full run, sure of her direction, and as she rose to the crest of the next hill, she spied the band of soldiers and, just beyond them, the ruins of an old fortress toward which they rode.

Samidar braced one end of her bow against her stirrup and strung it. Then, she selected an arrow from her quiver. The breeze ceased, and the air became still. Fitting the arrow to the bowstring, she drew back with a steady hand, judging the distance and the elevation. It was an impossible shot, but she let her breath out slowly and let the arrow fly.

The string made a soft hum. The arrow arced upward, becoming invisible against the dusky sky. Samidar fitted a second arrow to the string and with the same deliberate care, sent another slender shaft after the first.

Halfway up the next hill, a straggling soldier flung up his arms and tumbled from his horse. An instant later, his nearest companion did the same. They hit the ground together, and two riderless horses reared in panic. Samidar fired a third shaft as the rest of the soldiers spun about. A third man fell from his saddle, and chaos spread through the ranks.

Samidar smiled with grim satisfaction. By riding in a close group, the soldiers had made easy targets, but a fourth shot stood less chance of success, for now the soldiers spread out. Some raced for the fortress at the crest of the next hill while a few lingered near their fallen comrades.

She made no effort to conceal herself. When at last they spotted her, a single soldier broke away from the rest and turned his mount toward her. She could feel his angry gaze upon her as he drew his sword.

Either he's very brave or very foolish, Samidar thought. With men, it could be so hard to tell. She might have brought him down with another arrow, but she decided against it. Instead, she dismounted, hung her bow and quiver over the saddle horn, and waited.

The soldier spurred his horse suddenly, charging up the hill. *A fool then,* she decided, *and an amateur.* She noted how he held his weapon in his right hand, how he leaned forward in his saddle, and she stood her ground until the last possible minute. The soldier raised his blade, and still she waited. Then, just as the huge mount bore down upon her, she drew her own blade, stepped to the left, knelt, and slashed the horse's front legs.

The horse screamed and stumbled. Its rider flew over its head and smashed into the hard ground. Samidar moved swiftly. The man was nearly twice her size. She kicked him in the head, picked up his sword and flung it as far as she could. Then, straddling his chest, she pounded him in the face twice with the pommel of her sword and pressed the razor edge against his throat with both hands. His eyes widened with shock and terror as a thin line of blood formed below his chin.

"If you twitch," Samidar warned, "I'll cut your throat. Do you understand?"

The soldier exhaled. Samidar raised an eyebrow and applied a little more pressure to the threatening blade. He made a weak indication of agreement. "Why did you attack Shaloneh?" she demanded.

He answered with a bare whisper. "The bow," he answered. "The Death-God's bow in the temple."

Samidar ground her teeth as she leaned forward, her face close enough to the soldier that she could smell his leek-tainted breath. She remembered the immense idol in the temple at Shaloneh. *The temple of Hel—the temple of Death.*

The soldier squirmed beneath her, but only out of fear of the blade still cutting him. "The witch wants it," he volunteered. "The witch Persea. She believes the bow has the power to resurrect the sorcerer Christomerces."

Neither name meant anything to Samidar, and she shrugged. Too often, she had become caught up in the petty schemes of witches and sorcerers. She glanced up long enough to observe the few remaining soldiers dotting the opposite hill and the crumbling fortress beyond. She could feel its age.

She returned her attention to her captive. "One last question," she said, as an image of Jannica took shape in her mind.

"Shaloneh was a village of farmers, not a warrior in the lot of them. Who led the attack?"

The soldier trembled, and his eyes widened. "The witch gave the order," he said with pleading in his voice. "I had to obey!"

Samidar regarded him with disdain. With only five priestesses in the temple, twenty men could have seized the bow without all the butchery. She thought again of Jannica as her anger grew.

Somewhere inside himself, the soldier found a drop of courage. His hands came up suddenly to grasp her wrists, and he arched his back in an effort to throw her off. Samidar uttered a short curse and smashed her head down against his. The moonstone circlet shattered his front teeth. He gasped and spit blood. "Who are you?" he demanded, his heels kicking the ground. "*What are you?*"

In control again, Samidar remembered her words to the old temple priestess. "I have a hundred names," she answered, "but now my name is Vengeance." She leaned ever so slightly on the sword again, and the raider grew pale, sensing his end. Yet suddenly, Samidar threw her sword aside. The soldier looked relieved, but Samidar drew the strange, jeweled dagger from the silver sheath at her belt.

"This is *Demonfang*," she whispered, "and Persea is not the only witch you should fear."

The sound of shrieking filled the air. It came from nowhere and everywhere, as if a gateway to hell had opened. The sound echoed up and down the hills. It shook the nerves of the soldiers on the opposite hill as they fought to control their frightened mounts.

Demonfang shivered in Samidar's grip as she plunged it into the soldier's heart. For a moment, the shrieking stopped and silence fell over everything. Then, the soldier's mouth opened, and those same tormented shrieks and screams issued from him until death took his last breath.

Samidar wiped *Demonfang* clean on the soldier's tunic and returned the small blade to its sheath. "For Jannica," she murmured as she stood up. "And for Shaloneh." Still, it felt like only a small vengeance, and she was not satisfied.

Reclaiming her sword, she turned her attention to the soldier's horse. The poor beast lay in the grass breathing heavily, its front legs bloody ruins. She knelt down beside it, stroked its chestnut forelock, smoothed its mane, and apologized with soft words in its twitching ear. The creature calmed under her touch as if it knew and accepted what was coming, and when the time was right, Samidar covered its large brown eyes with a hand and made the mercy cut across its throat. The beast barely made a whimper, and she continued stroking and gently speaking to it until it was dead.

"Not a bad day's work for such a legendary warrior." The voice, feminine and mocking, spoke from behind Samidar. "Four peasant soldiers and a horse."

Samidar slowly rose without turning. She knew better than to meet a witch's gaze too quickly. "If you are Persea," she said evenly, "you have far more blood on your hands."

"You are too sure of yourself." Persea muttered a few words, her voice betraying her anger. In response, the grass around Samidar's feet shot upward. It entangled her ankles, crawled up her legs, encircled her waist. Then it began to tighten and constrict.

Demonfang shivered like a living thing in its sheath, but Samidar remained calm. She made a simple gesture, and the verdant blades of grass turned brown and crumbled away.

Now Samidar turned. For the barest instant, she hesitated, startled by Persea's appearance. *She looked exactly like Jannica.* Yet, Samidar knew it was not her beloved she faced, and the brown grass at her feet spread outward in a withering circle, a *dead zone* in which nothing could live.

The *dead zone* expanded swiftly, encompassing Persea. The witch screamed. Her blond hair turned gray, her brow wrinkled, and she began to age. "What have you done?" she cried as her heart-shaped face began to melt. She made a sharp gesture with both hands. The air crackled around Persea, and the *dead zone* lost its power.

Yet the spell had done its work. Samidar stared at the hag before her and gave in to a moment of doubt. Through all the wrinkles and liver spots, she still saw something familiar. "You can't be Jannica!"

Persea gave a bitter laugh. "You fool!" she hissed. "Did you think you were the only woman who was ever loved by the God of Death? Like you, I have lain beneath his black body and returned to the living world. Like you, I have his power." Her gaze burned with hatred. "I am Jannica's sister, and she was my twin."

"Liar," Samidar shouted. Raising her sword, she advanced across the dead ground. "If you had Hel's power, you wouldn't need the Bow of Shaloneh!"

Persea's aged face darkened as she gazed skyward. "You can't begin to guess my plans, Esgarian," she answered. "I lured you to Shaloneh to put an end to you. Jannica dreamed about you every night of her life, and because we were twins and close enough to share each other's thoughts, every night she forced those visions on me. *Every night!* She loved you, Frost called Samidar, and with just as much passion I grew to hate you."

Demonfang trembled violently as a rain of fire fell suddenly from the sky. Caught off guard, Samidar screamed and cursed as the flaming droplets struck her face and hands. Her hair began to smolder, and her armor smoked. Nearby, her black stallion whinnied and bolted. The dead grass caught fire, and Samidar stood trapped at the burning center of it.

"Join the rest of your dead Esgarian breed," Persea said, untouched by the fire. "I didn't mean for Jannica to die, but the result is the same if I'm finally free of you."

The flames took on an arcane life, transforming into wild man-shapes that reached for Samidar and attacked her. She fought uselessly as clawed hands carved burning scratches on her flesh, as flaming mouths bit her arms and legs. In desperation, she flung her sword at Persea, but the heavy blade missed, and the witch laughed at her.

Burned and bleeding, Samidar ran through the burning rain over smoking ground back down the hill the way she had come. She cursed herself and cried, her mind in turmoil, and through her pain all she saw was Jannica, who had called her *Beloved*.

As she reached the next summit, the burning rain ceased. Stumbling, she fell headlong to the ground and sobbed. Night fell, and a waxing moon with a peppering of stars lit the landscape. When she finally sat up, she nursed burned hands and wounds. Yet worse, she felt the bitter sting of loss and failure.

The stallion whinnied nearby, too nervous and distrustful to approach. Finding strength to rise, she talked to the horse with soft words. The skittish beast trembled when she reached out for the loose reins, but it did not bolt. Painfully, she put one foot into the saddle stirrup and swung into the saddle.

Her bow and quiver were gone. So was her sword. Except

for the dagger, *Demonfang*, she was weaponless. Despondent, she
turned her mount toward Shaloneh.

For two days and nights, Samidar lay semiconscious in the
dark recesses of the Temple of Death. Four priestesses had survived the attack on the village, and they treated her burns with
poultices and healing herbs. They cut her singed locks away,
leaving her hair mannishly short.

On the third day, she awoke to find herself in the same room
and the same bed she had shared with Jannica. The realization hit
her with a terrible force and she buried her face in bandaged hands.

Raxul, the oldest priestess, appeared in the doorway with
a basin of water. She placed it on the room's only table. Then,
without speaking, she also sat down on the bed and put a con-
soling hand on Samidar's shoulder.

"I failed," Samidar whispered as she stared at the floor. She
could not remember when she last had said those words or felt
such bleak defeat. "I ran away."

"You did what you had to do," Raxul answered. "Persea
tricked you."

Samidar hung her head again. "She looked like Jannica, and
when I struck at her, I suddenly felt like I'd stabbed myself in
the heart." She looked up bitterly, but in the priestess's face she
saw sympathy and calm. She sank down between Raxul's knees
and wept. "Tell me it wasn't Jannica."

Raxul explained in gentle tones. "We exiled Persea years ago
from Shaloneh. She shared Jannica's gift of sight, but she also
possessed an aptitude for the Dark Arts. We thought her long
gone from these lands."

"I had the advantage," Samidar whispered. "Something held
me back."

Raxul gave a low laugh. "Love held you back, Samidar." She
stroked Samidar's shorn hair with a gentle hand. "Jannica loved
you with all her heart. Although you only spent days together,
she knew you every night. I know you don't understand it, but
you loved her, too. You were fated to love her."

"It made me weak," Samidar answered. "Persea used it against
me."

Raxul lifted Samidar's chin. "It makes you strong," she corrected.

In the quiet lamplight, Samidar thought for a long time. She had lived without love for so long that she had forgotten the feeling. Now it crashed upon her like a wave. She ran one hand over the blanket and the bed she had shared with Jannica, and she struggled not to cry again.

She turned her thoughts, instead, to Persea and experienced a surprising moment of sympathy. What must it have been like for the sister, every night to share a vision of love that was never meant for her?

The thought sobered Samidar. She recovered herself a little and pressed Raxul's hand. "Tell me about Hel's bow, how it came to be in your temple and why Persea wants it."

A weak smile turned up the corners of Raxul's lips. "The bow represents a pact made by our forbearers with the Death-God. It's a very long story—almost a myth—but so long as we care for it and keep it safe in this temple, no child will be born stillborn in Shaloneh, and no mother will die in childbirth."

Raxul sighed, rose to her feet, and began to tremble. "But it also serves another purpose," she continued. "When someone dies, a priestess fires an arrow from Hel's bow, and where the shaft lands marks the burial spot. Without the bow, the ghosts of Shaloneh can never know rest."

Samidar thought for a long moment, taking in all that Raxul said. "It must have other powers," she murmured. "One of Persea's soldiers told me that she intends to use it to resurrect a sorcerer called Christomerces."

In the lamplight and shadow, it was hard to read Raxul's expression, but her old voice turned harsh. "Then Persea is a fool," she said. "Christomerces was the greatest sorcerer of his age. This world has never known another like him. He should not be disturbed or trifled with!"

"Then that crumbling fortress was his," Samidar guessed, "and his dead carcass lies there. I thought I felt something when I first glimpsed it. Persea hopes to learn from him or take his power."

"Christomerces is not dead," Raxul said. "His magicks made him immortal, but time is a subtle enemy. The stories say that eventually he wearied of the daily burdens of life. Unable to die, he cast a spell and surrendered himself to eternal slumber."

A draft seemed to blow through the small room, and the flame in the lamp fluttered. Samidar reached for *Demonfang*'s hilt, but the dagger was not at her side. She wore only nightclothes. With a glance at Raxul, she got up and opened a trunk at the foot of the bed. Her armor rested within it, cleaned of scorch marks and highly polished. The dagger lay on top of it, along with the Esgarian diadem.

"I will need new weapons," Samidar said.

Raxul pursed her lips. "You will have whatever you need from our storerooms and treasury. Over the years, people have made many offerings to the temple, and Persea's soldiers did not get everything. They didn't find our secret rooms." She held out a hand to Samidar. "But you should rest another day, at least."

Samidar moved to the basin of water on the table and, unwrapping the bandages from her hands, laved her face in the cool liquid. "I'm rested enough," she said, "and I won't be taken by doubt again."

"You're an Esgarian witch," Raxul said as she walked around the bed and placed a hand on the lid of the trunk. Before Samidar could react, Raxul wagged a finger. "We know you and know your legend. You carry the power of an ancient empire in your blood." She gazed directly into Samidar's eyes, as if daring her to deny it. "Still," she continued, "when the time comes to fight this battle, you will need help. Then, my sisters and I will be at your side."

Samidar's eyes narrowed. "What do you mean?"

Raxul looked down at the floor. "We failed our sister Jannica," she said. "We hid in the secret rooms when the soldiers attacked. Only Jannica, inspired by you, stood her ground and fought for the Death-God's bow. We failed her, and we failed our oaths as priestesses." She looked up again with a hard expression. "Now we will do our part to regain the bow and bring peace to the spirits of Shaloneh's dead." She stared down into the trunk and touched the moonstone circlet with the tip of one finger. "We lost more than just Jannica."

"But how can you help, Raxul?" Samidar asked. "You are priestesses, not warriors."

Raxul left the trunk and went to the door, yet she paused on the threshold without turning around. "Don't ask," she warned. "For us, there is only one road to redemption—and to vengeance."

At midmorning of the next day, Samidar rode out again from Shaloneh on her fine black stallion. Its eyes seemed to burn as she mounted, and it tossed its mane. A new sword of exquisite manufacture hung at her side, and on her right arm she wore a small buckler. Across her back, she wore a full quiver of arrows, and a new ash bow rested unstrung in a special holster beneath her left knee. She touched *Demonfang* on her belt. The dagger was as much a part of her as the air she breathed.

Raxul, Serafia, and all the villagers turned out in silence to watch as she departed. She studied the grim and worried faces, observed the children clinging to their mothers' skirts, noted the older men too weak or tired or injured to fight. The rest were farmers or woodsmen with no combat skills.

It was as if Persea's soldiers had deliberately targeted the able-bodied men of Shaloneh for slaughter. As she remembered Raxul's words and thought of the bodies laid out in the temple awaiting burial, the weight of her task seemed suddenly heavier.

At the edge of the village, she touched her stallion with her heels, and it lunged forward into the forest. Samidar leaned close to its neck, ducking low branches, feeling its thick mane in her face. The beast sensed the direction she wanted to go as if its mind and hers were linked, and she let it set its own pace as it weaved among trees and leaped muddy ravines.

Serafia's advice echoed in her head. *Follow the sun.*

The wild ride lifted her spirit, and the lingering pain of her burns faded away. The wind tingled in her short hair, and she felt somehow renewed, strengthened, and filled with purpose.

Tireless, her steed devoured ground with its smooth stride. By noon, she reached the edge of the forest and the beginning of the grasslands.

Then, without warning, *Demonfang* shivered as Persea spoke in Samidar's mind. *So, you've come back to play with me again.*

Samidar brought her mount to a halt and sat up straight in the saddle. Her gaze swept the countryside. "Did you doubt that I would?" she answered aloud.

Persea chuckled. *I like your new look.*

"I liked your gray hair and wrinkles," Samidar shot back.

However, Persea was gone from her mind, and the dagger became quiet again. Samidar stroked its jeweled hilt. She could almost feel the blade purring.

At a nudge, her horse started forward through the tall grass toward the rolling hills in the distance. By mid-afternoon, she came across patches of burned grass and, after that, a perfect circle of blasted, withered ground. Her *dead zone.*

In the distance at the summit of the next hill, silhouetted by a bloated setting sun, the ruined fortress of Christomerces loomed, its towers crumbled, its walls cracked by age. Yet, now that she knew its story, an air of awesome majesty clung to it. She wondered how long the sorcerer had been sleeping.

Demonfang gave a faint tingle. Samidar inclined her head slightly as she removed her bow from the saddle and strung it. Her stallion remained steady beneath her, almost as if it had been trained for war. "Persea is watching us, boy," she said to the horse. "I wonder what she thinks of you."

The fortress gates opened. Five soldiers charged out, quickly scattering as they rode toward her position. This time, though, Samidar did not wait for them. She bent close to the stallion's twitching ears. "Go!" she said.

As she raced down the slope, she gripped the saddle with her knees and drew an arrow. Without aiming, firing purely on instinct, she shot the nearest man. Before he hit the ground, she fired a second arrow, and another soldier fell.

The fortress gates slammed shut as a third soldier rode toward her with a drawn sword. Samidar charged straight at him. His blade whistled over her head as her great black mount slammed shoulders with the attacker's horse. Upset, the soldier lost his seat and fell hard to the ground. Drawing an arrow, Samidar twisted and planted a feathered shaft in his back as he tried to stand up.

Two soldiers remained, but they kept their distance, pacing their mounts before the fortress walls. Her stallion snorted a challenge and tore divots of earth as he stamped the ground, but Samidar held him back, suspicious, as she glanced upward.

High atop the ancient walls, she spied movement—archers! The air hummed with a sudden flurry of arrows. Samidar turned the stallion and raced back out of range. As she paused and wiped sweat from her face, the fortress gates opened again.

In Shaloneh, in the Temple of Death, four rope nooses dangled from a makeshift gallows hastily built on the spot where Jannica had died right before the idol of the Death-God. The bodies of the village's dead—Jannica among them—lay neatly placed around the construct.

In the near darkness, the four black-robed priestesses walked, each bearing a candle. One by one, they mounted the low platform,

Serafia first and Raxul last. One by one, they stepped upon a single long bench, placed the nooses around their necks, and tightened them, and one by one, they each blew out their candle.

When the last flame went out, they kicked the bench away together. A terrible gasping and choking echoed in the temple. Then followed an even more terrible silence.

Samidar could not count the number of soldiers who poured from the fortress gates. She fired three shafts in rapid succession, but there were not enough arrows in her quiver. Quickly, she cast a *dead zone*. The grass turned brown and died beneath her feet, and the effect spread outward in a widening circle. It would not be enough to combat an army, she knew, but it might buy her time.

The stallion, however, panicked as the ground decayed. He reared in sudden fear, nearly throwing her from the saddle. She cooed and stroked his withers, calming him.

The nearest soldier came on, the momentum of his charge carrying him across the *dead zone* before he could feel its effect. Samidar swung her bow like a staff, sweeping him from the saddle. As he hit the ground, he began to age, shriveling up like a grape in a hot sun. A pair of soldiers followed him. She blocked a sword stroke on her right with her buckler and with her left hand swung the bow again. The string caught the attacker's hand as he reached for her, and she flung him out of his saddle. He screamed as, like his comrade, he began to rapidly age.

But there were too many soldiers. It was only a matter of moments before they surrounded her. She drew her sword. At least, she would not run this time. "You are a coward, Persea!" she shouted in defiant anger.

Demonfang shivered against her side. Samidar assumed it was Persea answering her challenge. Yet, a mist rose up suddenly from the grass, a gray and chilly vapor that lent a sparkling rime to everything it touched. The horses went crazy. Even her stallion tried to bolt, but Samidar kept a tight grip on the reins as she shot a glance at the darkening sky.

Sundown.

The mist began to shift and transform. Something moved within the fog. Soldiers screamed and broke ranks as cold hands dragged them from their saddles, as invisible teeth closed on their throats.

Something passed in front of Samidar's face. She swung her sword at it and felt chill radiate along the length of the blade to her hand. She gasped, but kept her grip on the hilt. Something flitted by her again, a gray face that regarded her with dead eyes.

Raxul!

More faces and shapes emerged, and some of them formed a protective shield around Samidar. She knew them now, the priestesses and the village dead—all the ghosts of Shaloneh.

And there, with her sisters, was Jannica.

"Beloved!" Samidar cried, reaching a hand toward Jannica's misty shade.

Jannica smiled back with a dead smile.

Persea's soldiers were in full rout, but the ghosts pursued them, taking their full measure of vengeance. Not a man made it back alive to the fortress gates, and riderless horses scattered across the hillside.

The mist began to dissolve, and the ghosts of Shaloneh faded away. Raxul and Jannica lingered to the last and seemed to join hands in their final moment. Samidar blinked back tears, yet she knew the fight was still not over.

"Give me the bow, Persea!" she shouted. She had no doubt that the witch could hear her. She urged her stallion forward again toward the gates, picking her way carefully among the torn and shredded bodies.

A full moon, now just above the horizon, cast her shadow far before her. She glanced back over her shoulder to take note of it, effulgent and deep golden, a conjurer's moon.

She saw something else as well, drops of fire in the sky falling with smoky trails straight for her. Samidar raised her right hand, and the buckler on her arm seemed to catch the moonlight and direct it in a new direction. The reflected light brushed against the burning droplets and extinguished them.

"That trick won't work twice," Samidar murmured.

Persea's thoughts echoed in Samidar's mind. *Then look for me in Christomerces's tomb. I'll show you a new trick.*

Samidar reached the fortress gates and dismounted. She paused long enough to scratch the stallion's nose and pat its neck then hung her empty quiver and bow on the saddle. The gates stood open just wide enough to let her squeeze inside.

She drew her sword, but doubted she would need it. The

condition of several bodies inside the gate demonstrated that the ghosts had even taken care of the archers on the wall. She crept across a broken courtyard, past a dried-up fountain, as she wondered where a sorcerer's tomb might be.

Her buckler continued to glow, as if it contained a shard of moonlight. She held it before her to illuminate her way as she entered the largest of the many structures that made the fortress. Ancient tiles cracked under her feet; rats scurried from the light. Stranger things stirred, but kept to the shadows. She found a spiral staircase and began to climb, guided only by her instincts.

The highest point, she guessed. In slumber or in death, a sorcerer would still crave a view of the heavens upon which so many things depended. Their vanity would require it. So she climbed, and when she came to the highest room, she found the door invitingly open.

Stepping across the threshold, Samidar looked around. The room was colonnaded, and between each column a window stood open, unshuttered. The full moon's light spilled in from the eastward side, illuminating the layers of dust and bits of half-rotted furniture scattered about.

On one side a huge stone box stood, almost four times the size of any coffin, as large as any bed. Carved into the stone were rows of glyphs and symbols, some of them in Esgarian and other languages she recognized, but most completely alien. What disturbed her most was the way the box stood upright and open to reveal a perfectly preserved man with inhumanly handsome and sweetly composed features.

"It took me days to break the magical locks and wards on this room," Persea said. "Weeks more to crack the seals on his tomb."

Samidar turned toward Persea as she emerged from the farthest shadows with the Bow of Shaloneh in her hands and an arrow on the string. She wore Jannica's face again, but now Samidar knew it for the illusion it was. Persea bore only a faint resemblance to her gentler sister.

Persea clucked her tongue. "Two witches," she said. "We should have been friends. After all, like Jannica, I've also known you in my dreams. I would have shared Christomerces's knowledge with you."

Samidar sneered. "I doubt that."

"As it is," Persea shrugged, "you are an irrelevant annoyance.

When the full moonlight steals across the floor and touches Christomerces's tomb, I will resurrect him. In gratitude, he will teach me things and share his magic."

"He's not dead," Samidar said.

Persea laughed. "Of course he's dead. A thousand years and more dead! But I can awaken him. Just as a bow can take life, the Death-God's bow can give it back. It has more power than even the temple sisters know."

The moonlight flowed like milk across the dusty floor, and *Demonfang* began to shiver as the light touched the arcane sarcophagus.

"It won't be long now," Persea said. "All my dreams are coming to fruition."

"You're a fool," Samidar answered, wondering what she should do or if she should do anything at all. Something was building in the room, some force beyond her understanding. She felt the magic flowing from the Death-God's bow, from Persea, and from the sarcophagus.

"You didn't really think this arrow was for you, did you?" Persea said. With a quick move, she redirected her aim and fired the shaft straight for the sorcerer's heart.

Christomerces moved. His hand shot up and caught the arrow as his eyes slowly opened. He gazed at Persea, then at Samidar, and then outward, seeming to see beyond the fortress walls.

Samidar braced herself for some attack. When none came, she lunged for the Death-God's bow and ripped it from Persea's hands. Then she locked one arm around the blond witch's throat.

"I did it!" Persea gasped. "I did it! Hear me, Christomerces! I have raised you from the dead! Now teach me!"

Christomerces snapped the arrow between his fingers. His dry lips strained to move. When he spoke, dust issued from his long-unused throat. "The world is still the same," he pronounced as he closed his eyes again. "War and fighting. Nothing has changed. *You have not changed.*"

The heavy stone lid of the sarcophagus began to close.

"My Lord!" Persea screamed as all her magicks deserted her. "Don't desert me! Help me!"

Samidar tightened her grip on Persea as the witch struggled. "I'm sorry I haunted your dreams," she said with genuine sorrow in Persea's ear as she forced Persea forward, ever closer to the sorcerer's tomb. The immense lid continued to close. "You want a teacher? Then join him."

Persea screamed as Samidar pushed her into the closing tomb. To Samidar's astonishment, Christomerces awoke long enough to catch and wrap the witch tightly in his arms.

The great stone lid slid shut. *Demonfang* began to vibrate with an angry intensity as the glyphs and characters that adorned the sarcophagus started to shift and move. Magical wards and locks were closing once again.

Samidar shot a look toward the chamber doors. They, too, were closing, and she could feel the wards upon them. She flung Hel's bow and her sword into the corridor beyond and then launched herself in a long dive through the narrowing gap, rolling to her feet again just as the door sealed and faded away to become an unseen part of the bare wall.

Recovering the bow, sheathing her sword, she made the long descent down the spiral staircase. The moonlight played games with the shadows as she crossed the old courtyard, and she felt eerily alone. Yet, the black stallion waited outside the gate, and her mood lifted.

Slinging the Death-God's bow across her back, she mounted the stallion. "I'll call you Ashur," she said, "after an ancient Esgarian war god." She stroked his long neck before she gathered the reins. "Let's go home."

She turned Ashur eastward, toward the moon.

The people of Shaloneh were as silent and stoic as ever as she rode into the village and up to the temple. With the bow still upon her back, she dismounted and entered the Temple of Death. The sight of four priestesses hanging from their makeshift gallows shocked and saddened her, but Raxul had been true to her word. She already missed the old woman.

She also missed Jannica. For too short a time, Samidar had known love, that most valuable of gifts. She regretted that she had not recognized it sooner, but she would honor it and remember its sweetness.

As she counted the bodies on the temple floor, she felt the ghosts of Shaloneh around her. She owed them a debt. They had come to her, led by Raxul and the priestesses, in a moment of need. She would honor that, too. Going next to the temple store-rooms, she selected quivers of arrows and carried them outside.

The villagers gathered closer. A little boy crept forward and touched her hand shyly as he looked at her with questioning eyes. A wan smile crossed her lips.

A gasp went up from the villagers as she held up the Death-God's bow for all to see.

"Now, one at a time," she told them, "go inside the temple and bring out your dead."

The little boy stepped closer and in a quiet voice asked, "Are you the priestess now?"

Samidar rumpled his hair. Then, as someone carried the first body into the sunlight, she fitted an arrow to Hel's bow and aimed it skyward.

Deadfall

NANCY FULDA

JEFFRAN WATCHED THE LINE OF SCREAMING SAVAGES APPROACH. They poured from the sky-rafts in cacophonous waves, jumping off roughly lashed planks of amberwood to race barefooted across the dry yellow grass below. They were both male and female, pale and dark of complexion, a ragged aggregate from a dozen separate cultures. Jeffran's eye picked out grizzled elders, taut-faced children, one-handed cripples, and even a shorn-headed youth with slagging burns across his body.

They were conscripts, Jeffran had no doubt—hapless prisoners snatched during raids like this one, warped by some unspeakable mistreatment into this raging lust for slaughter. Jeffran's heart ached even as he checked the straps on his cuirass and tightened his grip on his spear.

By happy fortune, late afternoon winds had pushed the high floating logjams off course, causing the rafts to descend east of the village rather than atop it. There would be no repeat of the tragic direct assault that had cost Jeffran his younger brother so many long years ago.

Jeffran's patrol, firmly interposed between the small mountain town and its assailants, stood in ordered ranks beneath a crisp highland cloudscape. Golden sunlight caught the edge of their shields and cuirasses, set white shirts blazing against smooth tan skin. Crinkled auburn hair, worn long and loose in the style of the Holy Kingdoms, fell against scarlet half-cloaks.

The savages were almost upon them. Jeffran shifted his weight, calculating odds. His men were well-trained, but they were also spread thin, only three rows deep at the center of the line. The attacking wave would need to break against the spears and shields of Jeffran's soldiers, and do it quickly, lest they outwear his force by sheer numbers. Jeffran lifted his spear.

"By the Blood of the Emperor!" he bellowed, and surged forward. His soldiers sped beside him. They needed momentum, and a lot of it, to dampen the rushing assault. Too little, and the desperate savages would punch right through the defense.

Jeffran raised his shield as the lines closed. His lowered spear drove into the unarmored gut of an attacker. The impact wrenched his arm, and the spear splintered. He swore and reversed the stub of his weapon. Something crashed against his shield. He stumbled, stabilized by the line of soldiers behind him, and pushed the attacker away. Another savage—a young girl, hair wild above a grimly determined face—swung a cudgel at his head. Jeffran hesitated for a bare moment before thrusting forward, deliberately aiming for her thigh rather than her torso.

The lines held. Savages, unprepared for resistance by trained and well-equipped troops, dropped quickly, and the battle became a slaughter. *Run, curse you*, Jeffran thought as he cut down an old man wielding a corroded hunting knife. *Break and run. Don't waste your blood for this.*

But the attackers kept coming. They did not fight as a unit, as Jeffran's patrol did. Instead, they were a maddening mob of individuals. Some charged the shield line head-on. Others cut sideways, seeking a way around. A doomed few dropped to the ground and attempted to crawl beneath the spears of the defenders. Their eyes were gaunt, their faces lit by an eerie intensity that chilled Jeffran's spine.

A large, well-muscled warrior charged the line at full speed. The load cradled in his arms looked, at first, like a child but turned out to be a sawed-off hunk of amberwood. As he neared the shield line, the warrior jumped, tugging a release cord at his neck. A netted bundle of stones dropped from his back. Freed of this extra ballast, the warrior cleared the entire defensive line, soaring effortlessly over three rows of spears. He released the amberwood, allowing it to shoot upward, and yanked a broken broadsword from his belt. With a feral roar, he charged the unprotected rear of the defenders.

Jeffran cursed. Bellowing, he shouted commands for the rear line to about-face, but the noise of battle kept his voice from carrying. He dropped from formation, allowing the soldier behind him to fill his place, and moved to the back of the patrol.

A second warrior soared over the defensive line, releasing a second hunk of amberwood to drift skyward. Farther down the ranks, the man with the broken broadsword yanked his weapon across the backs of the soldiers' unprotected knees.

Jeffran flinched. He'd put his newest recruits in that back line. Eager lads, fresh from training, but unskilled in combat. He'd meant to keep them safe.

Another swipe from the broadsword. Three more men went down.

Jeffran leveled the spike of his broken spear, jumping backward to avoid an attack from the savage nearest him. A second blow thudded against Jeffran's shield. He made a jab with the spear, but his opponent stepped sideways, dodging.

They faced off warily. For all his skill leading soldiers, Jeffran had no prowess as a solo fighter. He was no match for this hulking brute, this leather-skinned monster with what looked like human bones knotted in his hair. Jeffran shifted the spear in his hand, sweat sticking along the back of his shirt.

Down the line, his new recruits had finally recognized the danger and were forming up to face the threat from the rear. But they were overcompensating, pulling too many men from the critical second line, leaving the foremost soldiers without support as they struggled to repel the continuing onslaught. Jeffran had to get over there, had to get them back in formation before the attackers pushed through.

Jeffran grunted, catching another attack on his shield. This time, instead of thrusting forward, he pivoted, whirling from the blow to his shield and spinning to strike backhand at the enemy's unprotected torso. He felt the spike hit flesh, heard the grunt that accompanied it, and threw his weight forward.

"Second line, hold!" he bellowed. "Third line, threat to rear! You there, with the axe! Get your menfolk out here and help hold the line!" This last was yelled to the village leader, who stood with a group of stalwart farmers. They'd gathered as a final line of defense for their wives and children, in case the savages broke through.

The tide of battle began to turn. Jeffran strode behind his soldiers like a tiger prowling its cage, directing concerted attacks on three more savages who attempted to jump the lines.

Abruptly, the savages retreated. They did not break in ones and twos, like warriors who had lost their courage. Nor did they back carefully away from the conflict. They simply whirled and fled, all at once, like a child's toys yanked backward by invisible strings. Jeffran forbore to pursue them, choosing instead to maintain the lines of defense until the amberwood rafts had risen from the plains and faded into dark smudges against the windswept heavens.

Turning to coordinate the care of the wounded, his foot caught against the impaled corpse of a fallen savage. The man was well-muscled, nearing middle age, and clearly from the Kindu principalities. His affixed earlobes and tumbling dark hair were unmistakable. Jeffran knelt to finger the tattered strips of cloth tied around the man's bicep, traditional local markers of a father with young children.

"How did they compel you to this monstrosity?" Jeffran murmured. "Why didn't you flee back to your family?"

There had been opportunities enough, in the mad hectic scramble of battle. Jeffran's troops would willingly have spared the lives of any who surrendered, yet no savage ever did. And the few piteous creatures whose wounds prevented them from retreating did not survive long as captives. They snarled and raged against their restraints, tearing their own bodies to ribbons in their frantic efforts to escape. Jeffran would have thought them soul-maddened, but they carried no signs of the dust.

His jaw tightened. Too many years. For too many years, this game of raid and rebuff, thrust and counterthrust had been played, with the cost measured in human blood. Jeffran had once believed there was no alternative, that even the Eternal Emperor's wisdom could not stem the savage tide. Now, though. . . . Over the past few months, disturbing rumors had trickled along the trade routes, secrets whispered from maid to water boy and back again in battered candlelit corners, with furtive sidelong glances to both sides. Secrets overheard by weary soldiers, on their way to or from some desperate mission.

Secrets that could change the world.

Jeffran grimaced and bent to straighten the tattered braided strips along the dead man's arm. He rose and wiped the blood from his fingers.

It was time to do more than merely listen.

✧　　　✧　　　✧

Jeffran approached the capital warily. He had been three weeks on the road, his horse muddy and dust-flecked, his patrol entrusted to the competent care of his second-in-command. His weapons thumped against his saddlebags, jangling counterpoint to the aching hollow uncertainty in his chest. Given the circumstances, the Eternal Emperor's servants were unlikely to condemn him for leaving his post. Mostly unlikely. Hopefully, anyway.

Jeffran frowned, his horse sidling impatiently on the rain-sodden trail, before snapping the reins and urging it down the incline. He spent the night in a seedy hostel and spent the morning tramping from one corner of the city to the next, until a snide half-blind quartermaster finally directed him to the proper administrative offices. A hot, sweaty afternoon, an endless line of supplicants, and one beady-eyed official later, Jeffran found himself kneeling before an elaborately robed man in the vaulted stone chambers of an audience hall.

"I know only what I have seen, Your Excellency," Jeffran said. His words rolled along the perilously high ceiling. "The deadfall savages are... uncanny. They run upon spears without flinching. The wounded crawl *toward* the battle, bleeding and ragged-throated, as though driven by some bestial urge. These poor savages are no willing murderers. I am certain of it."

The Eye of the Emperor, robed in swathes of peacock green, listened with a grave air. He bid Jeffran rise with a wave of his hand and turned toward the room's arched windows. His ancient eyes studied the fractured cloudscape beyond.

"Three years of peace," the Eye said. "The rebel faction appeased, the northern borders secured, no word from the floating islands except for itinerant tradesmen. The Holy Kingdoms had just begun to breathe easily... and now this."

Jeffran shrugged. "The western winds have always brought uncertainty, Your Excellency."

It was true. The floating logjams that drifted above the Emperor's kingdoms were a geography unto themselves. Some islands were uninhabited. Others held isolationist nations or warring tribes of cannibals. The deadfall savages were the most feral group. They occupied a series of unusually large islands that had drifted in, this time, from across the western seas. Their population was large; their supplies depleted from months spent hovering over saltwater. It was not surprising that they'd turned to pillaging as soon as they passed over land. And yet, the situation unnerved him.

"Your Excellency," Jeffran said cautiously. "There is talk among the patrollers to the north. They say there is a madman chained beneath the Emperor's palace. A man who froths and screams in the night, and claims the deadfall savages are filled with an unholy power."

He hesitated, knowing he was overstepping his bounds, but also unwilling to relent. This was why he had come. Best get it over with. "Your Excellency, if there *is* such a man, and such a power, my patrollers deserve to know of it. We give our lives to protect the frontier. We have a right to understand what we fight against."

Silence. Jeffran felt his heart hammering in his chest.

For a long time the Eye did not speak. Jeffran could not see, from the place where he knelt on the floor, what the old man saw beyond the window. Had the floating logjams finally reached the capital? They had trailed Jeffran on his three-week journey—dark shadows overhead, constantly distorting, like stains of blood upon a windowpane.

The Eye of the Emperor turned at last from the window. "You are a brave man, Jeffran of the Highlands. You left your troops and risked execution as a deserter in order to petition before a man who might have turned you away without a second thought. I almost did, except..." The Eye paused, tapping his fingers. "Perhaps it is fortuitous that you, of all patrol leaders, have chosen to ride to the capital with your concerns. I think... yes. You have made up my mind for me. Come."

Jeffran followed the Eye toward the back of the chamber and down a winding staircase. A pair of guards at the bottom—not mere administrative lackeys, but elite fighters with exquisite armor—parted to let them pass. A servant hurried from an alcove ahead, summoning handfire to light the way. The Eye smiled indulgently at Jeffran's startled expression.

"It is not a difficult skill to learn," the Eye said, nodding toward the heatless swirls of light above the servant's palm. "Alas, it would not be very useful to you on the frontier. Souldust falls infrequently there."

"I've no desire for magic, Excellency," Jeffran said, more gruffly than he intended. "The pretty tricks are not worth the cost."

The servant glanced sharply over his shoulder. "Not tricks," he said petulantly.

"Peace, Davothy," the Eye said in a soothing tone. "The patroller meant no insult." As they continued through underground tunnels, the Eye lowered his voice and leaned toward Jeffran. "Davothy was born as he is. His family placed him under my care, knowing that he would have a place of honor here in the capital."

Jeffran grunted noncommittally.

Davothy, his ears having clearly detected this exchange, turned to glower. "Not tricks," he said again. "Blessing. Where you live..." The servant paused, struggling to force out the slurred words. "I'm just stupid. Dim-witted boy, no good for nobody. Here"—he tapped his chest proudly—"I'm special. Do magic, earn wages." He gave Jeffran another glare for good measure, then whirled and continued his slightly lurching tread through the passage.

Privately, Jeffran thought that even a natural dimwit must take damage from souldust. The addiction alone was harmful. But this was the capital, where illusionists and fire-singers performed on every street corner, and where even respected scholars practiced occasional soulcraft. Jeffran's provincial attitudes were not welcome here, and so he kept his peace.

The tunnels grew darker, danker, with dripping patches of moisture on the walls. Shadowed sarcophagi revealed that they had entered the Emperor's catacombs, a restrictive labyrinth of tunnels that housed past rulers of the kingdoms. They came at last to a more well-lit area, with regular torch sconces on the walls and crisp, newly cut masonry.

"We are beneath the Eternal Emperor's palace," the Eye said. "Men awaiting justice are often kept here."

They passed another set of guards. Davothy extinguished his handfire and retreated to a wall alcove while the Eye spoke with a man at a broad, orderly desk. The man—who appeared to be some sort of warden—fetched a small set of keys and unlocked a narrow door of unspectacular construction.

Jeffran recoiled as the portal swung open. The tiny room stank of excrement. The sparse bedding had been shredded, the bed frame overturned, and jagged scratches marred the stuccoed walls. On a space of bare floor in the room's center, chained to a metal bolt that was clearly a recent addition, lay an emaciated man who did not acknowledge their entry.

Jeffran knelt beside the chained man, horrified by the staring eyes, the gaunt lines of cheek and jawbone. The prisoner's skin tones were those of the Holy Kingdoms, his tangled auburn hair a clear confirmation of ancestry. His clothing was in tatters, his hair snarled with fragments of broken bone. Faded remnants of war paint marked his cheeks and arms.

"Timoten?" Jeffran whispered. But the prisoner did not respond to the name.

"What is this?" Jeffran demanded, whirling to face the Eye of the Emperor. "This man is a citizen of the Holy Kingdoms. What has he done to deserve such treatment?"

"The chains are necessary," said the Eye, who remained at the room's entryway. "In his lucid moments, this man can be quite—"

A growl rose in the prisoner's throat. With a sudden lurch, he snapped bleeding fingers around the collar of Jeffran's shirt.

Jeffran yelped and jerked backward, but the prisoner forced him to the floor.

"Who are you?" the man demanded. "Why are you here? Don't you know I have to kill you? Stupid, abhorrent ground dwellers!"

A fist struck Jeffran's face. He floundered backward. The prisoner lunged, snarling, but snapped to a halt as the chains pulled taut. He raged, spine arching, and for a terrified instant Jeffran feared that his inhuman strength would rip the chains free of their mooring. Blood streamed down the prisoner's wrists. Bones snapped audibly as he threw his body against the floor.

Finally the man collapsed, whimpering. "I shouldn't have left," he gasped, lungs heaving. "Too much dust, it's all gone wrong. Jeffran! Help me, Jeffran!" He wept and clawed the ground.

The Eye of the Emperor said: "Jeffran. It is the only name he ever speaks. When you arrived to petition at my audience hall, your voice colored by the same highland dialect, I wondered at the coincidence."

"How did he come here?" Jeffran asked, voice rasping.

"He was found by a patrol near the Shan-ti border. Rather, he accosted them, clinging to their legs and begging for asylum. It seems he realized that he was among countrymen, and found courage to flee from the other savages." The Eye looked with pity on the trembling prisoner. "He claimed to have knowledge of critical importance to the Emperor, but when he was brought into the capital, he began raving. Our best physicians have been unable to ease his condition. He calls them 'irreverent bloodsuckers' and suggests a number of…intriguing alternate applications for their equipment."

Despite himself, Jeffran gave a wan smile. "Timoten never did like doctors much."

"You *do* know him, then?"

"Yes," Jeffran said. He lowered himself, exhausted, to sit beyond reach of the prisoner's chain. "He's my brother."

It took four men to hold Timoten down while the Emperor's physicians tended his wounds. When Timoten had screamed himself hoarse and the last of the broken bones had been set, a hunched, bird-boned matriarch murmured an incantation and passed a glowing palm across his chest.

Jeffran watched with gut-wrenching anguish. He had not seen his brother in fourteen years, not since the disastrous childhood raid that had separated them. Their mother's anguished cries had haunted Jeffran's dreams that night, and every night thereafter.

The matriarch finished her work and sat back, crooning to herself. Bone-knitting was intense magic, heavy on souldust and intellectually disastrous for those who practiced it. Timoten would not ordinarily have qualified for such attention, but the savage refugee—like a prized warhorse—could not be relied on to leave the injury undisturbed.

"Thank you," Jeffran said as he helped the old woman to her feet. "Your sacrifice honors us."

"That's all right, lovey." She patted his arm, eyes failing to focus on his face. "I'm bound for the grave. Didn't the golden birds tell you? No need for wits on the other side." She broke into an old sky shanty, rocking back and forth with the chorus.

Timoten, who had grown visibly more agitated at the old woman's arrival, at last ceased his screaming. He sank to the flagstones, hair falling in matted hunks around his face. "Too much dust," he mumbled. "Dust, dust, ashes and dust. He burns it like fire along my bones."

Jeffran leaned forward. "Who, Timoten? Who burns the dust?"

"He's always near. Behind the lines, whenever the rafts come down. Far enough to stay unbloodied. Near enough to dominate."

Jeffran leaned forward, urgent. "When the Emperor's soldiers found you, you said you knew something important. What was it, Timoten? What did you come here to tell us?"

Timoten wailed and yanked his hair. Eerie streaks of light pulsed along his skin. "It's no use," he cried. "There's too much of it. I can't break free. Jeffran! Where are you, Jeffran?"

"Timoten! It's me. *I'm* Jeffran."

"Dust, dust, ashes and dust..."

Jeffran paused. The Eye said Timoten had become incoherent when the Emperor's soldiers brought him to the capital. And his agitation had increased visibly when the ancient matriarch used souldust to heal him.

"You!" Jeffran said, whirling to address the warden. "Take the old woman outside."

The warden eyed Timoten uncertainly. "All right. I'll send a pair of guards to—"

"Don't send anyone. You city dwellers are all tainted with souldust."

"Souldust," the old woman said as the warden escorted her from the room. "Oh yes, the dust seeps into your soul. I had a patient once who...no. That was my husband. Is he dead? I think he died." Her voice trailed away down the hallway.

The glowing lines on Timoten's skin faded. The madness left his eyes. "Jeffran?" he asked, his gaze at last locking on his brother's. "Jeffran. Praise the kingdoms I found you. They're coming."

"The savages?"

"They mean to attack the capital."

"They'd be fools to try. They're no match for the Emperor's sorcerers."

"No, you don't see. You *must see*, Jeffran. The souldust. It strengthens his hold on us. You must warn the Emperor. If his soldiers loose magic against the savages—"

A signal horn blew, long and low, from the ramparts atop the Emperor's palace. Timoten's eyes rolled upward. He dropped in a trembling fit, spittle foaming from his mouth. Jeffran's blood froze. There was only one reason the horns would be blowing that particular signal, with quite that sense of urgency.

The deadfall savages were attacking.

Jeffran reached the ramparts as the first rafts were dropping, his patroller's insignia granting him access to the heights. A line of hard-eyed sorcerers stood ready to rebuff the attack. Their upraised fists glowed with souldust.

"Stop!" Jeffran shouted, but his words were lost in the throng of jostling soldiers. Brawny savages leapt from the descending rafts, dropping like scattered pebbles. Most were impaled on spears held by nervous soldiers. Others struck the ramparts and collapsed, bones snapping.

The sorcerers sent their first volley upward.

Flames erupted from outstretched fists, dazzling Jeffran's eyes and licking along the undersides of rafts. Savages pulled back from the edges, skin flaming. But, a moment later, the savages were jumping again, and this time something was different. They... glowed. A flaring network of lines lit their skin, brightest along their skulls. Moments before, overeager savages had broken bones when they jumped from the rafts. Now they landed in feral crouches, unharmed. They lashed out with cudgels and battle-axes.

A woman dropped onto the shield of a nearby soldier. She lunged toward Jeffran, snarling. He caught her club with both hands, intending to toss her aside, but she was unnaturally strong. She braced her legs against his cuirass and leapt from his chest, twisting midair to strike at the Emperor's sorcerers. Within seconds, she had razed the entire line, snapping bones and sending men tumbling to their deaths.

Jeffran whirled, intending to cut off the woman during her second pass, and found himself face to face with Timoten. His brother's face was contorted, his eyes blazing with mindless fury. Broken chains trailed from his forearms.

Jeffran backed away, hoping to avoid a confrontation. Timoten advanced, swinging the chains in a broad arc. Jeffran ducked, rolled to one knee, and scanned desperately for some avenue of escape. His eye caught on something unusual: a raft.

It hovered near the edge of the ramparts, the only raft that had not joined the battle. A massive figure stood at the center, with light blazing along its cranium.

He's always near. Timoten's words rang in Jeffran's memory. *Behind the lines. Far enough to stay unbloodied. Near enough to dominate.*

Jeffran didn't stop to think. He pushed himself upright, lunged to avoid Timoten's next attack, scooped up an abandoned shield, and charged toward the edge of the roof.

He honestly didn't know if he'd make the jump. Air whizzed beneath his boots, and the shield preceding him caught the edge of several blades. Then his feet struck the roughly lashed logs of the raft. He stumbled forward. Savages swung at him. He snapped a cudgel from the nearest belt and swung, eyes focused on the glowing skull of the savages' leader.

The cudgel *whizzed* through the air, snapping with crushing power. At the last moment, Jeffran's target raised an arm in self-defense. The cudgel descended, not on the unprotected cranium, but on the metal bracer strapped to his opponent's forearm. The bulky savage grunted, and the blinding patterns along his scalp dimmed slightly.

The other savages, who'd been moving to intercept Jeffran, halted mid-stride. They seemed disoriented. The glowing lines along their skin faded.

Looking more irritated than angry, the savage leader swatted Jeffran to the ground. Jeffran rolled, swinging at the savage's leg. Bone crunched beneath his cudgel. The savage roared and reached down to lift Jeffran by the neck. Jeffran struggled, throat collapsing beneath crushing fingers. His lungs burned. He could not draw air. The world began to go black.

Then something heavy thudded into the savage from the side.

Jeffran dropped, gasping. He struggled to his feet and saw Timoten crouching atop the fallen savage, severed chains trailing from both wrists. Timoten snarled and drew back an arm to strike, but the savage heaved sideways, knocking him aside. Timoten spun in air, chains flaring. Metal struck unarmored flesh. The savage grunted. He raised his head and stared at Timoten, light flaring with renewed brilliance along his scalp. Timoten faltered, hands grasping the sides of his head. He crumpled.

The savage leader smiled.

Then his expression froze, rigid, as Jeffran's cudgel shattered the bones of his skull.

Jeffran struck again, this time in the chest. He jumped away as his massive adversary toppled, but misjudged his direction. The savage's weight, now displaced from the center of the raft, set the entire surface rocking precariously. Jeffran's foot slipped off the edge.

Jeffran reeled, tumbling, catching a terrifying glimpse of the cobbles far, far below. He reached for the edge of the raft, but the distance was too great. His flailing hand swung through empty air...

And latched, palm to wrist, onto Timoten's outstretched arm.

"What will happen to them?" Timoten asked. He and Jeffran stood on the chaotic rooftop, still breathing heavily from the battle. Harried commanders paced and shouted, organizing the disarmament of the perplexed and occasionally weeping savages.

"They'll be returned home," Jeffran said, looking with pity on the sudden refugees. "Assuming no new savage leader arises to distort their minds."

"None will. The man you slew was soul-hungry, a demented sorcerer able to feed on others' souldust. There is not another like him on the islands."

"Emperor be praised. But Timoten, how did you remain free of the trance? By the time that monster was choking me, his influence on the savages had returned. How were you able to attack him?"

"I'd already jumped." Timoten shrugged and smiled wryly. "Hard to abandon a target mid-leap. You'd distracted him with your first attack. I broke free of his grip long enough to spring to your aid. Then, when I hit him, his concentration faltered again."

"Fair enough." Jeffran stretched his weary muscles and clapped his brother on the shoulder. "Come. The sooner I report back to the Eye, the sooner we may return to the highlands."

Timoten hesitated. "I'll remain here, I think. I'm...not quite ready to take up normal life again. There are things...memories." He shuddered.

Jeffran's hands opened and closed, helpless. "How can I help?"

"You have helped already, Jeffran." Timoten's gaze flicked over the crowded rooftop, chaotic but peaceful. "You have helped already."

Yael of the Strings

JOHN R. FULTZ

AMONG THE TENTS WHERE SOLDIERS WHISPERED OF SPIDERS AND warlocks, the minstrel walked and strummed his guitarra. He stopped here and there to tell a tale or sing a song that emboldened the hearts of his listeners. Wherever he wandered, the talk turned from nervous worry to headstrong bravado. Farmers' sons and unseasoned conscripts compared themselves with the heroes in the minstrel's songs. They looked for his cloak of crimson and gold when he passed near, waving him to their fires and offering mulled wine for their favorite tunes.

Yael Tarasca obliged them all. Such was the duty assigned to him by the Queen of Sharoc. For seven years she had retained Yael as her court minstrel, and she cherished the power of his voice. Yet now her soldiers needed Yael's presence far more than she did. "Such men as you are priceless in times of war," she told him, "for your tongue encourages others to spend their lives in service to the throne. Your songs make men hungry for glory. You will go with General Anco to the Valley of Ezerel."

So Yael had traded the comforts of palace life for a rude tent among the mud and piles of griffon dung. The Legions of Sharoc set their camp north of the valley, ten thousand tents and campfires beneath the rustling banner of the Lion and Hawk. Yael's boots of fine Sharoci leather were stained by the muck of the encampment, and he missed the nightly company of palace courtesans. His belly remained empty when he could not bring himself to eat the miserable rations of soldiers. General Anco and his lieutenants dined on sumptuous fare in a great silken pavilion behind the lines. Yet only the griffon-tamers, Knights of the Royal House, would get the fine foods imported from royal precincts. Yael contented himself with a ready supply of wine.

"Soon," he reminded himself while stalking from tent to tent, "the battle will be done and I'll return to the palace." Tonight he would get little sleep, for General Anco had ordered him to entertain the troops until dawn. Anco knew well the creeping fear, the gnawing dread that quivered in the stomachs of untested men on the night before a charge. He knew that Yael of the Strings would sing courage into his men. The minstrel counted himself lucky to bear such a duty. Most of the men he sang for tonight would die in the valley tomorrow. Far better to sing for the queen than to *die* for her.

Across the moonlit valley assembled the invading Legions of Ghoth. Behemoth spiders moved about their ranks on segmented legs thick as tree trunks. Strapped to the broad backs of the arachnids stood wicker pagodas with peaked roofs. Warlocks also walked among the Ghothians, grim sorcerers of the pureblood caste, each bearing the Mark of the Great Mother on his forehead. Rumor had it that such men shared their very thoughts with the great spiders. When the sun rose the Griffon and the Spider would converge, and a tide of blood would flow into the valley.

Yael shivered and turned his eyes back to the strings of his guitarra. He finished a performance of "The Hero's Blinding Blade" to cheers from nine soldiers gathered about a guttering flame. It was the sixth time he'd played the tune this night.

"Damn, but you're a fine singer," said a young man swathed in chain mail. He hoisted a tankard of wine and toasted the minstrel. His fellows joined the salute, and someone handed Yael a full cup. He drank the wine hungrily, and the blinking stars spun above his head.

"Do you know the 'Tale of Voros the Webcutter'?" asked another lad.

"Of course," said Yael. He was tired of that song, and the wine had loosened his tongue. "But everyone knows that tale. How about something new?"

The boy-soldiers exchanged nervous glances. "Like what?"

Yael smacked his lips and retuned the fifth string of his instrument. He launched into "The Ballad of the Summer Maiden." His audience listened, rapt with attention. A few more soldiers wandered over to join their fellows, hanging on the song's every word. When Yael finished there was applause, but no cheers. Half the men were weeping into their cups.

"Aye, Esmeralda, do I miss you!" sobbed a young man.

"I miss my sweet Jarethea!" moaned another.

"I might never see my wife and sons again," a soldier said.

Yael blinked. This was not the time for romantic ballads. These lads must be inspired to vanquish their foes, not too long for their distant loves.

So he launched into "The Tale of Voros the Webcutter," and the mood of the company improved immediately. He finished the song to another round of applause but refused another cup of wine. Despite the protests against his leaving, he made his way toward another group of soldiers gathered about another flame. There he gave a new performance, staying only long enough to banish the black moods of those who listened, then moving on to the next row of tents, the next fire, the next cup of wine.

The men of Sharoc listened to the minstrel's songs while oiling their blades, honing the heads of pikes, and tightening the straps of shields. Yael played, walked, played again. "The Lay of the Laughing Prince." "The Conquest of Altarro." "The Valiant Legions." Many more songs, and many of them two or three times apiece. Every tale he knew that quickened the blood, fired the spirit, and banished fear. He turned frowns into grins, worried looks to determined scowls, and unskilled boys into valorous warriors.

As he performed, Yael watched the full moon glide across the sky. When the bulk of the night was behind him, his fingers sore from plucking, his voice hoarse from singing, he came to one last fire. The men were busy slipping into breastplates and greaves, but he played "Swords of the Righteous" for them the best he could. His weariness crept into the song, but still they seemed to enjoy it. Anything to take their minds off the slaughter to come.

Someone offered him a piece of greasy flatbread as breakfast. He paused in his playing and accepted the tasteless fare. Sunrise was less than an hour away. A dim violet glow replaced the darkness along the eastern horizon. The clanking of metal and the shouts of captains rang across the encampment. Every man must now rise and make himself ready for the charge at dawn. Every man but the weary minstrel, who would remain among the tents and try to sleep while the blood tide rushed into the valley. His long night was over.

As Yael swallowed the last of his meal, a shadow fell across the encampment. Then the howling began, and the panicked screams of men rose into the darkness. The soldiers began twitching, falling, smacking at their legs and arms, as if a sudden madness had fallen upon them. Now Yael saw the masses of hairy spiders moving across the ground, each one big as a man's fist. They crawled up his tall boots toward his crotch. He leaped atop the wooden crate that had served him as a chair, scraping spiders from his boots with the flat side of his guitarra.

They came in a suffocating wave, an ocean of tarantulas invading the camps, seeking soft flesh with poison fangs. Yael stamped upon the crate, dislodging more of the deadly creatures. A few had already bitten deep into his boot leather. He slapped the remaining spiders from his legs, but more of them crawled up the sides of the crate.

The legions wailed and screamed as they drowned beneath the wave of venomous arachnids. Only Yael's elevated position on the crate and his well-made boots had saved him from the tiny monsters. The men around him were all dead or dying, their young faces purple and bloated by the killing venom. They fell to the earth clutching swollen necks, and they disappeared beneath a carpet of black spiders.

Yael kicked and stomped at the spiders streaming onto his crate. He would have smashed them with the guitarra, but he could not risk losing the instrument. It was made by the finest artisans in Sharoc, a gift to him from the queen herself. His boots crushed the tarantulas two at a time. If anyone had been watching they might have laughed at his absurd dance. Yet everyone was too busy smashing spiders, or dying, to notice that Yael of the Strings was dancing for his life.

Someone rushed by with a torch and swept it across the smothered crate. The spider-flesh ignited along with the crate itself. Yael stood as long as he dared on the flaming box while men rushed about him with torches, clearing out the spiders. They were knights in scalloped steel armor, more resistant to the fangs of their tiny foes.

"Goddess curse the Ghothian warlocks!" someone shouted as Yael leaped to the ground. The minstrel took a flaming brand from the campfire and quickly learned to maintain a spider-free zone about himself while the extermination of the crawling horde continued. Countless dead men littered the ridge, many of the tents were in flames, and the smell of roasting spiders filled the air like a cloying jasmine.

The sun rose full in the east, shedding flame across the sky. Yael glanced southward and saw the legions of Ghothian pikemen marching into the valley. After them came the ranks of gargantuan spiders. He could not see the Ghothian warlocks who had sent the plague of tarantulas, but he imagined them sitting in the pagodas rising from the backs of the eight-legged giants.

The knights had succeeded in burning and dispersing the swarm of tarantulas, but the losses among the footmen were great. The sneak attack had not been meant to damage the griffon riders. It had been aimed squarely at the masses of pikemen, most of whom weren't even strapped into their leather corselets yet. The spider plague had all but crippled the Sharoci infantry.

Even now the last tarantulas were scuttling into the weeds or tunneling into the earth itself. The advance of the Ghothians had begun, and now the Legions of Sharoc must rush to meet them or lose the valley in a single hour. Captains and generals shouted commands. Surviving soldiers forgot their dead comrades and continued their hasty preparations. Men took up pikes and short swords and pointed helms. They strapped on leather breastplates and formed into ranks as they were ordered. There were half as many in those ranks as there were yesterday. Dead men lay everywhere, their bodies swollen, their skin gone purple as grapes.

Yael stumbled through the chaos toward his private tent at the rear of the lines. A knight rode by him on a griffon, its wings still folded against the glistening coat of its leonine body. The griffon's claws sent mud spraying behind it, and its hawk-like head crowed with excitement. A long red plume rose from the knight's helmet. He raised a silver sword high as he shouted commands. The griffon-mount's passing almost knocked Yael over, but he stumbled onward in the opposite direction of every other man.

A war horn sounded somewhere, followed by two more. Men's voices raised in cries of anger, defiance, and raw bravado. At last Yael reached his modest tent. He collapsed on the cot, still clutching the guitarra to his chest. The thunder of griffons' wings filled the sky. The knights were launching. The charge had begun.

Yael clutched his instrument and thanked the Goddess that he was no soldier.

The flap of his tent opened. An armored knight without a helmet stalked inside. His iron-gray beard and long mustache were unmistakable. He was Sir Carracan, General Anco's first officer. He carried a footman's pike and a muddy broadsword in his hands, yet these weapons were not his own. They were far too crude for a rider of griffons, a commander of the queen's legions.

"Minstrel!" Carracan bellowed. "Up with your lazy ass!"

He tossed the pike and broadsword to the ground beside Yael's cot. He turned and exited the tent.

Yael sat on the edge of the cot. He stared at the rusted scabbard of the sword and the long pole with its razory iron head. His hands clutched the guitarra as if it would defend him from any enemy.

Sir Carracan returned a moment later with a bronze shield. On its pocked face were the images of Lion and Hawk. "Up, damn you!" shouted the knight. "You're fighting with us today!"

Yael shook his head, stood up to face the knight without realizing it. "Impossible," he said. "I'm not a soldier. I am, as you have said, only a tired minstrel."

Carracan snatched the guitarra from Yael with gauntleted fists. He raised the instrument high above his head so that it raked the canvas of the tent. Yael's breath stopped. The knight brought the guitarra down across his armored knee, shattering it into a hundred pieces. Its silvery strings, made from the best sheep's gut money could buy, snapped like the tender wood of its body.

"Today you're a soldier," said Carracan. "We've lost too many pikemen to those damn spiders. Every squire, cook, and boy who can lift a pike is joining the charge."

Yael could not have been more stunned if the knight had slapped him across the face. No words came into his mind. Only dread, and fear, and a terrible irony that crept like an arachnid across the back of his skull.

Carracan grabbed him by the shoulders and bellowed into his face. "Serve your queen, boy! Or I'll run you through right here." The knight placed a hand on the hilt of his silver sword. "Make your choice, warbler. Serve or die."

Yael bent and picked up the pike. It was longer than he was tall. He had studied fencing at the palace, as the upper classes were wont to do. But he had never fought for his life. Had never taken a life.

"I know not the use of this weapon," he said.

The knight showed Yael how to brace the pike for a charge. "Hold it like this. Run toward the enemy. And stick him with this end!"

Yael nodded. Carracan picked up the round shield. "And don't forget this. The spider-lovers will be trying to stick you, too."

Yael strapped the broadsword to his waist as Carracan gave him a last piece of advice.

"When the ranks have joined, the battle will turn to close-quarters fighting. You won't have room to use the pike anymore. That's when the sword comes in handy. Do not hesitate to kill these Ghothians, or they will kill you first. Do you understand?"

Yael nodded, his head swimming. Sir Carracan marched him out of the tent and sent him toward a group of pikemen jogging for the front line. Up ahead griffons filled the sky above the valley, already swooping to engage the great spiders. Yael joined the ranks of marching footmen. The smells of sweat and shit and fear suffocated him. The heat of the day rose with the sound of blaring horns, and the downward march began.

One of the pike-bearers marching beside Yael looked more like a stable boy than a warrior. He noticed Yael among the ranks. "Minstrel!" the lad called through the forest of raised spears. "Sing us a song for battle."

Yael's throat was dry. Fear had stolen his voice. He sweated and marched and said nothing.

"Sing a fighting tale!" called another. Others joined in. "Sing! Sing!"

Yael glanced about at their desperate faces. He saw the same sweat, the same fear as his own. He began singing "Triumph of the Red King," his voice pitched low and matching the cadence of the march. The men about him began to sing as well. It was a well-known song about a beloved king who marched into battle without his armor yet killed a hundred foes. His wrath was so great that no foe dared to approach him. His true armor was his courage and his noble spirit, and thus he survived to win the day.

The men of Sharoc marched toward the overwhelming ranks of Ghothians. Diving griffons harried the rows of colossal arachnids. Knights drove their lances into the bulbous monsters. The spider-beasts squirted silvery ropes of webbing into the sky, bringing knights and griffons tumbling to earth. The Ghothian pikemen closed about the fallen ones, stabbing them to death in seconds.

The marching armies grew closer and closer. They would meet in the valley's exact center. The spider-banners of Ghoth rippled in the autumn wind, and the yellow banners of Lion and Hawk streamed forth to meet them. At a certain distance, the archers on either side took to ground. Volleys flew into the sky, each a black rain of barbed death. The footmen paused, sank to their knees, and raised their shields for shelter. When the arrows had fallen, the footmen rose and marched again. Another volley shot into the sky, and the footmen paused again and raised their shields. A soldier next to Yael took an arrow in the eye and died instantly.

Again and again the arrows fell, until the two armies came together in a rush of shouting, charging pikemen. Then all sense of ranks and order was lost, and the slaughter truly began. The wicked pikes of the Ghothians impaled their foes, ripped sideways to spill guts from bellies. Others hooked men into immobile positions of lasting pain. In such cases the Ghothians pulled forth their scimitars and took the heads of wounded men.

Yael might have dropped his pike and run from the fray like a coward, but the press of men behind him made this impossible. So he marched into the forest of barbed and glittering blades aimed at his gut and face. The Ghothian pikes were grotesquely made, barbed and hooked to inflict maximum carnage. The screams grew louder. Dying men wailed and clutched at their spilled intestines on the ground as others trampled them into the mud.

Now came an opening, and Yael faced a howling pikeman of Ghoth. Like all his folk he wore a black turban instead of a metal helm. He thrust his hooked spear at Yael, who turned it with his shield and shoved his own pike forward. Yael aimed directly for the turban and winced when the blade of his pike punctured flesh and bone. The Ghothian died leaking blood from his nostrils, sinking to his knees.

Another Ghothian swept his scimitar at Yael's head. The minstrel's shield caught the edge of the blade. Yael's pike was caught in the dead man's skull, and already the field was too crowded to use such a long weapon. Yael grabbed at the hilt of his broadsword. The scimitar came at him again in a downward swing. Once more the shield saved his life. His arm went numb beneath it.

Yael swept the big blade from its scabbard. It was far heavier than the rapier he used for fencing. The scimitar resounded from his shield again and slipped sideways to slice his arm open below the shoulder. A shallow cut, but painful.

He drove the point of the broadsword forward with all his strength, as he had done with the pike. It caught his assailant in the shin, and the Ghothian howled. Yael sprang at him shield-first, knocking him backward across a corpse and landing on top of him. He drove his sword deep into the Ghothian's gut, far enough to pierce the earth beneath him, and he watched the eyes of his enemy grow soft. A great silence seemed to fall about him in the midst of the roaring chaos.

Yael stared into the face of the man he had killed. Only a youth, at least ten years younger than himself. Probably conscripted into the sultan's army. His skin was brown, a shade darker than that of most Sharoci, and his eyes were dark pools of light. But the light faded swiftly, until there was nothing but lifeless flesh beneath Yael's heaving body.

Time had slowed so that each moment was an eternity. The roar of battle was like the roar of the ocean in Yael's ears. Droplets of red blood spilled through the air like tiny jewels, splattered across the muddy ground. Dead boys lay all about him, their skulls and hearts and bellies split open, spilling the red secrets of existence into the black dirt. The whiteness of an ancient bone poked through the mud, a remnant of some historic battle. How many bones, how many skulls, filled the earth beneath this valley? The soil was rich with decayed humanity.

Suddenly, the rush of battle returned and the clashing of metal filled the air between the howls of desperate men and the sobs of the dying. The living men about Yael were moving away, fighting even as they moved, leaving him among a pile of corpses—both Ghothian and Sharoci. The ground trembled, and Yael heard an approaching thunderstorm. He rose to his knees and realized it was not thunder at all.

One of the behemoth spiders scuttled directly toward him, black legs stomping and thudding against the ground impossibly fast. Men were knocked aside or impaled on the sharp points of those legs. A pair of great mandibles clacked at the center of the arachnid's shaggy head. Rising on the hill of its back was an open-roofed pagoda. A dark and hooded figure stood there, gazing across the battle with flaming eyes. The master of the spider. A Ghothian warlock.

The beast raced toward the kneeling Yael, who could not stand or manage to raise his broadsword. The horrid head passed above him, mandibles dripping with purple poison. Somehow the beast and its driver had missed him among the piles of dead men. The spider paused and snapped up a fallen knight in its jaws, twin fangs piercing through armor, sinking deep into flesh. Beyond the knight a downed griffon attempted to tear its way out of a cocoon of webs. It howled and squawked as its lost rider died in the spider's jaws. Next the arachnid would turn on the trapped griffon and that would be the end of it.

The spider's distended belly hung above Yael's head. He was trapped in the prison of its legs, which rose about him like spiny pillars. He cast aside the bronze shield and wrapped both hands around the grip of the broadsword. He drove the blade upward with all his might. It pierced the outer skin like punching through boiled leather. Yael forced his legs to raise him up, driving the sword hilt-deep into the spider's guts. Green ichors spewed along his arms and into his face. He vomited but did not relent.

The beast quivered and jerked. Yael refused to let go of his blade. The beast rushed away from the pain in its lower quarters, and the transfixed sword ripped a gash half the length of its belly. A rain of translucent guts fell across the piles of corpses, and Yael barely avoided being caught in the sticky flow. He pulled the blade loose and ran, slipping between its legs as they spasmed and jerked.

As he ran free of its bulk, the monster crashed to the ground, still twitching yet wholly dead. Yael ran toward the griffon in its tangle of glittering webs. The corpse of the knight was still clasped in the mandibles of the dead spider. Yael glanced at the pagoda but saw no sign of the warlock.

The griffon's exertions with claws and beak were only drawing the webs tighter around its body. Yael cut at the thick strands of web with his blade. It was like cutting rope. Two or three slices broke a single strand here, another strand there. Still the griffon was not free, but he saw the black orbs of its eyes staring at him now through the sliced webbing. He swung again, and something grabbed him from behind.

The sword fell from his hand. Something had wrapped itself about his neck and lifted him off his feet. A stabbing pain seized his back, and he fell to the ground. He lay on his side, writhing and bleeding in the mire. The warlock stood over him, a curved dagger in his fist. The point of the blade dripped Yael's blood. The griffon stamped and cawed inside the net of torn webbing.

Stiffness grew in Yael's limbs as the warlock bent over him. The dagger was poisoned, there was no doubt of it. The Ghothian had stabbed him in the back. The blade did not sink deep, but the venom was coursing through his blood. He would be dead in seconds. Of that he was most certain.

The warlock pulled back his hood. He stared, bald and smiling, into the face of Yael. A mark in the center of his forehead resembled a spider tattoo. No, it was a birthmark. The Ghothian's eyes gleamed with barely contained fires. He spoke in Sharoci with a heavy Ghothian accent. "The great spiders are holy to us," he said. "Who are you to kill that which is holy?"

Yael stammered through swollen lips. "I'm not a soldier," he said. "I'm a singer of songs." His chest constricted. No air would enter his lungs.

The Ghothian's expression changed. His eyes narrowed, the fires inside them lowering. Yael did not understand this sudden concern. The warlock's long fingers reached out to remove Yael's helm and touch his sweating forehead.

"I hear them," said the warlock. His face was a mask of perplexed awe. "I hear your songs." He looked like someone who had made a terrible mistake. He muttered something that Yael could not hear.

A rushing shadow blotted out the sun. Something huge slammed into the warlock. It tore him away from Yael, who watched with unblinking eyes, struggling to breathe.

The griffon's beak tore off the warlock's arm at the shoulder. The dagger went flying to land somewhere among the heaps of dead and dying. Yael could no longer hear the roar of battle, but he heard the screams of the warlock as the griffon sank its talons deep. Shreds of torn webbing clung to the griffon's wings as it tore the Ghothian apart.

Finally, Yael saw the griffon's big black eyes staring at him once again. Blood dripped from the point of its great beak. Then his pain was gone and the world with it.

There was nothing but darkness, not even dreams.

✦   ✦   ✦

He did not awake nestled in the arms of the Goddess as the dead of Sharoc were supposed to. Instead he lay in a comfortable bed. By the silken sheets and the marble columns, he recognized the queen's palace. The smells of lilac and honeysuckle floated through the open window.

A bearded man snored in a deep chair beside the bed. Yael recognized Sir Carracan. The minstrel forced himself to sit upright against a mound of pillows, groaning at the fresh pain between his shoulder blades. The first officer awoke as Yael recalled being stabbed in the back. White bandages had been wrapped about his torso, and more about his lacerated shield arm. His body was clean, and the sunlight across the marble floor nearly blinded him. He blinked at Carracan when the knight offered him a cup of cold water.

Yael drank and Carracan spoke. "We held the valley, lad. Sent those spider-lovers scuttling southward. I saw what you did. So did many others. You've gone from singing about heroes to being one yourself."

"I only killed one spider," said Yael.

"Aye, but you saved a griffon. Her name is Yarvona."

Yael examined his chapped hands. A slight purple tinge discolored his fingertips.

"How am I alive?" he asked. "I was poisoned."

"The Goddess smiles on you," said Carracan. "Thousands died with that black venom in their veins, but She saw fit to spare you."

Thousands...

Yael recalled the perplexed look of the warlock, the final incantation the man had spoken before the griffon took his life. The Ghothian had changed his mind. Worked a spell to save Yael from the venom.

I hear your songs, the warlock said.

How could Yael explain this to Carracan? Or the queen? Or any of the Sharoci? He could barely explain it himself, but he knew it to be true. The warlock did not want to kill a singer of songs. The Ghothians obviously valued more than holy spiders and bone-filled valleys. It occurred to him that the Sharoci did not truly know their enemies, any more than the Ghothians knew the Sharoci.

"The servants will help you dress," said Carracan, stroking his oiled mustache. He wore a courtly robe instead of his silver armor. "The queen awaits your presence. I promised I'd bring you to her as soon as you woke up."

"I will need a guitarra," said Yael. "You broke mine."

Carracan looked genuinely embarrassed. "Yes, well, I'm sorry about that, lad. I'm sure there's another instrument to be found hereabouts. But you don't need it today."

Yael threw back the covers and placed his feet carefully on the marble floor.

"Of course I do," he said. "I'm a minstrel."

Carracan shook his head and grinned crookedly.

"No," he said. "You're a *knight*."

Outside the window a dark shape flitted between the palace and the sun. Yael heard the flapping of great wings. A griffon's cry resounded through the morning air.

"There's someone else anxious to see you, Sir Yael," said Carracan, pointing at the window. "Yarvona carried you from the field. She's your mount now. She has chosen you."

Yael sat back down upon the bed. He bent over the bowl of cool water, splashed some on his face. Inhaled fresh air.

"I don't know how to ride a griffon," he said. "Or how to be a knight."

Carracan wrapped a burly arm about Yael's shoulders. "And I don't know the first thing about playing the guitarra. We both have much to learn."

The first officer's booming laughter filled the chamber. "Sir Yael of the Strings," he called merrily as he exited the room. "The Singing Knight!"

Servants came forward to dress Yael in the finest silks.

The face of the Ghothian lingered like a ghost in his vision. *I hear your songs.*

Yes, he decided. *We all have much to learn.*

The Gleaners

DAVE GROSS

SOMEWHERE OVER THE NEAREST HILLOCKS, DOGS BAYED IN THE PRE-
dawn mist. Ambros kept his lantern hooded, directing the light
onto the wounded earth. The last thing he wanted was the war
hounds of some fallen knight to discover him and his companions.

The yellow light slid across the pale arm of a young soldier.
He lay on his side as though asleep, no wounds visible on his
body but his open eyes blank in death. Ambros shuddered at the
sight, thinking as he always did of that first time his mother led
him across a battlefield.

She drew him by the hand, guiding him around the severed
limbs and limbless trunks. The sudden pools and stenches frightened the boy, who had not yet seen ten years. When he balked,
his mother squeezed his hand and said, "We have to find your
father."

That was the only thing she said. Every time she rose from
turning over a corpse to see a stranger's face, she repeated it
like a prayer.

"We have to find your father."

Fifteen years later, Ambros had long since forgotten his father's
face, but he knew the man had answered the baron's call to
war. He did not remember, or perhaps he never understood, the
reasons for the war. He remembered only the stillness in the air
whenever anyone named the enemy: the Earl of the Ashen Citadel.

The legend had grown in the years since that first battle. The
conscripted forces always drove back the enemy, but they never
slew the earl, despite the baron's frequent claims to have quartered,

burned, or buried him alive. Sometimes the people even believed the claims, or perhaps their wishing only made it seem they did.

Every few years the earl returned like a plague, leaving black and red fields of corpses in his wake, until the common folk dared not utter even his title. The enemy was no longer "the earl" but "the witch" or "the necromancer."

Fewer now dared search the battlefields until after the baron's knights had reclaimed the area. Some sought in desperation for the bodies of their husbands, brothers, or sons. Others picked over the corpses for rings and coins and other valuable things. Like the meanest peasants at harvest, they gathered what was left after the reaping.

They were the gleaners.

"Bring the light," said Jurgen, a little too loud. Ambros pinched his tunic to feel the athame hanging from his neck. It gave him no comfort, but it reminded him of his purpose.

Ambros carried the lantern toward the sound of Jurgen's voice, careful to step over a corpse clad in a burlap tunic. The coarse hair on his pink shoulders gave the dead man the look of a slaughtered pig stuffed in a sack.

As the light revealed his brutal face, Jurgen gave Ambros one of his scrunch-mouthed smiles. Ambros could never tell whether the expression indicated pleasure in seeing him or a whiff of a bad smell. The big man poked at the body of a knight with the dead man's own mace. The eitr filigree gleamed blue even in the yellow light of the lantern.

"Jurgen," said Ambros. He kept his voice low, as much to avoid alerting the hounds they'd heard as to calm the giant. "Put it down."

Jurgen could claim an axe or cudgel belonged to him, but any commoner caught with a knight's weapon would be hanged. Ambros feared that Jurgen no longer understood the danger. The big man blinked constantly ever since a brawler creased his skull with a stool leg. Even with blood filling his eyes, Jurgen had ended that fight by slamming his opponent's head into the ceiling until the man's limp body slipped from his grasp. No one had attacked Ambros since Jurgen joined his battlefield gleanings, but the giant remained dangerous even to his friends.

Jurgen raised the mace as if to strike him. Ambros tried not to wince. These little games of menace were the price of his protection.

"Jurgen." Kaspar called from the gloom.

The giant's shoulders slumped as Kaspar stepped into the light. A foot and a half shorter than the giant, the slender man took the mace from his hand as easily as a mother might remove a twig from her toddler's grip. He carried the weapon in both hands and exchanged it for Ambros's lantern.

Ambros withdrew the silvered bowl from its bag and set it on the ground. As Kaspar held the lantern steady, Ambros laid the head of the mace in the bowl and held the weapon at a steady angle. He drew the athame from its inverted sheath on the thong around his neck. Its blade gleamed in sympathy with the eitr.

Starting from the lowest point of the filigree line, Ambros stroked the athame's sharp tip over the blue-gray substance. At the ritual knife's touch, the solid filigree returned to its natural liquid form. Ambros felt the deep, subtle vibration of the transformation through the athame. Its magic trembled in his fingers, shuddered in his bones.

He drew its point along the graceful lines of filigree, never wavering or slowing. Once the athame had begun working its transformation, to remove the tip even for an instant would break the disruption of the material and leave the remaining eitr in place, irretrievable.

When Ambros was done, star-colored liquid pooled in the silver bowl until there was nothing left of the filigree but a groove in the steel.

Working with deliberate speed, Ambros turned the mace and stroked the opposite side of the flange. A dram or so of the precious material flowed out of the surface of the mace and pooled in the bowl. He repeated the process for each of the other three sides of the mace, careful not to spill a drop.

Laying the mace aside, Ambros took a silver flask from the bag. He uncorked the mouth and poured the liquid eitr over the bowl's gentle lip and into the flask. Jurgen and Kaspar watched in silence, holding their breaths until he resealed the flask.

More than the gold coins and rings, even more than the knights' swords and the jewels they dared not steal, the eitr gleaned from enchanted weapons and talismans sustained Ambros and his friends. Rarely did they find as much as the mace contained. After his aunts had taken their portion to use in charms and remedies, the price the rest would fetch might feed the men for the better part of a year.

Kaspar nodded as he watched Ambros return the bowl and flask to the bag. Twenty years older than Jurgen and Ambros, Kaspar had joined them after they crossed paths on another battlefield six years earlier.

Gleaners usually did not speak to each other. Some raced from corpse to corpse to claim the choicest loot. Others fought over the bodies of knights. Others watched with cutthroat patience, letting the others do their work for them, for a while.

Kaspar had been one of the latter, appearing out of the smoke of a burning wagon like a vengeful phantom. He had his knife to Jurgen's throat before the big man saw him. Feeling the sharp edge against his larynx, Jurgen began to blubber.

"Wait," Ambrose had cried.

He had never understood why Kaspar hesitated then. When he paused, Ambros had no idea what to say or do to save Jurgen's life and his own. Ambros knew he couldn't overcome the interloper. And for all his strength, Jurgen was helpless as a child in his fear. Even if he weren't, Kaspar's knife would do its work before Jurgen could grip his throat.

Ambros plucked an eitr-painted talisman from his bag.

"Look," he said. "This is worth a bag of coins. It's yours."

Kaspar ignored the talisman. His gaze fixed on Ambros.

Panicked, Ambros explained the value of the eitr. "My aunts know its uses, and they know others who pay gold for just a drop or two. Take it, and let us go."

Slow and skeptical, Kaspar made a counteroffer. One man, even a giant, was not enough protection from rival scavengers. Ambros needed two guardians, as Kaspar had just proven.

Ambros wasn't sure there would be enough to split three ways, but he preferred the prospect of extra labor to the thought of defying the man with the knife.

Kaspar became their third partner.

The bargain lasted, even after they had quit the field and turned over their gleanings in exchange for coin. Split three ways, the profit was smaller. But they covered more ground and frightened off more rivals after the next battle. Those who did not flee at the sight of the giant took one look at Kaspar's cold eyes and decided their fortunes lay on the other side of the field.

The eitr secured, they continued their search. Ambros once

more carried the lantern while Jurgen and Kaspar spread out to either side. A thud followed by mush-mouthed curses told Ambros that Jurgen had tripped over corpses again. He climbed the nearby hillock to join the giant, but a premonition made him close the lantern's hood before he reached the crest.

Standing atop the promontory, Ambros saw the faint gray line of dawn to the east. Mist hugged the ground, pooling in the channels between the hills. Here and there, a lone tree or a crooked banner pierced the fog. He saw the silhouette of a weary mule struggling to escape its harness, the cart behind it half sunk in mud. The animal brayed, at first with a weakness, then with fierce panic. A dark shape the size of a wild boar charged into the beast, knocking it to the ground. A moment later, a second animal attacked. Even muted by the fog, the sound of bestial gorging sent a chill through Ambros's veins.

"What's that?" Jurgen's head whipped toward the sound as he freed himself from a tangle of dead bodies.

Ambros shook his head before realizing Jurgen wouldn't see the gesture. "Let's go the other way."

They climbed back down the hill, where Ambros once again opened the lantern's hood. They moved away from the dreadful sounds they heard and found a dying horse lying atop its dead rider. The animal's legs were shattered, slick with blood.

The horse wheezed and blew, too weak to scream. Jurgen's lip trembled.

Ambros went to the dead knight and found the sword lying under his cold body. He pulled it free and examined it, finding no eitr. He took the sword to Jurgen.

"You know what to do."

Jurgen tried to take the sword in two hands, but the grip was too short. He knelt beside the horse and stroked its neck. "Sorry," he said. "Sorry, sorry."

He stood and raised the sword. Ambros watched because he felt he should. When it was done, Jurgen turned to walk away, sword still in hand.

"Jurgen," said Ambros.

The giant shook his head as if waking from a bad dream. He threw the sword down and walked on.

Kaspar whistled like a nightingale. It wasn't a half-bad call, but Ambros never thought anyone would mistake it for a real bird.

He and Jurgen went to the sound. They found Kaspar crouched over a headless peasant, a pitchfork still in his grip.

Kaspar gave Ambros one of those looks he could never understand. It was as if he wanted the answer to a question he hadn't asked. Finally, Ambros gave up guessing. "What?"

Kaspar gestured to the severed neck. Ambros still didn't understand. He shrugged.

"Someone took this head after the battle," Kaspar whispered.

Once he pointed it out, Ambros saw how fresh the blood looked, and how little had poured out of the wound. He lowered his voice. "How long?"

"Minutes."

They heard another voice, this one sweeter than their own. It was the voice of a woman. "Manfred! Otto!"

"Looking for her sons," said Jurgen. He wiped his nose with the back of his hand. In the lantern light, Ambros saw tracks on the giant's dirty face. Jurgen loved a fight. He hated to kill animals, even for mercy.

"She shouldn't be out here alone," said Ambros. He thought of his mother, whom he had left with her new husband ten years ago. By the time he heard of her death, the murderer was already gone, conscripted.

"Forget about her," said Kaspar. "She's none of our concern."

Ambros didn't like it, but he knew Kaspar was right. The eitr from the mace was as good a find as they had ever had, but its presence hinted at more. One well-armed knight seldom went to battle without others at his side.

They resumed the search. Ambros heard the jingle of coins as Jurgen took a purse from a fallen soldier. Kaspar brought a dagger back to examine under the lantern, but it was only silvered, not enchanted. He made it disappear wherever it was he kept his other blade. Ambros had never figured out whether it was tucked into his belt or hidden up a sleeve. Sometimes he thought maybe there were several knives. Sometimes he thought maybe Kaspar was a magician.

They reached another edge of the battlefield, where they found fewer and fewer bodies until only the dew-kissed grass lay before them. They turned back, heading toward the center of the conflict they had heard from a safe distance the night before.

They found a crater where some spell had turned the men

standing there into a thin red spray surrounding the blast. Nearby they found the hacked bodies of men who had died long before the battle began, their withered flesh gray and tough as leather.

"The necromancer's men," whispered Kaspar. His sudden appearance startled Ambros. One look at Kaspar's face told Ambros that he had come to the lantern not to frighten him but for comfort. Dangerous as he appeared to others, Kaspar was no less dreadful of the enemy.

"It can't be," said Ambros, without much hope. "It was only last fall they found him at Whitepool."

"Who else conscripts the dead?"

No one, thought Ambros.

Jurgen came galumphing over, his thick hands cupping some small treasure, a terrifying grin on his face. Ambros knew the expression indicated joy, but only because he had known the man since they were boys.

"Eitr!" cried Jurgen. He held out his hands to reveal four talismans and a ring, all with intricate traces of silver-blue metal.

Kaspar shushed the giant.

Ambros raised the lantern over the jewels. It was indeed eitr in the filigree and mixed into the lacquered ornaments. Set upon the ring was a brilliant blue stone that drew Kaspar's hand like a moth to the light. He hesitated before touching it, deferring to Ambros and his athame.

Producing the bowl and flask once more, Ambros bent to do his work. Sometimes he had wondered why Kaspar did not simply kill him and steal the athame for himself, but he suspected the older man feared the magic of the ritual knife.

Ambros had feared it, too, at first. But once he learned its simple function, and his aunts had drilled him in the careful handling of the liquid eitr, which must never touch his skin, he shed some of his fear. Yet he knew the others watched him work as if he were performing magic. The truth was that he had simply learned a chore. He was privy to no mysteries. He knew no secrets, except the one: it is power to let others believe you know mysteries.

He laid the bowl on the ground and studied the ring. This one was tricky, because the filigree completely encircled the ring, winding around either side of the gem. Fortunately, there were only a few dead-ends in the design. Ambros could draw a single

stroke across most of the eitr, losing only the smallest fraction
inert.

After plotting the course in his mind, he placed the ring on
his thumb and set the athame against the filigree.

"What are you doing?"

So close and unexpected, the woman's voice startled him.
With a silent prayer that Jurgen and Kaspar stood ready to defend
him, Ambros continued to draw the tip of the athame across the
eitr. He dared not spare the woman even a glance lest he lose
the rest of the precious material.

He heard Jurgen stomping nearby. "You stay back," he said.
He sounded so angry that Ambros knew he was frightened. "Go
look for your husband somewhere else."

Ambros couldn't stand it any longer. He peered to the side,
hoping for a glimpse of the woman. What he saw almost made
him drop the ring into the bowl.

His first impression was of a famine-thin woman wearing one
of the wide skirts he had seen only in puppet shows of noble
ladies. But it was not a skirt that hung around her waist. They
were bags, all of different colors and materials. One was a burlap
sack stained dark red with its bulbous contents. Another looked
like silk, and upon its surface grew the blood-red impression of
a human face: chin, cheeks, nose, and brows.

All together there were five or six bags hanging from the
woman's waist, each sagging with the weight of a human head,
fresh carved from its body.

The woman didn't look strong enough to carry so much
weight. Her limbs were reed thin, although Ambros saw tough
sinews beneath her parchment-colored skin. Her hands were dark
with blood, her naked feet stained black. Only her hair seemed
out of place, long and dark, combed and clean as if just dried
from a river bath.

"Go away!" Jurgen insisted.

"Hush," said the woman. "Let him finish." Her voice was soft
as a summer breeze. Somehow it calmed Ambros even as her
appearance horrified him.

He finished his tracing, leaving only a few short curls of eitr
remaining in the ring's shallow trench. The woman stepped closer.
Jurgen moved to block her path.

"Let me see," she said.

"Nnn—" Jurgen began to protest, but he couldn't finish even such a short word. He stepped aside.

Ambros smelled blood and corruption as the woman moved closer.

He poured the precious eitr into the flask and sealed it. He returned the bowl to the bag but kept the flask in hand.

The woman was much shorter than he'd first thought, the top of her head barely as high as his chin. Her face looked younger, too, except for her sunken eyes and hollow cheeks.

She moved closer still. Jurgen raised a hand to grab her, but he withdrew it as if touching some unseen nettles. He sucked his fingers and stumbled back, eyes wide.

She moved her face close to Ambros's face, as if to kiss him. He felt dizzy, confused, unable to resist. But she did not touch him with her lips. She sniffed at his neck, then lower, above his heart.

"You have a talent," she said. "You are worth something more than these other scavengers."

"What do you want?" said Ambros. "Why are you taking these heads?"

Before she could answer, Kaspar's knife appeared at her throat. His fingers clutched her hair and jerked her head to the side.

"No!" cried Ambros. For no reason he could understand, he feared for Kaspar, not for the woman he threatened.

"She's taking them for ransom," said Kaspar, his lips close to the woman's ear. "Isn't that right?"

She smiled, her lips as sharp as Kaspar's blade. "No," she said, drawing out the syllable long and slow. "Not exactly." She looked at Ambros, seeming unconcerned about the knife at her throat. "Do you know what I'm doing?"

Ambros had no idea. His aunts had told him many mad stories, and like everyone he had learned even more tales of witchcraft from the pantomimes of traveling players. Then he remembered another puppet show, one about the necromancer, who lopped off the heads of his foes only to gather them afterward.

The woman's gaze pierced his thoughts. As her thin smile widened, Ambros felt as though she had somehow seen his crazed suspicion. If she said it aloud, if she proved she could read his mind, he knew he would go insane. To save himself, he said it first.

"You are conscripting soldiers."

Her smile widened more, impossibly more, and she bit her lower lip like a girl flirting with an older boy. She nodded, despite the tight dark line Kaspar's knife pressed into her skin.

Ambros raised the flask of eitr. "This is worth many bags of coins."

"It is worth far more than that," she said. "It is worth a man's life. A lord's life. A thousand lives."

"Take it. Just take it, and leave us in peace."

"Don't be stupid," snapped Kaspar. He slashed his knife across the woman's throat and shoved her to the ground.

Ambros gasped. Jurgen hopped and babbled, "Oh, no, oh, no, oh, no." Even Kaspar paled as he looked down at the woman, realizing he had done a thing more dreadful than murder.

The woman struggled for a moment, her body rising and falling as she tripped over the wet bags hanging from her waist. Her hand went to her throat, or so it seemed until she finally stood to reveal no blood flowing from her neck. No wound at all. She blew upon a whistle of bone.

Ambros heard no sound, but the hairs on his nape stiffened like pine needles. He felt a sudden warmth nearby and looked up at the closest hillock.

There stood a mastiff as large as a wild boar. Ambros blinked, unable to comprehend the other thing that was wrong about the beast. Before he understood, a man's head fell away and rolled down the hill toward him. Ambros felt all his muscles spasm at the sight of what lay beneath the place where the head had been.

Where a dog's neck should be, a great vertical maw ran between the mastiff's shoulders. Dagger-sized teeth interlaced as the weird mouth closed like a bear trap where it had a moment earlier held a man's head in place.

"Otto," said the woman. Ambros turned to see her point at Kaspar. "Fetch."

The mastiff charged. Kaspar stood fast. Holding his knife before him, he looked not at the beast but at Ambros. "I'm sorr—" he tried to say before the monster struck. Its wide maw opened, engulfing Kaspar's head.

"No, dog, no, dog, no, dog, no!" Jurgen screamed. He fell to his knees.

The woman pointed again. "Manfred, fetch!"

Jurgen never saw the second mastiff coming.

Ambros stared aghast at his friends' bodies. The mastiffs lingered near them, their headless bodies grumbling as they struggled with their meals. Instead of swallowing, the mastiffs opened their hideous maws. Kaspar's head appeared first, wet and bloody as a newborn, rolling until it faced forward before the jaws clamped down to hold it in place.

The man's eyes blinked twice, then opened wide to look at the woman.

"What is his name?" she asked.

"Kaspar." A moment later, the second mastiff choked, and Jurgen's face appeared upon its shoulders. Without waiting for the question, Ambros said, "Jurgen."

"Kaspar, Jurgen, heel."

The mastiffs obeyed, their human heads sniffing at the woman's dirty ankles.

Numb with terror and some nameless other emotion, Ambros turned, expecting to see a third mastiff rushing toward him. Again, the woman looked inside him and found his thoughts.

"You are not for the dogs," she said. "Come."

She offered him her bloody hand. Looking down at her, Ambros remembered looking up at his mother as she pulled him across that first battlefield.

"Come," the woman repeated. She took his warm dry hand in her cold wet hand and drew him away from the headless corpses of his friends. "I shall present you to the earl."

Bonded Men

JAMES L. SUTTER

A SINGLE ARROW IN FLIGHT IS ALMOST SILENT. PUT A THOUSAND of them in the air at the same time, however, and the whole sky sizzles like bacon fat on a skillet.

Crouched low, Coreo listened to that hiss, the sound of clothyard shafts piercing the very air itself. At last they hit, deadly metal drummers beating their thunderous tattoo on the thin layer of wood protecting the warriors.

"You love this part, don't you?"

Coreo looked up at Jain. The taller man's shield overlapped his own, forming a roof over their heads.

"You're smiling," Jain said.

Coreo shrugged. "As a child, I'd sit up all night listening to the rain pound the roof. It's soothing."

Jain laughed and reached down with his free hand, stroking the back of Coreo's neck. "Only you, Coreo. Only you."

Up and down the lines, screams rang out or died in bloody gurgles as the barrage found homes in flesh, yet the area just around the two warriors was a sea of tranquility. Packed tight beneath the canopy of their shields, the two hundred men of the Bonded Legion showed no signs of the panic reigning elsewhere among the troops.

"Hey, Coreo!" A grizzled soldier a few men over from their position stood with his tower shield held casually overhead, as if it were no heavier than a parasol. "When are you going to get Jain to leave off with that oversized butcher's cleaver? Makes it look like he's compensating for something."

It was an old joke. Coreo reached out and pointedly grabbed Jain's meaty thigh. "Trust me, Barcas, it's not compensation—it's an advertisement."

Barcas laughed. "I'll believe it when I see it!"

"The hell you will!" That was Barcas's own partner, a spear-man named Hosch. His elbow caught Barcas in the ribs.

"Besides," Barcas continued, ignoring the blow, "it's not size, it's how you use it." Barcas was a dagger man, who did his fighting up close and personal.

"Just keep telling yourself that," Jain said.

From the center of the shield wall, Captain Dorson's voice cut them off. "Infantry's broken ranks! They're charging!"

The waiting was almost over. Coreo looked to the other men. Some stood stone-faced. Others bore crazed grins. Coreo felt himself fall into the latter camp.

Jain caught his eye and leaned in, kissing him quick and hard. "Luck."

Coreo considered grabbing the big man's blond ponytail and bringing him down for another, but Dorson's bellow rang out again.

"Shields down!"

With a roar, the men of the Bonded Legion dropped their shields and leapt to the attack.

It was not the first exchange of the day. Already, the bodies of the enemy's giants—sent in first to soften up Loremar's lines with their huge spiked flails—lay putrefying in the sun's heat, their armor-clad forms providing makeshift fortifications. To either side, battle lines stretched across the field of knee-high grass, Loremar's soldiers a wave of green and black uniforms crashing against Eron the Pike's black and crimson. Horns and shouts split the air as spears pierced or splintered and both sides got down to the bloody business at hand.

There was no way to tell what was happening in the rest of the battle, but it didn't matter. If there was one thing the Bonded Legion could count on, it was that wherever the empire sent them would be the hottest part of the fight.

Ahead, a wall of men charged, racing across the last hundred yards of open field like a flash flood. Next to Coreo, Jain unsheathed his huge two-handed sword and lifted it over his head, screaming a wordless battle cry. The sight lit a fire in Coreo's chest—it was at these times that he loved the big Northman most.

Unsheathing his own sword—a short, wide-bladed weapon made for punching through leather and mail—Coreo joined the group's howl; a wolf pack descending on their prey.

Then the lines met, and the two charging forces became a seething, whirling mass of flesh and steel.

Unfortunately for Eron's men, chaos was where the men of the Bonded Legion did their best work. Even as the enemy commanders tried to maintain cohesion, the legion disintegrated, each Bonded pair spinning off to follow its own unique tactics.

Jain charged into the fray, massive shoulders swinging more than four feet of blade in a glittering arc, not so much slicing through the advancing footmen as smashing them out of the way. Coreo, sword in his right hand and a round fighting shield strapped to his left arm, slid in easily behind him, guarding the taller man's unarmored back. A blade came in from the side and he turned it easily, then stepped forward and rammed his blade into the wielder's stomach. No need to get fancy—a gut wound was almost always fatal. As quickly as he'd moved in, Coreo recovered, resuming his position in Jain's blind spot, turning with him as the big man continued to reap his bloody crop. He caught a brief glimpse of Barcas and Hosch, the latter using his spear to drag an officer from his horse while Barcas made short work of any who got too close, his twin daggers already dripping red. Then the crowd swirled again, and there was only the red and black of Eron's men.

Three came at Coreo at once, hoping to overwhelm him with sheer numbers. Coreo sidestepped the first blade, caught the second on his shield, and met the third with the flat of his own, angling so that his opponent's sword slid safely wide of Jain's calf. Hooking a foot behind the center soldier's ankle, he pulled, sending the man toppling into his comrade to the right, then slammed his shield into the face of the remaining soldier. Bone crumpled like eggshell and the soldier collapsed to the ground. One of the other soldiers lashed out in a clumsy overhand chop, and Coreo dodged out of the way, slipping past the man and sliding his sword up into the soldier's unarmored armpit.

Blood spurted and the man fell, twisting the gore-slick hilt of Coreo's blade from his grasp. Suddenly weaponless, Coreo turned to find himself face to face with the last enemy. The man smiled.

Coreo dropped to the ground. There was the briefest flicker of surprise in the soldier's eyes, and then his head flew clear as

Jain's sword came around in a flat arc, slicing cleanly through the man's neck.

Coreo recovered his sword and stood, Jain already turning back into position. Neither man said a word.

That was the part that no one outside the Bonded Legion ever understood. While two-man teams weren't unknown on battle-fields or in gladiatorial pits, a Bonded pair was so much more. By only accepting those warriors who were already committed lovers, the legion moved beyond simple tactics into a realm of perfect communication.

A bearded soldier lunged in beneath Jain's guard, and Coreo slid around his partner's side, catching the blade on his shield and stabbing the attacker in the kneecap. Then Jain brought his heavy blade down, and the beard became two. Coreo slid back out of his partner's way, feeling the heat radiating off the big man's tattooed chest, sweat mingling where their skin touched.

Men and horses screamed, and Coreo danced with his lover.

Then, suddenly, there were no more blades to block. Across the field, the battle still raged, yet right where Coreo and the other Bonded men stood, the enemy had swirled away, drawing back to seek easier prey. Coreo found himself standing with Jain and the rest of the legion amid a knee-high mire of gore and crimson uniforms.

"Legionaries! To me!" Captain Dorson and his partner, long-legged Raja, raised fists, the signal for the unit to form up. Jain and Coreo fell in alongside Barcas and Hosch, the dagger man with a long flap of skin hanging open on his cheek, but still grinning his manic smile.

Yet not everyone was present. Behind them, a familiar keen-ing rose above the din of the surrounding battle, and the whole unit turned toward its source.

Jesen, a two-swords man, knelt over the body of his partner. Karse, another northern warrior with one eye and an easy laugh, lay sprawled in the mud, a ragged red line carved across his throat. His good eye stared up at nothing.

Jesen's voice rose again in the high, oscillating tone. Two by two, the other Bonded pairs took it up, moving into a defensive ring around the man. Coreo put a hand on Jain's back, feel-ing the vibrations in the man's chest, a baritone counterpart to Coreo's own.

Still kneeling, Jesen reached down and touched two fingers to the blood coating Karse's neck and chest. Fingers spread wide, he then touched his own closed eyelids, drawing his fingers down and painting two bright red lines down his cheeks to his chin. The tears of the *kavapara*.

Dorson's voice broke through the chorus. "Cavalry incoming! Form up and follow me!"

Coreo glanced back at Jesen. The man stood and met his eyes, nodding. He could wait a few minutes.

"Move!" Dorson yelled.

Then they were all running, charging through the surrounding soldiers, not so much fighting as using their blades to part the sea before them.

The Bonded Legion was a legend: the greatest infantry unit in the Empire of Loremar, in which every man fought in perfect synchronicity with his beloved. Yet every unit has a weakness, and the problem with being a legend is that word tends to get around.

For the legion, that weakness was cavalry. Though they always traveled with long pikes for setting against charges, those had been abandoned with the tower shields in favor of giving the Bonded pairs the chance to use their individual strengths. Now Coreo wondered if that had been Lord Eron's plan all along—to draw them out with infantry, then trample them with cavalry. Regardless of skill and training, foot soldiers couldn't stand against a mounted charge without the proper precautions.

Off to Coreo's left, a low mound appeared, blood-slick steel shining. One of the fallen giants. "Captain!"

Coreo pointed, and Dorson followed the gesture. "Left!" the commander roared. "Take the high ground!"

The unit turned like a flock of birds, sandals biting deep into the gore-watered field. Those few enemy footmen who'd had the same idea fell easily beneath the unit's blades.

Standing, the giant would have towered higher than most castle walls, and even sprawled in death, its torso still rose nearly ten feet high. Its vaguely humanoid face was hidden behind a thick grille of steel bars, yet the ram-like horns curving out from holes in its helm were actually part of its skull. Crude armor plating covered its body, not so much worn as bolted and cauterized directly onto the beast's tough flesh. It appeared Eron the Pike was nearly as hard on his own troops as those of his enemies.

"Climb!" Dorson yelled, but the order was unnecessary. Already the first ranks were scrambling up the carcass, Coreo and Jain among them. Coreo reached down and lifted Jesen up as well. The *kavapara* said nothing, his chest heaving in rapid breaths, whites showing wide around the edges of his eyes. Jain squeezed the man's shoulder. "Just wait until after the cavalry charge, if you can."

Gaze still distant, Jesen nodded. "Good man," Jain said.

Any further conversation was cut off by a new thunder: the arrival of the cavalry, felt as much as heard. Those legionaries unable to fit atop the dead giant's torso turned, placing their backs to the corpse and setting themselves to meet the charge as enemy troops split to let the horsemen through.

Only they weren't horsemen—or rather, not in the conventional sense. Armored like a mounted knight in full plate, each of the charging warriors' humanity ended at the waist, flowing seamlessly into the chest and withers of a powerful destrier. The jet-black plate they wore stretched all the way back and down their flanks, jointed and overlapping to turn each heavy equine body into a steel juggernaut. Couched in the crook of each beast-man's arm was a long, barb-headed lance.

Jain swore softly. "Centaurs."

Coreo agreed. Normal cavalry was bad enough, but at least a knight could be unseated. A centaur *was* his steed, with a precision and grace no human rider could hope to match.

Still, the legion's tactic was a good one. With the giant at their back, the cavalry couldn't simply charge over the top of them, trampling or scattering them. They'd have to pull up short rather than charging full-on, or else risk losing or impaling themselves on their own spears as they drove through the legionaries and into the giant behind them.

"Brace!" Dorson yelled.

And then there was chaos. Even checking their momentum, the centaurs still slammed into the legionaries, some spears ending up stuck in the giant, others ramming home into human flesh. The legionaries, for their part, didn't wait for their attackers to recover, instead leaping forward, ducking low under lances as they cut at unprotected bellies or slashed hamstrings. Deprived of their natural advantage in speed, most of the centaurs dropped their lances and pulled out curved sabers, point-heavy weapons designed for taking off heads at a full canter.

The legionaries still atop the giant prepared to leap down and join the fray, but before they could, Jesen stepped forward and raised his blades. While Coreo had been fixated on the charge, the man had removed his cuirass and used the tip of one of his blades to slice the last of the *kavapara* marks—a rune of two interlocking circles—into the skin just left of his sternum, over his heart. He looked to Dorson.

The captain nodded.

With a scream that was equal parts rage and triumph, Jesen threw himself off the giant, slamming into one of the centaurs and knocking the beast-man sideways. Then he was up again, swords flashing, spinning left and right as he cut with whirlwind speed, heedless of his own safety. Behind him, the rest of the legionaries took up his cry, turning it into the keening ululation from earlier.

Coreo forced himself to watch. *Kavapara* was a beautiful, terrible thing. Deprived of his bondmate, Jesen would fight without rest or retreat until he was slain, joining Karse in the halls of the dead.

Though he knew it was selfish, Coreo hoped that when the time came, he died first—or perhaps that he and Jain could go down together, back-to-back.

But there was no time for sentiment. As Jesen disappeared into the fray, Dorson gave the signal and the rest of the legionaries hurled themselves into battle. Jain hit first, keeping his feet and swinging his sword around in a wide arc that hacked straight through a centaur's plate and into the flesh where man joined beast. Touching down a second later, Coreo darted right, deflecting the momentum of a heavy saber with his shield, arm going numb from the impact. Before the centaur could circle the awkward weapon back around for another blow, Coreo's sword carved a bright line across its flank, digging deep. The scream from inside the warrior's helmet was surprisingly equine.

"Coreo!" Jain was caught between two of the centaurs, struggling to counter both their strikes with his huge weapon. Without thinking, Coreo took two steps and leapt, hurling himself up onto the nearest one's armored back. It reared in surprise, and he grabbed the front of the thing's helm, both to help him stay on and to draw its head back, exposing the crack between helm and gorget. His blade slithered inside it, and then he was thrown free as the creature collapsed. On the other side, Jain had taken the brief respite to reverse his grip and stab backward with all his strength, plunging the great blade deep between two plates of the horseman's barding. Blood fountained.

Horns sounded. Coreo looked up, coming back from that still place his mind always went during battles, just in time to see a new wave of figures pour in from Lord Eron's side of the lines—lightly armored footmen who advanced quickly across or around the giant's corpse, wielding cudgels and—

"Nets!" Coreo shouted.

The legionaries closest to the newcomers turned to face them, but that only gave the centaurs the advantage once more. Sabers swung, biting deep, even as the slave-takers flung their nets. Packed in tight by the cavalry, men from both armies were unable to get out of the way, falling tangled in the thick ropes.

Standing back-to-back with Jain once more, Coreo managed to dodge the first net flung at him—but Jain wasn't so lucky. The big man's sword point caught in the loose weave, tangling hopelessly. Coreo lunged, arm and blade making a perfect line, and took the net man in the chest, careful to keep his blade parallel with the ground to avoid catching between ribs.

The back of his head exploded with pain. The world tilted, and then he was on the ground, seeing everything in sideways view as the soldier who'd clubbed him stepped forward and flung his net across Jain's suddenly unguarded back.

"Jain!" Coreo shoved himself up onto hands and knees, but there was something wrong with his balance, and the world tilted again, drawing him back down. Still he could see Jain. Like a great northern bear, the man surged against the net, slamming into the man holding its rope. Then another settled over him, pulling back the other direction, driving him down to one knee. A third man raised a cudgel in both hands. Again there came a sound of horns, ringing through the wool wrapping the battlefield. Jain met Coreo's eyes.

A boot caught Coreo in the side of the head, and the world went dark.

Seventeen.

Coreo stood in a circle with the others, yet there was no comfort in their presence. His right ear still made it sound as if everything were far away, but no amount of muffling could hold out the wailing ululation coming from the men's throats. From his own. When it was his turn, he took the knife and carved the joined circles into his breast, then dipped two fingers in the blood and drew them down his cheeks.

Seventeen pairs broken. Far more lucky enough to die together. If Loremar's army hadn't surged precisely when they did, the whole legion might have been slain or taken prisoner. As it was, Lord Eron's soldiers had been pushed back long enough for the survivors to retreat with the wounded. Of the seventeen new *kavapara*, four had partners among the dead. The rest had been taken by Eron's unexpected ploy with the nets.

Everyone knew what capture meant. Lord Eron the Pike hadn't earned his name by keeping prisoners. He simply liked to take his time.

Jain. Coreo closed his eyes, feeling the blood already cooling and drying on his cheeks, and passed the knife to the next man.

Horns. Drums. Shouts. Up and down the lines, soldiers readied themselves. After three days of repositioning and licking wounds, it was finally time for the next battle.

Coreo's last.

The keening song fell silent as Captain Dorson and Raja approached. The left side of the captain's face was one enormous purple bruise, but he still exuded his unyielding air of command. Instead of his sword, however, he carried an unfurled scroll. The rest of the legionaries, who had moved back to give the *kavapara* space, crowded close again, craning their necks.

The captain's voice was a whip crack. "They're not dead."

Silence. Then, "Sir?"

"*Lord* Eron sent us a message," Dorson said, holding up the letter. "The men he took haven't been killed—yet. He's offering us a deal: switch sides, and he'll return our prisoners."

A murmur burned through the ranks.

It was a brilliant move. The Bonded Legion wasn't just an elite unit—it was a symbol. If they defected at a crucial moment, it could break Loremar's lines. Demoralize the whole army.

None of it mattered. *Jain? Alive?*

Coreo heard a voice, and was surprised to recognize it as his own. "Why are you telling us this?"

Dorson looked from face to face among the *kavapara*. "Because those are your men out there," he said quietly. "And every warrior in this legion is your brother. I can't put the lives of thirteen men above the unit's honor. But if you choose to go, no one will stop you. Maybe Lord Eron will still release them."

Coreo looked around, seeing the truth in the eyes of the other soldiers, the question in the other *kavapara*. He thought of Jain—the golden curls of his beard, the stubborn set of his shoulders. So strong. So fierce.

So *loyal*.

He stepped forward. "We're *kavapara*. Our partners are dead, and so are we."

Captain Dorson reached out and clasped Coreo's wrist tightly. "Not yet, you aren't. Not by a long shot."

"Now!"

At Dorson's command, three legionaries lifted their spears, each flying a red-and-black uniform stripped from one of Eron's fallen soldiers. At the same time, the unit clustered together, forming ranks once more and marching straight into Eron's lines.

As promised, the soldiers there broke apart, letting the Bonded Legion pass with cheers and laughter. From behind came frantic shouts and horn blasts as Loremar's other commanders attempted to fill the sudden hole in their ranks. Eron's men closed in behind the defecting legion, pouring into the breach with a roar.

The screams and crashing of steel made Coreo's skin crawl, but he forced himself to stare straight ahead as he marched, not looking back at the results of their betrayal.

Lord Eron had set up a pavilion on top of a low, treeless hill toward the rear of the lines, safely out of the direct conflict and bordered on three sides by rocky cliff, giving it a commanding view of the surroundings. It was to this stony knob that the Bonded Legion marched, faces grim but backs straight. At the hill's foot, Eron's honor guard stopped them, forming a wall of shields and helms.

Eron had apparently decided to decorate. All around the edges of the hill, tall pikes stood upright in the dirt, impaling naked corpses so fresh that some still twitched. Coreo refused to let himself search their faces. Jain couldn't be among them. Not yet.

At the top of the hill, Lord Eron emerged from his tent. He was a surprisingly small man for a warlord, and wore simple black leather rather than the shining plate of Loremar's commander. Coreo was surprised to find that the Butcher Lord was actually rather handsome, with a thin moustache and slicked-back black hair. He smiled warmly as he surveyed the defectors, hands clasped casually behind his back.

"I'll admit," he said, voice carrying easily over the now distant sounds of battle, "I had some doubts. Would the famed love of the Bonded Legion really be enough to make them forsake their duty, surrendering their whole force—their whole *empire*—for the sake of a few men?" The smile broadened. "Yet here you are."

"Show us our men," Dorson called. "Prove that they're still alive."

Lord Eron inclined his head. "Of course."

He waved a hand, and several attendants leapt to one of the canvas-sided structures, pulling at knots and cords. A moment later, one whole side fell away, revealing that behind the stiff fabric was a huge cage of metal-reinforced wood. Inside, a group of men huddled together, naked except for their loincloths. Many were bloody, but all looked up in surprise as the canvas was removed.

One particularly large man, his head bandaged and beard flecked with dried blood, sat holding his knees to his chest. As he caught sight of Coreo, however, his slumped shoulders straightened.

Jain.

"As you see, they haven't been harmed any more than necessary to pacify them," Eron said. "I'm a man of honor. Despite the fact that you're now surrounded by my forces, my offer still stands: fight for me, as passionately as you fought for Loremar, and you will be reunited with your men. You'll be the shining spearhead of my invasion, with all the honors and privileges that entails. Neither I nor my soldiers will hold any grudges."

Dorson's thin-lipped expression didn't change. "We've already agreed to your terms. Give us our men."

Eron raised an index finger and waggled it admonishingly. "Please, Captain. I'm not a fool. Just because I'm a man of honor doesn't mean I expect anyone else to be so. Your men will be returned to you safely—*after* you've led an attack against the center of Loremar's lines. One so bloody and ruthless that there's no way they'd ever take you back, even if you tried to switch sides again. Though I imagine your defection already burned most of your bridges in that regard."

Dorson grunted. "Fair enough. But if it pleases you, my lord, I'd like to propose an alternative plan."

Eron's eyebrows rose. "Oh?"

The legion charged. There were no battle cries, no posturing— simply a wave of motion as more than a hundred men surged into motion. So disconcerting was the silence of their attack that many of Eron's honor guard stood frozen, not believing their eyes even as swords and axes rammed home between plates of armor, blood spurting out around hilts and shafts.

Then the moment of surprise was past. With a roar, the full weight of Eron's army crashed down on the legionaries.

Coreo was caught in a surging ocean of metal and flesh, awash in the hot stink of blood and shit as men gasped and died on all sides. He slammed his shield into the helm of one soldier, dropping him with a satisfying clang, then spun to slam his sword up under another soldier's tasset, through the underlying padding and deep into his thigh. It felt strangely naked to be fighting without Jain, but that was the nature of *kavapara*—you fought alone, letting your fury carry you.

Except that he wasn't *kavapara*. Not anymore.

They were hopelessly outnumbered. This deep in Eron's camp, Loremar's forces would never even know what happened to them, let alone be able to support them. Yet therein lay the legionaries' one advantage.

Eron had been so focused on cutting them off from any escape or reinforcement that he'd placed most of his forces behind the legionaries, leaving only a fraction standing between him and the presumably defeated men. That honor guard still outnumbered the legionaries three to one—but the Bonded men didn't need to kill them all. Only enough to break through.

Coreo let one man press him hard, feigning a stumble beneath the man's axe blows, then ducked sideways as Hosch's spear shot over his head and took the man in the throat. Coreo returned the favor by stretching out and cutting the legs from under another soldier who threatened the spearman. A savagely grinning Barcas streaked past him in a running crouch, face covered in blood and daggers in both hands. Then Coreo was back up and bringing his sword to bear on another man.

Foot by foot, the Bonded Legion moved up the hill.

Above, horns called for reinforcements, yet those reinforcements couldn't reach the command tents without first passing through the fracas. The same cliffs that defended the command tents made it impossible for Eron to retreat.

Another of Eron's soldiers fell, and Coreo was surprised to suddenly find himself in the open at the top of the rise. To his left, the honor guard was pulling back to form a defensive ring around Lord Eron and his retainers. Coreo ignored them and darted right instead, toward the cage.

The bars were thick wooden dowels wrapped with wire. Behind them, the men were standing now—not calling or pleading, but watching with silent anticipation. Coreo ignored them as best he could—*Jain!*—and focused on the door's locking mechanism. It was a simple bar of iron as wide as Coreo's forearm, slid horizontal across the door and locked with a padlock.

Damn. Coreo spun back toward the fight, and in a few seconds had what he needed: one of the honor guard's bardiches, its head a thick crescent blade on the end of an eight-foot pole. Sheathing his sword, he picked it up and swung it hard at the lock.

Chink! The blade hit with a shock that Coreo felt up through his shoulders, yet only grazed the lock.

With a growl, Coreo twisted again, throwing all his weight into a spin that whipped the blade around and—

Snap! The blade sheared through the lock's haft, its edge chipping horribly as the lock fell away. Coreo threw it aside and slammed the bar open.

Cheering men poured out, scooping up weapons and joining the fray. One of them grabbed Coreo and lifted him, squeezing the air from his lungs with arms like tree trunks.

"Jain," Coreo croaked.

Tears of joy streaked down into the big man's golden beard as he set Coreo back down and held him at arm's length. Jain's palms cupped Coreo's cheeks, smearing the painted tears of the *kavapara* and the real ones that had appeared alongside them.

"What took you so long?" Jain asked.

Coreo laughed, then drew his sword. "Some of us didn't get to sit around in a cage like a pampered songbird. Come on."

"Pampered!" Jain stooped and grabbed the chipped bardiche, snapping its haft to turn it into an axe. "I'll show you *pampered!*"

"I expect you will," Coreo said, and then they were back in the fight.

The battle had turned into a series of rings. The Bonded Legion had Lord Eron's retinue surrounded, yet at the same time was surrounded by Lord Eron's seemingly endless host. The thin ring of Loremar warriors fought in two lines, one facing out and one facing in, with only a few paces between them. Coreo and Jain moved up the shifting corridor and threw themselves at the remaining honor guard.

Jain's axe carved a swath, and Coreo followed it, keeping the enemy from getting inside the big man's guard while the heavy weapon reversed. His shield protected Jain's flank even as the man's axe deflected a blow meant for Coreo's head. They spun past each other, lunging in unison, and Coreo's heart pounded to their shared rhythm.

Then the last man before them fell, helm sheared halfway through by Jain's blow. Coreo leapt across the corpse and shoved aside panicked, perfumed courtesans.

Lord Eron's sword thrust at Coreo's left side, quick as a viper, and Coreo blocked it. He raised his own blade again just in time to see Jain step past him and slam a single meaty fist into the lord's jaw.

The nobleman fell like a sack of onions, collapsing to the dirt. Coreo wrapped his fingers in that greased black hair and lifted, hauling the man to his feet. Lord Eron shrieked, only cutting off as Coreo's sword touched his throat.

"Hold!" Jain's deep bass thundered over the sounds of battle. "Hold or your lord dies!"

Jain's words were picked up and repeated, rushing across the battle like a wind across waves. Slowly, the crash of combat faded to a ragged edge, distant yells, and the moans of the wounded. Those honor guard still left within the inner circle held their weapons ready, yet made no move to attack, turning their nervous attention on their lord. Beyond the line of legionaries, the rest of Eron's forces moved back warily.

"Good work." Captain Dorson limped through the press of bodies, leaning heavily on Raja's shoulder. The captain's left leg was a bloody mess, a leather belt cinched tight around his upper thigh. He motioned for Coreo to turn the captured lord to face him, and Coreo complied, twisting Eron's hair even tighter.

"Eron the Pike," Dorson said, "I hereby take you prisoner in the name of Loremar and the Imperial Council. Tell your men to stand down."

Lord Eron spat. "Why? Your men are surrounded. Even if you kill me, you'll never make it out alive. Every one of you will be butchered. My men will crack you open and nail your entrails to the trees."

"True," Dorson said quietly. "But you won't be here to see it. That's enough for me."

Eron glared, but Coreo could feel the man's body trembling. He let his sword slide up the lord's neck, shaving off the tiniest curl of flesh.

"I yield!" Eron called. "Stand down, all of you!"

There was a murmur and a rustle, but the honor guards lowered their weapons. Several legionaries began to move among them, removing weapons and binding hands.

Dorson turned away, finding another pair of men. "You—Kriesa and Falos. Go through that tent behind us and find something to make a hostage flag. Use the canvas if you have to. Salo and Ebermeir, find some furniture in there and rig up a sedan chair—I want to make sure that our guest is clearly displayed. Everyone else, get ready to form up and march out of here. Stay alert—it may be there are some here who don't care much for their lord's safety." The men he'd singled out nodded and turned away.

"Why?" Eron's voice was low, almost conversational, yet it carried.

Dorson turned back. "Beg pardon, your highness?"

"Why?" Eron asked again. "You were outnumbered. I offered you a fair deal. Instead, you put your entire command at risk and lost men you didn't have to." His eyes flicked from Dorson to Coreo, Jain, and others. "It should have worked."

Dorson laughed. "You don't know the Legion, then."

"But I had your men!" Eron's indignant tone sounded as if he thought he might argue his way to victory. "Everyone knows about Loremar's band of lovers. I wagered that you loved your own men more than you loved your empire, and I was right! Yet you fought anyway."

"So we did." Dorson gave the lord a smile, then turned it on Coreo. "Why is that, Coreo? Eron here had your man. Why'd you decide to fight?"

Coreo blinked. He was hardly a man for words. But…"Because I knew Jain wouldn't accept anything less." Behind him, Jain reached up and squeezed his shoulder.

"That's what your type never understands," Dorson said, turning back to Eron. "You think our love makes us vulnerable—that we'll be afraid to risk our partners in battle." He looked up at Raja. The lanky, black-skinned man smiled back at him and shook his head in amusement.

"Your soldiers," Dorson continued, "they've got wives back home. Children. Something to distract them, make them wish for the war to be over—one way or another—so that they can just *go home.* But us? Our partners are warriors. Everything we have is out there on that field, fighting beside us." He snaked an arm around Raja's waist and drew him close against his side. "Your men want to go home. Mine *are* home."

Lord Eron sniffed to show what he thought of that, and Coreo pressed his sword a little deeper, cutting him off mid-snort.

"Captain!" Four men came out of the tent holding an ornate wooden chair.

"Perfect," Dorson said. "Strap him to it. Get the other prisoners in a rope line behind it."

Several men moved forward, taking Eron from Coreo. Coreo let him go, wiping his hand on his tunic to try and remove the hair grease. Next to him, Jain laughed.

"A fine answer," the big man said, pulling him close again. "Very fine."

"Was I lying?" Coreo spoke directly into the big man's shoulder. "Would you still love me if I had turned coat to save you, rather than trying to break you out?"

"No." Jain's voice was flat, cold. Coreo felt a chill run through him. He pushed against the big man's chest, moving back until he could see Jain's face. The northman's features could have been carved out of stone.

Then he smiled, eyes crinkling and beard splitting wide. He ran fingers lightly through Coreo's sweat-soaked hair.

"No," the big man said again, softer. "But only because then you wouldn't have been you."

They kissed, beard meeting smooth-shaved chin. Around them, horns blew, and the Bonded Legion began to march.

Bone Candy

A Black Company Story

GLEN COOK

THE CAMPAIGN SEASON WAS OVER. THE WEATHER STANK. THE DARK Horse was packed elbow to asshole. There wasn't enough make-work to keep the troops busy. Markeg Zhorab's wife and sister had to help him serve. The wicked of mind hoped he would bring out his delectable daughter.

Otto checked his last card, cursed. A turn as dealer had not helped. His luck was still dreadful. "You're damned grim for a guy that keeps winning, Croaker."

"Bad nightmare last night. Still feeling it."

Silent signed, "Same one?"

"Third night in a row."

Otto grinned. "Your honey must be missing you." The old canard.

Silent signed, "Stop that."

My turn. I pounced, down with eleven. Otto cursed. Silent shook his head, resigned. Corey, in One-Eye's usual seat, pretended to wipe away tears. "When is the battlefield not a battlefield?"

"Huh?" Sergeant Otto grunted. "That some dumb-ass riddle?"

"One-Eye asked me that last time we talked."

Silent was the only wizard in the tavern. I asked, "Where *are* Goblin and One-Eye?"

Their apprentice, the Third, was missing, too. He did not usually stray far from the beer. Those two can drive anyone to drink.

217

Otto collected Silent's deal like he feared the cards would bite. "Them two are gone together, that could be bad."

Those two wizards are always up to no good but not usually together. The table fell into a deep disquiet. Corey muttered, "Definitely not good." Silent nodded grimly.

Zhorab delivered an untimely pitcher, muttered, "Flies." He hustled off, loath to leave his bar undefended.

I discarded. Corey snagged the card, spread a five-six-seven-eight, but nobody groused. Everybody suddenly had a whole lot of nothing to discuss. Cards and drinks had become totally fascinating.

Two Dead stepped into the room. Long, lean, skeletal, he needed more legs and eyes to complete himself.

Otto murmured, "When is the battlefield not a battlefield?"

That could be more than one question depending on how you heard it.

Two Dead. Real name, Shor Chodroze, wizard colonel from Eastern Army HQ with plenipotentiary powers. A blessing upon the Black Company bestowed by the Taken Whisper. He never volunteered anything about his real mission. He was said to be an unpredictably nasty sociopath. Our main wizards disappeared right after he arrived. He was Two Dead because when he rolled in with one oversize bodyguard, all bluster and self-regard, the lieutenant had declared, "That man ain't worth two dead flies."

Otto dealt. The rest of us shrank. Somebody was about to get unhappy.

I met Two Dead's gaze, as always amazed that he owned two good eyes. The left side of his face featured a lightning bolt of bruise-colored scar tissue, forehead to chin, but his eye had survived. I suspected a glancing upward thrust from an infantry pole arm.

He headed our way. And...something had him spooked. Not good, a sorcerer with the heebie-jeebies.

We were not the cause. He held us in abiding contempt. Still, he kept his bodyguard close. He knew his Company history.

Where was Buzzard Neck now?

Two Dead pointed at me, then Silent. "You two. Come with me. Bring your gear."

I always lug a bag. You never know when some idiot will need sewing up.

Silent took two steps out into the street, stopped dead. I banged into his back. "Hey! None of your mime stuff!" He had picked up the hobby recently.

This was not that. This was a response to the weather.

A wind hummed in from the north, flinging snow pellets into our faces.

The chill did not bother Two Dead. Nor had he been drinking. The cold shock had me hungry to piss, but Two Dead barked, "Come!"

I came.

Buzz awaited us in full battle gear, including a great goofy old-time kite shield. His expression was pinched. He had obvious stomach troubles.

He was a house in boots. Guys like him usually end up being called Tiny or Little Whoever, and are dim, but this walking building was supernaturally quick, monster strong, and twice as smart as the creep who employed him.

He was Buzzard Neck because his neck was long and crooked and included an Adam's apple like an Adam's melon. The name quickly shrank to Buzz.

He never said much. He was as well-liked as Two Dead was well-loathed. He claimed to have survived some of the shit the Company had, including the Battle at Charm.

Two Dead headed out. We followed, me hoping I would not have to hold it long.

Technically, we could have told Two Dead to go pound sand. He was not in our chain of command. But he was tight with Whisper, and Whisper was hungry for excuses to pound the Company. Also, he might be a cat underfoot for a long time. Not to mention, I was really curious about what could give the spider wizard the jimjams.

Aloe sprawls without being big, though it is the grandest metropolis for a hundred miles. Two Dead led us a third of a mile, to the lee of a redbrick box on whitewashed limestone foundations.

"There." He indicated a mound of brown fur in a dried-out flower patch. Wind stirred the fur and dead leaves.

I opined, "It don't look healthy."

Silent said nothing. Buzz clutched his gut.

I asked, "What is it?" Not a badger. It was too big and the color was wrong. Not a bear. It was too small.

"I don't know," Two Dead said. "It smells of sorcery."

Silent nodded. Buzz looked desperate to take a squat.

I stepped left, relieved myself at last. Steam rose to meet randomly falling snowflakes. Fat flakes. It must be getting warmer.

I eased closer. The beast was curled up like a pill bug.

Two Dead said, "There were two others. They scooted when they saw us."

Buzz said, "I didn't see them."

Two Dead said, "They ran a few steps and just faded out." He was nervous all over again. How come?

I asked, "What did they look like?"

"Giant beavers or woodchucks? They were gone too quick to tell."

Well. Beavers and groundhogs are somewhat less fierce than bears.

This one was not the right shade for a woodchuck. I didn't know about giant beavers, though.

I noted a stir not caused by the wind.

Silent offered a sorcery alert.

Two Dead said, "Something magical is about to happen." He did not mean magical in a wondrous surprise for the kids kind of way.

The moment disappointed. It expired without calamity.

I took a knee, faked veterinary skills.

The animal breathed slow and shallow and had a faint heartbeat. Hibernating? Some bears just drop in place when the sleepy season comes.

It didn't waken and shred me. Two Dead took that as license to revert to his old obnoxious self.

Silent and I hauled the beast on Buzz's shield. Buzz was too damned big to help. The downhill end had to carry most of the weight. Plus, he was having trouble keeping his trousers clean.

The beast sprawled on a table in my clinic. Two Dead perched like a spider on a stool close by, manfully keeping his yap shut. The captain and Otto were present as well. Like Two Dead, they kept quiet while the professional me worked. Buzz was off haunting a latrine.

"This is one ugly gob of snot," the professional said. Stretched out it looked more like a baboon than a beaver. Its face was a fright mask of scarlet skin. It had teeth fit for a crocodile. Its eyes were snakelike. Each foot included semi-retractable claws and a stubby but opposable thumb.

"It's starting to smell like a vulture's breath," Otto observed.

Its heart rate was rising, too. "The cold must have laid it down." Our vile weather might not be all bad.

The captain jiggered the flue on my heating stove.

"Then these things shouldn't be dangerous till the weather changes." It would, local boy Corey had promised. We would see one more spring-like week before winter came to stay.

Otto prodded, "Croaker?" There was work to do. Critical work. The Old Man was here his own self.

Did they know something? Two Dead certainly wondered.

The Old Man was all fired-up curious. "It's supernatural, right? What kind? Where from? Was it summoned? Is it invasive? Somebody talk to me." He was sure that Two Dead was to blame.

Two Dead shook his head. "I promise, it's new to me."

"Where are Goblin and One-Eye? Anybody know?"

Otto said, "They ain't been seen for days."

I reminded, "The colonel says there were more of these things. Better find the others while it's cold."

Otto mused, "Warfare by elliptical means?"

"When is the battlefield not a battlefield?"

We had crushed the Rebel in the region, a success that troubled some "friends." Vast incompetence and corruption had been turned up, which the guilty resented. Whisper's own discomfort was why we had Two Dead as a guest.

I had hoped the Rebel survivors would slink away to recruit, to train, to collect weapons and supplies, and to wait for us to be transferred. Informants said that quiet season would never come. Senior Rebels wanted Aloe back. The Port of Shadows might be hidden here.

Aloens did not understand that echo out of deep time. Rebel insiders did. The honest ones got so scared they sometimes came over to us.

I read a lot. I root around in folklore, legend, and local history. Port of Shadows references a plot to resurrect the Dominator, lord of the old Domination. He is still a demigod to some. The Port of Shadows is a gateway he can use to escape his tomb.

Some Rebel chieftains are closet Resurrectionists. The Lady has been plagued by them since she escaped her own grave, leaving him behind.

The Old Man and his cronies are worried, but they do not confide in the Annalist. The Annalist writes things down.

Might this monster be a Resurrectionist tool? Our enemies had not yet gone supernaturally asymmetric. Sneaking lethal paranormal uglies into an enemy camp was more like something we would do.

The captain leaned in, tempting the beast. He asked Silent, "Have Croaker cut it up to look at its insides? Or cage it and wait?"

Silent shrugged. He was out of his element.

The captain asked Two Dead, "Suggestions, Colonel?" while looking for some subtle tell.

The beast had been the sorcerer's discovery.

Two Dead remained unperturbed. He had come to us suspect. That would never change. "Let it live, but keep it cold. Find the others. Examine a healthy one." He eyed Silent.

Silent shrugged again, stubbornly frugal with his opinions.

I bent close, combed fur, hunting vermin. Fleas, ticks, lice, all tell tales. "This thing is getting warmer..." I reeled back, shoved by Silent. He pointed. Flakes of obsidian ash had puffed out of a nostril. "Hand me a sample bottle." Then, "Make that a bunch."

A black beetle stomped into the light, as shiny as the flakes. It glared around, measuring the world for conquest.

The Old Man asked, "That some kind of scarab?"

A second bug marched out, bumped into the first. Number one was in a bad mood. Bam! No threat display. No ritual dance. The bugs started trying to murder one another with ridiculous bear-trap jaws.

I whined, "Anybody got any idea what the hell?"

Nope. Two Dead, though, did snag my biggest glass jar, which he shoved over the beast's head. He packed the gaps with handy rags.

Otto took off in a big hurry, leaving the door halfway open. Snow blew in before Silent shut it.

Black flakes presaged the emergence of more beetles. These were not immediate bugacidal maniacs. They just wanted to leave. The jar frustrated their ambitions.

Then they went berserk. "What a racket." The captain was rattled, something you seldom saw.

The host animal began to deflate. Two Dead stuffed more bandages. A few beetles, struck brilliant, snipped cloth chunks with those nasty jaws.

"We need a container big enough for the whole thing," Two Dead said. "Maybe a pickle barrel."

Bam! Otto came back lugging a big tin box with a latch-down top that hailed from the commissary, where it kept grain and flour free of vermin.

"Perfect," Two Dead declared, nonplussed. This was too-quick thinking by people he wanted to be too dull to notice him nudging them onto a hangman's trap.

Otto said, "Push it in, glass and all." He positioned the tin so Two Dead could shove the beast in.

Two Dead held his paws up like a dog begging. He should soil his delicate fingers?

"Really?" the Old Man barked. "Push the damned thing!"

A particularly formidable beetle chose that moment to make his getaway via the beast's nether orifice. A Two Dead finger was nearby. It took a bite. Two Dead howled, "Oh, shit! Gods damn, that hurts!"

An even studlier bug tromped forth as the beast flopped forward. It had even more ridiculous jaws and a back end like a long, thin funnel. It flew at Two Dead, literally, wing cases flung high, ladybug style. It landed on the back of the sorcerer's left hand, grabbed hold, took a hearty bite. Then it stood on its nose, curled its tail down, drove its tip into the wound.

All that took only an eye-blink to happen. Two Dead shrieked again.

Silent crunched the bug.

Otto pounded the lid onto the can. The monster left several wriggling grubs on the table. The Old Man chased escaped beetles. Silent and I wrestled Two Dead into a chair. He began to shake. Shock? The bites did not look that bad. Silent hand signed, "It laid eggs."

The sealed tin sang like a metal roof in a hailstorm.

The Old Man killed one last fugitive bug, turned on the grubs. "Otto, take the can to the trash pit. Then get every swinging dick out looking for the other two animals. Hire tracking dogs." He moved over to watch as I dug almost invisibly tiny cream-color beads out of Two Dead's hand.

Otto left with the singing biscuit tin. And busted back in half a minute later. "Look what I found sneaking around with a sack of stolen bread and bacon." He had our apprentice sorcerer, the Third, by the scruff of the neck.

The kid was not happy. Truth be, he had had few shots at happiness since he got tangled up with Goblin and One-Eye.

The Old Man settled into a chair, leaned back, considered the Third. He put on his "I'm eager to hear how you'll try to bullshit me on this" face.

Silent passed me a jar of carbolic. I put bug eggs in, then dribbled liquid onto Two Dead's wounds. He squealed.

The Third volunteered, "One-Eye sent me to fetch food."

Really? That little shit is not big on bacon. On the other hand, the Third would devour it by the hog side.

I worked on Two Dead. Silent watched grubs in a jar. They behaved no better than adults. The Old Man glared at the Third. The level of noise outside rose. Otto had relayed the captain's orders.

Buzz stumbled in looking like death warmed over. His sojourn in the latrine had not helped much.

The Third said, "I was getting stuff for me. Otto spotted me before I started on One-Eye's stuff."

I observed, "The kid has his priorities straight."

Two Dead managed a ghost smile. His shakes continued.

The Old Man grumped, "Watch the colonel till you're sure he'll be all right. We don't hand Whisper any fresh excuses. You." He poked the Third. "You're with me."

Buzz wanted to fuss over his boss. Two Dead growled, "You look like a man with the drizzling shits, Tesch. Smell like one, too." He poked me with his unbitten hand. "I'll live. Help him."

I thought Buzz must have drunk some bad water. He ought to know better. I loaded him with liquids and orders not to stray far from the latrine. He was unhappy about not being able to stick close to Two Dead.

"Yet here you are alive and recuperating," I observed after Two Dead suggested that the Company might have rigged all this. "You probably conjured those animals yourself and just accidentally got the bad end."

That was plain chin music, ridiculousness in exchange for

absurdity, but Two Dead found something curious there. Like was he supposed to get it with the rest of us?

I was tempted to pin a target on Whisper's back. The more discord at HQ the less time those people would have to harass us out here.

I reiterated the common remark: "When is the battlefield not a battlefield?"

Two Dead eyed me. "An intriguing question, physician. Worth considering here, in these troubled times." He cocked his head, listened. I caught a vague hint of distant wind chimes. That rattled me. It tied into my recurrent nightmare somehow. "I'm going to lie down and brood on it." Two Dead indicated a cot.

I was snuggled into a cot and blankets myself. The captain poked me. "What's wrong with him?" Head jerk toward Two Dead, on his back, on his cot. Drool glistened on his ugly cheek. Snot hung from the nostril on that side. Dead sexy.

"What time is it?"

"Nighttime. We got the other beasts. What about Chodroze?"

"He was his old ugly self when I laid down." I set my feet on the cold dirt floor, rose with a groan, toddled over. Our chatter had not awakened Two Dead.

I felt the heat before I touched him.

The Captain said, "The dogs found them, unconscious from the cold. The men tinned them up and threw them in the fire pit."

"We need to pack Two Dead with snow. He's burning up."

"Whatever. Keep him healthy."

Two Dead had a weak, fast, irregular pulse and a dangerous fever. "I'll need help cooling him down." I started stripping him. That did not waken him. "What did the Third have to say?"

The Old Man looked like he had bitten into a chunk of alum candy.

Goblin and One-Eye *were* up to something. And he might not entirely disapprove.

Dead fierce, he snagged a bucket and headed outside. The weather had turned enthusiastically blizzardy.

He returned with a pail of muddy snow.

I indicated Two Dead's wounded arm. Scarlet threads ran up it from the uglier wound.

"Blood poisoning?"

"Some kind of poisoning. Blood poisoning isn't usually so aggressive."

Skin flexed near Two Dead's worst wound. I had not gotten every egg.

"Help me get him on the table. I'll clear the wound. You pack him with snow. Start with his head and throat. We need to cool his brain."

Move made. Snow packed and melting onto the floor to make mud. I dug with a scalpel. The Old Man hauled more snow.

"How about we just dump him in a snowdrift?"

"I need light to work." I had excised two thin grubs. They writhed in an alcohol bath. I was after what I hoped was the last.

"Those bitty things caused the blood poisoning?"

"Their shit is probably toxic."

"Ugly."

"Life is." In some forms, ugly for lots of us.

I fit puzzle pieces while I worked, hoping I was fooling myself, but afraid I was looking chaos in the crimson, googly eye.

"How come the tourniquet?"

"Keeping the poison contained. To avoid amputation if I can."

"That wouldn't be good."

No. "I should ask what he wants, worst case, but he won't wake up."

"We need more hands. Maybe Silent can get to him."

"I can't go. Where the hell is Buzz?"

"Buzz is in his rack, down and out and soaked in shit. He'd be dead if you hadn't given him that tea. Poor Corey is babysitting. I'll get another bucket, then head out on a recruiting tour."

So. Old Buzz came down with the drizzling shits right when his principal started dying from an infestation of supernatural parasites. That wanted a closer look. The timeline might tell us when Buzz picked up what was trying to kill him. Also, maybe who was there when it happened.

I winkled the last worm out. The Old Man brought more snow. I mused, "When is the battlefield not a battlefield?"

The captain eyed me oddly, shrugged, took off with his trained-bear shuffle.

The day's puzzle might have an explanation hidden inside the recurring question. That might put me eyeball to eyeball with a repellant cousin question that could have multiple readings as well. "When is my enemy not an enemy?"

Otto and his pal Hagop turned up. The captain had caught them trying to sneak off to town to help Markeg Zhorab get a little bit richer. They hauled snow.

We did not see the captain again right away. He went and stole a short nap. When he did turn up he had the Third in tow, all decorated with light shackles. "He's all we got. Silent is missing now, too."

The Third shook his wild shock of curls, lost in the insanities.

Answers had to wait. Two Dead was not improving. Snow packs were not enough. I told the Third, "I need the colonel awake. We need to talk. Amputation may be his only salvation. I can't decide that for him."

"Why bother? We could get shot of him."

"I save whoever I can." Not that I have not made exceptions. Not that Two Dead was insufficiently despicable to make the "he needs killing" list. "And he's Whisper's pet."

"Don't smell like that special a relationship to me." The Third eyed Two Dead. "It'll be tough. Feels like Silent put him in a coma for the pain."

"You can't bring him out?"

"Didn't say that. Said it's gonna be tough. Get ready for some serious screaming. His arm is gonna feel like it's on fire."

"Hang on then." I slathered Two Dead's forearm with topical painkiller. "All right. Go."

Two Dead surprised us. He did not let the pain unhinge him. He was creepy normal, disinclined to shed any limbs unnecessarily.

He was short four already, you asked me.

"I won't do it casually," I promised.

He was caught in a cleft stick. I had no reason to wish him well, but he did realize that I would not just maim him when death by inattention would be so much easier.

He played through the pain. "If it's the best choice, do it." His speech slurred. I kept feeding him painkiller tea.

The captain talked to him steadily, gently, casually, like he was Two Dead's cousin. He wanted to slide inside the sorcerer's head while he was addled.

I set up to cut, ever more sure that it could not be avoided. I listened. Two Dead made no sense. He was old, hardcore, and stubborn. The Old Man was unlikely to get much.

Then he did get something that I missed. He buttoned up and hit the weather and was gone for fifteen minutes.

I got Two Dead strapped down. The Third whined, "Can I go? I don't want to see this."

"You're going to be Company, you'd better get used to blood." Which sparked memories I would rather not have recalled. I have eaten a lot of bone candy with the Company.

There was no choice. Two Dead's body could not resist the poison. "Sorry, Colonel." Our senior sorcerers might have helped, but they were unavailable. Best not mention that. Two Dead supposedly had a fecund bent for paranoid violence.

He glared at the Third. The Third said, "I am sorry, sir. I'll do my best, but medical sorcery isn't among my skills."

Pain kept Two Dead from helping himself.

I asked the captain, "How goes the search for our favorite duo?"

"Still missing." He eyed Two Dead like he suspected a connection.

I asked, "Go ahead, Colonel? Final decision time."

Two Dead nodded grimly, probably rehearsing cruelties he would visit on those who had brought him to this, deliberately or otherwise.

"Would you like to remain awake during the procedure?"

"Put me out. Tesch won't shit himself forever. Anything goes wrong, he'll see that I don't walk the road to Hell by myself."

I smelled bluster and some graveyard sneaking-past, whistling.

"As you wish, sir." I soaked a bandage with pale green fluid. "Third, hold this over his face. Lightly! He has to breathe it."

The patient went under in seconds. "Third, Captain, watch me close in case there are questions later."

The Third narrowly avoided messing himself. He got the subtext.

I started. I talked while I worked. "Do Goblin and One-Eye being missing have anything to do with our beetle-infested weasels?"

No reply.

"There is something going on. I'm not blind."

"They could be up to something illegal," the captain said, carefully. "More likely, though, you're seeing something just because you want to."

The Third protested, "They were just trying to get the straight skinny on Two Dead and Buzzard Neck. They aren't what you think. Goblin knows Buzz from the Battle at Charm."

I suffered a half-ass flashback to my nightmare. It did not affect my work. That was old, familiar labor. I could hack off a limb while dead drunk or ready to collapse from exhaustion.

The captain shrugged. He was playing it close.

When is the battlefield not a battlefield? The enemy of my enemy is what and who?

When did those two wizards turn invisible? Right after Two Dead showed up. Because of Buzz? Was he more than just Two Dead's lifeguard?

All this drama, and our empire still controls half the world.

The Lady loves the chaos. While her underlings are backstabbing and undercutting each other they are too busy to move on her. She can focus on keeping her husband underground.

The Old Man wakened me again. "Going to sleep your life away?" He did not roll out the old saw about sleeping all I wanted after I was dead. He made a hand sign. Four men shifted Buzz from a litter to a table.

I asked, "What was that?"

"What was what?"

"Thought I heard wind chimes. Really faint."

"Maybe you're still dreaming."

Crap! I had been. The nightmare. The Lady was in there with somebody who moved in wind-chime tinkle... *Was* it a dream? Or something from the Tower? *She* does touch me strangely, at the oddest of times.

No matter. I was awake now. It was gone, and what was happening in the waking world seemed less rational than any dream. I had cooked up a fresh stew of weird ideas while I was off in slumberville.

I had a client. "Couldn't you clean him up before you brought him in? I'll need a month to air the place out."

Buzz might have been belly up now if I had not worked on him earlier. His situation was that grim.

Corey had helped bring Buzz in. The kid was dead on his feet. "I tried to keep him hydrated, but whatever I put in the top end came out the bottom like there was a pipe straight through."

"Let me check some stuff."

Buzz's pulse was fast and feeble. His temperature was fierce. I peeled back an eyelid. His pupil was a pinpoint. That did not add up. I smelled his breath, risky even when a patient is healthy considering the general disdain for hygiene. I said, "Poke." Surprised.

That raised me a crop of blank looks.

"It's everywhere. Big, waxy-leafed plant. Has shiny purple berries in bunches kind of like grapes. Nasty hard on your gut. Alkaloid. But they taste so bad you shouldn't be able to choke enough down to do this."

Corey asked, "So how did he get past the first mouthful?"

That would be the question. "I've never actually seen poke poisoning, but I'm sure this is it. Maybe it started out as something else. He didn't smell like poke before. There are stains on his lips that weren't there before. Somebody forced the juice down him." He must have been dead unconscious. Even a groggy Buzzard Neck would be hard to force.

I saw nobody looking so innocent he must be guilty, but the question was less who than why. Nobody hated Buzz.

Was the point to eliminate Two Dead's protection?

I set Buzz up so we could dump fluids in as fast as they left. I turned sleepy again. The captain observed. The Third assisted me, sort of. Corey snored his lungs out on a cot I wanted for me. Two Dead barely breathed on, awash in painkillers.

The Old Man asked, "You had a good dream? That why you want to get back to sleep?"

All I had left was a lingering nostalgia. "It was something about the Lady and the Tower."

"You don't usually dream about her, do you?"

I was once a prisoner in the Tower. I spent a lot of time around the Lady then, and that has cost me years of merciless teasing.

"I don't. No. Why?"

"Maybe she was trying to tell you something."

"Maybe," I admitted, reluctantly. The Lady randomly and wickedly flings fuel into the fire by contacting me.

"Remember what you can while there's something to recall."

"Too late, boss. It's gone. Only...Buzz was in it somewhere. He had on a smiley mask."

"Really? And us without a wizard to hypnotize you."

He *wanted* the Lady to have sent me a dream. "If Goblin was here, we could make him channel her." Goblin could provide an occasional direct link, letting the Lady use his mouth. That was rough on him, but I did not mind. It made for less strain on me. And *he* does not get accused of inappropriate fraternization when she uses him.

Two Dead groaned. The knockout painkillers were wearing off. I checked his dressing. "I've had the same nightmare every night since the wizards disappeared."

"But didn't say anything even though *she* was in there."

"*Because* she was in them."

"Yes. Let us not deliver live ammunition into the hands of anyone who might taunt us. Is there a connection?"

"Maybe." I had had no such suspicion before. We all dream. Sometimes we have nightmares. Those seldom make sense, the little we recall. I had never thought mine meant anything special. Now I got it. She had wanted to tell me something, but I would not listen.

It had been a busy double dozen hours since Zhorab whispered "Flies," the hours fat with events boasting an almost dreamlike lack of dynamic structure.

Two Dead lapsed into a deeper sleep after I applied another pad soaked green.

The door opened. Cold and snow and Otto burst in to bellow, "Look what I caught me this time."

He had a groggy Goblin by the scruff. The little toad sagged there, cross-eyed, his pupils not right. "What's wrong with him?"

"I thumped him some to make him cooperate. He maybe has a little concussion."

Some folks find Goblin or One-Eye getting thumped a blessed notion.

The wizard rasped, "He didn't have no call to attack me. I was on my way here anyways."

Nobody swallowed that.

The captain demanded, "Where you been? And why? Take into consideration my current lack of tolerance for your customary bullshit."

I checked Buzz again, then moved in on Goblin.

His eyes uncrossed. His little turd brain began to function, sort of. "The Lady touched me." He gave me an ugly look. "I was happy out there in my cave. But here she came because her honey bear was always asleep or drunk when she tried to get with him. I run off because when Chodroze turned up I remembered his sidekick from Charm. Him and me went eye to eye and claw to claw back then."

Buzz was on the other side, then? Not a window-rattling reveal. Others had shifted allegiance in preference to getting dead, Whisper herself included. I had helped set her up. She has nurtured an unreasonable animosity ever since.

Goblin said, "I needed privacy. I had to dip into the demon realms to winkle out the truth."

The Old Man made an impatient "Come on!" gesture.

"I also wanted out of sight so Tesch wouldn't remember me. Back then he was called Essentially Capable Shiiraki, the Spellsmith."

I remembered that odd name. "I thought he went into the mass grave with all the other Rebel wizards."

"His family thought so. But I found a surviving familiar who knew the true story. Adequately motivated, it barfed up the details."

"Adequately motivated?" the Old Man asked.

"I told it I wouldn't report it to the Lady. Seeing as how it had gotten dragged into the Tower after the fighting, it wasn't inclined to go back."

I understood that sentiment.

"What *is* going on?" the Old Man demanded. "You having had a heart-to-heart with this friendly devil."

"It's complicated and insane. Chodroze believes he was sent here to see if we've found the Port of Shadows thing. He is supposed to destroy it if he can. Messing with us was bonus fun. But Tesch had a darker mission. He was supposed to kill Chodroze and frame the Company for it. And get control of the Port of Shadows if it's real. *Not* to destroy it. And he had orders to take out the Company leadership if the chance presented itself."

I blurted, "Buzz was supposed to murder Two Dead?"

"Chodroze must've made Whisper really unhappy."

Two Dead was a long-time favorite of Whisper's. "She is one vindictive bitch."

She had loathed the world with smoldering fury since the moment she had become Taken. Taking made her one of the most powerful beings on earth but a slave of the Lady as well.

My drowsiness fled. "Two Dead might be the good guy? Buzz might be the villain?" Everything I had worked out must be wrong. "Where does One-Eye fit?"

The captain leaned in, daring Goblin to be less than completely forthright.

"I don't know anymore. He stuck with me at the start, but he grabbed his poison sack and took off when Tesch called up the infested *chinkami*. He knew what they were. Don't ask me how. The little turd knows way too much shit that nobody ought to. He said we would be in the shit really deep after the cold weather broke. That's the last we saw of him."

The captain asked, "You got that from the Lady?"

"Mostly I figured it out myself. She only touched me because her honey wouldn't listen. Going to suck to be you, Croaker. Your woman ain't happy." He grinned, showing teeth in desperate need of cleaning.

Why worry? She was weather. I would suffer through. "Instructive, though, eh? Her knowing what's going on out here when she's denned up a thousand miles away?" Some of us have trouble remembering what she can do.

The Old Man observed, "What is instructive is that while she sees every sparrow fall she mainly just lets them go *plop!* People like Whisper keep digging deeper holes by going right on pulling stupid tricks. They'll cry hard when she finally brings the hammer down."

That was long-winded for him. Remarkable things must be happening inside his head.

He fixed Goblin with his hard stare. "Tell me again, magic munchkin. Where is One-Eye? What is he up to?" He gestured. Otto moved over to wrangle the Third when the questioning turned to him. "What's the blowback likely to be once HQ hears that Buzz and Two Dead screwed the pooch?"

Goblin shuffled. "Some major ass-covering. Tesch will turn out to be some deep-cover Rebel mole. Chodroze was always a loose ballista who let personal grudges color his judgment. It will be all our fault, somehow."

I observed, "Same old, same old. How about if they both survive? Will that shift the battlefield under everybody's feet?"

"You pull them through, we could see some wicked real excitement on down the road. *She* might even show an interest."

The captain said, "We are the cow flop she uses to distract the flies out here."

Yes. Our big boss was running a long con. This was another knot in the cord. I said, "I *will* save them."

"Standing around with your thumb in your ass?" The Old Man turned to Otto. "Have him show you where he was supposed to take that food." He indicated the Third. "One-Eye will be there. Hurt him if you have to but don't break him. I want him helping Croaker. Goblin. You're Croaker's boy until Buzz and Two Dead are healthy enough to dance at his wedding."

Otto and crew found One-Eye snoozing in a derelict shack on the edge of town. They got his head in a sack and his hands tied before he could bark. Nobody came out of it needing splints or stitches.

The Old Man was in a foul temper. He stood back, iron gaze fixed while One-Eye received the Word. The little black man wasted no time getting his shit together. "Focus on Shiiraki. We can't do anything more for Chodroze except maybe add a slider spell to fight infection."

"Goblin did that. Laid on a sleeper, too. Corey can handle him. You fed Buzz poke juice?"

"After the *firenz* he got in some wine he thought would help with the shits. You can't taste *firenz* in sweet wine. It just gives you a stronger buzz. Blackberry is the best."

And was the same color as poke juice. "The juice disguised the real poison?"

"Yep. He got drunk. Did a major stupid. He was already messed up with the shits." Not exactly confessing. He ransacked my medicine stocks while he talked. "Here it is." He held up a phial of dirty brown powder. "This will neutralize the *firenz*. The poke will take care of itself, you put enough liquid through."

I did not know what *firenz* was. A poison, clearly. As Goblin did note, One-Eye knew a lot that nobody should. Came of being older than dirt, mostly.

The Old Man reminded One-Eye, "They need to pull through. The Tower is watching. The Tower wants it to happen."

Wind chimes sang on cue, louder than ever. Everyone heard,

not just the poor crazy Annalist. A lightning-bug flash in a corner turned into an expanding O-ring of sparkle. It reached a foot and a half in diameter. A dark-haired, to-die-for beautiful brunette teen looked out at us. She smiled a smile that lighted up the universe. She winked at me and pursed her lips in an air kiss that I would hear about forever. Then she faded without saying a word, leaving a tinkle, a hint of lilac, an impression that someone had watched from behind her, and a message clearly delivered to her favorite band of bad boys.

"Oh, my!" One-Eye blurted because the Lady had considered him directly and deliberately before flirting with me.

He had to improve his sense of discipline. And he would. For a while. But he was, is, and always will be One-Eye. He cannot be anything else.

He bustled around Buzz with Goblin and the Third helping. I decided to step outside. I had been too long safe from clean air.

It was daytime out there, still not thirty hours since Zhorab whispered "Flies." Snow no longer fell, but the wind remained busy. It was warmer. The ground had begun to turn to mud. The world felt changed. Definitely not new but forever changed.

The captain joined me. "I don't know what's happened, but we have stumbled into a fresh new future."

"It's that line. When is the battlefield not a battlefield? We'll win one big time without lifting a blade if those two survive."

"When."

"Yes, sir. When."

"A handy friend, Two Dead. He's almost Taken caliber but less subject to outside control. Buzzard Neck could be a useful badass, too."

"We should seduce them."

"We keep them alive, they're ours. *She* is counting on us, Croaker. Stuff like this is going to keep happening. When is the enemy not an enemy? When it's your friend patting your back with one hand while sticking a dagger in with the other."

"I'd best get back in there and supervise." It would not be impossible for One-Eye to precipitate a lethal mishap if there was something he thought needed hiding.

"Yes. No doubt One-Eye already thinks he sees some clever way to turn himself a profit." The Old Man clasped my left shoulder, touching me directly for only the third or fourth time in all the years we have known one another. "You played your part well. Go win us a brace of new magicians."

Yes. So. No direct confession, but...He had been part of a scheme with roots in the Tower. Somehow. Maybe *he* was the one romancing the crone.

"I'm on it, boss."

First Blood

ELIZABETH MOON

LUDEN FALL, GREAT-NEPHEW OF THE DUKE OF FALL, HAD NOT WON the spurs he strapped to his boots the morning he left home for the first time. War had come to Fallo, so Luden, three years too young for knighthood, had been given the honor of accompanying a cohort of Sofi Ganarrion's company to represent the family.

The cohort's captain, Madrelar, a lean, angular man with a weathered, sun-browned face, eyed him up and down and then shrugged. "We march in a ladyglass," Madrelar said. "There's your horse. Get your gear tied on and be at my side when we mount up."

The mounted troop moved quickly, riding longer and faster than Luden had before, into territory he had never seen, ever closer to the Dwarfmounts that divided the Eight Kingdoms of the North from Aarenis. His duties were minimal. When he first attempted to help the way he'd been taught at home, picking up and putting in place everything the captain put down, carrying dishes to and from a serving table, Madrelar told him to quit fussing about. Luden obeyed, as squires were supposed to do.

He had hoped to learn much from a mercenary captain, a man who had fought against Siniava and might have seen the Duke of Immer when he was still Alured the Black and an ally, but Madrelar said little to him beyond simple orders and discouraged questions by not answering them. Pastak, the cohort sergeant, said less. The troopers themselves ignored him, though he heard mutters and chuckles he assumed were at his expense.

Finally one evening, when the sentries were out walking the bounds, the captain called Luden into his tent. "You should know where we are and why," Madrelar said. He had maps spread on a folding table. "We guard the North Trade Road, where the road from Rotengre meets it, so Immer cannot outflank the duke's force. It's unlikely he'll try, but just in case. Do you understand?"

Luden looked at the map, at the captain's finger pointing to a crossroads. Back there was Fallo, where he had lived all his life until now. "Yes," he said. "I understand outflanking, and I can see..." He traced the line with his finger. "They could come this way, along the north road. But could they not also follow the route we took here, only bypassing us to the south?"

"They are unlikely to know the way," Madrelar said.

"What force might they bring?" Luden asked.

Madrelar shrugged. "Anything from nothing to five hundred. If they are too large, we retreat, sending word back for reinforcements. If they are small enough, we destroy them. In the middle..." He tipped his hand back and forth. "We fight and see who wins." He gave Luden a sharp glance out of frosty blue eyes. "Are you scared, boy?"

"Not really." Luden's skin prickled, but he knew it for excitement, not fear.

Madrelar grinned. "That will change."

The next day they stayed in camp. Madrelar told him to take all three of the captain's mounts to be checked for loose shoes. Luden waited his turn for the farrier, listening to the men talk, hoping to hear stories of Siniava's War. Instead, the men talked of drinking, dicing, money, women, and when they would be back in "a real city."

"Sorellin?" Luden asked, having seen that it was nearest on the map.

They all stopped and looked at him, then at one another. Finally one of them said, "No, young lord. Valdaire. Have you heard of it?"

"Of course—it's in the west, near the caravan pass to the north."

"It's *our* city," the man said. "Any other place we go, we're on hire. But in Valdaire, we're free."

"The girls in Valdaire..." another man said, making shapes with his hands. "They love us, for we bring money."

Luden felt his ears getting hot. His own interest in girls was new, and his father's lectures on deportment both clear and stringent.

"Don't embarrass the lad," the first trooper said. "He'll find out in time." His glance quieted the others. "You ride well, young lord. It is an honor to have a member of your family along."

"Thank you," Luden said. He knew the other men were amused, but this one seemed polite. "My name is Luden. This is the first time I have been so far."

Silence for a moment, then the man said, "I am Esker." He gestured. "These are Trongar, Vesk, and Hrondar. We all came south from Kostandan with Ganarrion."

Luden fizzed with questions he wanted to ask—was the north really all forest? Was it true that elves walked there? Esker tipped his head toward the fire. "Janits waits you and the captain's horses. Best go, or someone will take your place in line."

"Thank you," Luden said, and led the horses forward.

When he returned the horses to the hitch-line strung between trees, it was still broad daylight. He glanced in the captain's tent—orderly and empty. The men were busy with camp chores, with horse care, cleaning tack, mending anything that needed it. Luden's own small possessions were new enough to need nothing.

Luden spoke to the nearest sentry. "Would it be all right if I went for a walk?"

The man's brows rose. "You think that's a good idea? You do realize there might be an enemy army not a day's march away?"

"I thought...nothing's happening...I could just look at things."

The sentry heaved a dramatic sigh. "All right. Don't go far, don't get hurt, if you see strangers, come back and tell me. All right? Back in one sun-hand, no more."

"Thank you," Luden said. He looked around for a moment, thinking which way to go. Little red dots on a bush a stone's throw away caught his eye.

The dots were indeed berries, some ripened to purple, but most still red and sour. Luden ate some of the ripe ones, and brought a neck-cloth full back to the camp. At home, the cooks were always happy to get berries, however few. Here, too, the camp cook nodded when Luden offered them. "Can you get more?"

"I think so," Luden said.

"Take this bowl. Be back in ..." he glanced up at the sun, "a sun-hand, and I'll be able to use these for dinner."

Luden showed the sentry the bowl. "Cook wants more of those berries."

"Good," the sentry said.

Near the first bush were others; Luden filled the bowl and took it back to the cook. After that—still no sign of the captain—Luden wandered about the camp until he found Esker, the man who had been friendly before, replacing a strap on a saddle.

"If you've nothing to do, you can punch some holes in this strap," Esker said.

Luden sat down at once. Esker handed him another strap and the punching tools, and told him how to space the holes. Luden soon made a row of neat holes. "Good job, lad—Luden, wasn't it? Have you checked all your own tack?"

"It's almost new," Luden said. "I didn't see anything wrong."

"Bring it here. We'll give you a lesson in field maintenance of cavalry tack."

Luden brought his saddle, bridle, and rigging over to Esker where he sat amid a group of busy troopers. Luden had cleaned his tack, but—as Esker pointed out—he hadn't gone over every finger-width of every strap.

"You might think this doesn't matter as much," Hrondar said. Esker's friends had now joined in the instruction. Hrondar pointed to the strap that held a water bottle on his own saddle. "If that gives way and you have no water on a long march, you'll be less alert. Everything we carry is needed. Every strap should be checked daily to see it's not cracked, drying out, stretching too much."

Other men shared their ideas for keeping tack in perfect condition—including arguments about the best oils and waxes for different weather. Luden drank it in, fascinated by details his father's riding master had never mentioned.

Captain Madrelar found him there, two sun-hands later. "So this is where you are! I've been searching the camp, *squire*." The emphasis he put on "squire" would have sliced wood. "I need you in my quarters."

Luden scrambled to his feet, threw the rigging over his shoulder, put his arm through the bridle, and hitched his saddle onto his hip. The captain had turned away; Esker got up and tucked the trailing reins into the rigging on his shoulder. Luden nodded his thanks and followed the captain back to his tent.

There he endured a blistering scold for his venture out to pick berries and his interfering with the troopers at their tasks.

Finally, the captain ran down and left the tent, with a last order
to "Put that mess away, eat your dinner without saying a word,
and be ready to ride in the morning."

Luden put his tack on the rack next to the captain's, shivering with reaction. He'd been scolded plenty of times, but always
he'd understood what he'd done wrong. What was so bad about
gathering food for others and learning more that soldiers needed
to know? He hadn't been gossiping or gambling.

He looked around the tent for something useful to do. A
scattering of maps, message tubes, and papers covered the table.
He heard the clang of the dinner gong; he could clear the table
before the cook's assistant brought the captain's meal. He'd done
that before; the captain never minded.

Luden picked up the first papers then stopped, staring at a
green and black seal, one he had seen before. Had the captain
found it somewhere? It was wrong to read someone else's papers,
but this was Immer's seal. The *enemy's* seal. The hairs rose on
his scalp as he read. Captain Madrelar—the name leapt out at
him—was to put his troop at the service of the Duke of Immer,
by leading them into an ambush, four hundred of Immer's men,
within a half-day's ride of the crossroads Madrelar had shown
him. For this Madrelar would receive the promised reward and
a command. If he had been able to talk Fallo into sending one
of his nephews or grandsons along, then Madrelar should drug
or bind the sprout and send him to Cortes Immer.

Luden dropped the paper as if it were on fire and started
shaking. It was the most horrible thing he could imagine. The
captain a traitor? Why? And what was *he* supposed to do? He
was only a squire, and how many of these men outside, these
hardened mercenaries, were also traitors?

He had not understood fear before. He had thought, those
times he climbed high in a tree, or jumped from a wall, that the
tightness in his belly was fear, easily overcome for the thrill with
it. This was different—fear that hollowed out his mind and body
as a spoon scoops out the center of a melon. His bones had gone
to water. All he'd heard of Immer—the tortures, the magery, the
way Andressat's son had been flayed alive—came to mind. As
soon as the captain came back and saw that he'd moved things
on the desk, he might be overpowered, bound, doomed.

He had to get away before then . . . somehow. Even as he

thought that, and how impossible it would be, his hands went on working, shuffling several other messages on top of Immer's, squaring the sheets to a neat stack. He rolled the maps as he usually did, noting even in his haste the marks the captain had made on one of them. They were not two days' ride from the crossroads, but one: the captain had lied to him. He put the maps in the map-stand as always. What now? He glanced out the tent door. No immediate escape: the cook's assistant was almost at the tent with a basket of food, and the captain had already started the same way, talking to his sergeant.

Luden took the dinner basket from the cook and had the captain's supper laid out on the table by the time the captain arrived. When the captain came in, he stood by the table, hoping the captain could not detect his thundering heart. The captain stopped short.

"Who did this?"

"Sir, I laid out your dinner as usual."

"You touched my papers? When?"

"To have room for the dinner." Luden gestured at the stack of papers at the end of the table. "It took only a moment, to stack them and put the maps away. Just as usual."

"Hmph." The captain sat and pointed to his cup. "Wine. And water."

Luden poured, his hand shaking. The captain gave him a sharp look.

"What's this? Still shivering from a scold? I hope you don't fall off your mount with fright if we do meet the enemy." The captain stabbed a slab of meat, cut it, and put it in his mouth.

Madrelar said nothing more in the course of the meal, then ordered Luden to take the dishes back to the cook, and eat his own dinner there. "I will be working late tonight," he said. "It's dry; sleep outside, and don't be sitting up late with the men. They need their rest. We ride early."

Luden could not eat much, not even the berry-speckled dessert. What was the captain up to, besides betrayal? Were the other men, or some of them, also part of it? Was the captain really prepared to sacrifice his own troops? And why? Luden's background gave him no hint. He tried to think what he might do.

Could he run away? He might escape the sentries set around camp on foot, but the horse lines had a separate guard. He could not sneak away on horseback. And even if he did escape afoot, he might be captured before he reached home—they had ridden hard to get here, and going back would take him longer. Especially since he had no way to carry supplies.

What then could he do? He looked around for Esker, but didn't see him, and dared not wander around the camp, in case the captain looked for him. Finally, he went back to the captain's tent. A light inside cast shadows on the wall...two people at least were in it.

Outside, near the entrance, he found a folded blanket and a water bottle on top of it. The captain clearly meant for him to stay outside. He picked them up, went around the side of the tent, rolled himself in the blanket, and—sure he could not sleep—dozed off.

He woke from a dream so vivid he thought it was real, and heard his voice saying "Yes, my lord!" He lay a moment, wide awake, chilled by the night air. The dream lay bright as a picture in his mind: his great-uncle, the Duke of Fall, speaking to all the children as he did every Midwinter Feast. *It is not for wealth alone, or tradition, that the Dukes of Fall have ruled here for ages past, since first we came from the South. But because we keep faith with our people. Never forget what you owe to those who work our fields, who take up arms to defend us. They deserve the best we have to give them.* And then the phrase that had wakened him: *Luden, look to your honor.*

He was a child of Fallo; he was the only one of that House here, and these men around him—some of them at least, and maybe all but the captain—were being led to slaughter. He still had honor, and the duty that came with honor.

And he badly needed the jacks. He threw off his blanket and stood up. Overhead, stars burned bright in the clear mountain air; he could see the tips of the tallest mountains, snow at their peaks even in summer, pale against the night sky, and enough silvery light glimmered over the camp to show him the way.

He had taken but ten steps toward the jacks when someone grabbed his arm and swung him round.

"And where d'you think you're going?"

It was Sergeant Pastak. Had the captain set a watch over him? Of course: he would need to, just in case. And so the sergeant was in on it, also a traitor.

"To the jacks," Luden said, glad his voice sounded slightly annoyed.

"To be sure, the jacks," the sergeant said, with a sneer. "Young lads...always eager to go to war until they get closer to it. Thinking of that, are you?"

"I'm thinking I ate too many of those berries before I gave the rest to the cook," Luden said. "And I need the jacks."

The sergeant shook his arm; Luden stumbled. "Just know, lad, you're with a fighting troop, not some fancy-boy's personal guards. You're not running off home."

That was clear enough. He stiffened against the sergeant's arm and adopted a tone he'd heard from his elders. "I am not one to run away, Sergeant. But I would prefer not to mark my clothes with berry juice and have someone like you think it was fear."

The sergeant let go of his arm as if it had burned him. "Well," he said. "The young cock will crow, will he? We'll see how you crow when the time comes—if it does." He gestured, the starlight running down his mail shirt like molten silver. "Go on then. To the jacks with you, and if you mark your clothes red and not yellow, I'll call you worthy."

Red could mean blood and not berry juice. Luden held himself stiffly and stalked off to the jacks as if he hadn't thought of that. He was not the only one at the jacks trench, though he was glad to see he had room to himself. He did have a cramp, and what he had eaten the previous day, berries and all he was sure, came out in a rush. He waited a moment, two, and then, as he stood, saw another man nearby.

"All right, Luden?" It was Esker. "The berries were good, but I think they woke me up."

"I ate handfuls raw," Luden said.

"That can do it. These mountain berries—they look like the ones back in the lowlands, but they clear the system, even cooked."

Could he trust Esker? He had to do something, and Esker was the only one he had really talked to. "Esker, I have to tell—"

"I thought I told you to leave the soldiers alone, sprout!" It was the captain. No doubt the sergeant had told him where Luden was. "No chatter. Get to your blanket and stay there. And no more berries on the morrow." Luden turned to go. Behind him, he heard the captain. "Well, Esker? Sucking up to the old man's brat?"

"He had the gripe, captain, same as me. You know those mountain berries. I'd have sent him back in a moment."

Then murmurs he could not hear. Back near the tent, a torch burned; the sergeant stood beside it. Luden returned to his blanket and lay down, feigning sleep. He knew they would not leave him unwatched. Once again, sleep overtook him.

He woke to a boot prodding his ribs. "Hurry up. It's almost daylight."

Stars had faded; the sky glowed, the deep blue called Esea's Cloak, and the camp stirred. Horses whinnied, men were talking, laughing, he smelled something cooking. As he rolled his blanket, the captain stood by, watching. Luden yanked the thongs snug around it, and stood with it on his shoulder.

"Don't forget your water," the captain said. "You'll be thirsty later."

Luden bent to pick up the water bottle.

"Your tack's over there." The captain pointed to a pile on the ground; two men were already taking down the captain's tent.

Luden picked up his tack and headed for the horse lines.

"If you've no stomach for breakfast," the captain said, "put some bread in your saddlebags; you'll want it later."

He saddled his mount, put the water bottle into one saddlebag and then carried the bags to the cook for bread. Troopers were taking a loaf each from a pile on a table.

"Captain thought you'd like this," the cook said, handing him a spiced roll. "Gave me the spice for it special, and said put plenty of honey in it."

Luden's stomach turned. "It'll be too sweet if it's all I have. Could I have some plain bread, as well?"

The cook grinned. "You're more grown up than that, you're saying? Not just a child, to eat all the sweets he can beg?" He handed Luden a small plain loaf from the pile. "There. Eat troops' rations if you'd rather, but don't tell the captain; he only thought to please you."

"Thank you," Luden said. The sweetened roll felt sticky. He put both rolls in the other saddlebag, and then went to the jacks trench a last time. It was busy now; Luden went to one end, squatted, fished in the saddlebag for the roll, sticky with honey, that he was sure had some drug in it. He dropped it in the trench, then stood and grabbed the shovel, and covered it quickly.

"That's not your job," one of the men said. "Go back to the captain, get your gear tied down tight. Here—give me the shovel."

"I'll see him safe," another said. Esker.

Luden glanced in the trench; no sign of the roll. Unless someone had seen him drop it . . . he looked at Esker. "Thank you," he said. All at once it occurred to him that the formality of the duke's house—the relentless schooling in manners, in what his great-uncle called propriety—had a use after all. Underneath, he was still frightened, but now he could play other parts.

"Come on, then," Esker said. When they were a short distance from the trench, Esker said, "There was something you wanted to tell me last night. Still want to tell me in daylight? Is it that you're scared?"

As a rabbit before the hounds he wanted to say, but he must not. Instead, in a rush, he said, "The captain's going to betray you all to Immer's men; four hundred are coming to meet us."

Esker caught hold of his shoulder and swung him around. "Boy. Fallo's kin. That cannot be true, and we do not like liars."

"I'm not lying," Luden said. "I saw it—"

"Or sneaking."

"—a message from Immer, with Immer's seal."

Esker chewed his lip a moment. "You're certain?"

"Immer's seal, yes."

"I am an idiot," Esker said, "if I believe a stripling lad when I have ridden with the captain these eight years and more." He stopped abruptly, then pulled Luden forward. In a low growl: "Do not argue. There's no time; I can do nothing now. If it's true I will do what I can." Luden saw the captain then, staring at them both. Esker raised his voice. "Here he is, captain. Lad had a hankering to fill a jacks trench; Trongar saw him. I'm bringing him back to you." He sounded cheerful and unconcerned.

"I saw you head to head like old friends," the captain said.

"That, captain, was me telling him the *second* time that he had years enough for filling jacks trenches and you'd be looking for him. He's just young, that's all."

"That he is," the captain said, looking down at Luden. "Did you saddle that horse?"

"Yes, sir," Luden said. "And I thank you for that sweet loaf the cook gave me. Cook said you told him to put spice in it as well as honey."

The captain smiled. "So I did. You can eat it midmorning, when we rest the horses, since I doubt you've eaten breakfast after last night's adventure with berries."

"That's so, sir," Luden said. "It still gripes a bit."

"Today will take care of that," the captain said. "Riding a trot's the best thing for griping belly." He turned to the trooper. "Very well, Esker, I have him under my eye now; get back to your own place."

"Yes, Captain," Esker said. "Not a bad lad, sir. Just eager to help."

"Too eager," the captain said, "can be as annoying as lazy."

"True. So my own granfer told me."

Both men laughed; Luden's heart sank. He did not think Esker was a traitor, but clearly the man thought him just a foolish boy.

They were mounted when the first rays of sunlight fired the treetops to either side. When they reached the North Trade Road, their shadows lay long and blue before them. To either side, the forest thickened to a green wall and rose up a hill on the north side. Luden couldn't see the mountains now, but he could feel the cool air sifting down through the trees, fragrant with pine and spruce. Here and there he saw more bushes covered with berries. The captain pointed out a particularly lush patch.

"Tempted to stop and pick some?"

"No, sir."

"Good. Wouldn't want your belly griping again." A moment later, "Ready for that sweet bread yet?"

"No, sir," Luden said. "It's not settled yet."

"Ah. Well, you'll eat it before it spoils, I daresay."

The sun was high, their shadows shorter, when a man on horseback leading a pair of mules loaded with packs came riding toward them. He wore what looked like merchants' garb, even to the soft blue cap that slouched to one side. But it was the horse Luden noticed. He knew that horse.

That bay stallion with a white snip, uneven front socks, and a shorter white sock on the near hind had been stolen—along with fifteen mares—from a Fallo pasture the year before. Before that, it had been one of the older chargers used to teach Luden and his cousins mounted battle skills. Luden knew that horse the way he would know his own shirt; he had brushed every inch of its hide, picked dirt out of those massive hooves. And so the man riding him must be Immer's agent.

"Sir," he said to the captain. "That man's a horse thief."

"Don't be ridiculous," the captain said.

"I know that horse," Luden said.

"The world is full of bays with three white feet," the captain said. "It's just a merchant. Perhaps he'll tell us if he's seen any sign of brigands or—unlikely—Immer's troops."

"I'm telling you, I know that horse!"

The captain turned on him, furious. "You know *nothing*. You are a mere child, foisted on me by your great-uncle, Tir alone knows why, and you will be quiet or I will knock you off that horse and you can walk home alone."

Luden clamped his jaw on what he wanted to say and stared at the merchant instead. For a merchant, he sat the stallion very much like a cavalry trooper, his feet level in the stirrups, his shoulders square...and what was a merchant doing with the glint of mail showing at his neck? What was that combination of straight lines under the man's cloak? Not a sword...

The stallion stood foursquare, neck arched, head vertical, ears pointed forward. Luden checked his memory of the markings. It had to be the same horse.

Luden glanced at the captain, who raised his arm to halt the troop, then rode forward alone. Now was his only chance. Would the horse remember the commands? He held out his hand, opened and closed his fist twice, and called. "Sarky! *Nemosh ti!*"

At the same moment, a bowstring thrummed; Luden heard the crossbow bolt thunk into the captain's body, saw the captain stiffen, then slide to one side, even as the bay stallion leapt forward, kicking out behind; its rider lurched, dropped the crossbow and grabbed at the saddle.

"*Ambush!*" Luden yelled, "Ambush—form up!" He drew his sword and spurred toward Sarky; the stallion landed in a series of bucks that dumped its rider on the ground. Its tack glinted in the sun; instead of saddlebags, a polished round shield hung from one side of the saddle, and a helmet from the other. Bolts hummed past Luden; he heard them hitting behind him and kept going. Horses squealed, men cursed. The captain now hung by one foot from a stirrup, one bolt in his neck, two more bolts in his body; he bled from the mouth, arms dragging as his horse shied this way and that.

Luden had no time wonder why the enemy had shot the captain who'd done what he was hired to do. A crossbow bolt hit his own mount in the neck, then another and another. It staggered and went down. Luden rolled clear as the horse thrashed, but stumbled on a stirrup getting to his feet and fell again. He looked around—the old bay stallion was close beside him, kicking out at the fallen rider who now had a sword out, trying to reach Luden.

"Sarky," he called. "*Vi arthrin dekost.*" In the old language, "Lifebringer, aid me."

The stallion pivoted on his forehand, giving Luden the position he needed to jump, catch the saddlebow, and scramble into the saddle from the off side, still with sword in hand. The man on the ground, quick witted, grabbed the trailing reins and held off the stallion's lunge with the point of his sword.

"Here he is—Fallo's whelp—help me, some of you!"

Luden scrambled over the saddlebow, along the horse's neck, and sliced the bridle between the horse's ears. The stallion threw his head up; the bridle fell free. The man, off balance, staggered and fell backward. Luden slid back into the saddle just as the horse jumped forward, forefeet landing on the fallen man. He heard the snap and crunch of breaking bones.

Mounted soldiers wearing Immer's colors swarmed onto the road. Ganarrion's smaller troop was fully engaged, fighting hard—and he himself was surrounded, separated from them. He fended off the closest attackers as best he could, yanking his dagger from his belt, though he knew it might break against the heavier curved swords the enemy used. The horse pivoted, kicked, reared, giving him a moment to cut the strings of the round shield and get it on his arm.

He took a blow on the shield that drove his arm down, got it back up just in time, parried someone on the other side with his own blade, and with weight and leg aimed his mount in the right direction—toward the remaining Ganarrion troopers. The stallion, unhampered by bit or rein, bullied the other mounts out of his way—taking the ear off one, and biting the crest of another, a maneuver that almost unseated him. Arm's length by arm's length they forced their way through the enemy to rejoin the Ganarrion troop—itself proving no easy prey, despite losses of horses and men.

"Tir's guts, it's the squire!" someone yelled. "He's alive." A noise between a growl and a cheer answered him.

Luden found himself wedged between two of the troopers, then maneuvered into the middle of the group. He saw Esker; the man grinned at him then neatly shoved an enemy off his horse.

"We need to get out of here!" someone yelled.

"How? Which way? They're all over—!"

"Luden!" Esker shouted over the din. "WHERE?"

He saw other glances flicking to him and away as the fight raged. They were waiting—waiting for him to make a decision. *What* decision? He was only a squire, he couldn't—but he had to: he was Fallo here. "BACK!" he yelled. "Take word back—warn them! Follow me!"

He put his spurs to Sarky, forcing his way between the others to the east end of the group. Twice he fended off attacks, and once he pushed past a wounded trooper to run his sword into one of the enemy. When he reached the far end of the group, he yelled "Follow me!" again and charged ahead, into a line three deep of enemy riders. Sarky crashed into one of the horses; it slipped, fell, and opened a gap.

For a terrifying time that seemed to last forever, Luden found himself fending off swords, daggers, a short lance, hands grabbing for him, trying to keep himself and his mount alive. He felt blows on his back, his arms, his legs; he could not think but only fight, hitting as hard as he could anything—man or horse— that came close enough. The noise—he had never imagined such noise—the screaming of men and horses, the clash of swords. Someone grabbed his shield, tried to pull him off the saddle; he hacked at the man's wrist with his sword; blood spurted out as the man's hand dropped away.

Always, the stallion pushed on, biting and striking, and behind him now he heard the Ganarrion troopers. One last horseman stood in his way; he felt Sarky's sides swell, and the stallion let out a challenging scream; that rider's mount whirled and bolted.

"*Kerestra!*" Luden said. Home. Despite his wounds, the stallion surged into a gallop. Behind, more yells and screams and a thunder of hooves that shook the ground. Luden dared a glance back. Behind him were the red and gray surcoats of Ganarrion's troop—more than half of them—and behind them the green and black of Immer's. How far could they run, how far could Sarky run, with blood flowing from a gash on his shoulder, with thick curds of sweat on his neck?

Ganarrion's troops had the faster horses, and opened a lead, but Sarky slowed, laboring. Esker rode up beside Luden. "Only a little farther, and we can give your mount a rest. Were you wounded?"

"I don't think so," Luden said. "I was hit, but it doesn't hurt."

"We'll see when we stop. Where do we go from here?"

"Straight back to Fallo. Tell the first troops we see that Immer's on the way."

"I thank you for the warning," Esker said. "And more, for getting us out of that."

"It was mostly Sarky," Luden said. The stallion flicked an ear back at his name.

One of the troopers in the rear yelled something Luden did not understand; Esker did. "They've halted and turned away," he said. "They may come on later, but it's safe to slow now as soon as they're out of sight. But it's your command."

"Mine?" Luden looked at Esker.

"Of course, sir—young lord—I mean. Captain and sergeant are dead; you're the only person of rank. And you got us out of that."

"Then . . . can we slow down now?"

Esker looked ahead and behind. "I'd say up there, young lord, just over that rise. Shall I post a lookout there?"

"Yes," Luden said, wishing he'd thought of that. By the time they cleared the rise, the old stallion had slowed to an uneven trot. The troop surrounded them as the stallion stood, sides heaving.

"By all the gods, young lord, I thought we were done for!" said one of the men. "Esker told me what you said. I didn't believe it until it happened."

"Kellin, see to his horse. That's a nasty shoulder wound. Hrondar, we need a watch over the rise," Esker said.

Luden slid off the stallion; his legs almost gave way. The smell of blood, the sight of it on so many, men and horses both. Several of the men were already binding up wounds.

"You are bleeding," Esker said to him. "Here, let me see." He slit Luden's sleeve with his dagger, and there was a gash. Luden looked at it then looked away. "That needs a battle-surgeon," Esker said. "But we can stop the bleeding at least. Sit down. Yes, right down on the ground."

He called one of the other men over; for a few moments, Luden struggled to keep from making a noise. Now that he was sitting down, his arm throbbing, he felt other injuries. Esker looked him over, pronounced most of them minor, though two would need a surgeon's care, and offered a water bottle. Luden remembered that his was on the saddle of the horse that had fallen under him. Also that he'd had no breakfast and the loaf in his saddlebag was as distant and unobtainable as his own water bottle. Around him now, the troopers were eating.

"Here," Esker said, tearing off a piece of his own. "Eat this— too bad you lost the one the captain gave you—honey would be good for you about now."

"It was poisoned," Luden said. He bit off a hunk of roll.

"How do you know that?"

"The letter I saw, with Immer's seal. It wasn't just the ambush. He was also supposed to bring a member of Fall's family for them to take back to Cortes Immer."

"You—but he said you were a nuisance he had to bring along."

Luden shrugged. That hurt; he took another bite of bread. The longer he sat, the more he hurt, though bread and water cleared his head. He looked around. Kellin had smeared some greenish salve on Sarky's wounds. "Give me a hand," he said, reaching up.

Esker put a hand down, and Luden stood.

"How long do the horses need to rest?" Luden asked.

Esker stared at him a moment. "You don't want to camp here?"

"We don't know where they are. They could be circling round, out of our sight. We need to move—" He stopped. Sarky's head had come up, ears pricked toward the east. Other horses stared the same way.

"Tir's gut, we didn't need this," Esker said.

A shrill whistle from the west, from the lookout on the rise; Luden tensed. Esker grinned. "It's our folk," he said.

"Our folk?"

"Ganarrion." He leaned closer. "Your command, young lord, but we'd look better mounted and moving. Even slowly."

"I'll need a leg up," Luden said, then, "Mount up! We'll go to meet them." Esker helped him into the saddle; the others mounted, and the lookout in the rear trotted up to join them. Luden's head swam for a moment, but he nudged Sarky into a walk; the troop formed up behind him.

In moments, he could see the banner, larger than the one his own cohort carried: Ganarrion himself was with them. Behind

Ganarrion's company came another, Count Vladi's black banner in the lead. Ganarrion rode directly to Luden.

"Boy! What happened? Where's Captain Madrelar?"

Luden stiffened at the tone. "Madrelar's dead. He led us into ambush."

"WHAT?" Ganarrion's bellow echoed off the nearest hill.

"We were led into ambush; the enemy shot Madrelar, and we're all that fought free."

Ganarrion sat his horse as if stunned, then turned to his own company. "Sergeant Daesk, scouts out all sides, expect enemy contact. Cargin, fetch the surgeon; we have wounded." Then, to Luden he said, "You're Luden Fall, is that right? Prosso's son?"

"Yes, sir," Luden said.

"The duke told me to look for you. And that horse—if I'm not mistaken, that's one of the duke's horses, stolen a while back. And, no bridle? How did you—or I suppose the troop surrounded you?"

"No, my lord," Esker said. "Lord Fall warned us of the ambush then led us out, fighting all the way."

Lord Fall? He was no lord; he was barely a squire.

"Barely a squire," Esker continued, echoing Luden's thought, "but he took command when Madrelar and Pastak died, and led the charge that broke us out."

"And it was treachery?"

"Yes."

Ganarrion chewed his mustache for a long moment, staring at Luden then nodded. "Thank you, Esker." He gave a short bow. "Lord Fall, with your permission, I will relieve you of command. You and your mount are both in need of a surgeon's care, and I have need of those of your troop who are still fit to fight. Will you release them to me?"

Luden bowed in his turn; his vision darkened as he pushed himself erect again. "Certainly, Lord Ganarrion. As you wish." Then the dark closed in.

He woke in a tent with lamps already lit. When he tried to move, he could scarcely shift one limb, and he hurt all over. The memory of Immer's letter came first, and for one terrifying moment he thought he lay bound, already on his way to the dungeons of Cortes Immer. Then he heard voices he knew—Sofi

Ganarrion, Count Vladi, Esker. The events of the day reappeared in memory, hazy as if seen through smoke.

"It's unusual, certainly," Count Vladi was saying. "But I remember a certain young squire dancing with death when I was a captain in Kostandan...."

Ganarrion grunted. "I was young and foolish then."

"And brave and more capable than anyone expected. This lad was not foolish, for what other choices did he have? We shall have much to tell Duke Fall when we return."

Luden stood before the Duke of Fall, when he was again fit to ride and fight. Behind him were the men of Ganarrion's company; Sofi Ganarrion stood on his sword-side and his own father on his heart-side.

"Victory is sweet," the old man said, "but honor is bread and meat to the soul. Those who have both, even once in their lives, are fortunate beyond all riches. You *won* your spurs, Luden; I cannot give them to you. Let us say I found something of mine that I am too old to use, that might be of service to you."

He opened the box on the table between them and turned it around to show Luden. The spurs within were old, the straps burnished with wear. Luden's breath caught. The duke's own spurs? He didn't deserve—

"Men died, my lord," is what came out of his mouth before he could stop it. "Life was enough reward."

Duke Fall nodded. "You are right, nephew. And it is as much for your understanding as for your courage that these spurs are now yours. We will speak more later; for now, let your sponsors perform their duties."

His father and Sofi Ganarrion stepped forward, each taking a spur, then knelt beside him, fastening them to his boots.

BIOGRAPHIES

JENNIFER BROZEK is an award-winning editor, game designer, and author. Winner of the Australian Shadows Award for best edited publication, Jennifer has edited twelve anthologies with more on the way. Author of *In a Gilded Light*, *The Lady of Seeking in the City of Waiting*, *Industry Talk*, and the *Karen Wilson Chronicles*, she has more than fifty published short stories.

Jennifer also is a freelance author for numerous RPG companies. Winner of both the Origins and the ENnie awards, her contributions to RPG sourcebooks and fiction include Dragonlance™, BattleTech™, and Shadowrun™. Jennifer is also the author of the YA BattleTech™ novel, *The Nellus Academy Incident*.

When she is not writing her heart out, she is gallivanting around the Pacific Northwest in its wonderfully mercurial weather. Jennifer is an active member of SFWA, HWA, and IAMTW. Read more about her at www.jenniferbrozek.com or follow her on Twitter at @JenniferBrozek.

BRYAN THOMAS SCHMIDT is an author and editor of adult and children's speculative fiction. His debut novel, *The Worker Prince*, received Honorable Mention on Barnes & Noble Book Club's Year's Best Science Fiction Releases for 2011. His short stories have appeared in magazines, anthologies and online. In addition to *Shattered Shields*, he edited the anthologies *Space Battles: Full Throttle Space Tales #6*, *Beyond The Sun*, and *Raygun Chronicles: Space Opera For a New Age*. He hosts #sffwrtcht (Science Fiction & Fantasy Writer's Chat) on Twitter as @BryanThomasS. His forthcoming anthologies from Baen include *Mission: Tomorrow* (2015) and *Galactic Games* (2016).

ROBIN WAYNE BAILEY is the author of numerous novels, including the bestselling Dragonkin series, the Frost saga, *Shadowdance,* and the Fritz Leiber–inspired *Swords Against the Shadowland.* He's written over one hundred short stories, many of which are included in his two collections, *Turn Left to Tomorrow* and *The Fantastikon: Tales of Wonder.* He is a former president of the Science Fiction and Fantasy Writers of America and was a 2008 Nebula Award nominee. He lives in Kansas City, Missouri. His story for us is from his *Frost* universe.

ANNIE BELLET is the author of the *Pyrrh Considerable Crimes Division* and the *Gryphonpike Chronicles* series. She holds a BA in English and a BA in Medieval Studies and thus can speak a smattering of useful languages such as Anglo-Saxon and Medieval Welsh. Her short fiction is available in over two dozen magazines, collections, and anthologies. Her interests besides writing include rock climbing, reading, horseback riding, video games, comic books, tabletop RPGs and many other nerdy pursuits. She lives in the Pacific Northwest with her husband and a very demanding Bengal cat.

GLEN COOK was born in New York City, lived in southern Indiana as a small child, then grew up in Northern California. After high school he served in the U.S. Navy and attended the University of Missouri. He worked for General Motors for thirty-three years, retiring some years ago. He started writing short stories in seventh grade, had several published in a high school literary magazine. He began writing with malicious intent to publish in 1968, eventually producing fifty-one books and a number of short fiction pieces.

He met his wife of forty-three years while attending the Clarion Writers Workshop in 1970. He has three sons (army officer, architect, orchestral musician) and numerous grandchildren, all of whom but one are female. He is best known for his *Black Company* series, which has appeared in twenty-plus languages worldwide. His latest work is *Working God's Mischief,* fourth in the *Instrumentalities of the Night* series. His story for us is a *Black Company* tale.

LARRY CORREIA is the *New York Times* bestselling author of the *Monster Hunter International* series, the Audie Award–winning Grimnoir Chronicles trilogy, and the *Dead Six* military thrillers for Baen Books, as well as several novellas and novels set in the *Iron Kingdoms* for Privateer Press's Warmachine game. A former accountant, firearms instructor, machine-gun dealer, and military contractor, Larry is now a full-time author and lives in the mountains of northern Utah with his wife and children. "Keeper of Names" is the first story from the setting that will be featured in an upcoming epic fantasy series from Baen Books by Larry Correia.

DAVID FARLAND is a *New York Times* bestselling author with over fifty novel-length works to his credit. His latest novel, *Nightingale*, won the International Book Award for Best Young Adult Novel, the Next Gen Award, the Global E-Book Award, and the Hollywood Book Festival Award for Best Novel of the Year. Dave is currently finishing the last book in his popular *Runelords* series, and there will be no sequels. But this tale is set hundreds of years before the tales told in the *Runelords*, and is part of a prequel series. Enjoy!

NANCY FULDA is a Hugo and Nebula Nominee, a Phobos Award winner, and a Vera Hinckley Mayhew Award recipient. She is the first (and so far only) female recipient of the Jim Baen Memorial Award. She has been a featured writer at *Apex Online*, a guest on the Writing Excuses podcast, and is a regular attendee of the Villa Diodati Writers' Workshop. Visit her website at www.nancyfulda.com.

JOHN R. FULTZ lives in the North Bay area of California but is originally from Kentucky. His Books of the Shaper trilogy includes *Seven Princes*, *Seven Kings*, and *Seven Sorcerers*, available everywhere from Orbit Books. His short story collection, *The Revelations of Zang*, features the adventures of Artifice the Quill and Taizo of Narr. John's work has appeared in *Weird Tales*, *Black Gate*, *Space & Time*, *Lightspeed*, and the anthologies *Way of the Wizard*, *Cthulhu's Reign*, *Other Worlds Than These*, *The Book of Cthulhu II*, and *Deepest, Darkest Eden: New Tales of Hyperborea*. He keeps a virtual sanctuary at www.johnrfultz.com.

DAVE GROSS is the author of more than ten novels in settings from the *Forgotten Realms* to *Pathfinder Tales* to the *Iron Kingdoms* and various points in between. His short fiction has appeared in many anthologies, including *Shotguns v. Cthulhu* and *Tales of the Far West*. A former English teacher and magazine editor, he has dabbled in technical writing and computer game design. He now devotes his time to prose fiction. He lives in Alberta, Canada, with his fabulous wife and their above-average dog and cats. You can keep tabs on him at www.bydavegross.com.

JOHN HELFERS is an author and editor currently living in Green Bay, Wisconsin. In sixteen years working at Tekno Books, he co-edited twenty short story anthologies and oversaw the production of more than one hundred volumes in all genres. He has also edited more than forty novels. He's also published more than forty-five short stories in anthologies such as *If I Were an Evil Overlord*, *Time Twisters*, and *Places to Be, People to Kill*.

In addition, his fiction has appeared in game books, novels, and on websites for the Dragonlance™, Transformers™, BattleTech™ and Shadowrun™ universes, including the third novel in the first authorized trilogy based on *The Twilight Zone*™ television series, the YA novel Tom Clancy's *Net Force Explorers*™: *Cloak and Dagger*, and a history of the United States Navy.

He also wrote three novels in the Room 59™ espionage series for Gold Eagle/Worldwide Publishing and has written novels in their *Deathlands*™ and *Mack Bolan/Executioner*™ series. Currently he's working on several tie-in and original projects in both the adult and YA genres, including overseeing the production of new novels in the *Shadowrun*™ game universe.

He operates Stonehenge Art & Word, an editorial and literary fiction management company.

SARAH A. HOYT was born in Portugal (where her birth family still lives) and English is her third language (second is French.) This possibly explains why she's on the kill-list of most copy editors. To avoid them, she lives high and dry in Colorado with her husband, two sons and a variable clowder of cats, reading and writing, with an occasional leitmotif of pastel painting, sewing, or carpentry thrown in when someone complains she's been at the keyboard too long.

Her most recent books are *A Few Good Men* and *Noah's Boy* from Baen Books, and upcoming *Night Shifters*, *Through Fire*, and *Darkship Revenge*, also from Baen Books, along with indie *Witchfinder*, a Regency fantasy.

SEANAN MCGUIRE is the author of more than a dozen books, all published within the last five years, which may explain why some people believe that she does not actually sleep. Her work has been translated into several languages, and resulted in her receiving a record five Hugo Award nominations on the 2013 ballot. When not writing, Seanan spends her time reading, watching terrible horror movies and too much television, visiting Disney Parks, and rating haunted corn mazes. You can keep up with her at www.seananmcguire.com. Her story for us is an *October Daye* prequel story.

ELIZABETH MOON has published twenty-six novels including Nebula Award–winner *The Speed of Dark*, over thirty short-fiction pieces in anthologies and magazines, and three short fiction collections, most recently *Moon Flights*. Her most recent novel is *Crown of Renewal*. When not writing, she may be found knitting socks, photographing wildlife and native plants, poking her friends with (blunted) swords, or singing in the choir. She likes horses, dark chocolate, topographic maps, and traveling by train. Her story for us is the latest Paksenarrion tale.

CAT RAMBO lives, writes, and reads omnivorously in a candy-colored condo beside eagle-haunted Lake Sammamish in Redmond, Washington. Her short stories have appeared in such places as *Asimov's*, Tor.com, and *Clarkesworld,* as well as in three collections. Her most recent book is *Near + Far*, from Hydra House Books. Among the awards she's been shortlisted for are the Endeavour, World Fantasy, Locus, and Nebula. You can find more of her fiction and information about her online classes at www.kittywumpus.net.

GRAY RINEHART fought rocket-propellant fires, refurbished space-launch facilities, commanded the Air Force's largest satellite-tracking station, and did other interesting things during his rather odd US Air Force career. Now a contributing editor for Baen Books, his fiction has appeared in *Analog Science Fiction & Fact*, *Asimov's Science Fiction*, and elsewhere. Gray is also a singer/songwriter with one album, *Truths and Lies and Make-Believe*, of mostly science-fiction-and-fantasy-inspired songs. His alter ego is the Gray Man, one of several famed ghosts of South Carolina's Grand Strand, and his website is www.graymanwrites.com.

JAMES L. SUTTER is a co-creator of the Pathfinder Roleplaying Game and the Senior Editor for Paizo Publishing. He is the author of the novels *Death's Heretic* and *The Redemption Engine*, the former of which was ranked #3 on Barnes and Noble's list of the Best Fantasy Releases of 2011, and was a finalist for both the Compton Crook Award for Best First Novel and a 2013 Origins Award.

James has written numerous short stories for such publications as *Escape Pod*, *Starship Sofa*, *Apex Magazine*, *Beneath Ceaseless Skies*, *Geek Love*, and the #1 Amazon bestseller *Machine of Death*. His anthology *Before They Were Giants* pairs the first published short stories of science fiction and fantasy luminaries with new interviews and writing advice from the authors themselves.

In addition, he's published a wealth of gaming material for both Dungeons & Dragons and the Pathfinder Roleplaying Game. For more information, visit www.jameslsutter.com or follow him on Twitter at @jameslsutter.

WENDY N. WAGNER's short fiction has appeared in *Beneath Ceaseless Skies* and the anthologies *Armored* and *The Way of the Wizard*. Her first novel, *Skinwalkers*, is a *Pathfinder Tales* adventure. An avid gardener and fan of the sweet science, she lives with her family in Portland, Oregon. You can keep up with her at www.winniewoohoo.com.

JOSEPH ZIEJA is a veteran officer of the United States Air Force who still works for The Man. Joe likes to fool himself into thinking he can have four careers at once; in addition to using Powerpoint presentations to strike fear in the hearts of terrorists, and pursuing his dream of writing, he is also a composer and voiceover artist with his own studio in Virginia. Someday he'll learn that there are only so many hours in the day (and that terrorists aren't actually afraid of Powerpoint), but for now you can find a complete list of his published works, which include pieces at *Daily Science Fiction*, *Pill Hill Press*, and others, at www.josephzieja.com. His music and voice studio can be found at www.renmanstudio.com.

ACKNOWLEDGEMENTS

We'd like to thank Toni Weisskopf, Jim Minz, Laura Haywood-Cory, Tony Daniel, and everyone else at Baen Books for giving us this opportunity.

Thank you to all the wonderful authors for trusting us with your stories.

Thank you to Paul Goat Allen, whose post on the best military fantasy inspired the idea.